A Place Ca

Ellie Dean lives in a tiny hamlet set deep in the heart of the South Downs in Sussex, which has been her home for many years and where she raised her three children. She is the author of the Cliffehaven Series.

Also available by Ellie Dean

There'll be Blue Skies
Far From Home
Keep Smiling Through
Where the Heart Lies
Always in My Heart
All My Tomorrows
Some Lucky Day
While We're Apart
Sealed With a Loving Kiss
Sweet Memories of You
Shelter from the Storm
Until You Come Home
The Waiting Hours
With a Kiss and a Prayer
As the Sun Breaks Through
On a Turning Tide
With Hope and Love
Homecoming

Ellie DEAN

A Place Called Home

PENGUIN BOOKS

PENGUIN BOOKS

UK | USA | Canada | Ireland | Australia
India | New Zealand | South Africa

Penguin Books is part of the Penguin Random House group of companies whose addresses can be found at global.penguinrandomhouse.com

First published in Penguin Books 2023
001

Typeset in 11/12.5 pt Palatino LT Std
by Integra Software Services Pvt. Ltd, Pondicherry

Printed and bound in Great Britain by Clays Ltd, Elcograf S.p.A.

The authorised representative in the EEA is Penguin Random House Ireland, Morrison Chambers, 32 Nassau Street, Dublin D02 YH68

A CIP catalogue record for this book is available from the British Library

ISBN: 978–1–804–94255–0

www.greenpenguin.co.uk

Geoffrey (Ollie) Cater
1947–2020

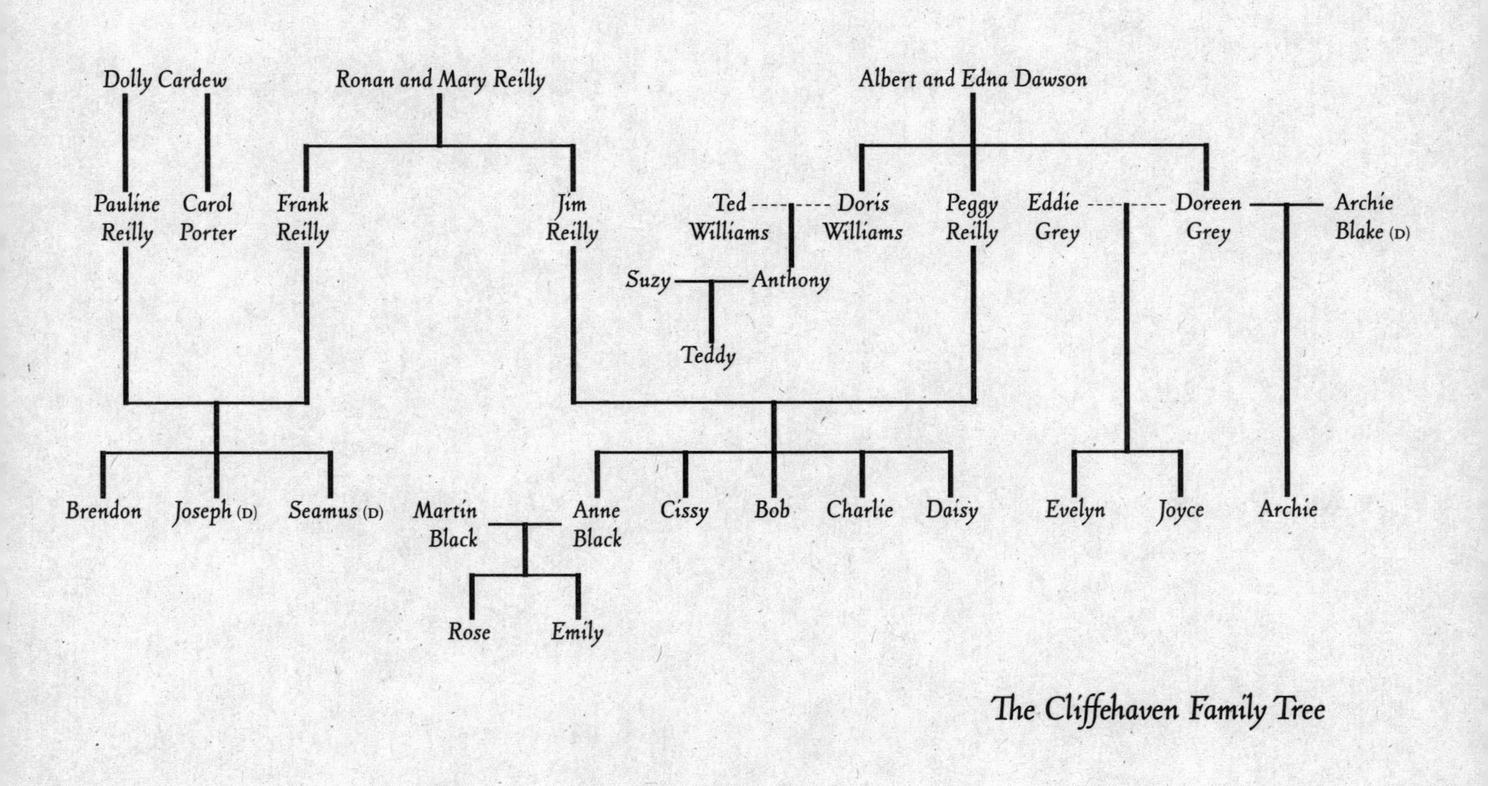

The Cliffehaven Family Tree

Dear Reader,

There was a point two years ago when I thought I would never write again, and this is why there has been a long gap in the Cliffehaven series. The loss of my husband to pancreatic cancer during the nightmare of lockdown and all the restrictions that entailed, left me feeling abandoned and unable to believe I could ever be creative again. It was an anniversary card that brought light back into my life and helped me to realise I was not alone, and that I did still have a future as an author. My darling Ollie had written it shortly before his death. He told me he loved me – said he'd understood the sacrifices I'd made to try and keep him alive – and that it was because he loved me so much, and was proud of all I'd achieved, he'd tried his very best to stay with me. While reading that card it was as if I could hear his voice and feel his presence again. I knew then that he would be watching over me and cheering me on as he always had in life. So, here is *A Place Called Home*. I do hope you enjoy reading it.

Ellie Dean x

Acknowledgements

I would like to thank Emily Griffin at Penguin Books, and my agent, Teresa Chris, for continuing to believe in me, and for their terrific support and encouragement during the writing of *A Place Called Home*. Following a tough two years in which I lost my husband and my belief in my ability to ever be creative again, it has been the love and support of my family and friends which has seen me return to my writing. Linda and Charlie, Tina, Ann, Val and Gerry who've had their own dramas, and of course my children. Without any of you, I wouldn't be where I am today – and I thank you.

1

September 1946

Dawn broke over the horizon and gilded the sails of the small fleet of fishing boats coming towards shore as the sprawling town of Cliffehaven slumbered in peace. The green slopes of the western headland gradually emerged from the night's dark shadows, and the white cliffs that towered above the eastern shore began to gleam as the squabbling seabirds circled the boats now anchoring on the shingle beach of the horseshoe bay.

The golden haze flooded the huddled rooftops, slowly bringing into focus the gaping wounds of bomb craters and the shattered skeletons of once elegant buildings that had lined the promenade and High Street. However, there were signs of regeneration in the new buildings, repaired streets and the clearance of bomb sites and, as the sun chased the shadows from the terraced Victorian villas that lined the steep hill climbing up from the seafront, it brought warmth to the fresh white stucco on the walls of Beach View.

Proudly standing three storeys above a basement, and surrounded by the blasted rubble of its neighbours, Beach View no longer bore the ugly scars of war, for Peggy Reilly had been determined that her husband Jim would not return from the Far East to face the evidence that she and their small daughter, Daisy, had come perilously close to losing their lives.

With the roof and chimney repaired, the light sparked in the new windowpanes and gleamed on freshly painted woodwork. The new front door had stained-glass panels at the top, a polished brass knocker and letter box; and the whitewashed concrete steps leading up to it were once again whole, the replacement lanterns set into the short pillars at the bottom exuding a sense of quiet elegance.

As the light slowly penetrated through the glass panels to the entrance hall, it sent a rainbow of colours over the polished blue and red Victorian floor tiles and the white paint of the walls and bannisters of the staircase where Cordelia Finch's stair-lift waited and brass rods gleamed against the dark red of the new carpet.

In the large front bedroom on the first floor, Peggy's eyelids fluttered open to the distant sound of the milkman's shire horse clip-clopping along Camden Road and Jim's gentle snoring. The snoring was a sound she'd missed for six years, and to hear it now was a balm to her soul. She lay there, snug and sleepily content in the big bed that had for so long felt empty, revelling in the warmth and solidity of the man beside her.

Her darling Jim: the man she'd loved with a passion from the moment they'd met; the man she'd waited for during the long and terrifying war years, and who, thank the Lord, had finally come home to her and their children. How she adored him. How lucky she was that their love had seen them through the dark days of separation and become more profound now he was home. He was her rock and her best friend, and although there were times when he exasperated her, she could forgive him anything.

Not wanting to disturb him, she turned onto her side so she could watch him sleeping. His broad back was still deeply tanned from the tropical sun, the muscles in his arms and torso clearly defined, and now his hair was longer, it curled enticingly into his nape and behind his poor damaged ear. Peggy was tempted to run her fingers through those dark curls, but managed to resist. Jim had actually slept through the night for a change, and she didn't want to wake him.

Peggy eyed the ugly scar tissue where the shrapnel had been removed from his back, and quickly pulled the bedding over it. She didn't need any reminders of how close he'd come to being killed and lost to her for ever. She nestled against him as the sun found a chink between the brocade curtains and filled the bedroom with golden light. It was so lovely to have the sun in the mornings after all those years of chilly dawns in the small, dark room off the hall. It had been a squash for her and Daisy in there, but now the heavy furniture was back in this room and it looked right.

She felt very lazy, which was most unlike her, but it was bliss to just lie listening to Jim breathing as the blackbirds and sparrows welcomed a new day, and the seagulls shrieked down by the beach, no doubt heralding the fishing boats' return from their night's work.

Her gaze drifted to what remained of his earlobe, knowing that although his wounds had been minor compared to some, there was unseen damage to Jim's heart and mind, and this worried her profoundly. Perhaps the undisturbed night was the beginning of the end of the nightmares he'd suffered since his return from Singapore three months ago. She prayed it was, for they left him dull-eyed and wrung-out, and even though he kept up the appearance of being his old, teasing, roguish self, Peggy knew him well enough to realise it was all an act. Whatever Jim had seen and experienced out in the Far East lived with him still, and he couldn't seem to shake it off no matter how hard he tried.

Her contentment in the moment fled, and she slipped out of bed, scooped up her clothes from the chair and padded in her slippers along the landing to check on little Daisy.

Her youngest child was almost five, and her room was a testament to her father-in-law, Ron's, hard work – as were all of the repairs and refurbishments to Beach View that had brought it up to date and made it far more convenient to live in now it was no longer a boarding house. There were two single beds so Daisy could have a friend to stay; the floorboards had been sanded and varnished; one of the walls was painted white, the others covered with nursery-rhyme wallpaper which went beautifully with the pink curtains. An old chest of drawers and bookcase had been painted white along with a large box for her toys, and there were colourful rag rugs on the floor. Peggy smiled and left the door ajar. It was little wonder that Daisy loved her room, for it was quite perfect.

Pausing on the landing, she looked up the stairs towards the large double bedroom at the top of the house which her younger son Charlie had commandeered as his own. At almost sixteen, he'd been most particular about how it was to be furnished, and now it boasted two single beds; a large wardrobe for his clothes and sports kits; numerous bookshelves to house his engineering manuals, comics, paperbacks and sports trophies; a desk and chair so he could do his homework in peace, and the big old wireless from the kitchen.

With no sound coming from up there, Peggy headed past the single room that was empty now her Polish evacuee, Danuta, had married Stanislav and moved into one of the tiny cottages down in Tamarisk Bay, and paused for a moment to listen at Cordelia's door. The elderly and much-loved Cordelia Finch had moved into that room many years ago as a lodger, and had opted to stay there as it was convenient for the bathroom and her stair-lift. Ron had given it a fresh coat of paint and new wallpaper, and Peggy had found some lovely material at the Sunday market which she'd had one of her factory machinists make into curtains.

As nothing was stirring, Peggy went into the refurbished bathroom and locked the door. But as she got ready for the day, she couldn't dismiss the awful, nagging worry over Jim. Her darling man was deeply troubled, but it seemed he was unwilling to talk about it to her, or to his brother Frank or his father, Ron, both of whom would have understood and perhaps been able to offer the quiet counselling and support she suspected he so sorely needed.

Perhaps he might open up to Martin, though? Her eldest daughter's husband had been through hell in that German POW camp, and he'd found solace in talking to his fellow flier, Roger Makepeace, who'd not only shared the privations of that camp but also the torture of the long death march through deep winter snows to safety.

'The bloody war has a lot to answer for,' she muttered crossly. 'It was bad enough having to face killing or being killed; now they're forced to relive every damned minute of it over and over again. It's no wonder they're sent half mad with it all.'

Peggy zipped up the pencil skirt and pulled at the hem of her knitted blue twinset, which seemed to have shrunk a bit in the wash. She clipped on earrings, dabbed on lipstick and powder, then dragged a brush through her dark hair, staring defiantly at her reflection in the bathroom mirror. If Jim wouldn't confide in her, then she'd jolly well find someone he *would* talk to.

It's a typical man thing, really, she thought wearily. *Women are far more sensible, and much more open to sharing their troubles. Men might call it gossiping, but there's nothing like a good natter over the teacups to put the world to rights.* It had never failed her yet.

Her frown remained as she headed downstairs past the stair-lift Rita and Pete had engineered to make Cordelia's life easier. Gossip and tea had seen her through the worst of times – had brought her closer to the evacuee girls who'd boarded with her, and to her daughters, Anne and Cissy. If women ruled the world there'd be far less war and more common sense.

Peggy couldn't resist taking a look at her lovely dining room which had sprigged wallpaper above the white dado rail and pretty yellow paint beneath it that went so well with the long, gold-coloured curtains that had cost her an arm and a leg to have dry-cleaned. Now the chimney had been repaired along with the crack in the marble surround, it was safe to light a fire in here once winter came. Peggy drew back the curtains and the sun streamed in to send fire through the gorgeous crystals of the chandelier that Ron had found in a house clearance the year before.

Her gaze swept from the smooth, varnished floor to the family photographs and brass candlesticks on the mantelpiece; her mother's ornate mirror above it all, and the colourful Egyptian rug that stood in front of the hearth between the two reupholstered chairs. The large dining table still bore the reminders of years of family meals and the chairs were mismatched, but somehow it didn't matter.

Peggy sighed with pleasure and headed across the hall to fetch the bottles of milk from the doorstep and breathe in the fresh, salty air. With barely a glance at the small room she and Jim had shared for years, she hurried into her kitchen and placed the bottles in the door compartment of the magnificent new fridge Anne and her husband Martin had given her. Switching on the smart Bakelite radio her daughter Cissy had sent down from London, she opened the yellow gingham curtains which matched the cushion covers she'd made for the kitchen chairs, then placed the kettle on the hob and, with a familiar thrill, turned to admire her pride and joy.

How clean, bright and spacious it was now the built-in larder had been pulled down and the large chest of drawers banished to Charlie's room. Jim's brother, Frank, had helped Ron build new white-painted cupboards above and below the lovely wooden worktop that stretched beneath the extended window to encompass the deep Belfast sink with its shiny brass taps. The walls were painted yellow to match the lino-leum on the floor, which made the room seem sunny although most of the day it was in shadow, and young Charlie had sanded down the battered kitchen table and chairs and painted them white.

The range still sat in the chimney breast, as a modern gas stove wouldn't have heated the water and the radi-ators, and although she'd really wanted to be rid of the sagging old fireside chairs, there'd been such an outcry at the idea, she'd had them reupholstered and jollied up with new loose covers. Now she was glad she had, for Jim still preferred to sit by the range of an evening rather than in the chilly dining room.

The kettle boiled and she made a pot of tea from leaves that had been used many times over. Placing it on a table mat, she sat down and lit a cigarette, her thoughts once more turning to Jim and how on earth she could help him.

'Whatever's eating you, dear?' chirped Cordelia as she came into the room with the morning newspapers. 'You look as if you have the weight of the world on your shoulders.'

'Just the usual worries over Jim,' she replied, pouring them both a cup of very weak tea.

Cordelia propped her walking stick against a chair and sat down to eye her with concern over her half-moon glasses. 'Another bad night?'

'Actually, no. He went right through for once, so I've left him sleeping.' Peggy took a sip of the tea which had very little in it to revive her. 'I do wish we could get better tea rations,' she muttered. 'The war in Europe has been over for more than a year, but the restrictions are getting more stringent by the week.'

'We just have to put up with it,' replied Cordelia calmly. 'At least our men are home and we're not being bombed every night.' She put the newspapers on the table and took off her glasses. 'I'm glad he had a good night,' she murmured. 'Poor Jim clearly hasn't got over whatever he's been through. Let us hope this one good night will lead to more and the nightmares become a thing of the past.' She reached for Peggy's hand. 'He'll come through, dear, so try not to fret.'

Peggy regarded her with infinite tenderness. Cordelia Finch was over eighty and had become an intrinsic part of the family, much loved by them all. However, the war years had aged her, made her frail, and this worry over Jim wasn't helping – especially coming so soon after the news of the tragic death of her nephew, Jock, on the infamous Burma railway.

'He's made of strong stuff, Cordy,' she reassured her; although she wasn't as certain as she sounded. 'I'm sure he'll pull through. I just wish he wasn't working with those ex-prisoners of war. Listening to their horror stories can't be doing him any good – not after all that ghastly carry-on in Singapore.'

'My work for the British Legion is not up for discussion,' said Jim from the doorway. 'And I'll thank you both to stop going on about it.' He plonked himself down at the table and reached for the teapot. 'And what's this dishwater supposed to be?' he complained with a grimace.

Peggy and Cordelia exchanged horrified glances as Jim emptied the teapot in the sink and started banging cupboard doors in search of the tea caddy. His work was always a touchy subject – as was the quality of his morning tea – and it seemed he was not in the best of moods this morning despite his long sleep.

Peggy swiftly found the caddy and carefully scraped out a spoonful of tea. 'That's it until next week,' she warned Jim. 'So please don't throw this away until we've got every last drop out of it.' She didn't add that chucking tea leaves down the sink wasn't at all helpful as they could block the pipes, but quietly cleared up the mess as she waited for the kettle to boil again.

'How's a man supposed to survive on these starvation rations?' he muttered. 'It comes to something when a decent cuppa can't be had first thing.'

Peggy had heard this moan before and ignored it. 'I'll see if I can get our egg ration later,' she said brightly to lighten his mood. 'You never know, you might get a fried egg tomorrow morning if you're lucky.'

'One egg each a week is hardly a bonanza,' he grumbled, pouring cereal into a bowl. 'It's a shame the hens are gone.'

'They were old and had stopped laying,' said Peggy calmly. 'At least they were good for the pot and kept us fed for a few weeks – and it was hardly my fault when the replacement ones were eaten by a fox.' She didn't remind him that it was through his carelessness that the coop door hadn't been shut properly.

'I'll have a word with Da and see if he can't persuade his pal Chalky White to sell us a couple of his,' he muttered moodily.

They'd discussed this before, but it seemed Chalky was loth to sell his hens, and no amount of cajoling from Jim and Ron would change his mind. Not wanting to get into an argument, Peggy left the table and hurried through the door down the concrete steps to her swanky new laundry room.

To her great surprise, it seemed Charlie was already up and singing dubious rugby songs as he splashed about in the deep tub of the new and fully equipped basement bathroom. *At least someone's cheerful this morning,* she thought before loading the twin-tub washing machine and switching it on. She gazed at it in admiration and gave it a gentle pat of appreciation. The days of handwashing and using the mangle were long gone, thank goodness.

'Don't be too long in there, Charlie,' she shouted through the bathroom door. 'Ron's expecting you in Havelock Road before nine.'

The singing stopped. 'It's all right, Mum. There's plenty of time yet.'

Peggy glanced at her watch and was surprised to find how early it still was. She left Charlie to his ablutions and, instead of returning to the kitchen and Jim's dour mood, went out of the back door into the garden which at this early hour was still in deep shadow.

The Anderson shelter had long since been dismantled and sent back to the council; the outside lav was gone, as was Ron's shed which he'd rebuilt in the garden of the Havelock Road house he and Rosie had recently bought. The chicken coop remained, however, but was looking rather sad as it awaited new tenants.

Once the garden had been cleared, Ron had extended the vegetable patch to its full capacity. It meant there was no lawn, and Daisy's sandpit was cheek by jowl with the stack of deckchairs stored beneath a sheet of tarpaulin, and the coal bunker. A line of slabs had been laid beneath the washing line to keep her feet dry, and there were pots of mint and rosemary beside the back door. It was still quite a crowded space and not very pretty to look at, but the fresh produce had seen them through the war, and still helped enormously to eke out the very tight rations.

Plucking a few of the late tomatoes from the vines, Peggy silently blessed Ron for all his hard work and care throughout the years, for she knew very little about gardening and couldn't possibly have managed to keep the vegetable plot going on her own.

The chill made her shiver and pull her cardigan more tightly about her as she returned to the basement. *Summer's definitely on the wane*, she thought as she checked on the washing machine before going back up to the kitchen. Another half an hour and she could transfer the load into the second tub which would spin the excess water out and make it far easier to carry to the line. It was such bliss not to have to wrangle with the mangle.

She was grinning at her own little joke as she entered the kitchen, so when Jim snaked out his arm and pulled her onto his lap she burst into a fit of giggles. 'Careful,' she spluttered. 'I'll drop the tomatoes.'

'Well, we can't have that, can we?' he murmured in her ear. He gave her a gentle squeeze and a hearty kiss before lifting her back onto her feet. 'Sorry I was a bit of a grouch earlier,' he said with the twinkle in his eyes he knew would charm her.

She patted his cheek. 'That's all right. You never were too sunny first thing, and it is still very early.'

She opened her lovely new refrigerator in search of the two rashers of bacon she still had left, and realised in horror that they'd gone. 'Who ate my bacon?' she demanded.

'Sorry, Mum,' replied Charlie from the doorway. 'I was starving after rugby practice last night. I didn't think you'd mind.'

She did mind but, unwilling to make a scene now Jim was in a better mood, she merely said, 'Next time, *ask* first, Charlie. You know how tight things are and bacon is as rare as hen's teeth these days.'

He dipped his chin so a lock of dark hair fell over his eyes. 'Sorry,' he muttered.

Peggy eyed her youngest son with exasperated affection. Although still in his teens, Charlie was as tall and broad as his father, with the same dark, curly hair and dark blue eyes. In his penultimate year at the grammar, he would be taking his School Certificate next summer, and if he passed all his exams and the RAF fitness tests, he would go on to university – paid for by the RAF. Once he'd gained his degree, Charlie would become a fully-fledged engineer and a valuable member of the airforce. Her little boy was on the cusp of manhood, growing like a weed and with his future all mapped out. It was hardly surprising he was forever hungry.

She turned back to the range, refusing to let her thoughts stray back to all those years he and his older brother, Bob, had been evacuated to Somerset, and their childhoods she'd missed. There was nothing she could do about the past, and she was simply thankful that at least Charlie was home now and after a tricky few months seemed finally to have settled down.

Peggy hunted through her cupboards and found a tin of baked beans. She decided to cook them up with fried bread and the tomatoes, though without bacon or eggs, it would be a pretty poor breakfast. She gave a sigh. Jim was right. It really did come to something when she couldn't put a decent breakfast on the table.

'Daddy!' Daisy entered the kitchen like a whirlwind and threw herself against a rather startled Jim before scrambling up onto his lap and shoving her rag doll into his face. 'Melia wanna say good morning,' she said firmly.

Peggy's heart melted at the sight. Daisy had been so wary of Jim when he'd first come home, and it had taken her a long while to get used to him. The main bone of contention had been Peggy's bed which she'd become used to sharing, but from which she had been fairly quickly – and firmly – ousted. But now she seemed to have accepted the status quo, and forgiven Jim for usurping her mother's undivided attention. And yet there were still moments when she eyed him warily – especially when he was in one of his moods, or suffering from yet another hangover – and she knew that Jim was struggling a bit to try and fathom out how to deal with her.

'Well, good morning, Amelia,' said Jim, giving Daisy and the doll a tentative cuddle. 'How's my best girl today?'

'I growed,' the child replied with great solemnity. 'I'm going to big school soon. Mummy said we go shopping for . . . for . . .' She frowned in concentration. 'Fruminorm,' she declared triumphantly.

Jim chuckled, gave her a hug and sat her in her own chair which was piled with cushions so she could reach the table. 'To be sure you'll be grand in your new uniform,' he replied. 'Now drink your juice.'

Having fried the bread and tomatoes and heated up the beans, Peggy placed the plates on the table, and cut Daisy's bread into more manageable pieces. As there hadn't really been enough to go round, she ignored the hunger pangs and sat down to her usual bowl of cereal and tried not to acknowledge the fact that Daisy's baby days were almost over. She would be five this December and once she started primary school on Monday, the years would fly past.

'Is that all you're having?' Jim asked.

'You know I never eat much breakfast,' she replied airily. 'This is more than enough.'

'There's nothing of you as it is,' he grumbled. 'At least have a bit of fried slice and some beans.'

She waved away his plate. 'Really, Jim, don't fuss. I'm happy with cereal and a bit of toast.'

She could see he didn't really believe her, so quickly changed the subject and turned to Charlie who was wolfing his food down as if afraid someone might steal it. 'You'd better go to the barber's, Charlie. That hair of yours is getting longer by the day.'

He shoved the drooping lock out of his eyes. 'Yeah, I know. I'll pop in there after I've been to Grandad's.'

'Is there much more work to do in Havelock Road?' she asked.

'Tons of it,' he replied, mopping his plate with a doorstep of bread. 'Poor Grandad's snowed under, and as I'm due back to school on Monday, I won't be around much to help.'

'Rosie's certainly cracking the whip,' said Jim, pushing his empty plate to one side. 'But, work permitting, Frank and I will help as much as we can. In fact, as it's Saturday, I'll go with Charlie and see what needs doing. Dad's getting too old to be climbing up ladders and painting ceilings.'

'I wouldn't let *him* hear you say that,' said Cordelia with a sniff. 'Ron still thinks he's in his prime.'

'Aye, that he does,' sighed Jim, 'but the fact is he's no spring chicken, and that's heavy work.'

The large Victorian house in Havelock Road stood on a corner plot within yards of the High Street and seafront. Almost hidden from the main road by a brick and flint wall, tall wooden gates and an overgrown hedge, it had miraculously escaped the V-1 bombardment which had devastated most of the other houses in this quiet, tree-lined corner of Cliffehaven – including Peggy's sister, Doris's – but it had been left empty for too long and by the time he and Rosie had bought it, there were more than a few signs of damp and decrepitude in the old timbers and walls.

Ron stood in the untamed front garden while the two brindled dogs, Harvey, and his pup, Monty, snuffled about in the brambles and long grass in search of anything they could chase. The lurcher in them meant it was in their nature to hunt, and just lately, Ron hadn't had the time to exercise them properly, so they were constantly restless and getting up to mischief.

He shoved back his moth-eaten cap and scratched his head as he regarded the huge roll of lino, pile of building materials and pots of paint stacked beneath a large sheet of tarpaulin in the garage. The work on the house was slow-going and arduous, but at least there were signs of improvement at last – a glimmer of light at the end of a very long tunnel.

The tiler had been to sort out the roof; the gutters and downpipes had been replaced and the chimney stack repaired. Drains had been mended and cleared, and the ancient wiring renewed to avoid the very real possibility of the place burning down. The inside walls had been freshly plastered, the ceilings repaired and painted. There were new cabinets in the kitchen to house a Belfast sink, washing machine and refrigerator, all of which – unbeknownst to Rosie – he'd managed to find on the black market at a good price.

Wisteria, honeysuckle and rambling roses had gone wild all over the front of the house to the point where they'd blocked the sun from the windows and started to damage the brickwork. Ron had pruned it all back, weeded out the honeysuckle which threatened to overtake the entire garden, and repaired the point-work and trellis. The window frames had been replaced, as had the front door, which was freshly painted a deep blue, and there was now a very smart brass door knocker in the shape of an anchor, which Rosie had picked up in a junk shop to remind her of her old home, the Anchor pub.

The walled back garden which gently sloped towards the promenade and newly mine-swept beach was laid to lawn and had been scythed down so it could be mown into attractive stripes, and Ron had planted fruit canes against the western wall of his small vegetable plot so they were sheltered from the wind and benefitted from the dawn to dusk daylight. He'd also laid a paved area outside the French doors of the drawing room so Rosie's garden chairs and table could be placed to make the most of the magnificent sea view and catch the sun throughout the day. Not that either of them had had much time to lounge about – but he supposed there was always next summer.

The area behind the garage had been fenced off to house his large ferret cage and shed, and he'd planted a line of frothy tamarisk to mask it all, safe in the knowledge they would survive the salty winds coming off the sea, and to remind him of his first home in Tamarisk Bay, where his eldest son Frank now lived.

Ron admired his handiwork. The outside was looking quite smart, even if he did say so himself, but there was still a lot to be done on the inside. Three of the four bedrooms were finished, as was the sitting room and bathroom. The central heating boiler had been fitted, but the dining room had yet to be started, and the radiators were waiting for the plumber who'd taken his family away on two weeks' holiday just as he was supposed to start fitting them. Luckily the summer had been unusually mild, if rather damp, but September had definitely brought a nip to the air, and he didn't fancy being in that large house with only the single fireplace in the sitting room to keep them warm through winter – especially as the price of coal had shot up.

He gave a deep sigh and wished Rosie didn't have such ambitious plans for the place. It left very little time to walk the dogs or exercise Flora and Dora, his ferrets, and by the end of the day he was often too tired to even bother going up the road to the Anchor for a restorative pint – let alone enjoy a bit of slap and tickle with Rosie. *Not that there's much chance of that,* he thought gloomily. Rosie was always out on some council business, or popping in to check on Ruby who'd taken over the Anchor. The girl was making a jolly good fist of it, as far as Ron could tell, and certainly didn't need Rosie sticking her nose in every five minutes.

Realising he was letting dangerous resentment creep up on him, Ron patted the pockets of his disreputable old trousers and pulled out his pipe and roll of tobacco. Perching on the top platform of his stepladder, he filled his pipe, his thoughts turning to the day's tasks.

He'd finished papering their bedroom walls late last night while Rosie was at yet another council function, and had been asleep by the time she'd arrived home. She was already out on more council business today, fighting the bureaucracy that was holding up the plans for a new council housing estate behind the station to replace the one that had been firebombed. His Rosie loved a battle, that was for certain, and he was proud of all she'd achieved, but he did wish she'd be at home more often. He missed her; missed the intimacy of a cuddle on the couch of an evening, and the companionship of sharing a meal or listening to *ITMA* on the wireless. As it was, they were like ships passing in the night, and it had become very clear to Ron that the honeymoon was well and truly over.

And that worried him, for although he'd encouraged her to follow her dreams, he *was* becoming resentful at being left to do all the hard graft while she concentrated on her civic duties and attended fancy parties at the Town Hall. He wanted her home; to appreciate him and become his soulmate again, not leave him with barely a kiss in the morning and an endless list of jobs to do. He gave a deep sigh. He still loved the bones of her and admired her drive and enthusiasm – but the work on the house and all this council stuff was forcing a wedge between them, and he wished wholeheartedly they could settle into retirement and have fun together like in their courting days.

He lit his pipe and sat there moodily contemplating the weeds and overgrown hedge that shielded the house from the road and passing traffic, then lifted his face to the sun and gave another sigh as he calculated how long it would take to lay the lino in the kitchen. The roll of linoleum was damned heavy, and it would be a job to get it from the garage to the kitchen without doing his back in. But he seemed to have no choice in the matter as there was no sign of Charlie, and Frank would be sleeping after his night's fishing.

He puffed on his pipe, eased his back and watched the two dogs that were now on their hind legs and whining as they looked through the trellis on top of the sturdy wooden gates. The gates had been the first thing he'd repaired, for if Harvey and Monty spotted a squirrel or bird, they'd be off like lightning, and it would be the devil's own job to round them up again.

Ron's pipe went out, so he jammed it back into his pocket and stood to stretch his legs and back. The delicate operation to remove the shrapnel had been a success, but all this heavy labour wasn't doing it any favours, and sometimes he was so stiff and sore, he could barely move. Deciding it was time to make another cup of tea, he was about to go inside when the gate swung open and the two dogs went into ecstatic yips and dances of welcome.

Ron grinned with pleasure, and some relief at his handsome son and grandson. 'Good timing,' he said. 'I was just about to make another pot of tea. Make sure you shut that gate properly, and while you're at it, you can bring in that roll of lino.'

2

Ruby moaned in her sleep, for she was once again in the icy wilderness of a Canadian forest. It was mid-winter, the snow so deep it almost reached the roof of the log cabin that had become her home since her marriage to Mike. The silence was profound, wrapping itself around her like a shroud, and emphasising the fact that she was very far from civilisation. The sight of such white emptiness was terrifying after being used to the bustle and noise of the East End, but she couldn't help but acknowledge its beauty. Yet it was a cruel beauty, for it separated her from Mike who was miles away at the logging camp with his father, and meant that when her time came, she would have to rely on his mother to help her give birth to her baby. No doctor could get to her through this, and the awful feeling of being trapped in this lonely, white world made her shiver with dread.

Heavily pregnant, and wrapped in many layers of clothing, she tentatively edged her way along the wooden veranda to the woodpile. Ruby watched herself slip. Saw herself slide awkwardly against the railings and go crashing down the steps. She knew what was to come – the pain – the blood in the snow – the death of all her dreams.

Ruby reared up in bed, eyes staring into the darkness, heart thudding, her breath sharp and painful in her chest as she tried desperately to escape the images which continued to haunt her even though two years had passed. Losing her baby like that was something she could never forget, and the pain had been intensified by the news that Mike had been killed in a logging accident shortly after. Canada had promised so much, but it had taken away everything she'd held precious, leaving her, once again, alone and fending for herself.

It was not quite dawn when she'd left her bed that morning, wrung out from yet another bad night, but determined to keep going and at least keep this part of their shared dream alive . . . The loss of her beloved Mike and their stillborn baby would be a sorrow she'd carry for ever – the rage against the isolation and impassable snow that had caused it all to happen was something she would never get over.

And yet those quiet hours following the bad nights hadn't been spent in idleness. Born and raised in the poorest part of the East End of London by a mother who'd regularly left her to her own devices, or dumped her with neighbours when she went off drinking with a new man, she'd forged an inner steel. Now she found that old habits die hard and it meant she'd put all her energies into scrubbing floors, whitewashing the tobacco-stained ceiling and walls of the Anchor's bar, repairing broken chairs and tables, making cushions for the settles by the inglenook, and polishing everything until it gleamed.

Dressed in old dungarees, baggy jumper, slippers and rubber gloves, she was perspiring as she stepped back and admired the freshly polished collection of brass and copper pots she'd hung around the cavernous fireplace. *There's no doubt about it*, she thought. *You can take the girl out of the East End, but the East End stays with the girl despite having left that old life at the start of the war.* Satisfied she could see her rather grubby reflection in them, she set to and cleaned out the hearth before relaying it in readiness for this evening. It was getting chilly once the sun went west, and a fire was always welcoming, but with the price and shortage of coal, it meant she had to keep her woodpile well stocked.

'Thank goodness for Frank,' she muttered, carrying the bucket of soot and ash out into the back garden. Depositing it around her carefully pruned rose bushes, she pulled off the rubber gloves and smeared away the sweat from her brow with the back of her hand as she admired the garden.

It was coming on nicely now that Frank regularly kept the grass cut and got rid of the brambles and nettles that had taken over; and the deep flower beds had been a riot of colour and glorious scent throughout the summer. There was a narrow paved area outside the back door where she'd placed a deckchair and camping table to catch the sun when she wasn't working, and instead of the unsightly and very unhygienic outside lav, there was now a neat brick extension off the hallway providing a proper inside toilet and wash basin.

Ruby smiled as she regarded the woodpile Frank had replenished only yesterday. She wasn't a bit fooled by his neighbourly help, though very grateful for it. He was clearly smitten with Brenda, her widowed barmaid, and managed to find any excuse to pop round when he thought she might be here. Ruby didn't mind at all, as she enjoyed a romance as much as anyone, and was perfectly willing to play her part in return for help about the place. Besides, she really liked Frank and was delighted he was no longer tied to that sour-faced bitch of a wife, Pauline, who she'd had the dubious pleasure of meeting when she'd been billeted with Peggy at Beach View.

Ruby's thoughts scattered as she heard the Town Hall clock strike ten, and she dumped the bucket and rubber gloves on the little table before hurrying indoors. She needed a good wash and to get changed into something decent if the pub was to open on time.

She opened the new door to her private rooms and ran up the narrow, creaking wooden stairs into the cosy lounge. She hadn't done much to change things up here, for she shared Rosie's love of flowery wallpaper and chintz fabrics, and the deep couches were supremely comfortable when she got the chance to actually sit in them.

Kicking off her slippers and wriggling out of the grubby dungarees, she stripped off her underwear and ran the water for a quick bath. The water wasn't that hot, so she didn't linger after she'd scrubbed the dirt away and washed her hair then, wrapped in a lovely big towel, she padded into the bedroom and opened the large wardrobe she'd bought in the market.

Like Rosie, she kept a set of clothes for when she was behind the bar, but instead of the tight skirts and rather revealing frilly blouses Rosie had favoured, she preferred well-cut slacks topped with a neat, short-sleeved white shirt. Her only concessions to glamour were a pair of high-heeled shoes, discreet gold earrings and a dash of scarlet lipstick. She might only be in her early twenties, and passable-looking, but she had no intention of giving the punters the wrong ideas just because she was on her own – this was a pub, not a knocking shop, and the quicker they realised it, the better.

Dressed and almost ready for the day, she checked that her nail polish hadn't chipped and slipped on her ruby engagement ring and gold wedding band. Brushing her long hair until it shone like cobnuts, she coiled it back from her face into a neat chignon. A dab of mascara on her lashes to enhance her green eyes, a puff or two of face powder, and a dash of lipstick completed her make-up. Tucking the crisply ironed shirt firmly into the waistband of her smart black trousers, she buckled on a broad leather belt, slipped on her heels, and took stock of her appearance in the long bedroom mirror.

Satisfied she passed muster, she swung a cardigan over her shoulders and made her way carefully down the stairs and locked the new door behind her. She'd come a very long way from the little girl who used to sit outside the pub waiting for her mother in the dark, and the young woman who trembled in fear at the sound of her first husband's footsteps on the tenement landing, and bore the brunt of his alcohol-fuelled beatings. The late and unlamented Ray Clark was in the past – a brief and violent marriage that had ended when the unstoppable force of his speeding motorbike had met an unyielding brick wall and broken his worthless neck.

Ruby shuddered as she was besieged by images of those mean streets where her mother, Ethel, regularly abandoned her until Ruby's step-father had come out of prison and made their lives even more of a misery. Life had been hard, but Ruby hadn't realised just how hard until she'd come down here and been billeted with Peggy at Beach View, and discovered another world. A world without fear – a world of love and encouragement, and finally, a real and lasting sense of home.

She took a deep breath and mentally shook off all memories of that time. She might still be young, but because of her marriage to Mike Taylor, she was now a woman of substance and in charge of her life. The fact that Mike had been killed less than a year after their marriage still haunted her, as did the loss of their precious baby, for they'd thought they would grow old together and have lots of children. But she'd learnt as a child that life wasn't easy and that fate had a nasty way of irreparably shattering the plans of mere mortals.

Impatient with these gloomy thoughts, Ruby whipped the towels from over the beer pumps and folded them away under the bar. Her life was here now, and she would make the most of it, for it was Mike's bequest which had bought this pub, and she was determined to make it a success.

As the Town Hall clock struck eleven-thirty, she crossed the brick floor to unbolt the front door. Wedging it open to let the fresh air in, she looked out into Camden Road and noted it was busy with long queues outside every shop. Having checked she had enough change in the till, she rubbed away a speck of dust from the bar, lit a cigarette and waited for her first customer.

She had no regrets about returning to Cliffehaven almost a year ago and buying the Anchor, for she'd worked in an East End pub and knew the life, and living in the isolated wilds of Canada hadn't suited her at all – in fact, she'd hated almost every minute of it. Mike had known how unhappy she'd been, and they'd made tentative plans to return to Cliffehaven and buy this place, so it was up to her to fulfil that shared dream. Now she was once more in the place she'd come to call home, and amongst those she loved. Cliffehaven had been her refuge when she'd fled war-torn London and the brutal Ray; Peggy and Ron Reilly her saviours. They had given her a home at Beach View and become closer than any family she'd known, and she knew she could never repay their love and kindness.

As if her thoughts had conjured her up, Peggy came through the door, laden with bags of shopping, and looking very smart in a two-piece suit, high heels and dinky hat. 'I can't stay long,' she said. 'Doris is minding Daisy while I finish my shopping. We've been to Plummers to get Daisy's school uniform, and you wouldn't believe the prices they're charging.'

Ruby leaned across the bar and welcomed her mother hen with a kiss on the cheek. 'Thirsty work, shopping,' she said with a smile. 'Wanna beer on the 'ouse to whet yer whistle?'

'Just a small one, though I shouldn't really.' Peggy dumped the bags on the floor, took off her gloves, and hoisted herself up onto the bar stool.

'There ain't no rush, is there? Not with your Doris in charge.'

Peggy sipped the freshly poured pale ale and relaxed. 'Not really. Jim and Charlie are over at Ron's helping out, Doris is treating Daisy to an ice-cream, and frankly, I could do with a bit of a sit-down.' She took another satisfying sip of beer, and then lit a fag. 'No Brenda today?'

'She's on tonight cos it gets ever so busy on match-day Saturdays.'

Peggy grinned. 'Frank still popping in regularly to do odd jobs, is he?'

Ruby chuckled. 'Can't stay away more like – especially if Brenda's here. Honest, Auntie Peggy, you ain't never seen the like of them two. Billing and cooing and trying to pretend they ain't head-over-heels.'

'Well, I'm glad for them both,' said Peggy. 'They deserve a bit of happiness, and he's well rid of Pauline.'

'Yeah, you're right there. I never did take to her.' Ruby was distracted by the sight of Stan coming into the bar. He was another of her favourite people, for he'd rescued her when she'd first arrived on the train and had helped see off the dodgy landlord who'd assaulted her. 'Watcha, Stan. How's yer trains?'

Stan leaned on the bar and grinned widely. 'They're running on time and coming in and out as regular as ever without anyone in the signal box. It's marvellous what modern technology can do.' Stan had retired from being stationmaster, but he still lived in the station cottage with his niece, April, and her baby.

He turned to Peggy. 'Surprised to see you in here so early,' he rumbled. 'Something up at Beach View?'

'I haven't turned to the drink, if that's what you're implying, Stan. Just resting my feet and enjoying five minutes' peace during a busy day.' She took a refreshing glug of her beer. 'How's April and baby Paula? I haven't seen them about much.'

Stan's ruddy face broke into a beaming smile of pride. 'Both doing marvellously,' he replied. 'April's still working at the telephone exchange, of course, and now courting a nice young fellow, and Paula has just turned three and is as sunny as a daffodil.'

'And he's all right with Paula not having a father to speak of?' asked Peggy with a worried frown.

'Oh, aye. He's a grand lad and accepts that accidents happen, and is as smitten with Paula as he is with April.'

'Oh, I am relieved,' sighed Peggy. 'That poor girl hasn't had much luck in her life – especially after her awful mother turned her back on her when she needed her the most.'

As Ruby placed Stan's beer in front of him and gave him his change, Peggy blurted out, 'Talking of awful mothers, Ruby, have you heard from yours?'

'No. And that suits me just fine,' she replied brusquely, turning to the four men decked out in woolly hats and football scarves waiting to be served. They were soon joined by others similarly festooned, and the noise level rose as expert opinions were voiced on everything from the skills of their team to the nefarious decisions of the referees. Match days were always busy, and Ruby enjoyed the cheerful bustle and noise after the long, lonely nights upstairs when she had too much time to think. And the last thing she wanted to think about was her mother, Ethel, who'd never shown her much affection, and had shamed her to the core by being sent to prison for stealing food meant for the Red Cross, and in turn, damaging dear old Stan's reputation. She'd vowed never to speak to her again after that, and wasn't about to change her mind.

She finally managed to grab a moment with Peggy who had now finished her beer and was gathering up her shopping. 'Sorry I was a bit sharp, Auntie Peg, but Ethel isn't someone I wanna talk about – not in here – and you can see how it is on Saturday mornings.'

'That's all right, dear, I do understand. It was tactless, what with Stan standing right next to me.'

'Don't worry,' murmured Ruby. 'It's all water under the bridge as far as he's concerned, especially now they're divorced.'

Peggy cleared her throat and edged closer to the bar so they couldn't be overheard. 'I only really came in to make sure you're coping, and to ask if you'd seen Jim lately.'

Ruby was immediately on guard. 'Why? Has he gone missing?' she hedged.

'Oh, I know where he is at the moment,' Peggy replied. 'It's the evenings I'm talking about. You see,' she added, lowering her voice further, 'he's been coming home late and is decidedly vague about where he's been.'

Ruby didn't want to lie to Peggy, but there again, she didn't want to tell tales about Jim, who had indeed become a fairly regular customer just lately. 'He nips in with Frank or Ron, sometimes,' she admitted hesitantly. 'He ain't playin' away, if that's what yer worrying about.'

Peggy glanced at Stan who was busy talking to one of the football supporters and edged closer. 'Just keep an eye on him, Ruby, love. And try to make sure he doesn't drink too much. Whisky gives him bad dreams.'

Ruby doubted very much if it was the whisky giving Jim nightmares. More likely, it was the traumas that had led to his drinking in the first place. Yet she nodded and assured Peggy that she would keep an eye on him – though how the hell she could do that was a mystery. The man was finding solace in the bottom of that glass, and if it gave him some respite from the awful things he must have seen out in Burma, then who was she to refuse him?

However, she'd seen how the drink could take hold and ruin lives – had witnessed Ethel being beaten by her step-father, just as Ray had abused her – and how Ethel's run-in with the drink had made her belligerent and up for a screeching scrap with anyone who looked at her sideways. She certainly didn't want that sort of trouble laid at darling Peggy's door. As they quickly embraced and Peggy tottered off with her shopping, Ruby wondered if perhaps she should have a quiet word with Frank when he came in later. Jim might listen to his older brother.

Jim stood in the kitchen doorway and admired the pale grey linoleum he'd helped to lay. His back ached a bit from the unaccustomed physical exertion, and his knees were creaking after being on them so long on that concrete floor, but it was a job that had saved his father the effort, so it was worth the minor discomfort.

'It's all looking grand, Da, so it is,' he shouted above the ear-splitting noise of the sander Charlie was using on the dining room floor.

'Aye. Grand enough,' he replied, wiping sweat from his neck with a grubby handkerchief. 'But I'll not be lying when I say I'll be glad when it's all done.'

'Well, I reckon we've all earned a pint,' said Jim, whose mouth was as dry as a desert.

'There's too much work to be skiving off to the Anchor,' rumbled Ron, 'and Ruby certainly won't serve young Charlie with any pint, even if he does look old enough. I'll freshen the teapot.'

Jim was about to suggest the Crown, where Gloria certainly would serve Charlie if they sat in the back room, and then thought better of it. It was a bit early in the day for drinking, and Peggy would blow a fuse if she even suspected he'd taken the boy there.

The awful racket of the sander came to an abrupt halt and Charlie emerged, his dark hair grey with wood-dust. 'The floor's done, Grandad, but it'll need a good clean before you varnish it. I'm sorry I can't hang about, but I need to get to the barber before rugby, and I'll have to wash first.'

Jim smiled at his youngest son and ruffled his filthy hair. 'I'll pop up to the ground later and see how you're getting on. Don't worry about that floor. I'll tidy up and put the first coat of varnish down.'

'That would be great, Dad,' Charlie replied, grinning. 'We're up against the Ditchling side today and they're a tough lot, so it should be a good match.'

He watched the boy hurry through the front door, banging it shut behind him. It was still something of a shock to see him so mature and self-assured when his abiding memory of him had been of a tearful little boy being evacuated to Somerset. In fact, his whole homecoming had been a shock, what with all the changes in the house, in Daisy and his other daughters – and in his Peggy, who'd lost her sweet curves, and had become rather alarmingly self-sufficient.

'Penny for your thoughts, son,' said Ron, filling his pipe with studied concentration.

'That lad of mine is almost a man,' he replied. 'It takes some getting used to, that's all. And what with Daisy starting school on Monday . . .' Jim hunted out a broom and dustpan, and without another word, went to sweep up the mess in the dining room.

He loved and admired his father, and could tell how hard he'd worked to bring Beach View up to date, so there was no way he was going to tell him that he really didn't like what he'd done, for the place was almost unrecognisable. Of course he understood how it had made life far easier for Peggy, what with all the gadgets in that fancy laundry room and posh kitchen, but it didn't feel like home – didn't begin to match up to the memories of the shabby old place he'd held so dear during his years away – and to his chagrin, he still felt like a visitor.

His mood darkened as he finished sweeping the dust from the floor, and he realised he was in for one of those days when all he really wanted was to shut himself away from everyone – to hide in the cocoon of darkness he'd wrapped around himself as protection from this new and bewildering world he'd found himself in.

There had been a lot of those since his return to Cliffehaven, and he'd done his best to hide them from the others. Yet trying to keep up the appearance of being his old self was exhausting, and he could only pray that if he kept up the pretence long enough it would become second nature, and ease him back into the ambitious, self-assured man he'd aimed to be on his return. Time was what he needed. Time and peace to come to terms with all he'd seen and done, and to adjust to living independently from the army life that had given him structure and purpose.

These thoughts unsettled him, for he was a man – a man with responsibilities – a husband, father and, God help him, a grandfather, with a wage to earn and a household to support. He had no business feeling like this when his family looked to him to take his place as head of the home. He knew he should take a leaf out of his father's book and just get on with things, thankful for all he had – after all, he reasoned, not everyone had come home to a decent, well-paid job, a faithful wife who loved him, and a home still intact. But just getting on with things wasn't that easy when his mind was in a fog, loud noises made him edgy, his sleep was disturbed by nightmares and the smallest task took huge concentration and effort.

It didn't help that his Peggy seemed to have coped extremely well during his absence, what with her job as manager at Solly's second garment factory and all the responsibilities of looking after Cordelia, the evacuees and raising Daisy throughout the war years. Now she was earning a good wage she'd grown more confident and assertive – perhaps even usurping his place as the main provider – and Jim couldn't quite banish the lurking suspicion that she didn't really need him at all.

Doing his best to shake off these disturbing thoughts, he wiped away the thick line of dust sitting along the picture rail and then got on his knees to sweep up in the corners and along the skirting board. *If I just concentrate on working hard, I'll get through this,* he thought. After all, he wasn't alone in this fog of confusion and unexplained fears. The POWs he helped with their numerous needs were haunted too, and closer to home, there was Martin and Roger – and even young Ruby, who sought oblivion from the past in hard work and a steely determination that he could only admire.

He finished cleaning and threw open the windows before returning to the kitchen for a mop and bucket. Despite the sunny day and the hard labour of the past few hours, he was shivering, for he still hadn't acclimatised to the British weather after all those years in the tropics. He dragged on a second sweater, thinking how ridiculous it was to be wearing sweaters, a thick shirt and fleecy vest in September, but he couldn't stand feeling cold all the time. The lack of decent food didn't help either, but that wasn't Peggy's fault, just the ridiculously strict rationing. He'd have given anything for a heaped plate of rich beef stew and dumplings with a mound of buttery mash on the side.

Catching a glimpse of Ron passing the window overlooking the side entrance, his thoughts on his stomach fled. Jim had always thought of his father as being ageless and sturdy – a tower of strength both in mind and body. And yet, in that fleeting, unguarded moment he'd noted there was more silver in Ron's thick dark hair, his shoulders were slumped, and his face lined with weariness.

Unwilling to accept that his father was getting old, Jim filled the bucket with hot, soapy water, picked up the scrubbing brush and mop and purposefully headed back to the dining room. The sooner this blasted house was finished, the better. His da had earned his rest and should be enjoying life, not slaving away here.

Peggy lugged her shopping back to the car which she'd had to park at the bottom of Camden Road. She'd rarely seen the place so busy, but that was probably something to do with the rumour of tinned ham in the shops.

She slid into the driving seat and shut the door with a sigh. It was another false rumour, of course, which she'd only discovered after half an hour's fruitless wait in a queue. But she had managed to persuade Doris to lend her some tea coupons, and collected the weekly ration of eggs, and Alf the butcher had slipped her a couple of bacon rashers from under the counter – so at least Jim wouldn't have anything to moan about tomorrow morning.

She didn't feel quite ready yet to face her rather too smug and bossy older sister, Doris. Lighting a cigarette, she stared out of the window at the blur and bustle of this busy Saturday morning, Ruby's words ringing in her head. She'd known they'd been meant to reassure her, but the thought that Jim might be roving had never occurred to her.

But surely not, she argued silently. He loved her – had proved it over and over again since coming home. There again, he'd said very little about his time in Singapore and the leaves he'd taken in India – and the nurses attached to the forces' hospitals. Then there was Elsa Bristow, who he *had* talked and written about and obviously admired. She'd always been suspicious about *that* relationship.

Peggy puffed on her cigarette, realised she was winding herself up like a clock and forced herself to calm down and think things through clearly. She wasn't a naive fool, and knowing Jim so well, with his charm, his flashing eyes and high libido, there had to have been some shenanigans during the years he'd been away despite his many denials. The idea of him being unfaithful was a knife to her heart, but she had to be realistic. She simply didn't want to know the details. What, if anything, had happened over there was in the past and best ignored.

She stubbed out her cigarette in the car's ashtray with some vigour and switched on the engine, determined to remain calm. Yet her thoughts were raging. If Jim Reilly had started acting the old goat, she'd have his guts for garters.

It was after twelve by the time the floor had been varnished, and the brambles and weeds banished from the front garden and gravel driveway. Jim had ordered his father to take the dogs for a run while he got on with it and, left alone to tidy up, cut the grass and dig over the flower beds, the job was soon done. The gravel needed replenishing on the driveway and there was a huge sack of it in the garage, but he'd do that once they'd finished tramping back and forth.

Tidying away the mower and gardening tools, he rearranged everything in the shed so it was easier to get at, tipped the garden waste onto the compost heap and closed all the windows. He'd come back early tomorrow to lightly sand that floor again and give it a second coat before papering the smallest bedroom.

With his thick overcoat warding off the chill wind now blowing from the sea, and his felt hat pulled low on his brow, he dug his hands in his deep pockets and headed for the sports ground. It was time to see how Charlie's team was faring, then nip into the Crown for a pint before tea. Gloria, the landlady, never asked him questions and always cheered him up, and because none of Peggy's friends went in there, there was little chance of her finding out. He didn't like hiding things from her, but what she didn't know wouldn't hurt her, and Gloria was always good for a laugh.

Doris had been entertaining Daisy for over an hour and was now at the point of losing patience with her sister. Peggy had promised to meet her here – had said she wouldn't be long – and now it was after two, and Daisy was fidgeting and beginning to whine most unpleasantly.

Doris wasn't used to small children and was a firm believer that they should be seen but not heard – unlike Peggy, who seemed to be very laissez-faire about how they should behave in public. 'Do sit still, dear,' she said, digging a clean handkerchief from her handbag to wipe the child's sticky face. 'Really, Daisy, you have made the most awful mess,' she complained, eyeing the smears of ice-cream on the dress and in her dark curls.

Daisy's big brown eyes regarded her with some defiance. 'I want my mum,' she said loudly.

'She'll be here soon,' replied Doris, aware that they were attracting po-faced attention from the other diners. It had clearly been a mistake to bring her up to Plummers' dining room for her ice-cream, and she wished now she'd taken her to the Lilac Tearoom where the customers were a lot less fussy.

'Sorry I'm late,' said Peggy, dumping herself into a chair and taking a delighted Daisy onto her lap.

Doris caught a whiff of alcohol and looked at her askance. 'Have you been drinking?' she hissed.

'So what if I have?' Peggy retorted. 'Half a beer isn't a crime, Doris.'

Doris tutted. 'It's a slippery slope when a married woman goes into a public house at this time of day – or any time of day, for that matter – especially if she's on her own.'

'And what if I was?'

Doris recognised the fighting light in Peggy's eyes. Not wishing to cause a scene in this hushed and genteel place, she decided to pay the bill and leave as quickly as possible. She dug into her expensive handbag for her purse and found the right coins. 'I must get home to John,' she murmured.

'You'll stay here and explain what you meant,' said Peggy, clamping her hand over Doris's wrist.

Aware of being surreptitiously watched by the other women nearby, Doris gritted her teeth. 'Let go of me, Peggy. This is neither the time nor the place.'

'Fine,' she snapped. 'We'll finish this conversation outside.' With that, she pushed back her chair and led a loudly protesting Daisy out of the restaurant.

Doris took a deep breath, paid the bill and reluctantly followed. She and Peggy had been getting along very well of late, and she really didn't want to fall out with her again. But Peggy seemed very on edge and determined to pick a fight.

Peggy rounded on her the minute she stepped outside. 'If I want a drink at lunchtime, then I'll have one,' she hissed. 'You're not my keeper, Doris.'

'I never imagined I was,' she replied with all the diplomacy she could dredge up. 'But don't you think you're protesting a bit too much, Peggy? Is there a reason behind this unusual behaviour?'

Peggy impatiently shook her head. 'I was thirsty after tramping up and down and standing about in endless queues, and I wanted something stronger than tea for a change. If that upsets you, then hard cheese.'

Doris sniffed and looked down her nose at her fiery sister. 'I knew things would change once Jim came home,' she said coolly. 'He's a bad influence and always has been.'

Peggy tightly folded her arms round her waist, her brown eyes bright with fury. 'I might have guessed you'd blame Jim,' she snapped. 'Well, for your information, this has nothing to do with him, so I suggest you keep your snooty nose out of my business and get on home.'

With that, she grabbed Daisy's hand and propelled her around a couple of men who were acting rather furtively in a shop doorway and then down the High Street towards the car. It was only when she was shepherding Daisy into the back seat that she realised she recognised both men, and thought it strange they should even know one another. But as it was none of her business, she turned her attention back to Daisy.

Doris stood on the pavement and watched her drive away. There was something wrong at Beach View, she just knew it. For how could such a simple remark set Peggy off like that?

Doris lifted her chin and strode in the other direction. She had never approved of Jim or his ghastly father, Ron, and she would lay odds that Jim's homecoming was at the heart of Peggy's frayed nerves. He always had been a fly-by-night with his ducking and diving, and Doris suspected he might be up to his old tricks again.

She was just walking past the alleyway which ran along the side of the Crown and led to the pub's back door when a movement caught her eye. Coming to a standstill, she recognised the back view of the figure hurrying down the alley and realised her suspicions about Jim Reilly had been right – although this evidence brought her no satisfaction.

The Crown was a rough den of iniquity, the brazen landlady a well-known purveyor of black-market booze and cigarettes – *amongst other things*, thought Doris with a shudder. If Jim was mixed up with her again it could only lead to trouble, and that was the last thing her sister needed. But what to do about it? She could hardly go in there and turf him out, or give him an earful. She had standards and a reputation to uphold – and frankly, wouldn't be caught dead in there.

These troubled thoughts remained with her as she walked up the hill towards home. Upon reaching Mafeking Terrace, she paused outside the spacious house she and John had had converted from their two adjoining bungalows, and realised she could tell no one what she'd seen, not even her darling husband John. But she had to do something. Her sister didn't deserve trouble laid at her door after all she'd been through.

3

Most of Ruby's customers had already left to attend the football match when she closed the door on the last of them on the dot of two o'clock. Heaving a weary sigh, she kicked off her shoes and slid her feet into the slippers she always kept beneath the bar. It had been a noisy, demanding session, and her feet were killing her after two and a half hours, but she wouldn't have had it any other way.

Swiftly collecting the dirty glasses, she lined them up on the bar and emptied the overflowing ashtrays into a bucket which she tipped into the rubbish bin. Retrieving her rubber gloves from the garden, she gave the tables a quick polish, straightened the chairs, then swept up fag ends and ash from the floor. Beer had been spilled here and there, and she'd mop it away later.

Returning to the bar, she checked the morning's takings and, after sorting out the float for the evening session, placed it all in a hessian bag. She'd stow it in the safe upstairs until Monday morning, and then take it to the bank.

Ruby was singing quietly to herself as she washed and dried the glasses, her thoughts happily centred on her healthy bank account. And yet, beneath that cheerfulness, she was constantly reminded that there had been a high price to pay for that bounty.

She hadn't known that Mike had written a will shortly after they'd married and sailed to Canada, so when he'd died in such a tragic and untimely way, it had come as a shock to discover that he'd left her his share in the family's prosperous logging business. Mike's family had immediately realised she would never stay in Canada and had generously bought the share from her – thus giving her the freedom to return home to England last year and make a new life.

Her hand trembled as she finished putting the glasses back under the bar. She'd have given up everything for Mike to still be alive – to be here – with her. 'Wishing don't change nothing,' she muttered crossly. 'Just be thankful you got all this and bloody well get on with it.'

She placed fresh towels over the pumps and gathered up the dirty ones ready to take upstairs for a wash. Once the bar had been polished to a shine, she brought up crates of beer and mixers from the cellar and then filled a bucket with hot water, added a splash of bleach and set about cleaning the floor. If she finished in time, she could still catch an hour or two of sun with a nice cuppa in the back garden.

Ruby had almost finished mopping the floor when someone banged on the front door. 'We're shut,' she shouted. 'Come back at seven.'

The muttered reply was inaudible and Ruby ignored it until the knocking came again – but louder this time. 'Oh, for Gawd's sake,' she muttered crossly, ramming the mop into the bucket, peeling off her rubber gloves and heading for the door.

The telephone began to ring just as the banging became even more demanding, and she angrily shot back the bolt to deliver whoever it was a piece of her mind. 'We're shut,' she barked on opening the door. 'Can't you . . .'

'There's no need to take that tone,' said Ethel primly.

Shocked into silence, Ruby could only stare in horror at the ragbag figure of her mother as the telephone kept urging her to answer it.

'Well, aren't you gunna let me in, gel? I ain't come all this way to be left on the bleedin' doorstep.'

As Ethel made to push past her, Ruby stood firm and barred her way. 'Then you'd better go back to where you come from,' she replied flatly. 'You're not welcome here.'

Ethel placed the battered suitcase onto the pavement and her haggard face crumpled. 'That's a fine thing to say to your own mother,' she whined, seemingly on the brink of tears. 'After all what I done for you.'

Ruby folded her arms, unmoved by this all-too-familiar display of crocodile tears. 'And what exactly have you done for me?' she asked coolly. 'Other than shame me, and bring about dishonour to an old man what done neither of us no harm.'

'I give birth to yer, that's what,' Ethel snapped, all pretence of tears vanishing in an instant. 'And looked after yer good and proper when that rotter Ray put you in the bleedin' hospital. As for what happened with Stan – that were none of yer business.'

The telephone finally stopped ringing, which was a relief, but Ruby could see they were attracting interest from the passers-by and had no wish to prolong this conversation. 'What do you want, Mum? I've better things to do than stand here arguing the toss with you.'

The thin, ravaged face crumpled again, but the eyes were dry and defiant. 'I put me 'ands up for what I done and served me time, Rubes. Stan's precious reputation didn't come to no 'arm.' She took a shuddering breath as if holding back more tears. 'But times is hard with no job or money coming in. I thought . . .' She licked her lips. 'I thought I could stay with you for a bit and perhaps 'elp with the cleaning and that until I find me feet again.'

Ruby's thoughts were in a whirl. Her mother was clearly down on her luck and in great need, and she did feel sorry for her. But if she let her over the threshold her settled life would be cast into chaos. Ethel had sticky fingers and certainly couldn't be trusted anywhere near money or booze – but she couldn't turn her back on her if she was destitute. Or was she? You never knew with Ethel.

'There's a Sally Army hostel just off the High Street,' she said. 'I'll take you there if you like. They'll give you a meal and a bed for the night.'

Ethel looked up at her as real tears began to roll down her cheeks. 'I never thought me own daughter would be so cold as to turn me away,' she sobbed. 'I got nothing and nowhere else to go, and I ain't eaten since yesterday.' Claw-like, nicotine-stained fingers clutched at Ruby's arm. 'Please, Ruby. I need 'elp. Really I do.'

Ruby wrinkled her nose at the ripe smell of old sweat and unwashed clothes emanating from Ethel. There was the whiff of drink on her too, and Ruby knew she was about to make a terrible mistake, but ignoring her better judgement, she took hold of the cold little hand and stepped aside.

'Just for the night, then you'll have to find somewhere else. I'll lose me licence if I let you stay and they find out you've got a prison record.'

Ethel sniffed back her tears, picked up her case and stepped into the bar. 'I'm ever so grateful,' she said humbly. 'You won't regret it, Ruby, I promise.'

Ruby suspected she would, but her conscience wouldn't allow her to leave Ethel to fend for herself in the state she was in. Having locked and bolted the door again, she was suddenly reminded of the bag of takings she'd left in full sight on the bar.

'Why don't you take the weight off and sit down while I get us both a lemonade?' she said, edging towards the bar.

'I'd rather 'ave a gin,' said Ethel, plumping down on a chair and removing her ratty fur coat.

'I thought you promised the judge you'd give up the drink?' said Ruby, hastily wrapping the money bag inside the bundle of bar towels and shoving it deep beneath the counter.

'Only cos I can't afford it,' said Ethel, her avaricious gaze roaming over the ornate mirror behind the bar where the bottles of spirits were lined up on glass shelves.

Ruby put half a measure of gin in a glass and drowned it in tonic. *But you've had at least one drink today already. No doubt you got some man to buy it for you after giving him a sob story.* With a glass of lemonade for herself, she slipped her shoes back on, sat down and put the drinks on the table.

Ethel grimaced at the taste of tonic, but it didn't stop her from swiftly emptying the glass.

Ruby took the opportunity to have a proper look at her mother, and was both shocked and saddened by how small and frail she'd become after her long prison sentence. Ethel was only in her forties but looked seventy. She'd always been skinny, but she'd never let herself go like this. Her hair was lacklustre, greying and thin, some of her teeth were missing, and her wan face was lined with experiences that surely hadn't been pleasant. But Ruby noted that her eyes were still watchful, and as sharp as a tack as they kept settling on her engagement ring and wedding band.

And yet, for all her wit and slyness, she hadn't been saved from destitution. The cotton dress was faded and grubby, there were holes in her stained cardigan and her shoes were falling apart. As for that ratty old fur coat, she remembered her wearing it in London before the war – swanning about like lady muck – now it was fit only for the rubbish bin.

'Had a good look, 'ave yer?' Ethel's expression was sour. 'It's all right for you. You always did land on yer feet.'

Ruby wouldn't be drawn. 'How long have you been out of prison?

'Three months,' she muttered.

'And how did you find me?'

Ethel shrugged and pointedly shoved her empty glass across the table. 'I come down to try and find work,' she said. 'Me throat's terrible dry, Ruby. Give us another drink.'

The last thing Ruby needed was her mother getting drunk and causing a scene. She pushed her untouched glass of lemonade towards her and, without offering one to Ethel, lit a cigarette. 'I'm surprised you dared show yer face here after what you done to Stan.'

Ethel's magpie gaze glinted at the sight of the gold cigarette case and lighter, and Ruby quickly slid them out of sight into her trouser pocket.

Ethel sniffed and pretended not to notice. 'Yeah, well, I thought Stan might put a bit of work me way seeing as 'ow we was married once and I took all the blame for selling that stuff.' She reluctantly took a sip of the lemonade and then abandoned it as if it was poison.

'Don't give me all that old pony,' Ruby snapped. '*You* thieved all that tinned food from the Red Cross store and factory canteen. *You* hid it away at Stan's – and it was *you* what sold it on the black market. It was you what was to blame. Not poor, innocent Stan.'

Ethel gave a snort of derision, pulled a tobacco pouch from her cardigan pocket and began to roll a cigarette. 'Me 'eart bleeds,' she said sarcastically.

Ruby could feel her temper rising as she watched Ethel strike a match and light the cigarette. 'So, what did he say when you turned up at 'is door?'

Ethel gave a hacking cough and then narrowed her eyes against the curl of smoke coming from the cigarette she'd jammed into the corner of her mouth. 'He weren't there. That tart April told me to sling me 'ook and slammed the door in me face like I was infectious or something.'

'April is not a tart.'

'Oh, yeah? One brown kid with no bleedin' father around, and 'er cavorting with some bloke while Stan's out? I'd say she's a tart all right.'

It takes one to know one, thought Ruby, who remembered all too well the different men who'd walked into and out of Ethel's chaotic life when her step-father had been serving time in prison. 'You still haven't said how you found me,' she reminded her.

The ash from Ethel's cigarette spilled down her front as she had another coughing fit, but she didn't seem to notice. 'I went in the Crown thinking Stan might be there, and met Phil Warner – a bloke what used to hang about with my old pal Olive. He told me about this place, and 'ow you'd fallen on yer feet good and proper.'

Her all-knowing eyes met Ruby's. 'Though how you come by the money for it, 'e didn't say,' she said slyly.

Ruby wasn't about to enlighten her. She glanced at the clock above the bar and went to discreetly retrieve the money bag and towels, and stow away the mop and bucket. 'I expect you'll want a bath, something to eat and a bit of a lie-down,' she said unenthusiastically, 'so let's get you settled in before I have to open at seven.'

Ethel pinched out the cigarette and jammed the stub behind her ear. Picking up her coat and suitcase, she followed her daughter, huffing and puffing up the stairs. Standing on the threshold to the lounge, she caught her wheezing breath and then gave a low whistle.

'Blimey, gel. Ain't this posh?'

'It's comfortable enough,' replied Ruby, guiding her further into the apartment. 'This is the kitchen. My bedroom's through here; this is the bathroom, and you can sleep in here,' she finished, opening the door to the spare bedroom.

Ethel eyed it with studied indifference. 'Very nice,' she said begrudgingly as she dumped her dirty case on the pink bedspread and glanced at the wallpaper and matching curtains sprigged with rose buds, and the fluffy bedside rug on the white-painted floor.

Ruby again caught the unpleasant tang of Ethel's body odour. 'I'll get you some towels and run the bath before we eat. You'll find soap and shampoo in the bathroom.'

Ethel grasped her wrist. 'Thanks, love. I knew you wouldn't let me down.'

'It's just for the night, remember,' Ruby replied firmly. 'We'll sort out something more permanent for tomorrow.'

While Ethel was splashing about in the bath, Ruby quickly hid the money away in the safe she'd had fitted under the floorboards of the kitchen larder. Her pearls and gold bracelets were already in there, so she added the lighter and cigarette case, knowing they would present an irresistible temptation to a woman like Ethel. With the lino back in place and the twenty-pound sack of potatoes sitting on top, it was well and truly hidden.

Ruby felt a little easier now her valuables were safe, but it left a nasty taste in her mouth to realise that her own mother was perfectly capable of robbing her blind, and would think nothing of it.

She reached into the small fridge for the pot of rabbit stew and dumplings she'd made the previous day. It could be heated up for supper, along with a few spuds and a slice of bread. Quickly peeling a large potato, Ruby cut it up and put the pan of salted water on to boil, checked the oven was on, and then set about laying the gate-leg table with cutlery.

Satisfied that she could do no more, she went into the sitting room, hid the bottle of gin from the side table behind the couch and plumped down into it to light a cigarette and ponder over the problem of what to do about Ethel.

Cliffehaven might have grown over the years, but it was a close-knit community and everyone knew everyone's business, so Ethel's dodgy reputation was already common knowledge. Apart from the Salvation Army hostel, there was nowhere else she could think of that might take her in, and Ruby wasn't about to pay rent for a room in a boarding house – neither would she give her a reference – for as sure as eggs were eggs, any such foolishness would come back to bite her.

However, she could pay for a train ticket to London. Ethel knew her way around there and, after all the years of ducking and diving, she was sure to find someone from the old crowd who'd give her a job and somewhere to stay. Yet it was odd she hadn't already tried that, for she was far more at home up there, and had made a lot of enemies here. She'd ask her after they'd eaten, she decided.

Her thoughts were interrupted as the telephone began to ring on the side table. Reaching across the arm of the couch, she picked up the receiver just as Ethel appeared wrapped in Ruby's best silk dressing-wrap and carrying a bottle of nail varnish, both of which she could only have found by going into Ruby's bedroom.

Ruby glared at her as she answered the telephone. 'Hello?'

The Cockney voice at the other end was immediately recognisable. 'It's Gloria. I tried earlier, but you must 'ave been busy. I need to warn yer, Ruby,' she hurried on. 'Ethel come into the Crown earlier and I seen her talking to that dodgy piece of work Phil Warner. And if she and 'im are in cahoots again, there could only be trouble ahead.'

Ruby watched as Ethel planted her skinny backside on the other couch and began to paint her bitten fingernails with Ruby's red polish. 'Yeah, I know,' she replied.

'You ain't let 'er in, 'ave you?' Gloria's rasping Cockney accent sharpened.

When Ruby didn't reply, Gloria gave an exasperated sigh. 'Bloody hell, mate. I know she's yer mum and all, but you're just askin' fer strife.'

Ruby realised she had to be careful what she said with Ethel earwigging. 'I'm aware of that. Thanks ever so much for calling. It is appreciated.'

'I'm guessing she's there and you can't talk proper, so I'll just say this, Ruby. If she or Phil Warner gives you an ounce of trouble, you call me. I'll sort them both out for you.'

Ruby smiled, for Gloria was made from the same East End cloth as her and Ethel, and had never stood for any nonsense. She could be a formidable opponent, which was why Ruby had deliberately forged a strong friendship with her. 'I'll remember that. Thanks ever so.'

She replaced the receiver and, ignoring Ethel's inquisitive look, went into the kitchen to get their supper.

Ron had spent a very pleasant afternoon tramping the hills to the east of Cliffehaven with his ferrets and dogs. He'd walked for miles, relishing the stretch in his legs, the fresh air and the glorious scenery as the dogs raced ahead of him. The sky seemed bluer than usual, the sea sparkling and calm as it softly broke on the shore, and Ron felt the weight of his responsibilities ease from his shoulders, leaving him clear-headed and vigorous again.

From the clifftops, he'd looked down to the line of fishermen's cottages in Tamarisk Bay and across to Cliffehaven which now sprawled into the hills above the horseshoe bay to the north, east and west. The town had grown, for there were new and rather smart detached houses on the estate once owned by the bankrupt Lord Chumley, and the fire-bombed council hovels behind the station had been cleared away in preparation for the new cheap terraces that would accommodate the previous tenants, as well as the influx of new ones.

As he waited for Flora and Dora to appear from the rabbit hole they'd dived into, he leaned back on his elbows and surveyed the Cliffe estate which nestled in the deep valley to the north of Cliffehaven. It encompassed woodland, salmon ponds, an enclosed pen to raise game birds, and several farms. Ron had many fond memories of poaching there – and of teaching his sons how to tickle a salmon, or grab an unsuspecting pheasant before it called out an alarm.

During the war years, the elegant mansion at the heart of the estate had first been taken over by the Yanks, and then turned into a sanatorium for injured servicemen who were in their final stages of recovery. The woodland had been harvested by the Women's Timber Corps. The patients and the women were long gone now, and Lord Cliffe had returned from his war posting in London to take up the reins again and restore everything to its former glory.

Ron noted that the high fencing around the place had been strengthened, and he'd heard that the eager young gamekeeper was as unforgiving and watchful as the old one. This didn't bode well, for there was nothing like a fresh salmon, or a nice fat pheasant for the table, and although Ron liked a challenge, he wasn't sure he was still up to giving a youthful gamekeeper a run for his money.

Flora poked her nose out of the hole, swiftly followed by Dora. It seemed each of them had caught a rabbit, so he quickly wrung their necks, stuffed them into one of the deep pockets of his ankle-length poacher's coat, and removed the purse nets. Once each ferret had received a congratulatory stroke, he eased them into their favourite deep pocket so they could sleep.

With the purse nets safely tucked away, he lit his pipe, his gaze travelling down to the valley where a farmer was ploughing to the accompaniment of a horde of screeching seagulls. From there, he looked further on to the distant airfield that had played such an important part in the defence of this corner of the world.

Ron could remember the runway being laid in haste at the start of hostilities in 1914, the control tower and huts being thrown up to accommodate the fledgling service of the Royal Flying Corps, which at the time was the air arm of the army. It had fallen into disrepair after the first war, but then quickly been brought back into use at the start of the second when it was realised how strategically placed it was for getting across the Channel, and for intercepting the German bombers on their way to London.

But those days were over once the heavy bombers landed elsewhere, and it had been abandoned by the RAF to quietly disappear back into the grassland from whence it had come. And yet change had come again through Peggy's son-in-law, Martin, and his fellow flier, Roger Makepeace. They had seen the potential in the place after they'd returned from the German POW camp to find so many other RAF personnel at a loose end, and had repaired the runway and control tower, hired a trained ground crew, and provided comfortable accommodation for their homeless families in the refurbished Nissan huts. Phoenix Air Freight had brought new life to the old place, and so far, business was booming.

Ron whistled to the dogs and began the steep descent towards the valley. Feeling free of constraints after the months of labour at the house, there was a spring in his step as he made his way towards the country lane which ran through the hamlet where Martin and Anne lived with their children and meandered on to the large town the other side of the hills. There was little need to hurry, for Rosie probably wouldn't be home for hours yet, and the dogs were enjoying themselves.

He returned the farmer's wave and sauntered on happily down the middle of the lane, feeling the sun on his face and enjoying the birdsong now the screeching gulls were occupied further away. Turning into the wide gateway, he made sure Harvey and Monty were following, and headed towards the reception hut which stood to the side of the far end of the repaired runway.

A huge DC-47 had just come to a halt in the holding area, the ground crew buzzing around it like flies as the powerful Pratt & Whitney engine fell silent and the propellers stopped turning. The second transport plane was already firmly tethered in its own docking bay, the cargo door open to unload several large crates.

Ron paused for a moment to watch the bustle, and then heard a shout. He grinned with pleasure as he realised it was Martin calling to him, and so hurried on in the hope there might be a cup of tea or even a beer to whet his whistle.

Martin certainly looked much better than he had when he'd first come home. There was colour in his cheeks and his eyes were sparkling above the luxuriant moustache, and although he bore the scars of his war on his face and hands, it seemed he was no longer aware of them. Ron strode forward and heartily shook his hand. 'Good to see you, son,' he said.

'It's good to see you too, Ron,' he replied. 'We don't often have the privilege of your company up here.'

'The animals needed exercising,' Ron said, 'and so do I, after being stuck indoors for weeks.'

Martin grinned. 'I won't ask how it's going,' he said. 'Your expression says it all. Come and have a beer.'

'To be sure that's music to me ears,' Ron replied happily. He followed Martin to the hut where a line of deckchairs had been placed outside and plonked himself down, careful not to squash the sleeping ferrets in his pocket.

Harvey and Monty drank water noisily from a fire bucket, and then went off eagerly to explore the hedgerow and water every blade of grass.

Martin returned with four bottles of beer and sat down beside him just as Roger Makepeace and young Charlotte climbed out of the recently parked plane. 'No Stanislav today?' asked Ron.

'He flew with me and then rushed home to Danuta,' replied Martin, chuckling. 'Our large and very loud Pole is still in the honeymoon stage, and we rarely see him when he's off duty.'

Roger's beaming smile and dashing moustache hadn't changed, Ron noticed as the man came to shake his hand. And neither had young Charlotte, who was still as pretty as a picture, and as slim as ever despite the fact she was the widowed mother of twins.

'Don't get up, Uncle Ron,' she said, leaning down to peck him on the cheek. 'I'm not staying. Kitty's been left with all four children today and must be on her knees by now, so I'm taking Roger home to do his fatherly duties, and to see to my two.'

'How's Kitty's new baby?' asked Ron.

'Thomas is both noisy and demanding,' she replied. 'Just like all boys,' she added, nudging Roger playfully with her elbow. 'Tell Auntie Peggy I'm sorry I haven't been round to visit lately, but it's been hectic here, and what with the twins and flying every day . . .' She shrugged. 'Well, you know.'

'She'll understand,' he replied, thinking how well the girl was doing, what with flying those huge planes and raising her children without Freddy at her side. The war had certainly brought changes to the lives of women. He sipped his beer and watched Charlotte drive away at speed. Perhaps that was part of the reason Jim couldn't settle, now Peggy was earning her own money at that factory and gaining confidence daily.

Dragging his thoughts back to the man beside him, he asked, 'How is that granddaughter of mine getting on, Martin?'

'Anne's due any day now,' he replied cheerfully. 'Now we've got Rose Margaret and Emily, we're hoping for a boy – though after being in young Thomas's company for half an hour, I'm starting to have second thoughts,' he added with a wink. 'That kid has more lung power than any plane.'

'Aye,' Ron muttered. 'I remember the days when my boys were little. I seemed to have a permanent headache.'

They sat in companionable silence, enjoying the peace of their surroundings and the cold beer as the dogs chased after something they'd discovered in the long grass.

'I get the feeling your visit today has a purpose,' said Martin a while later. 'Is there something on your mind, Ron?'

'There is, aye. But I don't know if I should really speak of it,' he replied, watching the dogs return from their fruitless hunt to flop panting at his feet.

'Whatever it is, it's clearly bothering you,' Martin said, reaching for his pipe. 'Better spoken about than left to moulder, Ron – you know that as well as I.'

'It's Jim,' he said flatly.

Martin took his time to light his pipe. 'I thought it might be,' he murmured.

Ron retrieved his own pipe and mulled over what he wanted to say as he filled it. 'When Jim first came home he was full of ideas and excited about working for the British Legion. There was a quiet maturity about him I'd never seen before, and a real determination to make a difference to their lives as well as his own. And I think, in some way, he wanted to make reparation for what had happened to them at the hands of the Japanese.'

'And now?'

Ron lit his pipe and puffed on it as he formulated an answer. 'He's doing his best to pretend everything is all right for Peggy's sake, and as far as I can tell, he's doing sterling work for the Legion. But it's as if he's withdrawing into himself, and in unguarded moments I've seen a darkness behind his eyes – one I recognise from my own experiences of war – and that really worries me.'

'It's the same for us all, Ron,' Martin said quietly. 'I suspect he's having nightmares about what he's seen and done – feels guilty because he survived when so many of his mates didn't – and is finding it difficult to adjust to family life again. I know I did.'

Ron nodded. 'Aye, me too, and from what Peggy's hinted at, that sounds about right.'

'He needs to talk to someone who was there,' said Martin. 'Like I did with Roger. It helped us both enormously.'

Ron looked at his son-in-law sharply. 'But you're all right now, aren't you?'

Martin grimaced. 'I still get what they call "flashbacks", but not as often, and mostly manage to get through the night without the bad dreams.' He took a long swig of his beer. 'The memories never really go, Ron – you must know that after what you went through in the first shout. They simply fade and hurt less with time.'

'Aye,' he sighed, remembering the horrors of the trenches and tunnels, the rats and mud which occasionally still came to haunt him. 'That they do.'

Martin finished his beer and opened the other bottles as Harvey dashed off into the nearby bushes, and Monty slowly followed him. 'I'd be very surprised if the Legion didn't offer help of some sort. After all, they're dealing with men who've been through hell and need all the help they can get to be able to live a full life again.'

'They do,' Ron replied, taking a sip of the fresh beer. 'I went up to the Legion social club the other night and spoke to the chairman – without naming names, of course – I don't want to put Jim's job in jeopardy. But Jim is refusing to admit he needs help.'

'Then there's not much anyone can do until he does,' said Martin on a sigh. 'You'll just have to keep an eye on him, and try to keep his spirits up when he gets depressed.'

'I can't see what he has to be depressed about,' said Ron gruffly. 'He's got a good job, a family who love him and a home any man would envy.'

'Depression isn't about the material things, Ron, and it's not even logical. You can be absolutely fine one day, and then wake up the next feeling as if the weight of the world is on your shoulders.'

Martin watched the smoke curl up from his pipe. 'It's an illness, according to my doctor, which brings us low for no apparent reason and plays havoc with how we see things and react to them. Churchill suffers from it, you know. He calls it his "black dog".'

Ron eyed him thoughtfully, wondering if he really had fully recovered or, like Jim, was merely acting a part. 'You seem to know a lot about it.'

'Apart from talking to Roger, who knew exactly what I was going through and why, my doctor was a huge help,' Martin said. 'He gave me several books on the subject which were most enlightening, and then prescribed a course of pills, which I have to say perked me up no end.'

'I'm not sure about the pills,' commented Ron, who didn't believe that pills could cure anything much. 'But the books might be a help.'

'I'll see what I can do. But he really should go and see Dr Freeman and have a talk with him. The man's forward thinking and much respected by his peers for his work with those suffering from what we used to call shell shock.'

Martin looked at his watch. 'I'm sorry, Ron, but I'd better get home or Anne will be on the warpath. Rose is overexcited about starting school on Monday, and Emily's being petulant because of it. Do you want a lift back?'

Feeling slightly better for having discussed things with someone as sensible as Martin, Ron shook his head. 'Thanks, but no. I've got a lot to think about, and walking helps.'

Martin squeezed his shoulder, and once the deck-chairs had been stacked away in the hut, waved a cheerful goodbye and drove off.

Ron whistled for the dogs, which seemed to have disappeared. 'Come to heel, you heathen beasts,' he shouted.

There was a rustle and scramble through the hedgerow, and a high-pitched yelp from Monty – and then an ominous silence.

Fearing one of them had been bitten by an adder, Ron quickly headed for the thick shrubbery. 'Will ye get outta there,' he roared, beating back the branches in search of them.

Another frantic thrashing in the undergrowth and Harvey appeared triumphantly with a plump pheasant in his mouth. Tail wagging in delight, he dropped the still-twitching bird at Ron's feet and sat waiting for his due praise.

'Well I'll be blowed,' breathed Ron, hastily wringing the bird's neck before stuffing it into another of his deep pockets. 'To be sure you're a fine fellow, so you are.'

With a glance towards the fields that belonged to Lord Cliffe, Ron patted the dog's head, and with a sharp order to both of them to come to heel, he hurried away from the crime scene.

There had been no sign of anyone watching, which was lucky, for it was illegal to catch or shoot the birds out of season, and if they were caught, he'd be up in front of the magistrate. It had happened before when old Simmons was on the bench, and he'd got away with it. But the new fellow wasn't half as obliging – or so he'd heard.

Once they'd left the airfield, Ron slowed to an amble down the quiet country lane, feeling rather pleased with himself and his animals. It had been a successful day, what with two rabbits, the pheasant, and a good airing of his troubles to Martin. Yet he was reluctant to get home to an empty house and the cold leftovers of yesterday's vegetable stew, which he really couldn't be bothered to heat up.

He took a deep, restorative breath of the country air and decided that a bag of hot chips drenched in salt and vinegar would be just the thing. And then remembered he'd left his wallet behind. With a deep sigh, he trudged on, thinking how hard done by he was.

4

Ruby had, with some difficulty, persuaded Ethel to unpack the battered case and put her dirty clothes in the washing machine. The filthy rags were hardly worth the soap powder, and it was likely they wouldn't survive the wash, but the thought of fleas and bedbugs getting into the flat made Ruby shudder. As for the fur coat, there wasn't much she could do about it, so after giving it a good shake out of the window, she hung it on the back of the bedroom door in the hope that whatever had lived in it was long dead.

Still draped in Ruby's expensive dressing gown, Ethel hungrily polished off two bowls of stew and three thick slices of bread which she ate in silence, too intent upon the food she was shovelling down to make conversation.

Ruby didn't begrudge her a morsel of it, and in fact could only feel terrible pity that her once fiercely battling and gobby mother had been brought so low. But she did wish she'd take more care, for now there were food stains all down the front of the silk wrap.

When Ethel finally sat back with a sated sigh, Ruby cleared away the plates and poured them both a cup of tea. 'The washing's done, so I'll hang it out when I go down to open up,' she said as they went into the lounge. 'I'll look out some underwear for you and a couple of other things you can use while it's drying.'

Ethel didn't reply as she plumped down into the couch and slurped the tea.

Ruby offered Ethel a cigarette and they smoked in silence, both of them feeling awkward to be in this strange position, and neither of them really knowing what to say to each other.

Ruby regarded her surreptitiously as the clock on the mantel ticked away the time and the silence stretched between them. They had never been that close, even when Ruby was a child, for Ethel had been a rough and careless sort of mother who was more interested in earning a shilling and having a good time than looking after her daughter. Ruby had lost count of the 'aunties' who'd looked after her when Ethel had done one of her disappearing acts. And yet there had been fleeting moments when it seemed that Ethel did actually care for her in her own way, and it was those that Ruby clung to now.

The irony of the situation she found herself in wasn't lost on her, for now it was Ethel who needed looking after, and Ruby wasn't at all sure how to do that – or, to her shame, if she even wanted to.

Ruby glanced at the clock. It would be opening time soon, so best to ask the question that had been on her mind since Ethel's arrival. 'I'm surprised you didn't stay up in the Smoke after you got released,' she said. 'You've got lots of friends up there.'

Ethel grimaced, stubbed out her cigarette and folded her arms. 'There ain't nothing left up there for me,' she said. 'The tenements have been blown to bits by Hitler's lot, and 'alf the East End's just matchwood and rubble now. I hardly recognised the place.'

'But surely there are still people there you know? Old pals who could help find you a job and a place to live?'

Ethel shook her head, her expression sour. 'Nah. Mostly all gorn, and them that's left are too bleedin' busy looking after theirselves to bother with the likes of me. I even went back to the canning factory, but they wouldn't take me on again. Said I were unreliable and needed a reference.' She snorted in disdain. 'Bits of bleedin' paper. What use are they when yer on yer uppers?'

She didn't wait for an answer but hurried on. 'I tried the Tanner's Arms where you was working before you come down 'ere, but what they was offering weren't worth me spit.'

Ruby raised an eyebrow. The Tanner's Arms was an old, established pub – rough and rowdy in the centre of Bow, but the landlord was a good bloke. 'What were they offering?'

'Washing glasses and cleaning. That Fred Bowman expected me to sleep in the bleedin' attic and all for two and a tanner a week. I told him where to poke it,' she added with some pride.

Ruby wasn't surprised, for Ethel always did have a mistaken sense of her own worth. But Fred was a good man and he and his wife had been kind to Ruby over the time she'd worked there, often hiding her in that cosy attic room from Ray when he'd come looking for her in one of his rages. At least Ethel would have had somewhere safe to live and work, and the Licensing Board would have turned a blind eye as they always did in that part of London, as trying to enforce the law caused more trouble than it was worth.

'Did your wage include meals?'

'Well, yeah,' Ethel admitted dismissively. 'But 'is wife's a filthy mare and the kitchen were disgusting. I wasn't about to eat anything she done.' She gave a vast yawn, hoisted herself out of the couch and drew Ruby's beautiful silk wrap more firmly about her naked body. 'Thanks for the tea. I'm off to bed.'

'Before you go,' said Ruby quickly, 'I'd prefer it if you didn't go into my room and borrow things.' She kept her tone mild in an effort to ward off any umbrage. 'If you need something, ask me first next time, eh?'

Ethel drew herself up to her full five feet and half an inch. 'I ain't nicking stuff if that's what yer implying,' she said haughtily.

'I never said you were,' Ruby replied mildly. 'But I'd appreciate it if you could stay out of my room, just as I won't come into yours without asking.' She regarded her mother steadily. 'Do we have a deal?'

Ethel nodded curtly and stalked away, slamming her bedroom door behind her.

Ruby gave a deep sigh, glanced at the clock and realised Brenda would be here any minute as it was almost opening time. She quickly hunted out some underwear and a nightdress for Ethel and told her she'd left them outside her bedroom door. Having checked in the mirror above the fireplace that she didn't look too frazzled, she bundled up the washing before hurrying down the stairs.

Pausing at the bottom, she was tempted to lock the door behind her as usual, and thus keep Ethel out of the bar. But then she'd probably sleep through the night after such a heavy meal, and Ruby felt uncomfortable at the thought of locking her mother in like a prisoner – the poor woman had served enough time behind locked doors.

Ruby kept an eye on the time as she hurried out to the back garden to peg up the clothes on the line. Most of it had fallen to bits, she realised sadly, and the underwear was in such a terrible state it wasn't even fit for cleaning rags. Chucking most of it in the dustbin, she returned to the bar, her mind going over what she could lend Ethel to see her through.

Brenda came hurrying through from the side door to hang up her raincoat and umbrella, and Ruby noted how lovely and girlish she looked despite being in her mid-thirties. Dressed in a pretty floral frock, with her gleaming brown hair neatly pinned back from her face, she radiated a happiness that warmed Ruby's heart.

'Hello, love. You're looking chirpy. Had a lovely day out with Frank?'

Brenda blushed and dipped her chin. 'We had tea together before he had to take the boat out again.' She glanced out of the window as she put her handbag under the counter. 'It's a bit late to be hanging out washing, isn't it? And the forecast is for more rain.'

Ruby shrugged. 'A bit of rain won't do much harm,' she replied. She saw Brenda's questioning look and realised she couldn't keep Ethel a secret. 'Me mother's turned up,' she said flatly. 'She's upstairs – and will hopefully stay there.'

'Oh lawks,' breathed Brenda, who'd heard all about Ethel from the local gossip. 'Is it wise to let her stay here?'

'I didn't really have much choice,' Ruby replied, heading across the room to unbolt the door. 'Hopefully she'll be gone tomorrow.'

Brenda fiddled with the string of amber beads round her neck, her hazel eyes regarding Ruby with concern. 'I am sorry she's landed on you like this, Ruby. We'd better warn Stan when he next comes in, because he definitely won't want to see her.'

'I suspect he already knows as she went round to his place looking for him and got a flea in the ear from young April. He'll probably give us a wide berth until she's gone – and, Brenda, please don't serve her any drink if she comes down. The last thing we need on a busy night is a scene.'

'Right you are,' Brenda replied uncertainly, 'but she's more likely to cause a scene if we refuse to serve her.'

Ruby gave a deep sigh. 'Then we'll just have to play it by ear, and hope she doesn't put in an appearance.'

It wasn't very long before they were both too busy to worry about anything but getting the customers served. Mostly male, they were a noisy lot but good spirited as the local team had won. Once they'd lubricated their throats with enough beer, the singing began to the accompaniment of someone bashing out the tunes on the piano Ron had bought to replace the old one which had been committed to a bonfire on VE night.

It was hard to hear anything above the racket as orders were shouted across the bar and cigarette smoke rose in a cloud to the ceiling. But Ruby and Brenda worked together in harmony, moving in well-practised unison behind the bar to fill the orders, clear dirty glasses and wipe spilled beer from the counter.

Brenda saw her first and gave Ruby a sharp nudge while cocking her head towards the hallway door.

Ruby followed her gaze and saw Ethel kitted out in Ruby's best black dress and high-heeled silver sandals. Make-up was smeared over her face and she was so drunk she could barely stand. With a stab of fury, she swiftly grabbed Ethel's skinny arm before she could slide to the floor. 'Upstairs,' she hissed.

'I wanna drink,' she slurred.

'You've had more than enough already by the state of yer,' retorted Ruby, steering her forcibly back down the narrow hallway towards the stairs – all too aware of the catcalls and coarse remarks coming from the men in the bar.

'Don't push me about,' Ethel snarled, wrestling to free her arm from Ruby's grip. 'Yer 'urtin' me.'

Ruby ignored the complaint and managed with some difficulty to get Ethel up the stairs. Virtually carrying her across the lounge, she finally got her into the spare bedroom and bundled her unceremoniously onto the bed.

The room looked as if a bomb had hit it. Looking round at the mess in disgust, she picked up the empty gin bottle from the floor, her frustration and anger sharpening. Ethel had not only found the gin she'd hidden behind the couch but burnt a hole in the rug with a careless cigarette – and been into her room despite being expressly told not to.

Now all her lovely clothes and shoes were scattered everywhere, the ashtray was overflowing and the empty bottle of cooking sherry was under the dressing table. Ethel had even been through her jewellery box, and her cheap earrings, beads and bracelets were strewn across the dressing table along with Ruby's make-up.

Ethel struggled to sit up and get off the bed.

Ruby pushed her back down none too gently. 'You ain't goin' nowhere, lady,' she snapped.

'I wanna drink,' Ethel muttered. 'You ain't got no right . . .'

Ruby was too cross to even listen. 'You just couldn't help yerself, could ya?' she yelled, her voice rising with every word. 'Well, you done it now, cos you'll be on the first bleedin' train outta here tomorrow. I ain't putting up with it. D'ya hear?'

Ethel cringed away, raising her arms protectively over her head to ward off the expected blows. 'I'm sorry,' she blubbered. 'I won't do it again. I promise. Don't hit me. Please don't hit me.'

Ruby's anger fled as swiftly as it had risen, and in its place came horror at how awful she was being. She looked down at her mother with heartfelt pity and deep remorse. 'I ain't never gunna hit you, Mum,' she said sadly. 'But you'd try the patience of a bleedin' saint, honest you would. Why couldn't you 'ave just left the booze alone?'

Ethel mumbled something and curled, whimpering, into the pitiful, protective ball that Ruby remembered from the bad old days.

Ruby felt heartsick as she regarded that frail, frightened and utterly helpless little body. Ethel was the sum of all that had happened to her over the years. Gone was the feisty battleaxe who'd given as good as she'd got; who'd made the best of things in a world of pain and poverty; who'd sought oblivion from it all in the only way she knew how. She'd been the victim too long, and now it was all she knew.

Ruby sat on the bed wanting to gather her mother into her arms and tell her how sorry she was for shouting at her.

But Ethel had passed out.

With a sigh of sad acceptance, Ruby removed the silver sandals, and gently turned her over so she could unzip the dress. Sliding it down the skinny body, she wasn't at all surprised to see bruises on her ribs and the scars of old beatings. There were also flea bites on her legs and a nasty ulcer on her thigh.

Ruby left her wearing the expensive bra, pants and slip and, making sure she was firmly wedged on her side in case she threw up, tenderly covered her with the blanket. She'd clear up the mess later, but first she'd confiscate the tobacco and matches to avoid having the place burnt down.

'I'll get Danuta to see to that ulcer tomorrow,' she murmured as the noise from the bar thundered up through the floor. 'But for now, I've got to get back to Brenda.'

*

Peggy was glad the day was over, for her scratchy mood hadn't been helped by Daisy's tantrum at bedtime. It had taken all of Peggy's patience to coax her out of wanting to wear her new uniform to bed, and to eat her supper without chucking it about everywhere. But once she'd had her bath and Peggy had read her a story, the child had finally settled down to sleep.

Leaving the nursery door ajar, Peggy went into her own bedroom and sat down at her dressing table to gaze out of her window. She should really telephone Doris and apologise for jumping down her throat like that, but it would only elicit more questions and needle her again, so perhaps it was better left until tomorrow.

She gave a sigh and dug into her apron pocket for her cigarettes. What she really needed was a few minutes' peace after the day she'd had, and now Daisy was settled she already felt much calmer. Once she'd lit a cigarette, she gazed out to the view she'd never had before the enemy bombers had blasted a jagged void through the lower terraces. Now she could see right down to the sea and the far horizon.

The sun was low now, the sea ruffled into white horses by a strengthening wind as the dark purple clouds rolled in, heralding yet more rain. The days were getting shorter and in less than a month the clocks would go back an hour and winter would be upon them. It was a depressing thought, for the summer had been a washout on the whole, with very few sunny days to take Daisy to the beach.

Peggy became aware of how quiet the house was, which was a bit unsettling, for she'd become used to the bustle and chatter of her evacuee chicks during the war years. They'd all flown the nest now and were living new and exciting lives – some of them as far away as Australia and America.

The thought of them all made her smile. There were babies, too, for Susie, Fran, Mary and Ivy had sent precious snapshots of their little ones which Peggy kept in a special album. And both Kitty and Charlotte had now produced two each, which she was lucky enough to be able to cuddle as they lived nearby.

Rita and her Australian flyer, Pete, had sent long letters from Cairns, with photos of the bush, the beaches and their large wooden house on stilts which they called a Queenslander. Peggy suspected they'd soon start a family as their fledgling motor repair business was starting to flourish. It would be lovely if they did, for it might encourage Rita's father, Jack, to go out there for a visit, instead of moping about here like a lost soul.

She reached into the bottom drawer of her dressing table and pulled out the album which was nestled beside the shoebox in which she stored their lovely letters and cards. She'd kept all Jim's in the same way during the war, and those many boxes were now stashed safely away in a trunk in the attic. She'd put them away because she realised she didn't need to read them any more now Jim was home – but perhaps one day, when they were old, she'd get them out again so they could reminisce and count their blessings.

Stubbing out her cigarette, she slowly flicked through the pages of the album, her heart warmed by the happy faces and sweet, gurgling babies in their mothers' arms. There were wedding pictures too, most of them taken here in Cliffehaven as, one by one, her chicks had found their Mr Right.

She chuckled at the one of Ivy and Andy, remembering Ivy virtually falling into the registry office with no shoes on after having run all the way up the High Street because she was late as usual. She and her fireman, Andy, were well and truly settled in Walthamstow with their little one – as were Sally and John, who'd just moved with Sally's young brother, Ernie, and their son, Harry, from their cramped cottage by the beach to a large detached house on the new estate in Cliffehaven. Frank's only surviving son, Brendon, was their neighbour with his sweet wife Betty and their little boy, Joseph.

And here was a photograph of Kitty and Roger on their wedding day, all kitted out ready for Kitty to fly them away on honeymoon. The loss of part of her leg hadn't stopped Kitty from pursuing her dream, and Peggy's admiration for her knew no bounds.

Photographs of Danuta and Stanislav brought back happy memories, as did those of Susie's wedding to Doris's son, Anthony, and Doris's own marriage to the delightful Colonel John White, who'd turned out to be an absolute treasure. And then there were the snapshots of Jane and Sarah's double wedding in the Singapore cathedral, their mother Sybil standing beside Jim and looking very glamorous in a huge hat.

'Happy days,' sighed Peggy, noting how devastatingly handsome her Jim looked in his tropical whites – surely a target for any woman with a pulse. She wished she could have been there, for she loved a good wedding – and there had certainly been a lot of them over the past six years.

She closed the album, tucking it safely away again with the shoebox. She missed all her girls but could take some satisfaction in knowing they were settled and happy – and taking full advantage of all the opportunities that were opening up now the war was over. They no longer needed her to fuss and fret over them, and the girls who still lived locally visited when they could, which was always a joy.

She sat there for a minute more, thinking about Kitty who'd had her second baby and would soon be back to flying those big planes; and April who was happily courting; Sally who'd been her first evacuee and who was about to have her second baby; her own daughter Anne who was about to pop with her third – and darling Ruby.

Peggy grinned. There were no flies on that girl, and she had no doubt that she'd follow in Rosie's footsteps and continue to make a success of the Anchor.

Hearing the chime of the distant Town Hall clock, she glanced at her watch and tutted. There was still no sign of Jim, and it was well past teatime. Leaving the bedroom, she slowly went downstairs to her kitchen. Charlie was nowhere to be seen either, and she could only assume he'd stayed on at the rugby club to celebrate or mourn the result of the day's match. Perhaps Jim was with him? She hoped so, for she'd rather that than him drinking himself silly at the Anchor.

Peggy straightened the cushions on the fireside chairs and sat down to listen to the Saturday evening recital on the BBC. Cordelia was out for supper at the Officers' Club with the dapper Bertie Double-Barrelled, who was also in his eighties, but as spry as a fifty-year-old, and still military in his bearing. She could have gone with them if she'd had a babysitter lined up for Daisy, but hadn't bothered as she'd expected to have a quiet evening in with Jim.

'Fat chance of that,' she muttered crossly, snatching up the basket of mending and promptly stabbing herself on a needle. 'That'll teach me to put the damned things away properly,' she hissed, sucking the afflicted finger.

As she began to darn one of Charlie's socks, she realised her bad mood had started after her visit to the Anchor, and Ruby's well-meaning words. It hadn't been helped by Doris getting all snooty about her being late to pick up Daisy and accusing her of drinking during the day – which of course, she had – but that was neither here nor there.

Peggy admitted silently that she'd flown off the handle far too quickly, so it was hardly surprising Doris had gone off in high dudgeon. But that was no excuse for her to blame Jim for what Doris saw as Peggy's downward spiral into bad habits.

There again, Doris had never approved of Jim, and it seemed she never would – but she had been right in thinking it was Jim who'd made Peggy edgy today – just not for the reasons Doris suspected.

Jim might have his faults. What man didn't? But although he'd often sailed close to the wind, he'd never really brought trouble home. On the odd occasion when she'd thought he might be on the brink of dallying, she'd nipped it in the bud quickly – and would do so again if there was the slightest hint of any hanky-panky.

She could feel her blood rising again so she got up to make a sandwich and a cup of tea. She hadn't eaten much all day, and that probably wasn't helping her bad mood.

The concert on the wireless had come to an end by the time she'd finished the corned beef and salad sandwich, and she was enjoying a comedy programme with a second cup of tea and a biscuit when she heard the back door slam. Thinking it was Jim or Charlie, she was about to uncover the dinner plates she'd left on the table when Ron opened the basement door and stepped in with both dogs, which immediately charged about trying to climb all over her.

'Oh, Ron,' she said in exasperation, wrestling the dogs away. 'Do mind my clean floor. Look at the mess you've brought in.'

'Ach, to be sure a speck of dirt will not be harming your floor, wee Peggy,' he replied with a wink. 'And 'tis not the welcome I was expecting when I come bearing gifts.'

She eyed his bulging poacher's coat suspiciously as the dogs began to sniff at the food on the table. 'It's a mite more than a speck, Ron,' she said, pushing the plates out of their reach. 'It's half the damned hills you've brought in with you.'

'I'll clean it up before I go,' he said airily. 'Are ye not wanting the gift I've brought?'

Peggy bit back a smile. The old rogue was still a charmer, even if he did drive her round the bend at times. 'That depends on what it is,' she replied.

Ron dug into his pocket and, with a flourish, pulled out the pheasant – which immediately set both dogs off into a flurry of barking. 'Quiet, ye heathen beasts,' he snarled before turning to Peggy with a broad grin. ''Tis a grand wee bird, Peggy. Harvey caught it for you especially.'

'I'm very grateful to him,' replied Peggy on a giggle. 'But there's not enough meat on that to feed us all. You'd be better off taking it home to Rosie.'

Ron shook his head. 'Of course there is, Peg. You need to put some meat on your bones, wee girl, and this fine bird will help with that,' he added, giving the plump breast a gentle squeeze. 'I'll pluck and gut it for you now, and then hang it for a few days until it's ripe and ready for you to roast.'

Peggy didn't want to appear ungrateful, but she'd spent too many years sharing her basement with Ron's ripening game, and really didn't want to start again now. 'I'd really rather not hang it,' she murmured. 'And honestly, Ron, you'd be better off taking it home for you and Rosie.'

But it seemed Ron was determined she should have it, for without a by-your-leave, he'd taken the bird to the sink and was busy preparing it.

The sight of her pristine draining board being covered in feathers and bloody guts, and her kitchen lino smeared with muddy footprints made her want to weep – and yet she was grateful for his kind thought, so managed to keep control of her feelings and waited for him to finish making a mess.

Harvey and Monty were very much at home now the excitement was over and both of them collapsed with little snorts of pleasure in front of the range fire.

Peggy gave up being cross and drank her tea. 'I don't suppose you've seen Jim, have you?' she asked finally.

Ron shook his head. 'I left him at the house lunch-time and have been in the hills all afternoon.' He stuffed some rosemary, sliced cooking apple and the wild berries he'd picked earlier into the bird and then hunted out string from the kitchen drawer, cut two lengths and trussed it.

'There we are,' he said proudly. 'All ready for the oven as you don't want to hang it.' He placed it square and bloody in the middle of Peggy's kitchen table.

'Urgh! For goodness' sake, Ron! *Do* mind what you're doing,' she snapped, snatching up the bird and quickly grabbing a cloth. 'I'll put it in the fridge and cook it tomorrow,' she said, holding it out of the reach of the dogs' inquisitive noses.

With the bird on a dish and safely inside the fridge, Peggy scrubbed the table clean with rather more vigour than was needed.

Ron eyed her sorrowfully. 'Ach, to be sure, Peggy, I'm thinking you're not in the best of moods today. I thought me wee gift would make you smile.'

She realised she was letting the side down by being so cross when it really wasn't called for. 'I'm sorry, Ron,' she said, shooting him a smile. 'You caught me on the hop, and I'd forgotten how quickly you can bring chaos into the house.' She patted his arm. 'I am grateful – really I am – and I promise to cook it tomorrow.'

'Mind you do. And eat a decent portion of it yourself,' he said sternly, his bushy brows waggling above his twinkling blue eyes.

Peggy nodded, although she was already thinking how she could eke it out for the others. There was a fair bit of meat on a pheasant, after all, and Jim loved a bit of game.

Ron cleaned up the mess he'd made on the draining board and wrapped it all in some old newspaper Peggy kept by the range. Throwing it into the waste bin under the sink before washing his hands, he fetched the mop and bucket from the basement laundry. Plonking it by the sink, he sat down. 'I'll clean the floor after I've had a cup of that tea,' he said.

She poured the tea and silently reminded herself to remove those remains from her bin the minute he'd gone. The last thing she needed was them stinking out the place.

Ron got his pipe going to his satisfaction and leaned back in the chair. 'So, Jim's not back yet?'

Peggy shook her head. 'I thought he might be with you – or with Charlie at the rugby club,' she replied. 'But he's most likely at the Anchor.'

'Aye, that'll be it. Young Ruby will send him home in one piece, never you mind.' He slurped his tea and then puffed on his pipe. 'While I was out on the hills I called in to see our Martin.'

Peggy looked at him sharply. 'You shouldn't be worrying Martin with our troubles,' she said. 'He has enough of his own what with Anne about to have her baby and those two little girls always fighting for attention.'

'Actually,' said Ron, inspecting his pipe, 'he talks a lot of sense. Martin understands exactly what Jim's going through and reckons he needs to see the doctor who helped him.'

'You know as well as I that Jim avoids doctors like the plague,' said Peggy. 'And he certainly won't thank you for discussing his business outside this house.'

'I'm not asking for his thanks, Peggy, but looking for a solution to the problem. I know he doesn't like going to doctors – to be sure, I'm not too fond of them myself – but this chap of Martin's does seem to have the answers. We both know how far that lad has come since he got back here – and it's the same for Roger.'

He drained his tea and rattled the cup in the saucer for seconds which Peggy obligingly poured.

'There are evidently books on the subject too, and I've asked him to get hold of them. Jim probably won't read them, but they might help us understand more of what he's going through.'

'Who's going through what?' slurred Jim, swaying rather alarmingly in the doorway at the top of the basement steps before staggering over to a chair and slumping into it.

Ron and Peggy could smell the booze on him and exchanged glances as the dogs went to greet Jim with great enthusiasm, and he just about managed to give them both a rough pat on the head without falling headlong off the chair.

'It's just some books Ron reckons he can lay his hands on,' said Peggy, who saw all the signs of a brewing row. She quickly uncovered the plate and pushed it towards him. 'I kept your tea for you. I expect you're hungry by now.'

Jim wrestled off his heavy coat and let it fall in a heap on the floor as he eyed the corned beef and salad with little pleasure. He nudged it away. 'I've already eaten. Thanks,' he added as an afterthought.

Peggy quickly removed both plates before Jim decided to feed the corned beef to the dogs, and shoved them into the fridge alongside the bird. Picking up his coat, she hung it on the back of the door.

'You should have warned me you were planning to eat out,' she said with all the calm she could muster. 'Where did you go?'

'Fish and chips,' he replied, his gaze sliding away. 'And don't worry about Charlie. He ate at the rugby club and stayed on for the fundraising dance.'

'He didn't say anything to me about a dance,' said Peggy, feeling rather miffed. 'I might have liked to have gone. It's been a while since we went dancing,' she added pointedly.

'It was for the youngsters,' he replied, fumbling to roll a cigarette and spilling tobacco on the floor. 'We'd have looked a bit silly surrounded by schoolkids.' He lit the cigarette on the third attempt and looked at Peggy through narrowed eyes. 'So what were you talking about when I came in?'

Peggy shot a nervous glance at Ron, for she'd hoped Jim had been side-tracked from that particular topic – but Jim clearly expected an answer. 'Ron thinks he might be able to lay his hands on some books which could help you understand things,' she said in a rush. 'We both know you aren't really yourself, and . . .'

'I'm fine,' he interrupted. 'And I'll thank you both to stop going on. I'm just tired, that's all.'

'I know you are, love,' soothed Peggy. 'And it's hardly surprising after all the disturbed nights you've had with those troubling dreams. We just want to help, that's all,' she finished lamely under his glare.

Jim mashed out the half-smoked cigarette in the ashtray and scraped back his chair to get to his feet. 'Well, I'm sorry if my bad dreams disturb you, Peggy. Perhaps you'd prefer it if I went to sleep somewhere else? I wouldn't want you too tired to go out to your important job, now would I?'

Stung by the barb, Peggy flinched. 'I didn't mean . . .'

'Oh, I think you did,' he retorted before stumbling out of the kitchen and slamming the door behind him.

Peggy gave a shuddering sigh. 'That's torn it,' she said, close to tears.

Ron patted her hand. 'It's the drink talking, Peggy. He'll sleep it off and won't remember any of it in the morning. He doesn't mean to be cruel.'

Peggy blinked back her tears and nodded. 'I know. But when he's like this he says things he'd never say sober, and it's the truth as he sees it, Ron. I do so wish there was something we could do to help him.'

'So do I,' replied Ron, with a worried frown.

It was an hour later when Peggy finally shut the door behind Ron and the dogs and traipsed upstairs. Ron had been as good as his word and cleaned up the kitchen, and the guts and feathers were now safely in the outside bin. Cordelia had returned from her evening out slightly tiddly from too much sherry, but there was still no sign of Charlie. Assuming he was probably staying with friends, Peggy wasn't too concerned, for he had a front door key.

Peggy reached the landing and peeked in at Daisy, who was sleeping soundly but had kicked her covers off. She pulled up the sheet and blanket, retrieved the new pencil case from under the pillow and crept back out.

Jim's loud snoring resounded like a chainsaw through the house as she used the bathroom – and continued on as she crept through the open bedroom door. Closing it behind her, she found him still fully dressed – shoes and all – flat on his back and spreadeagled right across the bed.

Peggy eyed the scene without much pleasure. The curtains were still open and the bedside light was on, so it was easy to see her way round the room as she got undressed, but Jim's drunken snoring would drive her potty if it went on for much longer.

With the curtains pulled against the wind and rain that was now lashing against the window, she unlaced Jim's shoes and eased them off before loosening his belt and trouser buttons. With a dressing gown over her nightie for extra warmth, she slipped into the few inches of bed Jim had left her and turned off the bedside light. She tried to pinch a bit of blanket, but Jim was lying on it, and it wouldn't shift.

Peggy gave up trying, hugged the dressing gown to her and lay there staring into the darkness. It was going to be a long night.

5

Ruby had bolted the pub door and spent the next hour helping Brenda to clear up the mess. When the bar was finally straight, she handed Brenda her money and bundled up the takings to put in the safe. 'Enjoy your Sunday,' she said, walking with her down the narrow hallway to the side door. 'Have you and Frank got anything nice planned?'

Brenda blushed prettily. 'We're meeting for something to eat at the Lilac Tearooms and then he's taking me to the pictures,' she said. 'The tide's on the turn so he won't be out fishing tomorrow night.'

'Oh, that's good. What are you going to see?'

'*The Man in Grey*,' Brenda replied, fetching her umbrella from the hall stand and slipping on her raincoat. 'I don't know what it's about, but I'm sure I'll enjoy it because I really like that James Mason.'

Ruby smiled. 'I'm sure you will,' she murmured, imagining the two of them canoodling in the back row and probably not really watching the film at all.

Brenda stepped into the covered alleyway and opened her umbrella before dashing out into the blustery rain, and Ruby locked the door behind her, not envying her the short run home – but rather jealous of the closeness Brenda had found with Frank.

Being part of a couple was what Ruby missed most of all, for the intimacy and warmth of having someone special to talk to and share things with was lost to her – and the simple but comforting thought that there was someone to come home to instead of an empty house and a cold, lonely bed. It was at times like this that she was all too aware of the huge void left by Mike's death.

Ruby squared her shoulders and opened the door to the flat. She was tired after a busy night and still upset by her mother's unwanted presence, but feeling sorry for herself wouldn't solve anything. Locking the door behind her, she tiptoed up the stairs not wanting to wake Ethel.

The table lamp's pink shade cast a warm glow into the sitting room, and all seemed quiet and as she'd left it, so she quickly stashed away the night's takings in the safe, shoved the door keys under her pillow and made a cup of cocoa. Not that she really needed any help to sleep – she was dead on her feet – but cocoa had become a cosy ritual that set her up well for the night.

She took the mug into her room and then listened for a moment outside Ethel's door. Thankfully she was snoring fit to bust, so would probably go through the night. Having washed and changed into her night-clothes, Ruby finally clambered into bed and leaned back into the pillows to enjoy her hot, milky drink. Within minutes of turning off the light she was asleep.

It was after two in the morning and the creak of the loose floorboard in the passage woke her instantly. Still befuddled by sleep, she sat up in bed. Someone was in the flat and creeping about.

Sliding out of bed, she reached for the cricket bat she kept next to it and, with her pulse racing, crept towards the door. It was only then that she remembered Ethel and realised it must be her moving about – not a burglar who'd somehow managed to get through two locked doors.

Feeling relieved and rather foolish, she put down the bat and opened the door to find Ethel standing there in the borrowed underwear looking distraught.

'Whatever's the matter?'

'I'm sorry, love. I don't know where I am. What am I doing here?'

'You're at the Anchor, Mum. In Cliffehaven. It's all right, really it is. I'm here.' She put her arm around the narrow, shuddering shoulders and was shocked to discover how cold her skin was. 'What's happened?' she asked quietly. 'Was it a bad dream?'

'I dunno.' Ethel shivered. 'I can't remember.' She looked down at her borrowed underwear and burst into tears. 'I think I've 'ad a bit of an accident,' she said on a sob. 'I'm ever so sorry, Rubes.'

Ruby took a deep breath. 'It's all right, Mum,' she said with more calm than she felt. 'You go and wash and I'll sort out the bed.'

Ethel nodded, and like an obedient child, tottered into the bathroom.

Ruby felt like crying too when she went into the spare room and regarded not only the sodden sheets and blankets, and the make-up smeared pillows, but the chaotic mess. What on earth had happened to her mother to bring her to such a pitiful state? The last time she'd seen her she was sober, neatly dressed and very much on the ball, even though she was a thieving toerag and on her way to prison. But this? This was far beyond anything she felt able to deal with. And yet deal with it she must.

Stripping everything off the bed, she bundled the linen into the washing machine and dropped the blankets into the kitchen sink. She'd take them to the communal laundry in the morning as it was open all day every day. The thought struck her that another accident was very possible and, not possessing a rubber sheet, she hurriedly dug out the sheet of oilcloth she'd bought at the market meaning to cut it into covers for her kitchen and garden tables. It would have to do for now.

Once she'd turned the mattress so the wet bit was at the foot of the bed, she spread out the oilcloth and covered it with a clean sheet. It wouldn't be very pleasant to lie on, but then neither was a sodden mattress.

With the bed freshly made, she gathered up her scattered clothes and jewellery, and carried them back to her room. Emptying the ashtray and collecting the empty bottles, she opened the narrow window to get rid of the smell and then went to see how Ethel was getting on.

Ethel was still in the sopping underwear and slumped on the bathroom floor with her back leaning against the bath. 'I don't feel well,' she moaned.

Ruby wasn't at all surprised, but she said nothing as she helped Ethel to her feet. 'Let's get these wet knickers off,' she murmured.

'Gerroff me,' barked Ethel, lashing out.

'Mum,' she said firmly, dodging the flailing hands. 'Mum, it's me, Ruby. You need to get these off.'

'Leave me be,' she snapped, giving Ruby a hard shove.

It was too late for a stand-up fight so Ruby let it go. 'All right, leave them on, but they won't feel at all nice, and I made up the bed all lovely and clean.'

'You ain't takin' me clothes off,' Ethel rasped, clearly still drunk. 'It ain't proper.'

'Right you are,' Ruby replied, gently taking her arm to steady her. 'Do you need the lav before you go back to bed?'

Ethel shook her head.

'Are you sure?' Ruby persisted. 'Only you don't want another accident, do you?'

Ethel shoved Ruby away from her with such force she was knocked against the doorjamb. 'I already said I didn't want the bleedin' lav,' she snarled. 'I ain't a kid. You got no right to tell me what to do.'

Ruby ignored the pain in her elbow and bit back a retort as Ethel weaved an unsteady path back to her bedroom. She watched her clamber into bed still wearing the sodden underwear, and realised Ethel was so far gone she probably didn't even notice.

She gently drew the blankets over her and tucked her in. 'Goodnight Mum,' she murmured before switching off the light.

Ethel grunted and Ruby heard the bedsprings creak as she settled down to sleep. The Lord only knew what state Ethel and the bed would be in in the morning, but Ruby was too tired to care.

She traipsed back to her own room, eyed the pile of clothes and shoes she'd dumped on the floor and then left them there. Pulling the covers to her chin, she curled onto her side and waited for sleep to return.

But the worry over her mother, the state she was in, and what to do about her kept her awake long after the Town Hall clock struck three.

Jim jerked in his sleep, for he was once more a battle-hardened member of General Slim's Chindit regiment and had been sent as part of a rearguard to mop up any retreating Japanese trying to get back to Burma from the battle of the Kohima to Imphal Road in India.

He could again smell the sticky mud that clung to his boots and the stench of rotting jungle vegetation, could feel the humidity of the drenching monsoon rain mingle with his sweat, and hear the ever-present whine of the mosquitoes as he marched in the long column of men, pack-mules and horses. His mates, Big Bert and Ernie, marched alongside him, but none of them could waste what little energy they had in talking, for they'd been behind enemy lines for weeks and were exhausted. And they all knew that with exhaustion came carelessness, and this was no place to drop your guard.

The heat and humidity sapped their strength and the terrain was nothing short of hellish, for they'd already crossed deep gorges, climbed precipitous cliffs and fought their way through dense jungle. Now they were weaving their way through the searing glare of a vast forest of lethal bamboo which bore ten-inch barbs that could rip through flesh and poke out eyes. Jim was rigid with tension, every sense on high alert, and as they suddenly came out of the bamboo and into a cool glade of thick jungle, he could feel his heart beating so rapidly it was making it even harder to breathe the soupy air.

The Japs came out of nowhere.

Jim hit the ground and squirmed for cover as machine guns rattled and grenades exploded. Firing back into the shifting shadows of the dense undergrowth, he caught sight of several Japanese moving towards Big Bert's position.

'Look out, Bert! On your flanks!'

Bert dispatched them with a wide sweep of the thundering Bren gun, but the enemy machine gun was still in action and Jim knew he had to get nearer to finish the bastard off before they were all mown down.

He began to crawl through the undergrowth as bullets zipped and thudded all round him. He felt the sting as one scored a burning path in his cheek and through his earlobe. It hurt like hell, but he ignored it and crawled closer to his target as the Gurkhas continued pounding the Japs with their Bren guns.

He could see the Japs manning the machine gun now, and as the noise of the battle filled his head, he lobbed a grenade straight at it, and hit the deck.

The explosion rocked the earth beneath him, bringing what felt like half the jungle raining down on top of him. He waited for the tremors to stop, but when he finally looked up it was to be faced by the dead eyes and gaping mouth of a decapitated Japanese head.

'Urrgh!' He reared up, swiping at his face and body to get rid of the blood and gore he could feel splattered all over him. But as the sound of battle continued, he realised he was still in danger so quickly huddled back into the safety of the undergrowth and grabbed his carbine.

'It's all right, Bert!' he shouted. 'I've got you covered!'

But instead of firing there was just an empty click. His gun had jammed, and he could see a Jap lining him up in his sights. He rolled into deeper cover, cursing the jammed gun, and praying Bert and the others had seen his predicament.

'Two o'clock cover, Bert!' he yelled above the roaring Bren guns and rattling machine-gun fire. 'Over here! Over here!'

'Jim! Jim, wake up!'

Jim froze at the sound of her voice and although her being there didn't make sense, he knew he had to protect her. 'Get down,' he yelled, grabbing hold of her and trying to shield her with his body. 'Cover, cover! We need cover over here,' he yelled.

'Jim!' she protested sharply. 'Jim, wake up. You're squashing me, and I can't breathe.'

The voice was louder and more commanding, and it brought a deeper terror. He clung to her, trying to bury them both in the tangled undergrowth as the bullets zipped and whined overhead.

'Shush, shush,' he whispered urgently. 'Stay still or the Japs will find you.'

'Jim,' she said firmly, fighting now to push him off. 'For God's sake wake up before you disturb the children. I'm not in danger. It's a dream!'

Jim opened his eyes and was suddenly aware that the sounds of battle had disappeared, and that instead of being entangled in the jungle, he was twisted up in sheets and blankets and Peggy was trying desperately to wriggle from under him.

He quickly released his grip on her and shook his head to clear the vestiges of the nightmare which still clung to him. 'I don't . . . I didn't . . .'

She rolled away trying to catch her breath. 'Mind your eyes,' she gasped. 'I'm going to switch on the light.'

Still befuddled from the nightmare and utterly confused by it all, the blinding light hit him with all the force of a searchlight, and he cringed away from it, rolling onto his side and burying his head beneath the pillow.

'Mum! Mum, are you all right?' Charlie slammed into the room with a wailing Daisy.

'Mummy? Mummy, I scared,' she hiccuped.

Jim heard their voices and felt Peggy leave the bed, but as much as he wanted to reassure his children, he found he was trapped in his nightmare and couldn't move.

'I'm fine, Charlie,' said Peggy almost matter-of-factly. 'Your dad has just had one of his dreams, that's all. Come on, Daisy, there's no need to be frightened, darling. It was just Daddy shouting in his sleep. He's not cross, and we're all safe.'

'It was a bad one this time, wasn't it?' said Charlie, his deep voice unsteady. 'His shouting woke me up, and he sounded so fierce, I was worried he might hurt you.'

'Your dad would never hurt me,' soothed Peggy. 'Not even in his worst nightmares. Come on now, let's see if we can make some lovely cocoa, shall we, Daisy? That will help us all get back to sleep.'

Jim heard their voices fade as they moved away. He listened as they went down the stairs, and the sound of his little daughter's sobbing tore at his heart. He had to find a way to banish these awful dreams, for it was hurting the people he loved most in the world, and the last thing he wanted was to bring his filthy war into their home.

And yet how to banish something that had insidiously become so much a part of him? He lived and breathed it in every unguarded moment, and at night it crept up on him in its full intensity. However, it wasn't always the battles that haunted him, but other lasting images that had been imprinted on his memory and from which there seemed to be no escape.

There was the seemingly endless parade of lost comrades hastily buried in barely marked graves; the sights, sounds and smells of lying in a muddy Flanders trench waiting for the German attack he knew would come; the heavy responsibility for the men in his platoon; starving women and children from the camps; terrified natives forced into slave labour – and the once-strong fighting men who'd been turned into barely living skeletons on the Burma railway.

Jim shuddered, rolled from the sweat-soaked pillow and tossed away the bedclothes to sit on the edge of the bed and try to make sense of the fact he was fully dressed, for he had no recollection of coming home, let alone going to bed.

He scrubbed at his head and face in a futile effort to block out the memories of not only the hand-to-hand fighting in Burma, but of the part he'd played in the last battle of the Somme as a raw and terrified eighteen-year-old.

Because of his youth and his father's determination to keep him from enlisting until the very last minute, Jim hadn't fought for long in the First World War, but it had been hell enough to etch the horrors of the trenches, the mud, rats, dead bodies and poisonous gas into his mind. Now, those memories seemed to have melded together in his nightmares, each as sharp and horrifying as if they'd happened only yesterday. And even in the bright light of his bedroom he could still hear the screams of dying men and the echoing rattle of machine-gun fire; could still feel the sticky blood-spatter of that dead Jap on his body.

He stumbled from the bed, stripped off his clothes and left them on the floor as he grabbed his dressing gown. He needed to wash away the remnants of the night and try to find peace. But he felt trapped. Trapped by the place he called home – and trapped by the people who loved him and wanted to understand what was happening to him but couldn't begin to fathom what was going on in his head. And how could they when it remained a mystery even to him?

He locked the bathroom door and while he waited for the bath to fill, drank from Gloria's quarter bottle of black-market whisky he'd hidden in his dressing-gown pocket. Sliding into the water, he let the heat and the whisky numb his mind and loosen the knots of stress in his neck and shoulders.

As the tension in his body finally eased and the nightmare faded, he scrubbed himself with soap and flannel until his skin felt raw – and although he knew the blood and gore was long gone, he could somehow still see it there no matter how many times he tried to rub it away.

He eventually discarded the soap and flannel and reached once more for the whisky. It was the only thing that helped him block it all out, and yet, deep down, he knew it wasn't the answer.

Jim leaned back in the tub and closed his eyes. It wasn't meant to be like this. His longed-for homecoming had been joyful, if rather overwhelming, and he'd had so many ambitious plans – so much to look forward to and embrace in this time of peace and new opportunities. His love and pride for Peggy and his children was as strong as ever, and his work with the POWs was good for his soul. Yet the routine and hardships of life in an austere and war-battered England had somehow taken the shine off his good intentions; the minefield of well-meaning questions about his war that he faced almost daily becoming impossible to navigate.

Which was why he'd taken to sneaking into the Crown. Gloria asked no questions, left him in the peace and tranquillity of her private sitting room whatever the time, and always had a supply of bootleg booze. He raised the bottle to her in a silent salute and took a drink.

His work with the Legion fulfilled the part of him that needed to make reparation for what had been done to those men who'd returned home broken in mind, body and spirit, and when he'd first started, he'd thought himself immune from the horrors they were trying to live with. After all, he'd reasoned, he hadn't been a POW, hadn't suffered life-changing injuries, or been forced into slave labour on that notorious railway.

But after tonight, he wasn't quite so sure. The chilling realisation that he too might be damaged by what he'd seen and done shocked him. Yet the possibility that he might destroy his family because of it was utterly sobering.

'Not me,' he muttered, letting the empty whisky bottle drop to the floor. 'I'm my father's son; tough in mind and body, a fighting man with medals to prove it – not a victim – never a victim.'

He hugged his knees, feeling the chill of night despite the warm bath. 'I'll beat this,' he vowed through chattering teeth. 'And I'll do it just as Dad and Frank did last time. With dignity. And on my own.'

Peggy had managed to scrape enough cocoa from the tub to make them a fairly decent drink, but as she brought the mug to her lips she managed to spill some down the front of her dressing gown.

'Whoops. Forgot where my mouth was,' she joked, hastily mopping at the stain, and hoping the children hadn't spotted how her hands were still trembling from the shock of what had happened tonight.

'Are you all right, Mum?' asked Charlie, who missed very little.

'I'm fine, really,' she replied, reaching for a cigarette. 'Just a bit unnerved from being woken up so abruptly.'

'He needs to get help,' said Charlie solemnly.

Peggy shot a warning look towards Daisy who was intent upon giving her rag doll some cocoa and making a frightful mess. 'I know, Charlie,' she said. 'But until he asks for it, there's nothing any of us can do.'

'Well, he can't go on like this,' he replied. 'And neither can you. You're already a nervous wreck, and he really frightened you-know-who tonight,' he added, nodding towards Daisy.

Peggy had been frightened too, but she'd never let her children know it. There had been a moment when Jim's crushing weight had threatened to squeeze the very life out of her, and her ribs were still aching from it – and his grip on her arms had been so strong she was sure he'd bruised her.

'We can't discuss this now,' she said briskly. 'It's almost three in the morning, and no one talks any sense at this sort of hour.'

'Then I'll talk to Grandad tomorrow,' he said. 'He always gives good advice, and as he and Uncle Frank went through the first lot, they'll know how to help Dad.'

But Jim had fought in the first war too, and from what she'd read and seen on the Pathé News it had been a hell on earth, but he hadn't come home and been tormented by nightmares then – so why now? Could Ron and Frank really help when they knew nothing of what Jim had been forced to see and do throughout all those years in India and Burma?

She realised Charlie was waiting for a reaction to his statement. 'Maybe,' she replied. 'But I'm not sure they're the right people to ask, Charlie. Theirs was a very different war.'

'There's no maybe about it, Mum,' hissed Charlie in exasperation. 'Of *course* they're the right people. War is war and Dad's really not right. Someone has to do something about it.'

Daisy's attention shifted from her doll to Charlie as his voice rose, and her little face puckered. 'Why is everyone so cross?' she whimpered. 'I don't like it when they're cross,' she added, sliding from her chair and clambering onto Peggy's lap.

'He's not really cross, darling,' she murmured, stroking back her dark curls and kissing away her frowns. 'He's just a bit tired after playing rugby and dancing with his friends.'

She stood and hoisted Daisy onto her hip. 'I think it's time we all went back to bed, don't you? Come on, Charlie. I'll wash the mugs in the morning.'

She turned off the lights as she left the kitchen and followed Charlie up the stairs. Upon reaching the landing she kissed his cheek. 'Thanks, Charlie,' she murmured. 'Try not to worry too much. It's very early days and I'm sure that once he really settles in, he'll be fine.'

'I hope so, Mum,' he replied. 'But I'm still going to have a word with Grandad.'

She watched him run up the stairs two at a time and waited for the sound of his door quietly clicking shut. He was such a good, intelligent boy, and she was so proud of him. But he had enough to deal with and his important exams were looming. It wouldn't be right to saddle him with worries over his father.

Peggy became aware of the sound of gentle snoring coming from Cordelia's room. At least she hadn't been disturbed by all the goings-on, which was a blessing – but then she could thank the fact Cordelia took her hearing aid out at night, and that she'd consumed a copious amount of sherry this evening.

Daisy was a heavy, drowsy weight on her hip now, so Peggy didn't want to disturb her further by washing her face or changing her sticky nightdress. She tucked the little girl into her bed and sat beside her, softly singing Daisy's favourite lullaby as she stroked the dark curls back from the cocoa-stained face.

'Linger longer, Lucy. Linger longer, Lou. I will linger Lucy, longer by the side of you.'

Three repeats of this worked its magic as always and Daisy plugged her thumb in her mouth before she fell asleep. Peggy softly kissed her sweet warm cheek and tiptoed out of the room.

Jim was waiting for her on the landing, his dark, tangled hair still wet from his bath. Peggy felt her heart miss a beat as she looked into his bloodshot eyes and haggard face, and caught the whiff of fresh whisky on his breath. She put a finger to her lips to warn him not to say anything, and gently steered him towards their bedroom.

'Did I frighten her very much?' he asked the moment she'd shut the door behind them.

Peggy decided to be truthful. 'You did a bit,' she replied. 'But I managed to distract her quickly enough.' She took a breath. 'But next time, it might not be so easy.'

He hung his head. 'I'm sorry, Peggy. But I can't promise it won't happen again, don't you see?'

She felt pain clutch her heart for what he was going through and leaned into him for a moment, hoping her warmth and love would somehow bolster his spirits. 'Yes, Jim. I do see, and that's why you've got to ask for help.'

He didn't reply, so she looked up at him and tenderly stroked back the lick of damp hair from his forehead. 'You can't go on like this, my darling. You'll make yourself ill.'

He lifted his chin and squared his shoulders. 'I know, and I'll do something about it, starting tomorrow.'

She grasped his arm to stop him turning away. 'Is that a promise, Jim?'

He shook off her hand and headed for the bed. 'I said I'd do something, didn't I?' he retorted. 'That should be enough.'

Peggy realised she'd get no more out of him tonight. She climbed into bed, yearning for him to hold her – needing the assurance that whatever they faced, they'd get through it together.

But Jim turned his back to her and she lay there feeling bereft and frightened for the future, not only of Jim's state of mind, but for their marriage.

6

Ron opened his eyes that early Sunday morning to find Rosie's beautiful face smiling down at him. 'Good morning, handsome,' she said brightly.

He gazed back at her with sleepy adoration. 'Aye, and a very good morning to you, my gorgeous girl,' he murmured, caressing her sweet face. 'You seem very cheerful today. Did you have a good time last night?'

She gave him a lingering kiss on the lips and then snuggled into his shoulder. 'It was just the usual council shindig, but I did manage to collar the mayor about the new council estate. He's promised to back my proposal for a more modern communal baths, so it was worth all the standing about swapping small talk and sipping cheap sherry.'

'I didn't hear you come to bed. What time did you get back?'

She giggled and gently poked a blood-red manicured fingernail in his ribs. 'A long while after you. I found you snoring away like a herd of hogs, and even a sharp dig in the back wouldn't wake you.'

'Sorry, Rosie. But I'd had a long, busy day.' He rolled over and lovingly stroked back a lock of platinum hair from her face. 'But I'm not tired now,' he said, wriggling his brows.

She snuggled closer, her blue eyes luminous with love. 'Oh, goody. I was hoping you'd say that,' she murmured.

Ron drew her into his arms and kissed her thoroughly, thrilled that she wanted him still, and very willing to oblige.

An hour later they were still in their dressing gowns and eating breakfast in the kitchen, the two dogs alert beneath the table for any dropped morsel or crumb. The sun was shining and the sky looked clear of cloud, promising a much better day.

'I don't think the dogs were too impressed to be let into the garden instead of having their usual walk,' said Ron, mopping his plate clean with a chunk of bread.

'It won't hurt them once in a while,' said Rosie. 'As it promises to be a nice day for once, I thought we could take them out on the hills this afternoon, and perhaps treat ourselves to afternoon tea in the Officers' Club garden afterwards. They'll let the dogs in as long as they're on leads.'

He eyed her from beneath his bushy brows. Rosie didn't like walking unless it was round the shops, so this was an unusual suggestion. 'There's still a bit of work to finish here,' he said, 'and the dogs had a very long walk yesterday. Are you sure you wouldn't rather drive out somewhere?'

Her blue eyes widened and she put down her teacup. 'Well,' she breathed. 'I never thought I'd hear you turn down the chance of going into the hills. Is there something wrong? It's not your back again, is it?'

He decided it was time to be honest with her. 'It's not been helped with all the lifting and bending, but it's just about holding up. I'm tired, Rosie – really tired. The work on the house has been heavy going, even with all the help from Jim, Frank and Charlie, and I'm ashamed to admit it, but I'm beginning to feel my age,' he confessed.

'You weren't feeling your age earlier,' she said with a naughty glint in her eyes.

Ron actually felt his cheeks redden. 'Aye, well that's different,' he muttered.

'Are you sure you're not just making excuses because you want us to spend the rest of the day in bed?'

Ron chuckled. 'Ach, Rosie, to be sure you're a wee tease, and there's nothing I'd like more. But Jim will be here soon to finish off that dining room floor, and I wanted to have a quiet word with him.' He winked at her. 'But hold on to that thought, wee girl. There's the rest of the day still to go yet.'

The teasing light in her eyes faded as she looked at him over the rim of her teacup. 'Is Jim still having problems then?'

Ron nodded as he filled his pipe. 'Aye. He's drinking too much, and not sleeping well. Poor Peggy's at her wits' end.'

He went on to tell her about his conversation with Martin, and described Jim's drunken arrival back home the previous night. 'I'm hoping that if we're away from Beach View and on our own, I can somehow get through to him.'

'Poor Peggy,' she murmured. 'She waited so long for him to come home – and now this. If you're going to be here with Jim this morning, I'll pop over and see her. She'll need a friend to talk to.'

'Aye,' he sighed. 'That she does. I know how you women talk about everything under the sun, and she might just be more open with you about how things really are than she has been with me. But I've seen for myself that things aren't right at Beach View.'

Rosie nodded, and then reached for his hand across the table. 'I'll go and see her and try to help if I can. But I want us to spend the afternoon and evening together, Ron.'

There was a determination in her tone that made him look at her more sharply. 'Well, of course,' he replied. 'We haven't had much time for ourselves just lately, and I was thinking that perhaps we could just lock up the house and go away for a couple of days.'

He smiled at her, a little disconcerted that she didn't seem too struck by the idea. 'I'm sure one of the family will look after the dogs while we're away. I don't know about you, but I need a bit of a break, and it will do us both good to escape. Get us back together again, if you see what I mean,' he finished lamely.

Rosie dipped her chin and began to fidget with the hem of the tablecloth. 'That sounds lovely, Ron, but it's just not possible,' she replied.

'Why not? The council won't miss you for two days, and most of the work should be finished by next weekend.'

'It's not that simple,' she said hesitantly, her gaze darting away from him. 'You see, there's this conference . . .'

He felt a chill of foreboding. 'You never mentioned a conference before.'

She took a sharp breath and met his gaze squarely. 'I know, and I wasn't really planning on going, which is why I said nothing,' she said in a rush. 'But they asked me to do a speech on the planning for new social housing, and as it's a bit of a project of mine, I couldn't really refuse.'

'I see,' he said gruffly. 'So when is this conference?'

'It starts tomorrow,' she replied, her gaze slipping away.

The news shocked him. 'And where is it?'

'Bournemouth,' she replied softly. Her eyes were bright with tears as she reached for his hand. 'I'm so sorry, Ron. I wanted to tell you yesterday, but you were out when I came home in the afternoon, and asleep when I got back last night.'

'Even so, that's very short notice, Rosie. How long will you be away?'

'Only until Wednesday,' she replied swiftly. 'And then we can plan a bit of a holiday together, I promise.'

'Aye, well, we'll see,' he murmured, the disappointment lying heavy on his heart.

He left the table and took his pipe out to smoke it in the back garden, only vaguely aware of the dogs following him. Staring out to sea, he replayed the morning in his mind and wondered if Rosie's lovemaking had merely been her way of softening the blow of what she must have known would be unwelcome news.

Fear gripped him, for he'd known it would be risky to marry a woman who was a decade younger – a woman who looked like a film star, was animated and intelligent, and who could have had any man she'd wanted. But it seemed she'd wanted him, and he'd willingly set aside his doubts and married her.

Now those doubts were crowding in again and, to his shame, a dart of burning jealousy. She spent more time with her fellow councillors than with him, and now she was going away to Bournemouth without so much as a by-your-leave. There would be other men there – younger, ambitious, well-dressed men who knew how to conduct themselves at fancy receptions and dinners – and he was all too aware that he didn't pass muster on any of those levels. In fact he was happy to admit that he was a plain-speaking, retired fisherman, poacher and general handyman, who felt out of his depth in the circles Rosie now moved within, but for her sake, and given half the chance, he'd do his best to fit in.

Her soft voice startled him from the dark musing. 'I truly am sorry, Ron,' she murmured, her arms sliding round his waist, her head resting against his back. 'I should have told you much earlier that going away was a possibility.'

Ron's heart melted. He loved her, would do anything for her, but realised in that moment that if he didn't tamp down on the rising jealousy and make a stand now, he could live to regret it – and ultimately lose her.

He turned in her embrace and held her hands. Looking down into her lovely face, he could see the distress and anxiety in her eyes, and felt a pang of regret for what he was about to say. 'I know you are, my love. And it's proud of you I am. But this can't go on, Rosie,' he said softly. 'Next time there's something like a conference, talk to me first. And I know I'm not one for the fancy parties, but now and again it would be nice to go with you to meet the people you work with.'

Rosie nodded, the tears sparking in her eyes. 'Oh, Ron. I didn't realise you felt so left out of things. I never asked you to come with me because I know you hate those sorts of gatherings. But from now on I will, I swear. But this conference is important, and it's a great honour to be asked to address it. I really can't turn it down.'

'Aye, I'm sure it is,' he replied, kissing away the tear that was glistening on her cheek. 'But you do realise, Rosie, that there will come a time when you will have to decide whether you're a wife or a councillor – because the deeper you get into this, the less we're together. And that isn't why we got married.'

Startled by his gruff tone, she looked up at him. 'Yes, I realise that,' she said. 'But I've always worked, Ron, and you knew I would carry on after I sold the pub. I'm still in my fifties and not ready to retire – and this seat on the council is important because at last I feel I'm really doing something good for the community.'

She caressed his grizzled chin and softened her tone of voice. 'It doesn't mean I love you any less or will let my work come between us. Our marriage means everything to me, and once this conference is over, I'll make sure I'm home more, and that you come with me to all the social events. I promise.'

'I'll hold you to that, my darling,' he said. 'And we'll talk more when you get back from Peggy's.'

She kissed him lightly on the lips and then glanced at her watch. 'Oh, my goodness. Is that the time? I'd better get dressed and be on my way.'

Ron's heart was heavy as he watched her go indoors. He knew she'd meant what she said, but he also knew how ambitious she was – how driven in her aim to make life better in this town for those who'd lost everything during the war – and how easy it would be for her to lose herself in her work and forget the promise she'd made.

He lit his pipe and sank down onto the garden chair. It was all very well trying to smooth things over for Peggy and Jim at Beach View, but there was a lot to be repaired here – and it had very little to do with plaster and paint.

Ruby's sleep had been fractured with dark memories of the old days back in the East End, and the sound of Ethel's rasping cough. As dawn lightened the sky, she impatiently threw off the bedclothes and prepared for what she suspected would be a long and emotional day.

After checking on Ethel who was thankfully still sleeping it off, she unloaded the washing machine and hung out the sheets and pillowcases to dry. The blankets were too heavy to do by hand, and too bulky for the machine, so she tied string around them and left them on the garden table to take to the communal laundry later.

The few bedraggled bits of Ethel's clothing she'd left on the line were still soaked through after the rain, so having tidied away all her things she'd dumped on the floor the previous night, she began to hunt out something for her mother. It was patently clear that Ethel would not be leaving on the first train out of Cliffehaven today, and so there were plans to be devised, telephone calls to make, and a very serious conversation to be had.

As it was Sunday, and her only day off, Ruby had plenty of time to pick out the basic necessities. She chose a couple of pairs of plain white cotton knickers; a petticoat; two skirts; a blouse and a jumper. They'd probably be a bit too big as Ethel had become so thin, but they were better than nothing, and a belt round the waist would keep the skirts up. Their feet were the same size and so she dug out a pair of flat pumps she rarely wore, thinking Ethel would find it easier to walk in them than heels.

Having sorted out the clothes, she added a string of blue beads because Ethel liked bright colours, and managed to find a cheap pair of earrings and bangle to match. Feeling a bit mean for doing so, she nevertheless locked her bedroom door behind her and tucked the key in her pocket. She placed the clothes, shoes and beads on a kitchen chair, then set the table for breakfast before tackling the filthy tidemark Ethel had left in the bath.

Once the flat was clean and tidy again, she made a cup of tea, lit a fag and plumped down onto the couch. She checked the time and was surprised at how quickly it had flown – and that Ethel still seemed to be asleep. Her conscience pricked and she got up again to check on her, fearful she might have choked in her sleep.

But all was well, so she returned to the sitting room and opened the windows that overlooked Camden

Road to let in the fresh air. Flicking through her address book, she reached for the telephone and dialled the number.

'Hello, Danuta. I hope I didn't wake you. This is Ruby.'

'Hello, Ruby. No, no. I was awake already,' she replied. 'Is there a problem?'

'I'm so sorry to trouble you, Danuta, but my mother is here, and she has a nasty ulcer on her leg which needs to be treated. I realise it's Sunday, but . . .'

'It is no problem, Ruby,' she broke in. 'I am on duty today anyway. I will come in one hour and a half.'

'That's ever so kind of you. Thank you.'

'I did not know your mother arrive,' Danuta said carefully.

'It was certainly unexpected,' replied Ruby drily. 'And I'd prefer it if you could keep her visit to yourself. I don't want the gossip to start all over again and risk the licensing people getting to hear about it.'

'I not gossip, Ruby,' she said firmly. 'I will be with you in one hour and a half.'

The line disconnected abruptly and Ruby replaced the receiver wishing she hadn't said anything about gossip. She knew Danuta well enough to realise that of course she took her job as district nurse and midwife very seriously and would never in a million years start tittle-tattling about her patients.

She finished the cup of tea and stubbed out her cigarette before reaching for the telephone again. Getting through to the exchange, she recognised April's voice immediately and almost put the receiver back down, embarrassed by the fact her call was about Ethel. But as April had already had a run-in with her, what did it really matter?

'Hello, April, love. Could you put me through to the Sally Army hostel?'

'Oh dear. So she found you then?'

'She certainly did. I'm sorry if she was rude to you, April.'

'I rather think it was the other way round,' replied the girl. 'It was a bit of a shock seeing her again after so long. How she had the nerve, I just don't know.' She paused. 'Sorry, I know it must be difficult for you. I'll put you through to the hostel. And good luck.'

The number rang for some time and Ruby was about to hang up when it was finally answered by a man who was clearly out of breath. 'Cliffehaven Salvation Army Refuge,' he said. 'Arthur Banks speaking.'

'Hello, Mr Banks. This is Ruby Taylor, the landlady of the Anchor. I was wondering if you had room to take in someone for a couple of nights?'

'We're full at the moment, but there might be a space later today,' he said, the sound of him turning pages coming down the line. 'Could you give me some details of the person who needs refuge?'

'She's a single lady who's very much down on her luck,' hedged Ruby, unwilling to reveal too much in case he'd heard the past gossip about Ethel. 'I can't keep her here, and she really is in need of somewhere to stay for a while.'

'I see. So this lady just turned up and asked you for help?'

'Sort of,' said Ruby. 'Look, do you have a place for her or not?'

'As I said before, we are full at the moment, but if a vacancy comes up, then I will telephone you. Can I have the lady's name please to pencil her in?'

'Ethel Sharp,' she replied, choosing to use her old name and not the one she'd gained by marrying Stan from the station.

'That name sounds familiar,' Mr Banks murmured. 'Never mind, it'll come to me sooner or later.' He cleared his throat. 'There's just one other thing I think you should know, Mrs Taylor. We run a dry hostel here.'

Ruby couldn't fudge it by lying about Ethel's drinking. 'Oh dear. That could be a problem. But I'm sure she'll abide by your rules if you can give her a place,' she said, hoping her fib wouldn't land her in even deeper water.

'I am sorry, but if you can't guarantee she'll keep to the dry rule, then I really can't take her.' He paused for a breath. 'I could telephone a colleague who runs a general hostel for the homeless if you like – but drinking would still be frowned upon unless the lady is prepared to attend our special prayer and counselling meetings to help her turn away from the evils of alcohol.'

Ruby realised she was on a hiding to nowhere. 'Is there anywhere else I can try that would take her in?'

'I'm sorry, but with so many families living on the streets, very few places take in alcoholics. They cause trouble, you see, and with young children about . . .'

'Thanks anyway,' she said, and abruptly ended the call.

'I heard all that,' said Ethel, coming into the sitting room. 'Trying to get rid of me already, eh?'

'Don't be like that, Mum, she said wearily. 'This is a pub and you've got a prison record. As I explained yesterday, I could lose my licence having you here.' She saw Ethel wasn't impressed, and hurried on. 'I tried the Sally Army hostel, but they're full, so we'll have to think of something else.'

Ethel plonked herself down on the couch beside her. 'It's nice to feel wanted,' she said sourly. 'Anyway. I need a fag. Where's me baccy?'

'It's here,' Ruby replied, taking it out of the side-table drawer. 'Sorry I hid it away, but I was worried you'd burn the place down, the state you was in last night,' she said carefully.

Ethel pulled a face, choosing to ignore the barb. 'I don't like them hostels anyways,' she said as she expertly rolled a cigarette. 'Full of tramps and drunks what nick yer stuff or try to 'ave their filthy way with yer.'

She lit the fag, blew out a stream of pungent smoke and had a good cough. 'And then there's the God botherers what are twice as bad. Tellin' folk what to do and what not to do. I like a drink, I admit. But I could give it up tomorrow if I wanted.'

Ruby reached for her hand. 'Then why don't you?' she asked softly. 'All that booze ain't doing you no favours, you know.'

Ethel snatched away her hand. 'There ain't no one to care what I does. And anyway, the drink helps me get through the day.'

Ruby took her hand again. 'I know you think I don't care, Mum, but I do – really. It hurts me to see you like this. Would you give it up for me?'

'I might,' she said without conviction.

Ruby regarded her mother, and realised it would be a long road to sobriety for her, and one she would probably find almost impossible. 'That would be really good if you could, Mum. Because you see, the drinking makes it really difficult to find you a place to stay. Have you ever thought of joining . . .?'

'I ain't an alcoholic, if that's what yer implying,' Ethel snapped. 'I don't need to go to meetings to talk about meself or listen to others prattlin' on.'

'So, you have been to a meeting then?' Ruby pressed. 'You did at some point realise you might have a problem?'

Ethel smoked in silence, her gaze firmly fixed away from Ruby, her expression obdurate.

'Mum, do you remember anything about last night?'

'Nah. Not really. Only that bed's bloody uncomfortable. Why?'

'It doesn't matter,' sighed Ruby, and changed the subject. 'I've put some clean clothes out for you in the kitchen. They might 'ang off yer a bit, but they'll do until we can get to the shops.'

'Where's me own stuff?'

'I'm sorry, Mum, but most of it fell to bits when I washed 'em.' She glanced at the mantel clock. 'Look, why don't you go and have a nice wash and get dressed, then we can have a bit of breakfast before the nurse comes to look at your bad leg.'

'There ain't nothing wrong with me leg other than a bit of a sore. And a drop of gin dries it up a treat. I don't want some stranger poking and prodding me about.' Her gaze sharpened through the curl of cigarette smoke. 'How did yer know it were there?'

'I saw it when I had to undress you last night – and then again when you woke up all confused at two in the morning.'

Ethel quickly looked away. 'I don't remember,' she muttered.

Ruby took a deep breath and forced a smile in an attempt to lighten the mood. 'Come and see what I've picked out for yer, then after you've washed and dressed we can have some scrambled egg on a fried slice. How about that?'

Ethel grimaced. 'If yer want,' she said ungraciously. 'But not if it's that powdered muck. Gives me indigestion.'

She followed Ruby into the kitchen, eyed the pile of clothes with little pleasure, then snatched them up and slammed her way into the bathroom, locking the door behind her.

Ruby folded her arms and leaned against the sink. It seemed her mother was determined to be unpleasant.

But, like it or not, they were stuck with each other until she could come up with somewhere for her to live – and although the Licensing Board might have something to say about it, she was not going to throw her mother out onto the street.

To his shame, Jim had feigned sleep as Peggy lay like a stone next to him, for he hadn't known what to say or do to make things better between them. He would have liked to cuddle her but feared she'd reject him, and anything he said probably wouldn't be believed. She was hurt and angry – and she had every right to be because he'd been a bloody fool. He could only hope she'd eventually forgive him his outburst and appalling behaviour, and understand that he was battling not only the things going on in his head but the stubborn male pride he couldn't seem to shake off.

He'd lain awake as Peggy finally fell asleep, and must have drifted off eventually, for when he next opened his eyes the rising sun's glow seeped around the curtains.

He looked over his shoulder and felt a deep ache of love for his little Peggy who was curled like a small child against his back, her dark curls spread against the pillow. But then he saw the livid bruises on her arms and was shocked to the core by what he must have done to her while in the throes of his nightmare. He'd never laid a finger on her before – and never would – and yet the twin demons of drink and nightmares had led to him hurting her.

Tears welled as deep remorse weighed on his heart. She was so precious and didn't deserve the hurt and worry he'd caused, and in that moment he wanted more than anything to take her into his arms and hold her – to protect her – not only from himself, but from the rest of the world. Most of all, he wanted to tell her how sorry he was and that he meant to keep his promise and ask for help.

And yet she was sleeping so peacefully that it would be cruel to wake her, so he carefully left the bed and drew the covers over her shoulders. Quietly pulling on his clothes, he tiptoed out of the bedroom and made his way downstairs, relieved that no one else seemed to be stirring, for he wasn't ready to face anyone just yet.

He had a hangover, which was no more than he deserved, so he hunted out the packet of aspirin and put the kettle on. As he opened the fridge door he was taken aback to see a pheasant sitting there, all ready to cook, and could only suppose his father had brought it last night, for there were no such things in butcher shops these days.

'Good for you, Da,' he murmured. 'That'll be a real treat.'

Once he'd made a pot of tea – remembering to use the old leaves – and the aspirin began to ease his headache, he went outside to the vegetable plot and chose carrots and a cabbage to go with the bird. Taking a deep breath of the salty early air, and feeling all the better for it, he returned to the kitchen to prepare the vegetables for lunch so that Peggy wouldn't have to.

Once the potatoes and other vegetables were in pans of salted water, he laid the table for breakfast and cleaned up the mess he'd made in the sink. With the peelings thrown on the compost heap, and the kitchen tidy again, he made himself some toast, hunted out a pad and pencil, poured a second cup of tea and sat down to write Peggy a letter.

He wrote from the heart, and when it was done, he folded it in two and placed it beneath Peggy's packet of cigarettes so she'd find it the minute she came down.

Now he'd bared his soul, Jim left Beach View feeling lighter in spirit. It promised to be a lovely day, his hangover was almost gone and the work at Havelock Gardens would be finished very soon. He dug his hands deep into his overcoat pockets and softly whistled a tune as he strolled down Camden Road. He still couldn't get warm, but at least the sun was shining, and the elderly ladies in their Sunday best hats made a pretty picture as they chattered like sparrows and headed for the church.

He saw Fred the Fish scrubbing his shop window display counter and waved a greeting, and then waved again when he saw Alf the Butcher doing the same. His father's two old pals had become like uncles over the years and were known to talk the hind legs off a donkey given half a chance, so he didn't stop.

Yet, as he strolled past the Anchor, he hesitated, for the upstairs windows were open and he could hear Ruby talking quite loudly to someone. *Hello,* he thought with a grin. *Has our Ruby got herself a man tucked away overnight?* And then he heard another voice, a rough female one with a whining Cockney accent and unpleasant tone.

Jim frowned. Whoever it was, it was no concern of his, and he should have known Ruby wasn't the sort of girl to let a man over her threshold so soon after losing her husband. He walked on, remembering what Peggy had told her about the girl, and came to the conclusion that some friend from the old days must have come down from London for a visit.

Reaching the fire station at the end of Camden Road, he stopped for a few minutes to chat to John Hicks who was the senior fire officer, and whose wife, Sally, had been Peggy's very first evacuee. John had lost part of his leg when he'd sailed with the flotilla of boats sent to Dunkirk to rescue the stranded soldiers from the beaches, but it hadn't stopped him pursuing his career in the fire service.

'How's the leg holding up, John?'

'Very well, thanks. I've been given a very smart new prosthetic, and it's a marvel for what it lets me do.' He raised his trouser leg to proudly show it off.

They chatted for a bit, catching up on news of family, and then John returned to overseeing the washing down of the fire engines by his crew. Wishing him and his Sally well, Jim strode across the street and then stood on the corner of Havelock Gardens to look at the sea and watch the gulls swarming over the fishing boats which had been hauled over the waterline at the far end of the beach.

His brother Frank would probably be down there with his son, Brendon, preparing to go out once the tide was favourable. Frank had invested in larger and more up-to-date boats since getting compensation for the ones the Government had requisitioned as minesweepers, and had taken on a whole new crew. It seemed that the family tradition his Irish grandfather, Joseph, had started back at the beginning of the century was still going strong. Jim grimaced. The fishing life had never been his cup of tea, as he preferred to keep his feet on solid ground.

As Jim approached Ron's house he heard the dogs barking and could see the high wooden gates tremble as they pushed against it in their eagerness to welcome him.

'Get down, you two, and let me in,' he said, gently pushing them back as he opened the gates.

Harvey rushed out, closely followed by Monty, and Jim spent a moment making a fuss of them before he ordered them back into the garden and firmly fastened the gate again.

'I thought it must be you,' said Ron, emerging onto the front step. He glowered at him from beneath his shaggy brows. 'How's the head?'

Jim dared to meet his gaze. 'Still on my shoulders,' he replied flippantly. 'But only just.'

'Well, you certainly made a show of yourself last night,' rumbled Ron. 'If you've a bad head this morning, you've only yourself to blame.'

Jim dug his hands back into his pockets and shuffled his feet. 'Aye. I'm aware of that, Da, and I'm sorry. It won't happen again.'

Ron's blue gaze was piercing. 'It's not me you should be apologising to,' he said sternly. 'Peggy doesn't deserve to have you coming home like that and saying hurtful things.'

Jim stared at his father, his pulse quickening as he tried desperately to remember what he'd done after leaving Gloria's sitting room. But it was all a blank. 'What did I say, Da?'

'You were nasty about disturbing her sleep with your bad dreams, and threatening to sleep in another room – and you were snide about her job at the factory.'

'Oh, Lord,' Jim breathed. 'I don't remember any of it.'

'I'm not surprised,' growled Ron. 'You'd clearly had enough to sink an entire ruddy fleet, and made yourself look a complete eejit.'

Jim flinched as Ron took a step closer, his expression darkening as he jabbed a meaty finger in his face. 'I'll have no son of mine talking to a woman like that – least of all to Peggy. You will show her the respect she deserves, and as you obviously can't hold your liquor and be civil, I suggest you stick to tea.'

Duly chastened, Jim nodded. He'd rarely seen his father so angry, and although the old man was in his late sixties, Jim had no doubt he was still capable of giving him a thick ear.

'Yes, Da,' he said meekly. For all his experiences in Burma and India, facing his angry Da was just as intimidating as any bayonet-wielding Jap.

Ron glared at him and then gave a sharp nod. 'Good. Come on then, there's work to be done before Rosie gets back.' With that he turned and went indoors.

Jim followed him, and silently gathered the things he needed to finish the dining room floor. He'd never felt so ashamed, and if his father ever found out about the bruises on Peggy's arms, there really would be hell to pay.

With the dogs now banished to the back garden, he concentrated on lightly sanding the floor, and then gave it the final coat of varnish, aware that his father seemed to be in an extremely bad mood this morning. There were curses and bangs coming from the spare bedroom above him, which made him wonder if he and Rosie had rowed earlier.

Having finished the dining room and cleaned the brush of varnish, he went upstairs to see what was causing Ron so much fury.

'Damn and blast the bloody thing,' roared Ron as something crashed to the floor.

Jim hurried along the landing and found Ron standing by an overturned stepladder and a puddle of paint, and clutching at his hand. 'What happened here, Da?'

'I was trying to open the ruddy tin and stabbed myself with the ruddy screwdriver. Then knocked the whole ruddy thing over.'

Jim quickly righted the tin of paint, grabbed the sheets of newspaper that had been put down to protect the freshly sanded floor and began to mop up. Dumping the sticky mess in a nearby bucket, he finished cleaning what he could, but the stain on the floorboards would always be there even if it was sanded again. Rosie would blow a fuse.

'I don't know what's got you in this foul mood this morning, Da, but you'd better go and put that hand under the cold tap,' he said, glancing at the steady flow of blood staining the filthy handkerchief Ron had tied round it.

'It's all right,' Ron muttered. 'And it's hardly surprising I'm not in the best of moods, what with a son who can't hold his drink, and a ruddy wife who keeps swanning off to ruddy conferences.'

Jim didn't really have an answer to this, realising that anything he said would only infuriate the old man further. So he reached for his father's hand and inspected the deep cut in the palm. 'This is far from all right,' he said. 'And that disgusting handkerchief is probably infecting it. Come on. Let me help clean it up.'

Ron snatched back his hand. 'I'm not a child,' he snarled. 'I'm perfectly capable of doing it myself.' He stomped off into the bathroom and stuck his hand under the cold tap, wincing as the icy water hit the raw edges of the cut.

'You'll probably need a couple of stitches in that,' said Jim.

'I'll stick a plaster on it for now,' said Ron.

'A plaster isn't going to help it heal, Da. It's too deep and needs stitching.'

Ron carefully dried his hand and wrapped it in one of Rosie's pale pink towels. 'You should take your own advice,' he said gruffly. 'It's no good putting a sticking plaster over your wounds, boy. You need to let the poison out so you can heal yourself.'

'And what do you know about it, Da?' Jim asked quietly. 'You weren't there. You didn't see what I saw – didn't do what I had to do.'

'I saw enough back in the trenches and tunnels to give me the sort of nightmares you've been having,' said Ron, perching on the lavatory lid and reaching into his pocket for his pipe. 'I remember the shell-fire, the clouds of sulphur yellow gas, and the faces of my pals who didn't come through.'

Jim remained silent as his father awkwardly lit his pipe, his left hand still swathed in the towel. He hadn't known his father was still haunted by his experiences in the first war, and it made him fear that he too might live the rest of his life crippled by the same thing.

'When I was digging tunnels and laying mines on the Somme, I could hear Fritz laying his own mines right next to me in the darkness,' Ron continued. 'One tremor from a shell-blast; one false move and we'd have both been buried alive. The claustrophobia still wakes me sometimes even after all these years.'

'I didn't realise,' Jim murmured. 'Why have you never told me about this?'

'The same reason you won't talk about your time in Burma,' said Ron, his steady gaze holding Jim's. 'We're a stubborn proud lot, us Reilly men, raised by strong women who expected us to never show weakness even in the face of overwhelming troubles. It can be a blessing, son. But it can also be a great curse.'

'Aye,' murmured Jim in agreement.

There was a long moment of silence between them as Ron carried on puffing his pipe, arms folded as if he was waiting for something.

Jim lit a cigarette and then perched on the side of the bath. 'I dream about the fear,' he began hesitantly, 'the knife-edge tension of creeping through the jungle, feeling the watching eyes, knowing that at any moment the Japs will strike, your heart hammering, the air so thick with damp heat you can't breathe. And then the awful noise of the Bren and machine guns that gets into your head until you think it'll burst.'

Ron puffed on his pipe and ignored the throbbing ache in his hand as his son finally opened his heart and tentatively began to heal his own, deeply painful wounds.

7

Peggy had woken to find Jim's side of the bed cold to the touch, and assumed he'd woken earlier and was probably down in the kitchen nursing a sore head. 'Serves him right,' she muttered as she headed for the bathroom to wash and get ready for the day.

It was only when she'd stripped off her nightdress and looked in the mirror that she was faced with the horrifying reality of Jim's unintentional assault on her the night before. The tops of her arms were livid with bruises, and there were shadows of more on her ribs. 'Oh lawks,' she breathed. 'No wonder I was aching so much.'

She hunted through the bathroom cabinet and found some salve she used when the children knocked themselves and gingerly dabbed it on her arms and midriff. It didn't sting, but ponged a bit and felt unpleasantly sticky when she drew her clothes over it. No one must ever see the marks, she decided, so instead of the short-sleeved blouse she was planning to wear, she pulled on a light sweater.

Eyeing her reflection in her dressing-table mirror some minutes later, she realised that no amount of make-up would hide the dark circles under her eyes, or the very real worry etched on her face. But a dab of rouge would bring colour to her cheeks, and a slash of scarlet lipstick might make her feel a little better. Clipping on her earrings and brushing her hair into better order, she slipped on her high heels. They were more for bravado than comfort, but she needed something to bolster her spirits before she faced Jim.

Daisy was still asleep, and so it seemed were Cordelia and Charlie, so she went down to the kitchen, her nerves jangling at the thought of Jim waiting for her to have another row.

Yet to her enormous relief the kitchen was deserted, the table was all set for breakfast, and there beside the hob were saucepans of freshly prepared vegetables. 'Oh, Jim,' she breathed. 'You really do know how to apologise, don't you?'

She put the kettle on the hob and reached for her packet of Park Drive, which seemed to be sitting on top of a piece of folded paper. Curious, she picked it up, and as she began to read what Jim had written, she sank into the chair, tears streaming down her face.

My darling girl.

How can I put into words my deepest regret for having hurt and frightened you? I adore you with all my heart and would never wish to harm you or our children. But when the dreams take me over it's as if I'm back there fighting for survival, with all the noise of guns and planes and the screams of dying men, and there seems to be no escape from the terror of it all.

I have too many memories and images in my head, Peggy. They consume me, and I don't know how to get rid of them. But I make a solemn oath to you now that I will find a way, for after last night, I realise I'm as damaged by my war as the men I'm trying to help at the Legion, and I never <u>*ever*</u> *want to hear my little Daisy sobbing in fear again – or my son, my lovely, caring son, being made to witness his mother in distress.*

I left you sleeping so peacefully, it would have been cruel to wake you, but I wanted so desperately to hold and kiss you and tell you I'm deeply sorry for everything I've put you through these past months. I shall go to Da's and finish the work as I promised, then come home. Sober. Repentant. And with a heart full of love.

Ever yours,
Jim xxxx

Peggy read it through again and dried her tears. 'Bless you, love,' she murmured, tucking the precious letter into her skirt pocket. 'Of course I forgive you. Don't I always?'

She had just freshened the pot of tea Jim must have made earlier when she heard the back door slam and light footsteps running up the basement steps. Fervently hoping it wasn't Doris, she called out, 'Hello? Who's there?'

'Only me,' said a smiling Rosie as she came into the kitchen. 'I thought I'd pop in and see how you're doing,' she murmured, giving Peggy a hug.

Peggy was delighted to see her best friend, but very surprised she'd come visiting so early. She knew Rosie of old, and she never got up before nine on a Sunday. 'Good timing,' she said. 'I've just made tea – although it's probably very weak.'

Rosie stepped back from their embrace and regarded Peggy thoughtfully. 'Have you been crying, Peg?'

'It's nothing serious,' she replied. 'And you look as if you've shed a tear or two this morning. What's up?'

Rosie settled into a chair, lit them both a fag and placed her cigarettes and lighter on the table. 'Ron blew a fuse because I'm going to a conference in Bournemouth tomorrow,' she said. 'I tried to take the sting out of the news, really I did, but earned a lecture on how to be a good wife instead.'

'Oh dear,' Peggy sighed.

'Yes, well . . . It was stupid of me not to warn him about it much earlier, but I honestly hadn't been meaning to go until they asked me to give a speech.' She tapped ash into the glass ashtray. 'He'll be grumpy for the rest of the day, I bet.'

'I hope not,' said Peggy. 'Jim's going to be spending the morning with him, and if he's got the hangover he deserves, it could end up being a right how-d' you-do.'

'Oh lawks,' breathed Rosie. 'Aren't men just the absolute end? Honestly, Peg, I could swing for Ron sometimes. He can be so pig-headed.'

'It's the same with Jim,' she replied. 'Last night he had one of his bad dreams. Woke the entire house and scared poor Daisy. Charlie was quite grim afterwards, and of course Jim was in the sort of mood that I hardly dared open my mouth before he jumped down my throat.'

'Is it really that bad, Peggy?' Rosie's blue eyes were full of concern. 'Ron told me he came home worse for wear last night, and I think he's meaning to try and get him to open up this morning. He wants to help, you know.'

'I admit I was really at the end of my tether this morning until I found this waiting for me.' Peggy pulled Jim's letter from her pocket.

Rosie took it and read to the end before handing it back. 'Oh, Peggy, what a lovely note. It really seems as if he's willing to try and get help. Perhaps last night brought things to a head for him, and he realises the situation can't possibly go on.'

'What situation?' Doris stepped into the kitchen unannounced.

'Nothing,' said Peggy, quickly stuffing Jim's letter back into her pocket. 'I do wish you'd knock before barging in,' she said crossly.

'I don't *barge* anywhere,' said Doris rather grandly and plumped down on a kitchen chair, placed her expensive handbag on the table and removed her kid gloves. 'I will overlook your rather rude welcome as I realise you're not yourself at the moment,' she said to Peggy. She eyed Rosie. 'It's a bit early for you to be out and about, isn't it?'

'I might say the same about you,' retorted Rosie, who rarely let Doris get away with being sniffy with her.

'I am on my way to church,' she said, the feathers in her fancy hat fluttering as she spoke. 'And as I was passing, I thought I should drop in and see if my sister was in a better temper today.' She sniffed delicately. 'But it seems she's not.'

'Look, Doris,' said Peggy, handing her a cup and saucer. 'You clearly came for a purpose, so will you just get on and tell us what it is?'

Doris poured the tea, looked at it in disgust and proceeded to ignore it as she lit a cigarette. 'You were very short with me yesterday, when there was absolutely no need,' she said. 'I have, for some time, had the feeling things aren't going well here now Jim's home, so I've come to offer my support.'

'That's very kind of you, Doris. But we're all fine.'

Doris regarded her evenly. 'I think not, Peggy,' she said. 'There are dark rings under your eyes, and you look worn out. And there's this *situation* you were both discussing. He's not up to his old tricks again, is he?'

Peggy folded her arms and glared. 'I don't know what you mean by that, but if you think he's messing about with other women or doing business on the black market, then you couldn't be more wrong.'

'Then how come I saw him sneaking into the back door of the Crown yesterday? It was well past closing time – but of course a little thing like that wouldn't stop Gloria from peddling her illicit booze,' Doris added with disdain.

This was news to Peggy, but she was damned if she'd let her sister know that. 'I expect he just wanted a quiet drink after working at Ron's place all morning,' she said. 'And he knows better than to ask Ruby to serve him out of hours.'

'Gloria is certainly obliging in many ways,' said Doris cattily. 'But he's heading for a fall if he thinks he can get away with it for much longer. This town has eyes and ears, and gossip soon spreads, Peggy. You should put your foot down.'

Doris was winding her up like a clock again, and Peggy could barely contain her fury. 'If Jim wants a drink at Gloria's, or anywhere else for that matter, then he has a right to one. That man fought for years in conditions that would defeat lesser mortals. So what if he drinks a bit?' she snapped. 'He's bloody well earned it.'

'All right, Peg,' murmured Rosie, putting a warning hand on her arm. 'Enough said, I think.'

'Yes, you're right,' she replied, her temper ebbing. She looked at her po-faced sister with her immaculate make-up and expensive clothes, and wondered, not for the first time, how they could be so different. 'I'm sorry for shouting, Doris, but you really do get on the wrong side of me at times.'

'That's no excuse for losing your temper,' she replied coolly.

'No, it isn't. But Jim's been having terrible trouble with nightmares and can barely make it through the night. You see, he's haunted by what he's seen and done out in the Far East, and is really struggling to make sense of it all.'

'I'm sorry,' Doris murmured. 'If I'd known, I wouldn't have said anything.'

'And why should you? It's not something we shout from the rooftops,' said Peggy.

'He needs help, then,' said Doris bossily. 'Surely the Legion has people he can talk to?'

'Yes, they do, and he's promised me faithfully that he'll ask for help. And this time I believe him, because last night was particularly bad. So please don't come round here accusing him of things and making snide remarks. You have absolutely no idea what he's going through.'

Doris looked rather chastened for once. 'Of course,' she murmured. 'I am sorry, Peggy. I didn't mean to interfere, but I was worried about you. Is there anything I can do? I could talk to John and see if he knows someone who might help.'

'Please don't, Doris. I know you're just being kind, but the fewer people who know what's going on with Jim the better until he's ready to talk about it.'

Doris looked at her slim gold wristwatch. 'I'd better be going or I'll be late for mass. Why don't you get your coat and come with me? Father Finlay always gives most delightful and uplifting sermons.'

Peggy shook her head. 'Thanks, but Daisy and Charlie will be up in a minute and I have lunch to get ready.' To soften the rejection, she patted Doris's hand. 'Maybe next week?'

Doris collected her bag and gloves and gave Peggy a swift hug, then nodded goodbye to Rosie and left the house.

'Well, that was an unexpected surprise,' said Rosie drily. 'Good old Doris, eh? Still clinging on to her snooty, bossy ways regardless of the fact she's been taken down several pegs over the last few years. I honestly don't know how you put up with it.'

'Years of practice,' said Peggy flatly. 'More tea?'

*

Ethel emerged from the bathroom in Ruby's pale blue pleated skirt and navy sweater. She'd added the beaded necklace, bracelet and earrings, and brushed her hair, so was looking much more presentable.

'What you give me these bloody ugly shoes for? Yer know I likes a pair of heels.'

'I thought they'd be easier to walk in,' said Ruby, turning from the stove. 'Anyway, you look proper nice this morning, Mum,' she added cheerfully. 'That blue really suits you.'

Ethel just grimaced as she sat down and poured tea into a cup.

Ruby had decided Ethel needed feeding up, so had scrambled her one precious egg with milk, and a dab of her rationed butter. She also buttered the slice of toast and presented it to Ethel, hoping she'd enjoy it. Watching her wolf it down in silence, she sipped her tea, glad to have done something to please her at last.

Ethel finished the meal and added two teaspoons of sugar to her tea before drinking it down. 'Oh, that's better,' she sighed, reaching for her tobacco pouch. 'Nothing like a proper breakfast to set me up fer the day.'

'You'd better give me your ration book, and I'll sort it out so you can use it here,' said Ruby. 'The way things are at the moment, it'll be impossible to feed us both on my allowance.'

Ethel lit her fag and then was consumed by a bout of phlegmy coughing. 'I lost it,' she rasped eventually. 'I've been meaning to get another one, but keep forgetting.'

Ruby looked at her in astonishment. 'Then how have you managed? You can't get nothing without them stamps.'

Ethel shrugged. 'There's always a way,' she said mysteriously. She took another puff of her roll-up and stifled a further fit of coughing. 'Anyway, you're nicely set up 'ere by the looks of it. You can afford to get extra on the black market.'

Ruby shook her head. 'I'm not starting that game,' she said firmly. 'Rules are rules, and I ain't risking my licence for a bit of hookey meat and veg.'

'You and yer bleedin' licence,' Ethel sneered. 'Times is hard and rules are there to be broken if you know what's good for yer,' she added, squinting against her cigarette smoke. 'Besides, you got an 'usband somewhere. How come he ain't 'ere providing for yer?'

Ruby felt a stab of something akin to disgust at having to talk about Mike to her mother. 'My husband died two years ago,' she said quietly.

'I'm sorry to hear that,' Ethel replied without a glimmer of emotion. 'Good-looking fella by the looks of them photos you got in yer room. He was a Yank, weren't he?'

'Mike was Canadian.'

Ethel shrugged. 'Same difference. At least he married yer, not like most of them fly-by-nights. And he were clearly rich by the looks of all this. You done well, gel, and he's a definite step up from that bastard Ray.'

Ruby was so furious she was trembling and unable to speak. Pushing back her chair, she grabbed the dirty dishes and dumped them in the sink. Tears threatened as she filled the sink with hot water, for Ethel was as insensitive as ever, the words coming out of her mouth without a thought for how hurtful they might be.

Thankfully, Ethel seemed to realise she'd said too much, so stayed silent as she took a tea towel and started drying the clean dishes.

The heavy silence was broken by knocking on the side door. 'That'll be Sister Danuta,' said Ruby. 'The district nurse,' she explained to a clearly confused Ethel. 'I'll go down and let her in.'

'What sort of name's that, anyways? Foreign, is she?'

Ruby looked stern. 'She's Polish, and you're to be nice to her. Understand? She's a friend of mine, and is here to help you, so watch yer mouth.'

'All right, keep yer 'air on,' Ethel muttered sourly.

Ruby ran down the stairs and opened the door to find Danuta as neat and pretty as always, looking very efficient in her dark blue uniform, hat, pristine white apron, and carrying her medical bag.

'Thanks ever so for coming. Mum's upstairs.'

Danuta stepped into the hall and closed the door behind her. 'I am sorry for being sharp with you this morning,' she said, placing a gentle hand on Ruby's arm.

'No, it's me what should apologise. You know I never meant you was a gossip, Danuta. But Mum's driving me round the bend, and I'm not thinking straight.' She drew her closer. 'She's not the easiest person to deal with,' she murmured. 'So please don't be offended if she starts kicking off.'

Danuta frowned. 'What is this kicking off? She will kick me?'

'Nah,' Ruby said hastily – though she wouldn't put it past her. 'She likes saying things to cause trouble. Nasty things. Just try and ignore it, love – it's the only way to deal with 'er.'

Danuta lifted her chin and squared her shoulders. 'I have met other patients like this. I can deal with her. You not worry, Ruby.'

Ruby led the way upstairs to find Ethel sitting on the couch smoking another cigarette and coughing fit to bust. 'Mum, this is Danuta. Why don't you put that fag out and go with her into the bedroom so you can be a bit private?'

'I'll stay 'ere if it's all the same to you,' she replied with a baleful glare at Danuta.

Ruby fetched a bar of soap and a clean towel for Danuta, and then sat at the kitchen table to keep an ear open in case Ethel's gobby attitude caused offence.

'Ruby tells me you have an ulcer on your leg,' said Danuta. 'May I see it, please?'

'If yer want,' Ethel replied gruffly. 'But you wash yer 'ands first, lady. I don't know where you been before you come here.'

'I will wash my hands when I have had look at ulcer,' said Danuta, completely unfazed by Ethel's rudeness. 'You will please lift skirt?'

'Bleedin' foreigners,' muttered Ethel as she lifted the hem of her skirt and stuck out her leg. 'Can't even speak the King's flamin' English.'

Danuta ignored the sting of her insults as she looked at the ulcer and then headed for the kitchen sink to wash her hands. 'It is infected and I will need to treat and dress it,' she said, returning to reach into her medical bag for her stethoscope. 'But first I would like to take your pulse and listen to your chest.'

'What for? It's me bleedin' leg, not me chest.'

'It is your leg, yes,' said Danuta calmly, taking Ethel's wrist firmly in one hand and checking her watch with the other. 'But it is important to understand why you have ulcer. And you have bad cough.'

'It's the fags,' said Ethel.

'I am thinking you are right,' murmured Danuta as she listened to Ethel's wheezing chest through the stethoscope and then gently pressed down the bottom lids of her eyes. 'You are very underweight and anaemic,' she said almost to herself. 'I think you have not been taking care of your health, Mrs Sharp.'

'You wanna try taking care of anything where I been,' snapped Ethel, swatting away Danuta's hand. 'Just get on and see to that ulcer, or sling yer 'ook. I've had enough of this poking and prodding.'

'Mum,' warned Ruby.

Ethel rolled her eyes and gave a great sigh, but said nothing as Danuta treated the ulcer and began to dress it.

Danuta drew the skirt back over Ethel's legs. 'Do you have more ulcer anywhere?' she asked.

Ethel avoided looking at her and shook her head before reaching once more for her tobacco pouch.

'That is good,' said Danuta, returning to the sink to wash her hands again. 'Ruby,' she said quietly, 'I will make appointment with the doctor for tomorrow. Your mother is most unwell, and I do not like the cough.'

'Do you think it's serious?'

Danuta bit her lip. 'I am not doctor, but she is too thin, the cough is very bad, and the ulcer is a sign that her blood is not good. It is very important she see the doctor first thing tomorrow. I will arrange it.'

'What are you two whispering about?' shouted Ethel from the other room.

Ruby exchanged a knowing look with Danuta and they both left the kitchen. She sat down next to Ethel and took her hand. 'We were talking about you, Mum,' she said quietly. 'Danuta is worried about you, and is going to make an appointment for you tomorrow at the surgery.'

Ethel snatched away her hand. 'I ain't going to no doctor,' she snapped. 'And you can't make me.'

'If you don't go, then you can't stay here,' said Ruby firmly. 'You're not well, Mum, and you need to see a doctor. And don't worry about the cost, because I'll pay.'

'It's a load of fuss about nothing, and . . .' A fit of coughing interrupted her.

'You make that appointment, Danuta, and I'll get 'er there,' said Ruby.

Danuta nodded, packed up her medical bag and headed for the stairs. 'I will telephone to let you know what time,' she said before running down the stairs.

Ethel shrugged off Ruby's embracing arm from her shoulders. 'Leave it out,' she grumbled. 'There's no call for getting soft. What I need is a stiff drink. That'll put me to rights.'

'No,' said Ruby. 'What you need is fresh air and a break from them fags.' She snatched the cigarette from her and stubbed it out before pulling a reluctant Ethel to her feet. 'Come on. We're going to the laundry, and then I'll treat you to a coffee and a bun at the Lilac Tearooms.'

'I don't wanna go anywhere,' whined Ethel. 'Leave me be, Rubes.'

'You're coming with me like it or not,' Ruby replied, hating the bossy manner she'd been forced to take with her mother. 'I ain't leaving you here on yer own. Gawd knows what you'll get up to with the place full of booze.'

'You can't make me,' retorted Ethel, her arms folded, expression belligerent.

Ruby stood firm. 'You either come with me or I lock you in up here. Your choice.'

Ethel gave it some thought. 'All right,' she said with little grace.

Jim had become so focused on trying to explain what he was going through that he hadn't really looked at his father throughout his long, rambling speech. But when he finally lifted his gaze from his knotted hands and saw Ron's ashen face, he realised with a jolt of guilt that the stoic old man was in awful pain.

With gentle determination, he pulled his barely protesting father from his perch on the lavatory seat, guided him carefully down the stairs and helped him on with his coat. Ron was unsteady on his feet – probably through the quantity of blood that was now soaking the towel – so Jim kept a steadying hand under his elbow as they walked towards the Cliffehaven General, praying that Ron would be all right.

They were almost there when they saw Danuta emerge from the Anchor's side entrance.

'I hope there's nothing wrong with our young Ruby,' muttered Ron, who was trying to walk more steadily.

'We're probably about to find out,' replied Jim as the girl made a beeline for them.

'What is matter with your hand, Uncle Ron?' she asked immediately.

'Ach, it's just a scratch. Nothing for you to worry about. Is young Ruby all right?'

'She is very well,' the girl replied, reaching for Ron's wrist and holding it in an iron grip as she unwound the towel and looked at the wound. 'You must go immediately to the hospital,' she said, replacing the blood-sodden towel. 'That will need cleaning properly and several stitches.'

'Yes, we know,' said Jim. 'We're on our way there now. But,' he hurried on, 'if Ruby's all right, then it must be her friend who's visiting. I hope it's nothing serious.'

'I just go to see my friend Ruby. It is not permitted?' she asked, her gaze meeting his squarely.

Jim realised he'd overstepped the mark and put his hands up in surrender. 'Sorry,' he said. 'None of my business.'

'No. It is not. Now I must go. I have many more calls to make and Stanislav will expect me home for our midday meal.' With that, she hurried off to her little car.

'She's a fierce little thing, isn't she?' chuckled Ron. 'I certainly wouldn't want to get on the wrong side of her.'

'That reminds me,' said Jim, watching the girl drive away. 'Peggy will be cooking that pheasant you took round, and if I'm not back in time there'll be hell to pay. We'd better get a move on.'

'Aye. Rosie will soon be on her way home too.' Ron held his injured hand to his chest and took a sharp breath as the pain throbbed right through him. 'Ach, to be sure it's a ruddy nuisance. How could I have been so careless?'

'It's easy to have accidents when your mind is on other things,' said Jim, who'd had his fair share of careless moments in the past.

They walked onto the forecourt of the Cliffehaven General and past two ambulances to climb the steps into the reception hall. Knowing the way to the accident and emergency department as they'd both been regular visitors over the years, they turned left into the short corridor and were soon at the swing doors.

'It looks busy,' said Ron, peering through the windows. 'Perhaps I'll come back tomorrow.'

'Oh no you don't.' Jim took hold of his arm, well aware of his father's dislike of hospitals, doctors and anything medical, and steered him through the doors into the crowded room and up to the queue at the desk. Once the receptionist had taken down Ron's particulars, they managed to find a couple of chairs and sat down.

'We could be here for hours,' grumbled Ron. 'And there's all that mess to clear up as well as walking the dogs.' He eyed the other people who were waiting. 'To be sure it's a waste of me time.'

'Stop moaning, Da,' said Jim, retrieving a discarded newspaper from a nearby chair. 'Have a look at the football results. You never know. You might have won something on the pools.'

'I doubt it,' he rumbled, ignoring the proffered paper. 'Never won a thing and I've been doing them for years.'

Jim skimmed the headlines pertaining to the Nuremberg trials which had been going on for almost a year, and the Tokyo Trial which had begun back in April. He had little interest in either, for they merely underlined the fact that man's inhumanity to his fellow man – regardless of nationality – was a flaw in the human race that would never be eradicated. He turned to the sports pages, and then set the paper aside.

Ron gave a deep, impatient sigh, dug in his coat for his pipe and then saw the 'no smoking' sign on the opposite wall. With a grunt of annoyance, he shoved it back in his pocket, folded his arms as best he could and glared at anyone who dared catch his eye.

'Look, I know you hate it here, Da, but it's important you get that seen to. And all the huffing and puffing won't shift this lot any quicker.'

Ron didn't reply.

Jim realised he was on a hiding to nothing, so changed tack. 'Thanks for hearing me out this morning, Da,' he said quietly beneath the buzz of chatter surrounding them. 'I do feel as if a weight has been lifted off my shoulders.'

Ron stopped glowering at everyone and regarded Jim with deep affection. 'I'm glad, son, and when you need to talk again – which you will – you know where I am. You can't do it on your own, you know.'

'But you did,' Jim replied.

Ron shook his head. 'You might think that, but I had friends to talk to when I needed them. Chalky, Fred the Fish, Alf the Butcher, and Stan from the station – we were all there, you see – all pals in the same regiment.

We'd gone through it together, watched each other's backs and supported one another when the going got really tough. So it was only right we should rely on each other in the same way once we made it home.'

He took a deep breath before carrying on. 'None of us liked the thought of being weak or self-pitying, or thought of as less of a man because of what we were feeling. But we did recognise the need to share our experiences, and by doing so, we faced our demons and learnt how to live with them. As you will in time.'

'I never knew,' murmured Jim. 'You always seemed so strong, so capable of carrying on once we all got back. It was as if you hadn't been touched by any of it.'

'I wouldn't have been human if I'd not been affected,' said Ron with a tremor in his voice. 'None of us came through unscathed despite appearances to the contrary.'

'Frank too?'

'Oh, aye. Your brother too – but like you, he came home to a wife and young family. They became your focus – the means by which you could both bury the past and look to the future.'

Ron gave a sigh of deep regret. 'I had hoped it would remain buried, but when Hitler started another war, it brought it all back. You were forced to go into the killing fields again, and although Frank never saw action this time, he was dealt the cruellest blow when his two boys were killed on the minesweepers.'

Jim dipped his chin in shame and humility. He'd been so occupied with his own terrors that he hadn't given a thought to what his father and brother must have gone through. 'I'm sorry, Da. Truly I am,' he murmured.

Ron placed a meaty hand on Jim's knee. 'I know, son. I know.'

8

Rosie was just returning home from Beach View when she saw Ruby emerge from the side entrance of the Anchor looking strangely furtive. When she was swiftly followed by someone Rosie knew all too well, she understood why. Puzzled and somewhat perturbed, she hurried down Camden Road to waylay them.

Ruby had clearly seen her, for she was trying to hustle a recalcitrant Ethel across the road.

Rosie closed in on them quickly. 'Hello, Ruby,' she said, eyeing both the unwieldy bundle of blankets Ruby was holding and Ethel who was fidgeting beside her.

'Watcha, mate,' Ruby said too brightly. 'Sorry, can't stop. I gotta get this lot to the laundry.'

'Hold on a minute, Ruby.' Rosie caught her arm. 'What's she doing here?'

'Mum's just visiting for a bit,' she replied, her gaze slipping away.

'You realise what'll happen if the Licensing Board hears about it?'

'Yeah,' she replied, looking furtive again. 'Look, Rosie, keep schtum about it, will ya? It's just a short visit, and no one needs to know nothing.'

Before Rosie could reply, she was jabbed in the ribs by Ethel's sharp finger. 'Yeah, you mind yer own business, you old tart,' she rasped. 'It ain't your pub no more.'

Rosie ignored the painful jab and the insult to keep her focus on Ruby. 'Does anyone else know she's here, Ruby? You know what the gossips are like.'

Ruby seemed to think about this, and Rosie suspected Ethel's arrival had already got the jungle drums going.

And yet Ruby seemed determined to keep to her story. 'Like I said, Rosie. It won't be fer long.' She passed the blanket bundle from one hand to the other. 'Now I gotta get on.'

Rosie watched them hurry across the road to the twitten that would lead to the corporation laundry. She caught Ethel shooting her a baleful glare from over her shoulder before following Ruby, and knew there'd be trouble before long. Ethel attracted it like flies to a dung heap, which could only spell disaster for Ruby.

She shook her head, baffled as to why on earth the girl was risking everything by having her mother here. However, Ethel was the only family Ruby had left, and maybe she really was only here for a bit of a rest cure. She certainly didn't look very well. Rosie could only hope Ruby saw sense and sent Ethel on her way the minute she recovered, for although she was family, that woman was capable of doing a great deal of damage to everything the girl held dear.

With that worrying thought needling her, she purposefully carried on down Camden Road, intent upon getting Jim home before Peggy's lunch was ruined. What the two men thought they were doing this late on a Sunday morning was beyond her, but whatever it was, it was time to call a halt. Sunday lunch was sacrosanct at Beach View, both men knew it, and Peggy had had quite enough to cope with for one day.

She was just passing the hospital when she spotted two men who looked distinctly familiar coming out of the main entrance. 'What on earth?' she breathed, noting the sling and heavy bandaging on Ron's left hand. She ran across the road and met them in the car park.

'Hello, Rosie,' said an ashen Ron with only a glimmer of his usual bravado. 'Fancy seeing you here.'

'I might say the same to you,' she replied. 'What on earth have you done to yourself?'

'Ach, just a minor run-in with a screwdriver,' he said airily. 'Nothing to worry your pretty head about.'

'Don't patronise me, Ronan Reilly,' she retorted, taking his arm as he swayed alarmingly. 'You look like death warmed up, and they don't give you a sling and a bandage like that for a scratch.'

She kept a tight hold on Ron as she turned to Jim. 'What really happened, and what did the doctor say?'

'It's as Da said, Rosie,' he replied. 'He stabbed himself with a screwdriver trying to open a tin of paint. The doctor cleaned and stitched it, and gave him a tetanus jab, with some penicillin. They wanted to keep him in but of course he refused, so he's been told to rest for a day or two.'

Rosie gave a sigh. 'I'll make sure he does, and by the way, Jim, your lunch is almost ready. You'd better get home before Peggy feeds it to Charlie.'

'I was going to walk Da home,' he said. 'He's lost a fair amount of blood and is a bit woozy.'

'That's all right. I'll get him back.' Rosie tucked her hand more firmly into the crook of Ron's uninjured arm and gave it a gentle tug. 'Come on, you big brave soldier. You can tell me all about it on the way.'

'Now who's being patronising,' he muttered.

Rosie let the remark pass without comment, waved goodbye to Jim and steered Ron towards home. She had to fight off the dogs who were so pleased to see them they were in danger of knocking Ron's bad hand. 'Get down,' she ordered sternly, and shut the gate.

They rushed to wait for her at the front door, and bounded in the moment it was open, no doubt hoping for something to eat.

Rosie was on the point of releasing Ron's arm to go and feed them when he stumbled on the top step and almost fell. It was only a matter of luck that he didn't bring them both tumbling down, but Rosie had quickly braced herself and held tightly to his arm to keep him upright. She waited for him to get his balance, fretting all the while that something serious must be happening to him, and then helped him indoors.

'What on earth did the doctors give you?' she asked as she guided him into the sitting room and helped him sink into the couch.

'Like Jim said, tetanus and a painkiller and I think penicillin,' he slurred. He closed his eyes and rested his head back against the cushions. 'Whatever it was cost me an arm and a leg – and to be sure, wee girl, it's knocked the stuffing out of me so it has.'

As the dogs whined with concern at Ron's unusual behaviour, Rosie wrestled to get his coat and shoes off and then adjusted the cushions so his head was resting more comfortably. She could see his eyelids were drooping, so quickly fetched a blanket from the airing cupboard and tucked it round him.

Running her fingers gently through his tangled dark hair, she planted a soft kiss onto his rather hot forehead. 'I'll get you a cup of sweet tea,' she murmured. 'It might perk you up a bit.'

'Ach, no need to fuss,' he said drowsily. 'I'll be right as rain in a minute.'

Rosie doubted that, and by the time she returned with the tea he was fast asleep with the dogs curled up beside him on the couch. They weren't usually allowed on the furniture, but she let them stay as they clearly wanted to comfort Ron.

She sat and drank her tea and then eventually realised he'd probably be out of it for some time and therefore any plans they might have had for the rest of the day were cancelled. She eyed the coat she'd left on the arm of the chair. Something was sticking out of the pocket and for once it wasn't a ferret's nose – but something red and unpleasantly matted. Pulling it out, she gasped in shock. It was one of her very best towels, and it was absolutely smothered in dried blood.

'Good grief,' she muttered. 'What on earth did you do to yourself, Ron, to bleed this much? And of all the towels in the house, did you *really* have to choose this one?'

Her question remained unanswered but for a loud snore, so she left him to slumber on and went to soak the expensive towel in cold, heavily salted water. It was part of a beautiful bale that Ron's friend, Dolly, had given them as a wedding present. *Still,* she thought. *I should be grateful that he picked a hand towel and not one of the huge bath sheets.*

After many rinses, the water finally ran clear and she washed it in hot soapy water before hanging it out on the line to dry. On her return from the side garden, Rosie found both dogs sitting there looking piteous. She suspected that with all the hullabaloo, the men had forgotten to feed them, so filled their bowls, topped up their water and went back into the sitting room to check on Ron.

He was still snoring, but his colour was marginally better, so she left him there snug beneath the blanket. But she was intrigued about what had happened this morning, so she walked from room to room in search of any sign that might explain it. She admired the newly varnished floor in the dining room, and then went upstairs to their bedroom.

All seemed to be as she'd left it, so she went into the bathroom and gasped in horror. It resembled a slaughterhouse. There was blood smeared on the bath, the taps and the wash basin. Bloody fingerprints marked the wooden lavatory seat and chain-pull, and there were more spots drying on the linoleum.

'You certainly spread it about, didn't you?' she sighed, reaching into the cupboard under the basin for her cleaning materials.

It took a while to bring the bathroom back to its usual pristine state, and by that time, Rosie was hot, bothered and feeling decidedly grubby. She needed a bath, really, but having just cleaned it, she instead made do with a thorough strip wash and wrapped herself in one of Dolly's lovely big towels.

Feeling marginally better, she padded barefoot into the small spare bedroom to fetch the suitcase she kept in the built-in wardrobe and froze in the doorway.

The stepladder was on its side, the can of paint sitting on a bed of wadded newspaper, its lid askew, paint drips all down the sides, the discarded brush beside it. And on the freshly sanded floor was the evidence of spillage which someone had unsuccessfully tried to clean up with the rest of the newspaper she'd put down to protect it. She found that screwed up and sodden with paint in a nearby bucket.

She stood and looked at it for a long moment and then grabbed the suitcase from the cupboard, turned on her heel and shut the door behind her. Jim could jolly well come back later to clean it up. How two men could make such a mess in one morning was a mystery to her, but once Ron was more with it, he had a lot of explaining to do.

Feeling cross again, she threw the case onto their bed and unfastened the leather straps from their buckles. She was due to leave for Bournemouth first thing in the morning, and with all the bother, she hadn't prepared a single thing, let alone remembered to have her hair and nails done at Julie's salon in the High Street.

Pulling skirts, dresses, blouses and sweaters out of the wardrobe, she dumped them on the bed and then hunted out the shoes and handbags she wanted to take. There was a welcoming dinner on the first evening and a cocktail party on Tuesday night. She would definitely need two elegant dresses for them, something smart but feminine for the conference itself, and some casual slacks and a sweater in case she had time for a stroll along Bournemouth promenade. She'd heard that the famous resort was very smart, with palm trees, manicured gardens, and acres of sand lining the shore, and was quite looking forward to seeing it all.

And then cold and shocking reality struck. 'What the *hell* do I think I'm doing?' she breathed, sinking onto the bed. 'I can't possibly go with Ron in this state.'

She heard the echo of his voice from their conversation this morning, 'There will come a time when you'll have to choose between being a councillor or a wife.'

And the time had come – right this minute – and no matter how important the conference was, or how much she'd been looking forward to the trip, she wouldn't enjoy any of it knowing she'd heartlessly left Ron alone and unwell.

She closed her eyes and buried her face in her hands, horrified that she'd even contemplated going. This wasn't like her – not like her at all – and the realisation of how much damage her selfish ambition was doing to her marriage appalled her. Ron was the love of her life, the man she adored and who adored her to the point where he'd given her the freedom to pursue her new career on the council.

But at what cost to them and to their marriage? His gentle recriminations this morning should have alerted her to the way he really felt about things, and now they tore at her heart. He'd felt shut out, ignored and used as a workhorse to bring the house up to her high expectations, and she'd overlooked all the signs and taken him for granted.

She scrubbed at her face, took a deep breath and got to her feet. She'd never do that again, she vowed silently. Her marriage was too important, and Ron too dear.

Gathering up her clothes, she hung them back in the wardrobe. Once everything was put away, she fastened the buckles on the case and left it in a corner. Aware that Ron was still downstairs, she quickly got dressed in slacks and a light sweater, slipped on her flat shoes and went to check on him.

He was still asleep, the dogs having returned to their vigil on the couch beside him now they'd been fed. Softly kissing his brow which felt slightly cooler than before, she went into the hall and reached for the telephone. The call she had to make wouldn't be easy, and it would mean letting down the mayor who'd been one of her most stalwart supporters, but Ron was her priority, and from this moment on, always would be.

Jim entered the kitchen almost sheepishly, his gaze flying immediately to Peggy who was busy at the range. 'That smells wonderful,' he said, cautiously giving her a kiss on her cheek.

She giggled delightfully. 'You were very nearly late,' she replied. 'Perhaps you could get the bird out of the oven and do the carving while I drain the veg.'

Jim drew the roasting pan out and carefully placed it on the trivets to avoid damaging the wooden work surface. 'It's a good fat bird,' he said, his mouth watering as he carved the succulent meat. 'Plenty for everyone, so I hope you're all hungry.'

'What on earth were you doing fattening up birds in Hungary?' asked Cordelia. 'I thought you'd been down at Ron's place?'

Jim grinned and caught Peggy's eye as Charlie explained to Cordelia what had really been said. 'I love you,' he murmured beneath the laughter and chatter. 'And I'm sorry.'

'I love you too,' she replied softly. 'And thank you for that sweet note.'

'I meant every word in it,' he said. 'And I started today by talking with Da.'

'Are we going to get any lunch today?' asked Cordelia impatiently. 'Only we're in danger of starving to death over here while you two bill and coo.'

'To be sure, Cordelia, I'll not have you starving,' Jim joked, imitating his father's Irish accent. He placed a laden plate in front of her and gave her a hearty kiss on the top of her silvery hair. 'There you go. Get stuck into that.'

Cordelia rolled her eyes dramatically. 'Like father like son,' she muttered without rancour before looking at Charlie over her half-moon glasses. 'Take note, young man,' she said sternly. 'Roguishness runs in the family – so be warned.'

Charlie just grinned as he poured water from the jug into everyone's glasses.

When all the food had been dished up, Jim and Peggy sat down and tucked in. Jim noticed that Daisy kept eyeing him thoughtfully and decided he'd say nothing for now, but he would take her to one side later so he could reassure her that he wasn't as frightening as he'd seemed last night.

'So, have you finished over at Grandad's?' Charlie paused from shovelling his food down as if it might be the last meal he'd ever have.

'There was a bit of an accident, so the spare room isn't finished,' said Jim. He went on to tell them about Ron's hand and the paint that had been spilled on the floor. 'I'll have to pop down again later to try and sand it off, because I'm sure Rosie isn't best pleased with the mess we made.'

'Was there a lot of blood?' asked Charlie, who was always impressed by such things.

'A fair bit,' said Jim. 'Oh Lord,' he breathed. 'I've just remembered how we left the bathroom. Da spread the red stuff everywhere and I was in such a hurry to get him to the hospital I didn't have time to clean it up. Rosie will go ballistic.'

'It sounds as if she has more to worry about than a dirty house,' said Peggy. 'Poor Ron must be feeling very groggy.'

Jim nodded as he finished the last mouthful of delicious food. 'I was surprised he took it all so badly,' he said. 'I've never seen him that pale and unsteady before.'

'He hates hospitals,' said Cordelia. 'The big softie.'

Jim shook his head. 'No, Cordelia, I think it's more than that. He was really shaky, and Rosie had to hold on to him all the way home. He really should have taken the doctor's advice and gone in overnight.'

'I'll tell you what,' said Peggy. 'We'll go down there once we've cleared this lot away. I don't like the sound of that at all, and Rosie's supposed to be going to Bournemouth tomorrow morning.'

'Whatever for?' asked Jim.

'Some conference linked to her work on the local council.' Peggy gathered up the plates. 'But if Ron's as bad as you say, I'm sure she'll cancel.'

Jim hoped very much that she did, for otherwise he would think a great deal less of her.

*

Rosie had been keeping a close eye on Ron, and began to get concerned when his breathing became laboured, and angry red blotches appeared on his neck. She hurried across to him and touched his face to find he was burning up. Opening his shirt, she saw more red blotches on his chest.

'Ron. Ron, wake up,' she urged.

But he clearly couldn't hear her. His breathing was shallow and rapid; he had a temperature and she definitely didn't like the look of those red marks.

Dashing into the hall, she rang for an ambulance, then went to unlock the gate, leaving the door open before she shooed the dogs into the kitchen and shut them in. They already knew something was up for they were whining and scratching at the door.

With her focus on Ron's welfare, she quickly soaked a flannel in cold water and went back to him to try and cool him down. 'It's all right, my darling,' she murmured, placing the cold flannel on his forehead. 'Help is on the way.'

The clamour of the ambulance bell drew nearer and the dogs began to bark hysterically from behind the kitchen door. Rosie waited with Ron, who was still unaware of anything as he struggled to breathe.

Two sturdy men appeared in the doorway, took one look at Ron and hurried towards him. 'How long has he had trouble breathing, Mrs Reilly?'

'For the last ten minutes or so.' She quickly went on to explain about his hospital visit and the medication he'd had.

'It looks like a bad reaction to the penicillin,' said the more senior of the two men. 'We'd better take him in immediately.' He ordered the other man to fetch the stretcher, and while he waited, took Ron's pulse and temperature, and inspected the blossoming blotches on his chest, neck and face, his expression grim.

Rosie's heart was thundering, and she thought she might faint through fear. 'Is it serious?' she breathed.

'It can be if not treated quickly,' he replied solemnly. 'Luckily the hospital is only down the road. Don't worry, Mrs Reilly, we'll get him there in time.'

In time? Dear God, did that mean he could die? Rosie's legs almost gave way through sheer terror as she watched them lift Ron onto the stretcher, but with a huge force of will she managed to stay upright and follow them outside, only just remembering to grab her keys and bag on the way before slamming the door behind her. The dogs were still barking, but they were the least of her worries.

She was about to clamber into the ambulance when the senior man stopped her. 'Sorry, missus, but you'll have to walk. No room in here.'

She stood on the pavement, close to tears as he slammed the door shut. And then, galvanised by the urgency of it all, she began to run as the ambulance did a rapid U-turn at the top of the cul-de-sac and roared past her, bells clanging, on the way to the hospital.

She was out of breath and had a stitch in her side by the time she reached the hospital grounds, but she kept on running as she saw Ron being lifted out of the ambulance.

'Rosie! Rosie! What's happening?'

She turned and almost fell into Jim's arms. 'It's Ron,' she gasped. 'Bad reaction to the penicillin.' She wrested herself from his embrace. 'I've got to go to him.'

Aware only of the figure on the stretcher, Rosie dashed up the steps and ran down the short corridor to the emergency department. Almost collapsing against the reception desk, she could barely speak coherently. 'My husband . . . Just coming in . . . Reaction . . . Penicillin.'

A nurse came and put her arm round her. 'It's Mrs Reilly, isn't it?' she asked calmly. 'Your husband is being looked after now, so why don't you sit down and I'll get you a nice cup of tea.'

Rosie didn't want tea. She wanted to be with Ron. But she knew better than to argue, so she obediently sat down and burst into tears.

'I'm here, Rosie,' said Peggy. 'It'll be all right, really it will.'

'How can you know that?' Rosie sobbed. 'The ambulance man said he could die if they got to him too late. Oh, Peggy,' she wailed. 'He can't die. Really he can't.'

'You're getting yourself all het up,' said Peggy. 'And that won't do Ron any good at all. Here, take this and try to pull yourself together, love.'

Rosie took the handkerchief and made a huge effort to calm down, but it wasn't easy, for all she could think of was how bad Ron's breathing had been, and the solemn way the ambulance man had warned her of the danger he was in.

The nurse returned with a cup of tea. 'The doctor is with your husband now,' she said. 'I'll let you know when you can see him.'

'I should have done something sooner,' said an ashen-faced Jim. 'I knew he wasn't right when we left here earlier.'

'You weren't to know,' soothed Peggy before turning again to Rosie. 'How did you know something was seriously wrong?'

'He was finding it hard to breathe and there were red blotches all over his face and chest and he was burning up and . . .' Rosie burst into tears again. 'It's all my fault,' she sobbed. 'I should never have planned on going to that bloody conference. I'm sure that's what upset him – made him careless with that screwdriver.'

'It wasn't you who gave him the penicillin,' said Peggy firmly. 'As for his accident with the screwdriver

– well, that's par for the course with Ron. I've lost count of the times I've had to bring him in here. The man's a walking disaster,' she added with a reassuring smile.

The nurse returned. 'Your husband's breathing is much easier now, so you can go in and see him for just a minute.' She looked at Peggy and Jim. 'Sorry, just Mrs Reilly for now. The doctor insists.'

Rosie shot to her feet. 'Thank you, nurse.' She followed the girl through the door to the treatment area and met the doctor as he came from behind the screens that had been placed around the bed. 'How is he?' she asked immediately.

'He's on the mend, Mrs Reilly. Luckily we got to him in time. But he will have to be admitted so we can keep an eye on him.'

'But he will recover fully?'

'He'll be as right as rain in a few days,' he reassured her. 'And now we know he's allergic to penicillin it will be marked up on his medical records.'

He looked down at her solemnly. 'He's had quite a rare and very serious reaction, Mrs Reilly – what we call anaphylactic shock – so we've given him a drug called epinephrine to open his airways and help him to breathe more easily. The red patches will be itchy for a bit, but they'll fade in time with no lasting effect.'

Rosie nodded her understanding, though the thought of him being so close to dying made her tremble. 'How long will he have to stay?'

'At least a couple of days, Mrs Reilly. He will have to have a series of tests to check that his heart and lungs are working as they should, but he seems to be very fit for a man of his age, so I'm sure there's nothing for you to worry about.' He looked at his watch. 'I have other patients to see, but you can sit with him until he's taken up to the ward.'

Rosie thanked him and stepped nervously round the screens, not sure what she might find. But Ron was propped up by a stack of pillows and seemed to be almost his usual self as he raised his hand in greeting.

'Hello,' he wheezed. 'Sorry for the scare.'

She took his hand which now felt dry and only slightly too warm. 'You frightened the life out of me,' she replied. 'I thought I was going to lose you.'

'Ach, you'll not lose me that easy, wee girl,' he rasped, his breathing still rather laboured. 'To be fair, Rosie, I frightened meself, so I did. I knew coming here was a mistake.'

'This time it saved your life,' she said flatly. 'And you should be thankful they knew what was wrong with you.'

'Aye,' he murmured gloomily, scratching at his chest. 'Now I have to put up with staying here while they poke and prod me about like a piece of meat.'

'Oh, Ron. Please promise me you'll behave yourself. You know what happened last time with that run-in with Matron.'

He grinned. 'Aye, but thankfully the old battleaxe has retired.'

'She probably wanted to avoid any further shenanigans from you,' she teased. 'For a man who hates hospitals, you do spend rather a lot of time here.'

Their conversation was interrupted by the two porters folding back the screens and wheeling in a trolley. 'Hello, Ron,' said Harry Fuller cheerfully. 'Back again?'

'Can't stay away from the blooming place, Harry my friend,' Ron wheezed. 'Where are you taking me?'

'Spencer Ward. Men's medical. You'll be all right there, matey. The luscious Sister Morgan's in charge,' he added with a wink and hand gestures to suggest Sister Morgan had an hourglass figure.

Rosie was far from impressed by this. 'I'll let you get settled in and come at visiting time later,' she said. 'Is there anything you want apart from nightclothes and your washbag?'

'Aye. Me pipe and tobacco. If I'm to be stuck in this place, I'm entitled to a few pleasures.'

Rosie doubted that smoking would be allowed, or would do his lungs any good, but she nodded and stepped back as the porters wheeled him away, extolling the sister's feminine assets.

With a deep sigh, she traipsed back to the waiting room to tell Peggy and Jim that although it had been a close-run thing, he seemed to be on the mend.

9

Ruby had clearly picked the worst time to go to the laundry, because it seemed as if half the women in Cliffehaven were in there having a fair old gossip. The large, steam-filled room echoed with their chatter and laughter as the industrial-sized machines whirred, and irons hissed over damp linen.

But as Ruby stepped inside, the sight of Ethel brought a deathly silence, drawing suspicious glances and quite a few glares. Ruby lifted her chin and warned her mother not to provoke trouble, then quickly dumped the blankets in the huge machine, added soap powder, slotted in the right coins and turned it on to do a full cycle which would take about three-quarters of an hour.

The questions came at her like battering rams, and she tried to give the same answer she'd given Rosie and keep her patience. But it was utter bedlam, and in the end she had to almost drag Ethel out before she got into a fist-fight with one particularly belligerent woman who seemed determined to settle some old scores.

'That was a bad idea,' she muttered, towing Ethel along with her. 'And you don't 'elp by causing a ruck.'

'It weren't me what started it,' she snapped. 'That fat cow never liked me.'

'I suspect she has her reasons,' Ruby replied. 'The washing won't be done for a bit, and as it seems your arrival will soon be the talk of the town, we might as well get something to eat at the tearooms and face it out.'

'I'd rather have a drink back at the pub,' Ethel said sourly.

Ruby knew she would, but that was definitely not in the plan for the day. She hurried a whining Ethel down Camden Road, hoping they wouldn't bump into any more people who would remember her mother, but it seemed luck was not on her side, for coming away from the hospital was a very worried-looking Peggy.

'Oh Gawd,' she breathed. 'That's torn it.'

'I dunno what yer moaning about,' said Ethel through a fit of coughing. 'That Peggy Reilly's about the only decent person in this bloody place.' She stepped forward. 'Hello there, Peg. Nice ter see yer again.'

Peggy's stunned expression said it all, but she quickly recovered. 'Hello, Ethel. Ruby didn't tell me you were visiting.'

'It were a surprise. I decided to come down to get some good fresh air in me lungs and make sure me daughter was all right.'

Peggy glanced at Ruby with questions in her eyes. 'That's nice,' she murmured.

'Is something up, as you've been to the hospital, Auntie Peg?' asked Ruby with concern.

'Ron's had a bit of an accident so he'll be staying for a while. Nothing too serious, so don't worry. He'll be out and causing mischief again before we know it,' she added with a lightness that belied the lines of worry in her face.

Ruby suspected things were rather more serious than Peggy was letting on. 'I hope he gets better soon, Auntie Peg.'

The Town Hall clock struck the hour, and Peggy stiffened. 'Sorry, Ruby, love, but I must dash. I need to get back to Daisy.' She shot a stiff smile at Ethel. 'Enjoy your little holiday,' she said and hurried off.

Ethel looked puzzled as she followed Peggy's bustling progress along the street. 'She were a bit off, which ain't like her,' she said.

'She's probably worried about Ron. I shouldn't take it personally. I wonder what he's done to himself now?'

Ethel shrugged. 'Who cares?'

Ruby cared a great deal and decided she'd telephone Peggy later to find out what had happened, and to put her straight about Ethel's unwanted visit.

She crossed Camden Road and opened the door to the Lilac Tearooms, making the little bell above it ring jauntily. It was still a bit early for afternoon tea, but as neither of them had eaten since breakfast they were ready for cheese on toast and a slice of cake with a pot of tea for afters.

Peggy had been shocked to see Ethel – not only because she looked dreadful, but because she'd had the nerve to come back to Cliffehaven, and then compounded it by moving in with Ruby. She'd found it hard to be polite to the woman she'd helped all those years ago, and who'd let her and those she loved down so badly. Poor Stan had been an emotional wreck for weeks after she'd been arrested, thinking his reputation had been ruined by marrying such a thief and liar, and dear Ruby had vowed to have nothing to do with her ever again after her own reputation had been tainted by their connection. So what on earth had possessed the girl to take her in?

She shook her head as she walked up the twitten that ran along the backs of the houses. After all, Ethel was Ruby's only family – and the woman certainly didn't look well. Knowing Ruby's soft heart, the silly girl had fallen for whatever sob story Ethel had given her, and Peggy could only hope Ethel's stay here was a very short one.

Reaching the gate, she could hear Daisy having the most appalling tantrum, so she set aside all her other worries and hurried up the path, through the back door and up the basement steps to the kitchen.

'Mum, Daisy's being a complete pain,' complained a clearly frazzled Charlie over the noise. 'And I can't do a thing with her.'

Peggy took in the scene at a glance.

Daisy stood by the table, her dolls and colouring books scattered around her as she repeatedly stamped her feet and screamed at the top of her voice. Cordelia had almost certainly switched off her hearing aid, for she was reading her library book and taking no notice, and poor Charlie was clearly on the point of tearing his hair out.

Peggy went straight to Daisy, firmly grasped her arms and looked straight into her furious face. 'Stop this at once,' she ordered.

'Won't,' she yelled back. 'I want my new colouring pencils and Charlie won't give them to me.'

'You *will* stop, or I shall take those pencils back to the shop. And the new case to put them in,' said Peggy, giving her a gentle shake.

'But I want them,' Daisy stormed, her little face turning quite puce.

'No, Daisy. What you want is a smacked bottom. And that is what you'll get if you don't stop behaving like a brat.'

Daisy folded her arms and glared at her mother with all the fury she could summon, her dark brown eyes glittering with furious tears. 'I'm not a brat, and I don't want a smacked bottom,' she retorted. 'I want my pencils.'

'Right,' said Peggy whose patience had now been stretched to the limit. 'In that case you will sit down at the table and not say a word for ten minutes after you've said sorry to Charlie for being so horrid.'

'Then can I have my pencils?' she asked with wide brown eyes and a cajoling smile.

If ever there was a child that took after her father, it's Daisy, thought Peggy, not at all moved by this show of wanton manipulation. 'Not today,' she said firmly. 'You'll have them tomorrow – but only if you're good for the rest of the evening.'

Daisy climbed into her chair, crossed her arms on the table and sank her chin into them with a martyred sigh. 'Sorry, Charlie,' she mumbled into her cardigan sleeves.

'He didn't hear that,' said Peggy. 'Say it properly – and as if you mean it.'

Daisy lifted her head and looked at Charlie through her long, dark eyelashes. 'Sorry, Charlie,' she murmured sweetly.

Peggy knew the sweetness was as false as the apology, but for the sake of peace and harmony, she let it go. 'Now you'll sit there in silence until the small hand on the clock gets to there,' she said, reaching up to tap the six. 'One peep out of you, and you'll go to bed with no tea.'

It was a threat she'd rarely carried through, but it seemed to have the right effect on her little daughter who liked her food and knew there were iced biscuits tonight as a treat.

Peggy gently touched Cordelia's arm. 'It's safe to turn on your hearing aid again, Cordy,' she mouthed, making winding movements by her ears.

'Thank goodness for that,' the elderly woman sighed. 'I didn't realise Daisy could imitate an air raid siren quite so well. Positively ear-splitting. I'm surprised the whole town didn't hear her.'

She set her book to one side and fiddled with her hearing aid. 'I don't like telling tales, but she's been a proper little minx from the moment you and Jim left the house, and poor Charlie has had to have the patience of a saint.' She looked towards the door and frowned. 'Where is Jim, anyway? You haven't lost him, have you?'

Peggy told her and Charlie what had happened to Ron. 'Jim went home with Rosie to clean up the mess they left, and to walk the dogs which must have their legs crossed by now.'

'I'll go and help him,' said Charlie. 'It'll be a relief to get away from Daisy and to stretch my legs.' He grabbed his jacket from the hook on the door and looked at his mother with an understanding that surpassed his years. 'I'll bring him straight home when we're finished.'

She nodded, thankful that all the pubs were shut on a Sunday. She didn't want a repeat of last night even though Jim had promised to stay sober. Good intentions were all very well, but Jim had yet to prove he meant to keep them.

Ruby knew the situation with Ethel couldn't go on much longer, for even in the hushed and very relaxed atmosphere of the Lilac Tearooms, her mother's presence had made things awkward. Ethel's need for a drink had become apparent in her short temper and shaking hands. She hadn't helped matters by glaring at everyone and complaining loudly about the weakness of the tea and the staleness of the cake – both of which had been perfectly fine.

She'd paid and got Ethel out of there only to have to run the gauntlet of the women at the laundry when she collected the blankets. By this time Ethel's need for a drink had made her quite vicious, and she'd deliberately started a slanging match that would have turned violent if Ruby hadn't managed to haul her out again.

Feeling thoroughly fed up with everything, Ruby unlocked the side door of the pub and found a note which Danuta must have put in the letter box earlier. 'Danuta's got you a doctor's appointment for eight-thirty tomorrow morning,' she told Ethel, slipping the note into her trouser pocket.

'I wanna bloody drink,' snapped Ethel. 'Can't you see I need to have something?'

Ruby could, and knew she'd have to relent soon or there would be real trouble. 'Perhaps later,' she said. 'For now you can help me hang these blankets out.'

She headed for the back garden, closing her ears to Ethel's constant whingeing. 'And then we can listen to the wireless for the evening. There are a couple of good things on tonight.'

Ethel looked singularly unimpressed, but she helped with the blankets and then traipsed upstairs after Ruby. Plonking herself onto a couch, she rolled a cigarette and then had a prolonged coughing fit.

'Give the fags a rest, Mum, for goodness' sake. They clearly ain't doing you no good.'

'You won't let me 'ave a drink, now yer on about me fags,' growled Ethel. 'You're worse than the bleedin' God squad at the hostel.'

'Well, if you won't listen to me, perhaps you'll listen to the doctor tomorrow,' retorted Ruby, twiddling the knobs on the wireless to get a decent reception.

The dulcet tones of Alistair Cooke heralded the start of his *Letter from America*, and Ruby sat down to enjoy her favourite programme in the hope that the rest of the day would prove to be less fraught.

*

Jim had escorted Rosie home, made her a cup of tea and gently ordered her to sit down and try to relax until it was time to visit Ron. Once he was satisfied that she was comfortable, he'd gone upstairs to discover that she'd already cleaned up the chaos in the bathroom, but there was still plenty to do in the small spare room.

Having put the paint-soaked paper in the rubbish bin, cleaned the brush and stowed away the step-ladder, he was about to start the noisy sanding machine when he heard heavy footsteps on the stairs.

'Hello, Dad. Thought I'd come and help clean up.'

Jim beamed with pleasure as Charlie came into the room. 'This paint needs to be sanded off as best we can, and then the boards will have to be varnished again before painting the skirting boards. The wallpaper will have to wait for now.'

'I doubt we'll get it all out,' said Charlie, eyeing the stain. 'Most of it has sunk right into the wood.'

'Aye, so it has, but we'll give it a go, eh?' He handed the machine to Charlie before getting down on his hands and knees with a sheet of glasspaper to erase the lighter splashes.

He surreptitiously watched his son concentrating on the task, and wondered if Peggy had sent him here to keep an eye on him. He wouldn't have put it past her, and really he couldn't blame her if she had. He'd made promises before and broken them. But it was different this time because he'd seen what the drink and the nightmares had done to his loved ones, and he never wanted to see Daisy's terror, Peggy's tears or Charlie's disgust ever again.

But the sound of the sander was going through his head, making it ring and bringing back the memories of the enemy Zeros as they swooped in with the sun behind them to strafe the men running for cover over the paddy fields. He could almost hear the whine and thuds of the bullets as the planes returned again and again to mow them all down with their deadly machine guns.

His pulse racing, he quickly left the room and went downstairs to stand on the front doorstep and gulp in the salty air. He just wanted the noise to stop – to deaden the effects it was causing – and yet there was no doubt that it brought back the adrenaline rush of those moments when death was raining down and it was every man for himself. He'd known nothing like it since the end of his war, and to experience it again made him feel strangely alive.

'You're losing your mind, Jim Reilly,' he murmured. 'Get a bloody grip.'

'Are you all right, Jim?'

He turned sharply to find Rosie standing at his shoulder. 'It's the noise,' he replied. 'Goes right through my head.' He lit a cigarette and inhaled deeply before stuffing his trembling hands into his pockets.

'Through mine too,' she said. 'It would probably be a lot easier just to leave the stain there and put a rug over it.'

'You might have to anyway,' he replied. 'It's pretty well dried in.' He looked at his watch just as Charlie switched off the machine. 'I'll go up and varnish, and then me and Charlie will take the dogs out for a short run. I'd like to come with you to see Da, if that's all right, Rosie. He put the wind up me today, and no mistake.'

'Of course.' She smiled and patted his arm. 'I'll ring Peggy to let her know you won't be back until after visiting.'

Jim nodded, fetched the pot of varnish from the kitchen and returned to the spare room. It seemed there was some sort of conspiracy between the women to keep tabs on him, and although he didn't much like the thought, he realised he'd have to put up with it if life was to continue without more drama.

Cliffehaven General was run as a charitable institution, funded by donations and payments made by those who could afford their treatment. Ron was stuck in the hospital bed feeling very hard done by, for the almoner had decided that as he and Rosie owned their own house and Rosie had a good income, his bill for treatment would be presented to him on his discharge. The blotches on his body were itching, and although the pretty little nurse had smeared some sort of sticky cream all over them, they now stank to high heaven and were still driving him potty. He needed his pipe and tobacco, and wished he'd thought to ask Rosie for something to read, because although he'd only been in here a matter of hours he was being driven round the bend by boredom.

He leaned back against the pillows with an impatient sigh and regarded the other men on the ward with little hope of any excitement. There was nobody he knew, or who even looked as if they might provide entertainment during his stay. Half of them seemed to be asleep, and the rest were so old they needed help to get out of bed.

His gaze shifted to the sister in charge. He'd forgotten her name, but his porter pal, Harry, had been right about her being a right little smasher. She had curves in all the right places and a naughty glint in her eye, but something told him there was steel behind that sweet smile and that she wouldn't stand for any nonsense – rather like his Rosie.

He closed his eyes, thinking he might try to sleep for a bit despite the awful itching. He still felt light-headed, and his breathing continued to be ragged and painful, but the bed was surprisingly comfortable and it was blissfully quiet.

'Time for your pills, Mr Reilly.'

Ron dragged himself back from the rather pleasant doze he'd fallen into and eyed the nurse with little favour. 'I was asleep,' he grumbled.

'That's very good, Mr Reilly, but Sister said you must have these pills now, and then I'm to give you a lovely bed bath.' She dragged the screens across, making the castors squeak horribly against the highly polished lino.

He glared at her from beneath his brows. 'I'll have your pills, but I'll not be having any bed bath.' He swallowed the pills with a glug of water and pulled the bedclothes up to his chin to ward off any future attack upon his person.

'Come on, Mr Reilly, please don't make a fuss,' she wheedled, tugging at the sheet. 'Sister said you need to have a proper wash before visiting, and you can't stay in your underwear.'

'I'm perfectly capable of going for a wash in the bathroom,' he rumbled. 'And my underwear is staying put until my wife comes in with my pyjamas.'

She leaned closer, her voice barely above a whisper. 'Please, Mr Reilly. I'm already in trouble with Sister Morgan, and she'll tell me off something rotten if I don't do as she's asked.'

Ron realised she was just a probationer, and probably not much older than Charlie. She was clearly in awe of Sister Morgan, but there was absolutely no way he was going to allow her to strip him naked and wash him.

He threw back the covers and swung his legs out of bed to grab the hospital dressing gown from the nearby chair. 'I'll go and have a word with Sister and then wash in the bathroom,' he said, suddenly rather light-headed.

The nurse hovered nervously, casting repeated worried glances towards the sister, who was talking to a patient at the other end of the ward. 'Oh dear,' she murmured. 'I really do think that's a bad idea, Mr Reilly.'

Sister marched towards them, starched apron crackling, the wings of her white cap fluttering with every purposeful step. 'What is the meaning of this, Nurse Harris?' she demanded, barring Ron's escape from his bedside.

'It's not her fault,' said Ron stoically as he fought off a sudden wave of vertigo. 'I'm perfectly capable of washing myself and prefer to do it in the privacy of the bathroom.'

The blonde, blue-eyed beauty merely smiled at him with icy intent. 'I think not,' she said, steadying him firmly as he stumbled into her. 'Back into bed, Mr Reilly,' she said briskly, 'and behave yourself.'

'I'll not . . .' Darkness eddied through his head and the world seemed to tilt most alarmingly. 'I think I'm going to be . . .' he managed before his stomach rebelled and he threw up all over the bed, the sister and himself.

'Clean this up, nurse,' said the senior nurse who was clearly far from amused. 'And when you've done that, give him the bed bath. Time is marching on and we can't have this mess on show for the visitors.'

Ron felt not only foolish, but absolutely furious that he'd let the side down and caused more work for the poor little probationer. He wanted to apologise to her, but the world seemed to be spinning out of control and his stomach was heaving again.

The nurse scuttled off to the sluice room to fetch what she needed, and Ron was left to the mercy of the arctic harridan.

She removed her ruined apron with a grimace and set it to one side before propping Ron upright and holding a bowl beneath his chin. 'I've heard about you and your shenanigans, Mr Reilly,' she said quietly. 'In fact you are quite infamous. But I will not stand for it on my watch,' she said sternly, the blue eyes like shards of flint.

Ron was too busy trying to overcome the awful nausea to defend himself, and just wished she'd stop talking and go away.

But it seemed the young woman hadn't finished with him. 'You will behave yourself on my ward and do as you are told. Otherwise, I will have to inform Matron,' she said calmly.

Ron dared to look her in the eye but found no sympathy in those icy depths.

'I do not make this threat idly, Mr Reilly,' she continued, holding his gaze. 'If you think I'm being hard on you, then you've yet to meet our new matron.'

'She can't be any worse than the last one,' he mumbled, breaking eye contact.

Sister Morgan chuckled. 'She was a pussycat compared to the one we've got now. So be warned, Mr Reilly.'

Duly warned and feeling far from well enough to argue, Ron closed his eyes and surrendered.

Rosie was ready and waiting by the time Jim and Charlie returned from walking the dogs, and having locked the animals indoors, she walked with them to the hospital.

Having found Spencer Ward in the maze of corridors and staircases of the vast building, she braced herself for what she might find. A poorly Ron wasn't the easiest person to care for at the best of times, but he'd proven to be an absolute pain in the rear end during his previous hospital stays, and she was dreading to hear what he might have been up to this time.

Jim seemed to read her mind. 'He's only been in for a few hours, Rosie. He can't possibly have caused trouble already.'

'I wouldn't put it past him,' she replied shortly and pushed her way in through the swing doors as the bell rang at the start of the visiting hour. The tide of visitors swirled around her as she paused to find Ron's bed.

She saw him waving impatiently at her and quickly led Jim and Charlie over. 'How are you feeling?' she asked after kissing his forehead which felt unpleasantly clammy.

'Like I've been pulled through a hedge backwards,' he replied sourly. 'I've suffered no end of indignities already. You've got to get me out of here, Rosie.'

'I'll do no such thing,' she replied calmly. 'You're still clearly unwell, and this is the best place for you.'

'Home is the best place,' he replied, winking at his son and grandson. 'Can't you have a word with the sister and get me discharged?' he wheedled.

Rosie looked down at him with a smile and shook her head. 'You've been here less than four hours, Ron. A couple of days more won't do you any harm, so buck up and accept it's necessary.'

'But the dogs will need walking, the ferrets haven't eaten, and there's the rest of the work on the house to finish. And what about that conference?'

'Jim and Charlie have walked the dogs, Charlie can sort out the ferrets, and the work's done bar a bit of paper and paint. And I've cancelled the conference, so there's absolutely nothing for you to worry about,' she said firmly, and began to unpack the holdall she'd brought from home.

'Here are your pyjamas and washbag; your slippers, hairbrush and dressing gown. I've put in a couple of the books you've said you wanted to read, today's newspaper, and your pipe and tobacco. Though I doubt you'll be allowed to smoke it in here,' she added, looking around her at the oxygen bottles, and catching the frosty gaze of the glamorous sister in charge.

'Looks like you've fallen on your feet having that one to boss you about,' joked Jim. 'Quite the looker, isn't she?'

'She might look the part, but she's a harridan at heart,' grumbled Ron.

'Da,' sighed Jim. 'Surely you haven't upset her already?'

Ron shrugged and looked at his grandson. 'Be warned, Charlie my boy. Just because they look like that on the outside, doesn't mean they're pretty inside. That one's an ice queen.'

Charlie grinned. 'What did you do, Grandad?'

'Refused to have a bed bath,' he replied, reaching for his pipe and tobacco. He glowered at Jim who seemed to rather like the idea of having such a thing. 'Threatened me with the new matron, so she did,' he continued, getting into the stride of his story. 'Reckons she's worse than the old one – but I doubt she is – no one could be worse than that dragon.'

'Mr Reilly?'

They all turned to look up at the tall, thin woman in the navy-blue uniform and starched white cap who had appeared silently at the end of the bed. With a hatchet face and a beak for a nose, the mouth was a thin line of disapproval, the eyes gimlet sharp – and none of them dared speak.

'Aye,' said Ron warily as the others stared at her in awe.

'I am the matron of this hospital,' she said, her tone flat and without any hint of warmth. 'And I will not tolerate my ward being disrupted by recalcitrant patients. Should you disobey my nurses again, I will have you removed to a side ward under my sole charge. Is that understood?'

Ron nodded, for once unable to think of a quip as those beady, unrelenting eyes held him prisoner.

She advanced on him and snatched the pipe and tobacco from his hands. 'There is no smoking in here. I will leave these with Sister Morgan, and *when* I give you permission to leave your bed, you will smoke it in the day room.' With that, she glared sternly at them all to ensure her message was received and understood, turned on her heel and marched down the ward to a quaking Sister Morgan.

'Whew, what a tartar,' breathed Jim.

'No wonder you want to get out of here,' said Charlie sympathetically.

'If it means you'll behave and get better quickly, then it's all to the good,' said Rosie, and then burst into giggles. 'Oh, Ron, I do wish I'd brought the box Brownie. Your face was an absolute picture.'

Ron grimaced and scratched furiously at his itching chest. ''Tis no laughing matter, Rosie, girl. To be sure I'd rather face the Hun. Given half a chance, that Medusa could have killed Hitler with one glance.'

'It's a good thing he's already dead then,' said Charlie through his laughter.

Ron folded his arms and tried desperately to ignore the awful itching. 'You'd be laughing on the other side of your face if it was you stuck in this ruddy bed, helpless and ill and at the mercy of women like that,' he said moodily.

'Then you'd better make sure you hurry up and get better,' said Rosie, who was still amused by the whole thing. Poor Ron, she thought affectionately. Would he never learn that women like Matron could never be beaten?

10

Peggy and Cordelia had already eaten their tea and Peggy was feeling wrung out after dealing with another tantrum from Daisy. She'd only just settled her into bed and come downstairs when she heard the back door slam. It was Jim and Charlie back from the hospital, but they seemed to be in quite high spirits, so Ron must be doing all right.

'How is the old rogue?' asked Cordelia from her fireside chair. 'Causing trouble, I wouldn't mind betting.'

'Aye, Grandma Cordy, that he is,' said Jim on a chuckle. 'But I think he's met his match this time. The new matron could turn a man to stone.'

'That should be interesting.' Cordelia gave a naughty grin. 'I've heard from Bertie that she runs a very tight ship and even the consultants are terrified of her.' She sighed wistfully. 'Oh, to be a fly on the wall when those two clash.'

'Their first encounter was less of a clash and more of a submission from Grandad,' said Charlie cheerfully. 'I don't think I've ever seen him lost for words like that.'

'But how is he really?' asked Peggy as Jim gave her a quick hug and a kiss on the cheek.

'Not as well as he makes out,' he replied, stealing a biscuit from the tin. 'And those hives are driving him mad, which probably isn't improving his temper. Matron took his pipe and tobacco away too, so he's well and truly stuck, poor old devil.'

'How long do you think he'll be in for?'

Jim shrugged. 'Who knows? But I wouldn't put it past Dad to already have an escape plan brewing.'

Peggy giggled. 'Unfortunately he doesn't have Rita and her motorbike to aid and abet him this time,' she said. 'Do you remember me writing and telling you about that little escapade?'

Jim grinned. 'I certainly do, and I'll never forget the image you painted of him clinging onto the back of that bike with his leg sticking out a mile in the plaster cast as Rita hurtled down the road.' He pinched another iced biscuit and began to rummage in the fridge. 'What's for tea?'

'The corned beef salad you didn't eat yesterday.' She saw him grimace. 'I'm not having it go to waste and there's no other alternative,' she said firmly. 'And those biscuits are Cordelia's, so leave them alone.'

'Sorry, Cordy,' he said. 'I didn't realise.'

'My great-niece sent them over from Canada, so they are for everyone.' She picked up her knitting which was in its usual tangle. 'Oh dear, I seem to have gone wrong somewhere.'

'It's no good asking me, Cordy,' he replied. 'I don't know one end of a knitting needle from the other.'

'Neither does she,' said Charlie under his breath so as not to cause her offence. 'Her knitting gets worse by the day.'

Jim shot him a warning glance and joined him at the table. 'I was hoping Daisy would still be up,' he said to Peggy. 'I wanted to have a little chat with her after the trouble I caused last night.'

Peggy had put some fresh salad on the plate to try to make the meal look more plentiful and appetising – though it was neither, really. 'There's plenty of bread for once, so you can fill up on that,' she told them both.

'As for Daisy . . .' She let out a weary sigh as she sat down. 'She's been a proper little madam all day, and played up something rotten when I was trying to get her to bed, but thankfully she's finally gone to sleep.'

'She's overexcited about going to school tomorrow,' said Cordelia, 'but they won't tolerate the sort of carry-on we've had to put up with today, I'll be bound.'

'I'll make it up to her in the morning, then,' Jim said, making a doorstep sandwich with the hated corned beef. 'Can't you find something else in future, Peg? I had enough bully beef in the army to last me a lifetime.'

'It's cheap, available and fills your stomach,' replied Peggy. 'Just be thankful there is anything for tea after that huge and extravagant lunch.'

'Peggy, dear, can you turn the wireless on? It's time for *It's That Man Again*. And this knitting is all wrong. I wonder if you could help me with it?'

Peggy rolled her eyes at Jim, turned on the wireless and took the knitting to see how on earth she could unravel it. 'What's it supposed to be, Cordelia?' she asked with a frown.

'A jacket for Anne's new baby,' she replied. 'Now shush. The programme's started.'

Duly chastened, Peggy tried her best with the knitting, but found the only answer to the tangle and dropped stitches was to take it all off the needles and start again. It was a familiar ritual that had been played out regularly throughout these past years, but happily accepted as part of family life.

They sat and listened to the comedy show, and once the programme had ended, Charlie pushed back from the table. 'I need to sort out my stuff for tomorrow,' he said, 'and get used to being out of bed early to catch the bus.' He kissed his mother and Cordelia goodnight, winked at his father and thudded up the two flights of stairs to his room.

'I hope he didn't wake Daisy,' Peggy fretted. 'I've really had quite enough of her for one day.'

Jim glanced across at Cordelia who was busy collecting her book and glasses in preparation for bed. 'Have you had enough of me too?' he asked Peggy softly.

She blushed. 'Never,' she breathed, holding his gaze and reading the message of love and desire in his eyes.

'An early night then?' he murmured, reaching for her hand.

'That would be lovely.'

Ethel had begun to prowl around the flat, opening cupboards and slamming drawers in an increasingly desperate search for a drink. Ruby tried to ignore her and concentrate on her wireless programme, but it was proving impossible.

'What are you looking for, Mum?' she asked although she knew. 'Your baccy is here.'

'I want a drink,' Ethel snarled, coming to jab Ruby painfully in the shoulder before bursting into tears. 'Please, Rubes,' she wheedled, dropping to her knees at Ruby's feet. 'Just one little drink. That's all I'm asking. I got such a thirst, and me belly's crawling for the want of it.'

'Oh, Mum,' sighed Ruby, gently drawing her to her feet and giving her a hug. 'You've been so good all day. Can't you try to go without?'

'No.' She lifted her tear-streaked face, the need clear in every haggard line. 'I need it, Rubes. Really I do,' she sobbed.

Ruby hated seeing her mother like this but realised the addiction had her so tightly in its grip that there'd be no relief until she'd got what she needed. 'All right, Mum,' she said with great reluctance. 'I'll get you something.'

Ethel moved quickly out of the embrace, her eyes already bright with hope as she licked her lips in anticipation. 'Gin? Whisky?'

Ruby shook her head. 'I can't afford to give the spirits away now they're so tightly rationed. But I've got a good strong brown ale.'

'Anything,' she gasped, wringing her shaking hands. 'Anything, Rubes, then I promise I won't ask again.'

'Stay here and I'll fetch it.' She pressed Ethel down into the couch and handed her the roll of tobacco and box of matches to keep her occupied before she ran down to unlock the door and go into the bar.

Ethel was miraculously still on the couch when she returned minutes later with four bottles of Newcastle Brown, but she leapt up to follow her to the kitchen and snatched the bottle from Ruby's hand the moment she'd opened it. Drinking it straight out of the bottle, she glugged it down to slake what must have been the most awful thirst.

'Take it easy, Mum, and try to make it last,' said Ruby softly. 'Because I ain't going down to get more tonight.'

Ethel finished the first bottle and wiped her mouth with the back of her hand before opening the second. 'Yeah, all right. Just need a bit of a top-up and I'll be fine,' she muttered.

Ruby watched as she quickly drained the second beer, gave a satisfied burp and reached for the third. At least she'd slowed down a bit, for this time she poured the thick brown ale into a glass and carried it over to the couch. It was heart-breaking to see this once feisty woman brought so low, and Ruby could only pray that the doctor might have some advice on how to try and wean her off it – or at least deal with it somehow before she bankrupted her bar stock.

As the evening dragged on the silence stretched between them. The wireless burbled in the background, but neither of them was really listening to it. Ethel had quietened down considerably now she'd got what she needed, and she sat smoking, coughing and drinking, lost in her own world.

Ruby could think of nothing to say, though watching her now, she wished they could cuddle up together for a proper mother and daughter talk so she could begin to understand precisely what Ethel had been through during the years they'd been estranged.

But Ethel had never encouraged what she called 'being soft' and certainly wouldn't appreciate any show of emotion now – and any advice Ruby might offer would definitely be ignored.

Ruby sighed inwardly. Even a well-meaning lecture on the evils of drink would be like water off a duck's back, for she'd probably heard it all before. And she suspected her mother had already given in to the demons because she was exhausted from fighting – not only them, but authority and the harsh reality of a life lived forever on the outer edges of society.

An hour later, Ruby noticed that Ethel had finished the beer and was now drooping towards sleep. Stifling a yawn, she retrieved the cigarette that was about to burn Ethel's fingers and stubbed it out. 'Come on, Mum,' she said quietly. 'Let's get you to bed. We've got an early start tomorrow, remember?'

Ethel stared at her groggily and allowed Ruby to help her to her feet. 'I can manage,' she slurred, pushing Ruby aside before staggering into the bathroom.

Ruby took the opportunity to check that the bed was still dry, and waited outside the bathroom in case Ethel needed help.

'What you waiting for?' Ethel said, emerging at last in the borrowed nightdress.

'I wanted to wish you goodnight,' she replied, opening her arms to give her a hug.

Ethel ignored the gesture and walked straight past her. 'Yeah. Goodnight,' she said before shutting the bedroom door in Ruby's face.

Ruby stood there as she'd done so many times as a child, left wanting the warmth and affection she craved, and hurt by her mother's rejection. The familiar emotions brought back too many bad memories, and to experience them again after all these years proved to be just as painful. And yet she couldn't understand why she should still be affected by Ethel's selfish disregard, for she'd never been a mother who cuddled and kissed and made her feel anything more than a hindrance – unless she needed her for something. It was a lesson she should have learnt long ago, but it seemed to Ruby that the yearning for even the slightest acknowledgement from Ethel was deeply ingrained.

She blinked back the tears and returned to the sitting room. Having turned off the wireless, she sat down and reached for the silver-framed photograph she kept next to the telephone on the side table.

Her darling Mike grinned back at her, looking so happy and handsome in his uniform. How cruel fate had been to snatch him from her so soon after they'd begun their life together in Canada. She held the picture to her heart, leaned back into the cushions and closed her eyes. How she needed him now – to hold – to talk to – to just be here.

She must have fallen asleep, for when she opened her eyes, the mantel clock was softly chiming midnight. Kissing Mike's picture, she put it back on the side table and got to her feet to stretch and yawn. It had been a long, fraught day in which she'd got very little done, and there were certain things that couldn't wait if she was to open the pub tomorrow. But first she had to make sure Ethel was sound asleep.

Ruby tiptoed into the narrow passage and listened at her door. Satisfied that she was happily snoring, she collected the bunch of keys from under her pillow and went quietly down the stairs.

Locking the door into the hall behind her in case Ethel woke and decided to wander about, she headed for the dusty, cobwebbed cellar and unlocked the heavy oak door, which creaked alarmingly. The single low-watt light bulb only deepened the many shadows cast by the heavy oak beams, and Ruby shivered. She'd always found it creepy down here, but it felt more so in the dead of night when she could hear the rustle of mice, and perhaps the echoes of those who'd once used this place for other, more nefarious purposes.

The Anchor had been built almost two centuries ago as a coaching inn, and there were stories of local smugglers using it to store their booty of brandy, tobacco, silk, cotton and lace which they'd brought ashore from France. There were also tantalising rumours of a network of tunnels that connected the cellar to the old church which had been flattened by a doodlebug in the war, but Ruby had yet to find any sign of them. She suspected Ron knew more than he was telling, but he had always claimed ignorance of such things and wouldn't be drawn on the subject – which actually made her even more intrigued.

Ruby remembered hiding here during air raids. They'd been frightening times, but Rosie and Ron had made it as comfortable and cosy as possible with old sofas and rugs on the hard-packed earthen floor, and a plentiful stock of beer to keep them singing through to the all-clear.

But for now she had work to do. There were crates of bottled beer and mixers to bring up to the bar, and the barrel of bitter was down to the last dregs so it needed changing. The drayman was due on Thursday, and as Ron was in hospital, she'd have to see if Frank would be about to help steady the heavy barrels down the chute and roll them into place.

Ruby picked up the first of the crates and climbed the concrete steps up to the bar. It was a nuisance not having a man to help at such times. She'd advertised for someone to come in part-time, but the only ones who'd turned up had proved to be unsuited to the task. Some thought they were God's gift to womankind and saw her as an easy target; others wanted a full-time job which she couldn't afford, or were too shifty to be trusted with either the till or the stock. In the end, she'd had to rely on Frank or Ron, but they weren't always around, so she'd have to keep advertising and just hope there was someone out there who'd fit the bill.

As she went up and down the concrete steps and slowly restocked the bar, her thoughts strayed to the exchange she'd had earlier with Ethel. She hadn't been lying when she'd said she couldn't afford to give away drinks of gin or whisky, for unlike Gloria at the Crown, she wasn't running a thriving black-market outlet – and didn't intend to.

However, rationing meant the prices had rocketed, especially on the spirits, and even the beer wasn't as plentiful or as strong as it used to be, since it had been watered down. Customers were getting thinner on the ground except on match days as everyone was being careful with their pennies, and too many were still out of work. Rosie had warned her it would be tough trying to run a pub in these austere times and she'd been prepared to work hard and be canny with her money, but the added pressure of Ethel threatening to drink her profits dry certainly wouldn't help.

Once she'd sorted everything out in the bar to her satisfaction, she locked the cellar door and then went into the garden to bring in the blankets before they got any wetter from the heavy dew. Tiptoeing back upstairs, she put them on a clothes horse in the bathroom in the hope they'd dry.

Another listen at Ethel's door told her she was still snoring, so she went to the safe to collect the Saturday takings and stow away the keys to the cellar. She hid the takings in a handbag which she stuffed at the bottom of her bed, and planned to make time tomorrow morning to get the cash to the bank.

Ruby finally climbed into bed at two o'clock, exhausted by the emotional traumas of the day, her head buzzing with all she had to do tomorrow. Ethel would need constant watching, which would be almost impossible during opening time, so she'd have to give Brenda a call, although she didn't usually work on Mondays as it was one of their quietest days. If she couldn't come in, then she'd have to ask Gloria for the loan of one of her staff – which would be a big favour in Gloria's eyes and one she would expect to be returned twofold since Ethel was the reason behind the request.

Sleepless and anxious despite being so tired, Ruby punched the pillows and shoved her feet against the handbag of money until it was in a far corner of the bed. She then remembered that she hadn't telephoned either Peggy or Rosie. Both deserved an explanation, but what on earth could she say?

She closed her eyes. The plain fact was that Ethel was here needing sanctuary and help with all that ailed her. And yes, she was a selfish, ungrateful liability and posed a threat to everything Ruby had here – but at the heart of it she was still her mother, and therefore her responsibility.

11

Peggy woke to the sounds of the milkman's plodding horse and the screaming gulls. She lay curled next to Jim, reluctant to leave him and the lovely warmth of their bed where they'd made love so sweetly the night before, and reaffirmed the ties that bound them in soft words and heartfelt promises.

She had lain awake for some time after he'd fallen asleep, and as far as she was aware, he'd gone through the night without any bad dreams. Whether that was because he hadn't been drinking, or because of their lovemaking, she wasn't sure. But the unbroken night should certainly leave him more rested.

She glanced over his broad shoulders to look at the bedside clock. Startled to see how late it was, she gave him a gentle nudge. 'Time to get up, Jim,' she murmured.

He rolled onto his back and smiled sleepily at her as he stretched out an arm and pulled her close. 'Good morning, Mrs Reilly,' he murmured with a glint in his eyes that bode mischief.

'And good morning to you, Mr Reilly,' she giggled. 'It's no use you getting ideas – I can hear Daisy moving about next door.'

He ignored her and nuzzled her neck as his hand caressed the curve of her hip and thighs. 'Are you sure?' he whispered.

He was making her tingle from her neck to her toes, and it would have been so easy to give in to the delicious sensations he was arousing, but there simply wasn't time. 'Positive,' she replied, pushing against his chest. 'We've both got to get to work and Daisy starts school today. And you said you wanted to talk to her, remember?'

He gave a sigh. 'Aye. That I did.' He kissed her, then rolled away and flung back the bedclothes. 'I'll use the downstairs bathroom so you can see to Daisy, and then I'll make a start on breakfast.' He looked around the room. 'Where's my clean shirt?'

'Hanging in the wardrobe along with your suit as usual,' she replied. 'And there's clean underwear in the drawer if you bothered to look,' she teased. 'I thought you army types were trained to be observant,' she chuckled as she put her arms around his waist and hugged him.

'Oh, we are,' he replied, kissing the top of her head and cupping her behind in his big hands. 'And I am observing a very desirable woman at this moment, so why look for shirts and socks?'

'Just hold those thoughts until tonight,' she retorted playfully, before wriggling away from temptation and leaving the room.

'Mummy, Mummy, look. I dressed myself.' Daisy spun round in delight and almost tripped because she had her shoes on the wrong feet.

'Well done, love,' said Peggy, blinking back her tears. Her baby girl was looking so very grown-up in her navy-blue uniform skirt and white blouse, the neat white socks carefully folded at the ankle. *Where have the years gone?* she wondered.

'Let me do those shirt buttons up again, because they're a bit higgledy-piggledy, aren't they, and then we'll sort out those shoes.'

'I'm a big girl now,' said Daisy, fidgeting with impatience as Peggy dealt with the buttons and pulled the navy V-neck sweater over her head for added warmth. 'Can I wear my blazer?'

'I think it might be better if we leave off the blazer until after you've eaten your breakfast,' said Peggy carefully. She buckled up the shoes. 'There. Those feel better now, don't they?'

Daisy nodded and ran to the low chest of drawers to get her hairbrush. 'I want a ribbon like Rose Margaret,' she demanded.

Peggy smiled. Daisy adored Anne's little Rose who was the same age, and liked to emulate her, so she brushed the lustrous dark hair and held it back from her face with a rubber band before tying on the blue ribbon which matched the uniform skirt and jumper. It probably wouldn't stay in for long, but that really didn't matter much. Tantrums were not to be risked this morning.

As Daisy twisted and twirled in front of the mirror to admire herself, Peggy marvelled at the strangeness of fate which had given her a daughter and a granddaughter within a few months of each other. Unlike Anne's Rose Margaret, Daisy had not been planned, and the pregnancy had come as a shock to them all – but particularly to Cissy, her younger daughter, who hadn't approved at all and considered her parents to be far too old to be carrying on as they obviously had.

Peggy smiled at the memory, for Cissy had eventually come round to the idea, and of course she herself had revelled in the chance to have a little one again, knowing it would be her last – and all the more precious because she was a constant reminder of Jim's penultimate leave home before he was sent to India.

Bob and Charlie had been very good about it all, but then they'd already been evacuated to Somerset, so didn't have the embarrassment of their rather mature and very pregnant mother turning up at the school gate.

Peggy sighed. The war years had been hard enough with Jim being sent to the Far East, but with Anne, baby Rose Margaret and the boys evacuated to the farm in Somerset, and Cissy joining the WAAF to live up at the airfield, she'd felt bereft. And although things were very different now, she still found it difficult to let go of the apron strings.

Cissy was always a constant source of worry now she lived in London, Anne was expecting her third baby any minute, and Bob was still in the West Country, managing the farm and courting a local girl. They were all growing up too fast, and now it was Daisy and Rose's turn to take their first step away from home and babyhood by starting school.

She snapped out of her rambling thoughts, realising time was fast slipping by, and bustled Daisy into the bathroom. She covered her clothes with a towel and stood over her as she washed and brushed her teeth. They came out of the bathroom to find Cordelia waiting for them on her stair-lift.

'Well,' she said, admiring Daisy. 'Don't you look smart? I thought you'd like a ride this morning as it's a very special day.'

'Yes please, Gan-gan.' Daisy clapped her hands in delight, for this was a treat she hadn't had in a while as she was getting a bit too big for it.

'Be careful, Daisy. Remember Gan-gan's legs aren't as strong as they were.'

'I know,' she huffed. Then with all the delicacy of a gazelle, the child perched very carefully on the old woman's lap.

'If you could just keep an eye on her while I get ready, Cordy, that would be a huge help. I'm in danger of running late.'

Cordelia waved her stick in acknowledgement, told Daisy to hold on tight and lowered the lever beside the chair. The contraption made its stately progress down the stairs, Daisy giggling in delight all the way.

Peggy dashed back into the bathroom to have a strip wash – there wasn't time for a bath – and get ready for the day. Emerging some minutes later, she went to her bedroom to dress in the smart pencil skirt, blouse and jacket she kept for work. She fastened her much-mended and third-best lisle stockings to the suspender belt, then slipped her feet into the low-heeled shoes that were so comfortable for a day trawling a factory floor.

Brushing her dark hair, she was a bit disconcerted to notice a few wisps of silver glinting amongst the curls, but chose to ignore them for now. A trip to Julie's salon next weekend would sort them out, and she might even treat herself to a manicure.

She finished putting on her make-up, clipped on the fake pearl earrings and grabbed her handbag, before remembering to hunt out the box Brownie camera. This first day of school had to be recorded like all the others, and if she could persuade Charlie to stand still for five seconds, it would be rather nice to get a picture of him too.

She checked there was a roll of film in the camera and then went to retrieve Daisy's rag doll from her room. She'd forgotten her in the excitement, but as she took Amelia everywhere, it would be a small comfort for her once she was at school.

It seemed that Charlie had also risen early, for he was already dressed and eating cereal as Cordelia was sipping tea and scanning the morning newspaper in between responding to Daisy's excited chatter.

Peggy knew it wouldn't last, for as the days shortened and winter came, they'd all be reluctant to leave their beds and it would be the devil's own job to get them where they needed to be each morning.

She gave Daisy her doll and then smiled at Jim, whose hair was still damp from his wash, and hastily put a tea towel over Daisy's new clothes so she wouldn't drop her cereal all down them.

She glanced at the kitchen clock. 'Before you go, Charlie, I want to take your photograph.'

'Whatever for?'

'As a keepsake,' she replied. 'In fact, I'll probably get two copies if it turns out all right so I can send one to Bob.'

'Why?'

Peggy rolled her eyes. Charlie was always monosyllabic in the mornings. 'Because he hasn't seen you since May and I'm sure he'd appreciate it. I'll send him one of Daisy in her uniform too,' she added. 'He'll be amazed by how much she's grown since he saw her last.'

'Can I have my picture tooken too?' asked Daisy excitedly.

'Taken, darling. It's taken not tooken,' Jim corrected fondly.

Daisy looked at him with big, solemn brown eyes. 'I love you, Daddy,' she said. 'I'm glad you're not cross any more.'

He bit his lip and went slightly pink. 'I love you too, sweetheart,' he replied, softly kissing the top of her head. 'Now hurry up and finish your breakfast so Mummy can take your picture.'

Aware of the time ticking away, Peggy quickly downed a cup of tea and ate a piece of toast before chivvying Charlie and Daisy out onto the front steps. She fussed with Daisy's blazer and beret until she got them both just right, and then dared to tweak Charlie's tie so it covered the top button of his shirt. Noting his grumpy expression, she didn't attempt to get his hair out of his eyes, for he'd never liked anyone messing about with it.

'Say cheese,' she ordered, holding the little camera at waist height and trying to focus on them through the viewfinder on the top. Hoping her hand was steady and she'd got them where she wanted them, she pressed the button.

'And once more, please. Charlie, you're squinting.'

'I've got the sun in my eyes,' he grumbled.

She quickly took another shot before he got totally fed up and walked off. 'All done,' she said brightly.

'Good,' muttered Charlie, turning back into the house.

By the time she and Daisy had returned to the kitchen there was no sign of him, and Jim was slipping on his suit jacket.

'Charlie didn't want to miss his bus,' he said, reaching for his briefcase. 'And I have to go too. There's a staff meeting at nine, and I'm expected to be there.'

He kissed Peggy and then hugged Daisy. 'Enjoy your first day of school, Daisy, and I want to hear all about it when I come home tonight.'

'You have a good day too, Jim,' said Peggy, thinking how handsome he looked in his demob suit and how much she adored him.

Jim said goodbye to Cordelia and then walked swiftly out into the hall and down the front steps to the Austin which had been provided by the Legion to enable him to get back and forth to headquarters and visit the men under his care.

Peggy turned to repair her lipstick, checking her reflection in the glass of the clock-face. 'Have you got any plans for the day, Cordy?'

'I thought I might get Bertie to drive me to the hospital so I can visit Ron,' she replied. 'And then he can take me out to tea at the golf club.'

'Let's hope he hasn't already made other plans,' chuckled Peggy, knowing that Bertie had better things to do than chauffeur Cordelia about, although he'd never once complained. 'It's promising to be a very pleasant day for his usual round of golf.'

Cordelia sniffed. 'That's as maybe. But there's far more entertainment to be had visiting Ron than tramping about a golf course.'

Peggy laughed. 'That's not fair, Cordy. Poor Ron.'

'All's fair in love and war,' she replied enigmatically and returned to perusing the obituary column of her newspaper to see who she'd outlived.

Peggy noticed that her fingers were blackened from the cheap ink and even cheaper two sheets of recycled paper that constituted a broadsheet these days, and hoped she would remember to wash it off before going out with Bertie Double-Barrelled, whose army background made him quite pernickety about appearances.

'I'm off then,' she said, picking up Daisy's tiny case containing her pencils and pencil case, and some sandwiches and juice for her lunch. But Cordelia had switched off her hearing aid, so she left her to the newspaper.

She helped Daisy down the deep steps to the basement. 'Do you want to go to the lav before we leave?'

Daisy shook her head and clutched her precious doll to her chest.

They got as far as the gate, and it was no surprise to Peggy that Daisy then decided that perhaps she did need to go after all. Peggy took the doll, lit a cigarette and waited for her daughter in the chilly shadows of the twitten, remembering all those other first days of school.

Anne had been as excited as Daisy, and had loved school so much she'd trained as a teacher and had worked all through the war in the Somerset village school, returning to Cliffehaven Junior until this last pregnancy meant she had to give it up.

Cissy hadn't liked school at all, for she was always preoccupied with thoughts of being a famous star of stage and screen, and was forever getting into mischief. Bob had been quite stoic, putting up with having to go until something better came along – and he'd finally found his niche on the farm in Somerset. Peggy was still amazed by that, for she'd never thought of him as a farmer. As for Charlie, well, he seemed to relish the challenge of school from the first day, and because he was doing so well at the grammar, she had very little trouble getting him there.

Daisy ran down the path and took charge of her doll again. Peggy stubbed out her cigarette and held her hand as they went down the twitten and crossed over into Camden Road.

There were still bomb sites on both corners, but there was talk of plans to build some terraced houses in their place, though when that might be was anyone's guess, for there wasn't much money about and building materials were as rare as hen's teeth.

The shops were still shut, but Fred the Fish and Alf the Butcher waved and wished Daisy luck as they prepared for the day's business. Despite the early hour there was already a steady stream of women heading towards Solly's huge clothing factory for their day shift, and lots of chattering children on their way to the school.

The original school building had been so badly damaged during an air raid that it had been pulled down and rebuilt. The new building was much bigger, for it had been extended beyond its original plot to encompass that of the big block of flats which had also been bombed. The playground was at the front, and at this moment was teeming with children noisily playing football, skipping or just racing around yelling. Peggy certainly didn't envy the teachers who would have to deal with them.

She felt Daisy tighten her grasp on her hand. 'Mum? I don't want to go,' she said, cowering away from a group of jostling boys that raced past, kicking a tin can.

Peggy had guessed this might happen but knew the reluctance wouldn't last for long. She handed Daisy the little case. 'Look, there's Rose Margaret waiting for you by the gate. Don't you want to go in with her?'

Daisy clutched her doll and case even tighter and looked torn between wanting to go home, and spending time with Rose.

Rose won by running towards her and grabbing her arm. 'Come on,' she shouted, her voice high with excitement. 'Miss Bell's waiting for us.'

The two little girls ran into the playground towards the plump and motherly Miss Bell, who had taken over Anne's position as teacher to the reception class. They didn't even bother to look back, let alone wave.

'So much for first day nerves,' said Peggy, feeling a bit tearful and put out. 'I'm glad they're starting together, though. It'll make it easier for them to settle in.'

Anne put her arm around her mother's shoulders. 'I'd have thought you'd had enough first school days under your belt to not bring on the tears, Mum,' she teased gently.

Peggy dabbed her eyes and watched the two little girls scamper into the building with Miss Bell. 'Silly, isn't it? But it's always hard – as you'll find out when your last one walks through these gates.'

'It's understandable, Mum, and I do sympathise,' Anne said. 'But I haven't really had time to think about anything much this morning except getting here in one piece and on time. Emily's ferociously jealous and in a terrible bait about Rose starting big school. I had quite a tussle to get her into the crèche this morning.'

Peggy looked at her lovely, very pregnant daughter and noted the dark shadows under her blue eyes. 'You look tired, love,' she said sympathetically. 'These last weeks are exhausting, aren't they?'

'They certainly are,' she replied, easing her back. 'I shall be glad to get home and put my feet up. I've got the house to myself as Martin's flying to Germany and isn't expected back until late tomorrow, so I've promised myself to do absolutely nothing all day but read and sleep and eat biscuits.'

Peggy laughed. 'Lucky girl. I've got a factory full of women waiting for me who will have the usual moans and arguments, and a stack of inventories to go through.' She took her daughter's hand. 'But should you need me while Martin's away you know where I'll be, and now I've got the car back on the road, I can easily get to you.'

'Thanks, Mum,' she replied with a loving smile. 'But I'll be fine. There's a few more days before this one's due,' she said, running a gentle hand over her large stomach.

They both heard the school bell ringing and watched the children make a mad scramble indoors.

'Let me give you a lift to the factory, Mum,' Anne offered. 'It's on my way home and will save you the walk.'

'That would be lovely,' said Peggy. 'I am running a bit late.'

They walked to the small black car parked at the kerb and climbed in.

Anne concentrated on her driving as they went down the hill and then turned right into the High Street. 'How's Dad doing?' she asked.

'Better, I think,' said Peggy. 'He slept well last night and seemed quite eager to get to work this morning.'

'That's good,' said Anne. She turned left for the steep climb up the hill to the vast industrial estate which had been Cliffehaven's hub of wartime industry. 'But don't expect too much too soon, Mum. It took Martin a long time to get over his war experiences, and even now there's the occasional bad night.'

'I realise it will take time for Jim to come to terms with things,' said Peggy. 'But every good night is a step forward, don't you think?'

Anne turned the car at the bottom of Mafeking Drive so she'd be facing down the hill again, and parked outside the factory gates. 'Let's hope so. Martin told me Grandad came to see him the other day, and they discussed the best way forward. Do you think Dad will ask for help?'

'He and Ron had a long heart-to-heart yesterday, and I think it did him a lot of good.' Peggy realised Anne knew nothing about Ron being in hospital, and quickly told her what had happened.

'He's not liking it much – as usual,' she said finally, 'but he is in the best place.'

Anne giggled. 'I doubt he thinks that,' she said wryly. 'I'll try and pop in just before I pick up the girls from school. Poor Grandad, he's his own worst enemy, isn't he?'

'He certainly is.' Peggy kissed her cheek. 'Take care of yourself, darling, and thanks for the lift.'

The large Victorian house that contained the doctor's surgery looked over the recreation ground. It hadn't changed much since Ruby had first come here from London, for the lovely old house had fortunately been left unscathed during the war and still stood proudly in the quiet, tree-lined avenue on the western edges of the town. The surrounding trees seemed a little taller, and the hedge thicker, but the front garden was still immaculate and the paintwork fresh.

The only real changes had come in the surgery staff. According to the brass plaque on the wall outside the entrance, there was a Dr Darwin, a Dr Preston, and a Dr Robinson. Ruby wondered what they were like, and which one had actually moved into the spacious rooms on the first and second floor, for it suited someone with a large family.

She could remember the lovely, gentle Dr Sayer who'd since retired and moved to a bungalow in the next town, and his rather good-looking son, Michael, who'd married the snooty nurse, Eunice Beecham, and taken over the practice. She'd heard that Michael, Eunice and their children had moved to a swanky part of London shortly after the end of the war, and that he was now in private practice.

Ruby had no idea which of the doctors they would be seeing, but at least she'd managed to get Ethel here. She tried to concentrate on the glossy magazine as she sat in the waiting room beside Ethel who was on the fidget. It had been a struggle to get her here on time, and the only way she'd managed to persuade her out of the house without a fight was to give her a bottle of brown ale, and promise another on their return. It had gone down so fast it could barely have touched the sides, and Ruby doubted she'd even tasted it. At least it had done the trick for now – but there was the rest of the day to get through yet.

Ethel threw the magazine she'd been flicking through onto the low table and crossly folded her arms, her expression stormy. 'How long 'ave we got to sit 'ere?' she grumbled for the umpteenth time. 'What's 'e up to in there? I ain't got all bleedin' day.'

'It won't be much longer,' murmured Ruby, hoping this was true, for Ethel was making a show of herself and the other people in the room were beginning to tut and cast them dirty looks.

Ethel took out her tobacco, plucked out a roll-up she'd prepared earlier and lit up despite the fact she was sitting right beneath a large poster warning of the dangers of smoking. The first drag elicited a prolonged and violent bout of coughing that bent her almost double.

Ruby gave her a handkerchief, retrieved the cigarette and stubbed it out in the ashtray. 'Leave it out, Mum,' she urged in a hiss.

'What you do that for?' rasped Ethel, making the woman next to her cringe and clutch her handbag.

Ruby was saved from answering by Danuta emerging from one of the four rooms that led off the waiting room. 'Dr Darwin will see Mrs Sharp now,' she said.

Ruby clutched Ethel's elbow and got to her feet.

'So sorry, Ruby,' said Danuta quietly, 'but it is just your mother for now. He will see you immediately after he has examined her.'

'I ain't goin' in on me own,' snapped Ethel.

'I will be with you, Mrs Sharp,' said Danuta, firmly taking her arm. 'Dr Darwin just wants to listen to your chest and give you the once-over.' She smiled into Ethel's scowling face. 'Ruby will come as soon as he's finished. I promise.'

Ethel glared at her and then grudgingly let her lead the way into the other room.

Ruby didn't fancy the doctor's chances of getting her mother to cooperate, for even as she sat here in the hushed waiting room, she could hear Ethel's strident voice issuing a string of curses and threats between bouts of violent coughing.

She avoided catching anyone else's eye and picked up a magazine, pretending to read an article about this winter's new fashions, but actually focusing on what might be happening behind that closed door as Ethel finally stopped shouting and there was an ominous silence.

As the minutes ticked by and people came and went, Ruby became more and more tense. What on earth was going on in there? Surely a quick examination couldn't take this long? She looked at her watch, fretting over getting to the bank and then back to the pub before Brenda turned up.

Danuta finally appeared and beckoned to her.

Ruby quickly discarded the magazine and stepped into the examination room, her anxiety increasing tenfold at the other girl's solemn expression, and the sight of a distressed Ethel huddled into the depths of an upholstered chair. 'What is it?' she breathed. 'What's wrong with her?'

'Dr Darwin will explain,' Danuta replied just above a whisper. 'I am to give your mother some tea and stay with her until you are finished.' She crossed the room and tapped on another door. 'Dr Darwin is very kind man,' she murmured. 'He will see that Ethel is well looked after.'

Ruby didn't like the sound of that at all, and although she'd have preferred to go and console Ethel, she didn't have a chance because Danuta had opened the door and Dr Darwin was approaching her from behind his desk.

'Mrs Taylor,' he said with a melodious, deep voice that held the attractive burr of Scotland. 'It's a pleasure to meet you at last. I've heard many good things about you since you took over from Rosie at the Anchor. Please come in and sit down.'

Her first impression was of a man in his mid-thirties who epitomised everyone's idea of a family doctor, and a safe pair of hands. He wore twill trousers, a plain shirt, dark tie, highly polished brown brogues and a tweed jacket; was of medium height and weight, with brown hair and eyes and the tan of someone who enjoyed the outdoors.

And then he smiled at her and, despite her awful worry over Ethel, she couldn't help but smile back, for the warmth and sincerity of it drew her to him and immediately eased the tension in her spine.

He didn't go behind the desk but pulled his chair to one side so there were no barriers between them.

Ruby tensed again, knowing without any doubt that he was about to tell her something bad.

'Mrs Taylor, I'm sorry, but your mother is very ill,' he began. 'However, I think you already realise that?'

Ruby nodded, her gaze fixed to his face in search of clues to what he was trying to tell her.

'I have given your mother a thorough examination and taken samples of blood, urine and sputum. But I would like her to go to the hospital for further tests, and have asked Sister Danuta to accompany her there this morning,' he continued, his expression giving little away.

Ruby finally found her voice although her rapid heartbeat was making it hard to breathe. 'What do you think's wrong with her?' she managed.

He lifted his hands and sighed. 'Apart from being malnourished, very underweight and anaemic, the beatings she has sustained over the years and the alcohol she consumes have taken their toll.' His brown eyes held her in a kind, steady gaze. 'I understand from Sister Danuta that she's recently been released from HMP Holloway after quite a long sentence. Your mother has confirmed she's been living rough ever since.'

'I knew about the prison, but only suspected she'd been living rough,' said Ruby, looking down at her hands twisted in her lap. 'We've been estranged for some years,' she added softly.

'I can understand that,' he murmured. 'It can't have been easy for either of you.'

Ruby didn't reply, as it had been easier for her than for Ethel, but she was relieved he didn't probe into the reasons for their estrangement.

He shifted in the chair. 'The conditions in Holloway are only marginally better than living on the streets,' he said softly. 'The damp and cold, the dirt, diseases and lack of decent food and medical intervention are all conducive to bad health, and I'm sorry, Mrs Taylor, but your mother is now extremely ill.'

Ruby swallowed the lump in her throat and looked back at him as the truth she'd been trying to ignore sank in. 'She ain't going to get better, is she?' she whispered.

He held her gaze, his expression full of sympathy. 'The prognosis isn't hopeful, I'm afraid.' He sat forward. 'But we mustn't get ahead of ourselves, Mrs Taylor. There are tests to be done by the experts at the hospital, and medication to ease some of the distressing symptoms she's dealing with. We will know more once we have a fully detailed picture.'

'What do you think is wrong with her?'

'I would like to have the results of the tests before I can give you a firm diagnosis,' he hedged.

Ruby held his gaze. 'But you suspect something serious, don't you?'

He was not to be drawn. 'There could be several reasons for her current situation,' he said, 'but as I said before, I'd prefer to wait until . . .'

'Yeah, I know what you said,' she snapped. 'What I want is a straight answer to a straight question. Is it cancer?'

He let his breath out in a deep sigh. 'It is one of the possibilities,' he admitted reluctantly. 'But not a certainty,' he added firmly.

He leaned towards her again, his expression intense. 'Your mother is a fighter, Mrs Taylor. Her body may be struggling, but her spirit is still very much to the fore, and while we wait for the test results, it's important to keep our focus on maintaining your mother's care, comfort and quality of life.'

Ruby burst into tears, and because she'd given her handkerchief to Ethel earlier, he dug into his pocket and handed her his – a pristine white square of tweed-scented cotton, which she clung to like a lifeline.

'You're right about Mum being a fighter,' she sobbed. 'There's nothing she likes more than a good scrap. I'm ever so sorry if she was rude to you.'

'I took no offence,' he said easily. 'It's just her way of hiding her fear.'

Ruby realised he was right, but that didn't begin to help her absorb the possibility that Ethel could be beyond help. 'Will she have to stay in hospital once she's had these tests? Or can I look after her at home?'

'I really do think the hospital is the answer for now,' he replied. 'They can attend to her needs day and night, and provide the medication to boost her weakened immune system and deal with any pain she might be experiencing.'

'She never told me she was in pain,' Ruby said, struggling to contain her tears.

'She's a proud and feisty woman who would regard admitting to pain as a weakness. It's how she's withstood the beatings, the congestion in her lungs, and the awful discomfort from the ulcers which have recently erupted. Habits of a lifetime are hard to overcome, even in the direst circumstances, Mrs Taylor.'

Ruby absorbed the shocking news that there had been more than one ulcer, but recognised that he was right in his diagnosis of her mother's bloody-minded character. 'I feel as if I've let her down so badly,' she said. 'I was rude and bossy and unkind to her, and I could see she weren't well, though I put that down to the drink. But it's obvious now that she come 'ere cos she thought I'd look after 'er, and I couldn't even do that properly.'

He placed a warm, dry hand over hers. 'You weren't to know, and are certainly not to blame, Mrs Taylor. Your mother's unwillingness to admit she needed help is part of the problem, as are her chaotic lifestyle and bad habits which have brought her to this sorry state. Even if she'd come to you sooner, things had already progressed to the point where any help would be severely limited. But you were right in bringing her to me – and together, we'll do our very best for her.'

'Are you sure I couldn't have done more in the short time she's been with me?'

'Positive.' He squeezed her fingers and sat back. 'I have already telephoned the hospital and made arrangements for her to be admitted to Clarice Burnette Ward after she's had the tests. Sister Danuta will be with her throughout to explain what's happening and keep her company until she's settled in. Are there any questions you'd like to ask?'

'Why can't I go with her for the tests?'

'It's better to let Sister Danuta accompany her – even if she does complain about it vociferously,' he said with a smile. 'Danuta, as I'm sure you know, stands no nonsense, and I think your mother is a little in awe of her, whereas she might play up with you.'

Ruby nodded. It was a distinct possibility. She dried her eyes and squared her shoulders. 'Can I go and see 'er this afternoon?'

'I'd leave it until this evening,' he replied. 'She'll be tired after all the tests and will probably need to rest.'

'She'll need a drink and a fag more like, if I know her,' said Ruby, trying to make light of the ghastly situation – and had to battle against tears again.

'She'll be permitted a little of both during her stay – but under strict supervision,' he said. 'Her alcoholism will be recognised, and there's a day room for when she wants a cigarette.'

'Blimey,' she breathed. 'I didn't realise. But that's good, because without a drink she can be really hard work.'

He nodded and then got to his feet. 'I'm sorry, but I have to cut this short for now as I have a full surgery this morning. But if you wish to speak to me at any time, you only have to ring reception and I'll make sure to get back to you as quickly as possible. I will keep close watch on your mother, Mrs Taylor, and let you know the results as soon as I have them – I promise.'

It was a struggle to stand up, for every part of her was aching and stiff as if she'd aged years in these past few minutes. 'Thanks ever so much, Dr Darwin,' she managed as she shook his warm, firm hand. 'You've been ever so kind.'

'I want you to promise to eat properly and get plenty of rest,' he said, still holding her hand. 'I know you're very worried, but you'll need strength of mind and body to meet what I suspect will be tough times ahead.'

She dredged up a smile and reluctantly withdrew her hand from his. 'Yeah, I know. But me and tough times are old acquaintances. I'll manage.'

They were brave words, but Ruby was trembling inside as she walked out of his consulting room in a daze and managed to pay the receptionist the sixpence for the consultation and get outside without collapsing into a heap and making a fool of herself.

Yet, stepping out into the manicured front garden, she became shockingly aware of the melodious bird-song and the clear blue sky, the sounds of young boys' voices as they played football in the recreation ground, and of someone nearby playing the most glorious sonata on the piano.

Ruby froze on the gravel path and watched the gulls swoop and soar, their white wings gilded by the bright sun that warmed her face. It should have been raining and ominously silent with thunderclouds looming from a dark sky, the whole town shrouded in shadow. But it seemed life was going on regardless. No one cared that Ethel might be incurably ill, or that her own battered heart was, once again, being torn apart.

She stumbled along the path and sank onto the bench that had been placed in a sheltered corner, buried her face in her hands and wept for all she'd lost – and for what she might yet lose.

12

The smaller of Solly Goldman's two factories had been set up towards the end of the war in a fair-sized unit that had once been used to make parachutes. There were good facilities as Solly was a great believer in keeping his workers happy so they didn't disrupt his profit margins – but also because he hated conflict, and had realised that contented workers were less likely to go on strike. .

There was a cloakroom with lavatories and wash basins as well as lockers and pegs for clothes, and a small recreation room with tables and chairs for those who didn't want to go to the large communal canteen during their breaks.

The main body of the factory was a vast room with a vaulted tin roof which contained lines of work stations for the machinists beneath the bright hanging lights. There were heaters set up for when winter came, and a loud-speaker system had been put in place so the women could listen to the BBC Light Programme as they worked.

The cutting table was placed at the back of the room and behind that was a door leading to a warehouse filled with bolts of cloth, and a smaller room for checking the quality of the garments before they left the building. This, in turn, led to a wide metal door that could be rolled up to reveal a ramp and loading bay where the lorries came to load the stock for sale, and unload the bolts of fabric.

Peggy's office was a self-contained area partitioned off with hardboard to one side of the main room. She had a door she could lock, and there was a broad window looking out over the factory floor so she could keep an eye on what was happening, and a smaller one which gave her a view of the bomb site that had once been a council estate. It wasn't the best view in the world, but at least she could open the window when it got too warm.

The small room wasn't sound-proofed, so she worked to the constant background noise of whirring machines, wireless programmes and the loud chatter of the machinists. However, she barely noticed it any more and felt quite at home with her desk, comfortable chair, filing cabinets and telephone. There was a spider plant thriving in a pot on the windowsill, and a large calendar and clock on the wall along with a huge board showing all the workers' names and the times of their shifts.

Peggy had had very little opportunity to think about anything other than her work this morning, for it had taken the first half-hour to sort out a minor accident in the washroom, another to follow up accusations of pilfering from the cloakroom which turned out to be a case of forgetfulness on the part of the complainant, and the rest to sorting through the sales and purchase invoices with the accountant – of which there were many.

The factory was doing very well now they were making baby and toddler clothes along with bed-linen for prams and cots – and they were about to start a new line in christening gowns. England was certainly having a baby boom now all the men were home, and Solly had somehow known it was coming and had got into the market well before many others in the rag trade. His main factory in Camden Road made maternity dresses and copies of the latest women's fashions, which were proving very popular after the austerity of wartime make-do-and-mend utility clothing.

Although children's clothes were free from restrictions, nothing else could be bought without the hated clothing coupons, and because there was an ongoing problem with the supply of materials which were at a premium right now, the prices were quite high. Imports from abroad were haphazard at best and of poor quality at worst.

A lot of the mills in the north and the Midlands were still struggling to get their looms going again – whether through lack of building materials to repair bomb damage or a dearth of suitable staff, Peggy wasn't sure, but it was difficult to keep the warehouses as fully stocked as Solly would have liked.

As her lunch hour approached, she gratefully left John Farley to the account books and picked up her bunch of keys and handbag. She'd been in such a rush this morning she'd forgotten to bring the sandwiches she'd made when she was doing Daisy's lunch box, so would have to go to the canteen.

She smiled and exchanged a few pleasantries with some of the women as she walked through to the exit, and discovered to her delight that it had turned out to be a lovely day. Hurrying over to the canteen, she bought a cheese and tomato roll and a cup of tea, and went over to Jack Smith who was sitting outside his garage workshop in the sun.

'All right if I join you, Jack?'

His pleasant, open face broke into a welcoming grin and he patted the seat of an ancient kitchen chair. 'It's a free world, Peg. Help yourself.'

She sat down and took a sip of her tea. 'Have you heard from your Rita lately?'

'I got a letter this morning,' he replied. 'She and Pete are really making a go of things out there by the sound of it. And Australia seems to suit her,' he added wistfully.

Peggy knew he was missing his only daughter dreadfully, but had had to accept the fact she'd fallen in love with an Aussie flyer and was now living on the other side of the world. She regarded the line of used cars for sale and the gloomy workshop with all its hydraulic lifts and heavy tools that smelled of engine oil, petrol and grease.

'You must be making a good living here,' she said. 'Why don't you go over and spend some time with them?'

He took a deep breath and tossed away the dregs of tea from his mug into the nearby drain. 'I've said I'll go one day, but I'm too busy here to just shut up shop and risk someone else pinching all my customers.' He lit a cigarette and stared into space. 'It sounds all right out there, though. There's space for a man to breathe, and exciting opportunities for those who want them.'

'I read there's a scheme that's been set up by the Australian government which would cost just ten pounds for you to go out there,' she said helpfully.

He chuckled. 'Yes, I've read all about that and Rita has mentioned it many times. But it's for people who want to emigrate out there permanently, and at forty-nine, I'm a bit long in the tooth to be considering such a radical change.'

'Well, it's just a thought,' she said, opening her roll and finding the merest sliver of cheese hiding behind rather soggy tomatoes, which was a bit of a swizz as it had cost her thruppence-ha'penny. She ate it anyway because she was very hungry, and then washed it down with the last of the very weak tea. Lighting a cigarette, she closed her eyes and enjoyed feeling the sun on her face after a morning indoors.

'How's your Jim?'

'Enjoying his work and doing his best to come to terms with things,' she replied, 'though he's got a long way to go before he's his old self again. But he and Charlie are getting on like a house on fire, and Daisy is slowly getting used to having him around. She adores him, which is lovely. By the way, Daisy started proper school today.'

'Crikey, I didn't realise she was old enough. Where have the years gone, eh?'

'Those were my thoughts exactly.'

They shared a smile and then fell silent with their own thoughts. She had known Jack since childhood, and he was probably the closest person to a brother she would ever have. He'd married young as they all had back in those days, but his lovely wife had died when Rita was still pre-school age. He'd struggled to raise her on his own, and Peggy had done what she could to help him – and when their house was bombed while he was fighting in Europe, she'd willingly given Rita a home. His little tomboy had turned out more than all right. In fact, she'd learnt his trade so well, she'd left these shores as not only a wife, but a first-class motor mechanic.

Remembering Rita in her First World War flying jacket and goggles, tearing about the place on her Triumph and terrifying anyone who was unlucky enough to ride pillion, made Peggy grin. 'Is that bike of hers still going?' she asked.

He laughed. 'Oh, yes. She's juiced it up by all accounts and it's going a treat. She's bought another one to go racing on the dirt tracks, determined to beat Peter at his own game, but I think she's met her match there.'

He got up and stretched. 'You stay there as long as you like, Peg, but I'd better get on. The customer will be back for his car soon and I haven't quite finished the service on it.'

'I must go too,' she said, looking at her watch. 'Come and see us again soon. Jim would be glad of your company, and there's always a place at our table.'

'I will, Peg. No worries, as they say down under.' He hitched up his oil-stained overalls and returned to working beneath the car bonnet.

Peggy took the empty mug back to the canteen and was about to return to her office when she saw Doris coming down the wooden staircase from the office she shared with her husband John who was the administrator for the factory estate.

She waited as Doris carefully negotiated the stairs in her high heels, and rather envied the fact that her sister always looked as if she'd just stepped out of a beauty parlour. Her hair and make-up were immaculate; her clothes were smart and probably more suited to a ladies' luncheon at the Officers' Club than a poky office on an industrial estate. But then that was Doris. She had very high standards, and nothing and no one was going to change her.

'I just wanted to say sorry for barging in the other day,' she said. 'I got the wrong end of things, and certainly hadn't meant to cause trouble.'

'That's all right, Doris. I know you only had the best intentions,' Peggy replied smoothly, knowing full well Doris had tried to stir up trouble between her and Jim.

'How is he doing?'

'He's very chirpy today, thanks. Which is more than I can say about his father. Ron's in hospital.' She quickly went on to explain what had happened. 'But I'm sure he won't be in there for long. You know how much he hates anything medical.'

Doris sniffed delicately. 'When my John had trouble with his back the staff at the General were absolutely wonderful. It's a shame some people don't appreciate the work they do there.'

'Quite,' said Peggy, not wanting to add fuel to the fire. 'Look, sorry, I can't stop. I've got to get back to work, Doris. Thanks for the quick chat.'

'Of course you do,' she said, with a hint of a sneer. 'I'm sure the entire factory would collapse if you weren't always there.'

'Don't be catty, Doris. It doesn't suit you.' Peggy walked off before Doris could reply.

Jim managed to get through the endless staff meeting without losing track of what was being said, although everyone did seem to like the sound of their own voice, which was tedious. He grabbed his briefcase and was following the others out of the room when his senior supervisor called him back.

'Jim, a word before you leave, if you wouldn't mind.'

'What is it, Colonel?' he asked warily.

The older man relaxed his usual rigid stance and his smile was warm. 'Everything all right at home, Jim? Only I've noticed you've been a bit on edge lately.'

Jim was disconcerted by the man's direct approach, but not altogether surprised. Colonel Harry Field might be over seventy and long retired, but those keen grey eyes missed very little when it came to the welfare of the people working under him.

'Everything at home is fine, sir,' he replied, snapping to attention. 'It's just taking me a while to settle into civilian life again, that's all.'

The older man smiled. 'At ease, Jim, you're no longer on the parade ground.'

'Sorry, sir,' blustered Jim. 'Old habits die hard.'

The Colonel sighed. 'They certainly do, so it's quite natural for you to take time getting used to things. I felt like a fish out of water for quite a while after I was put out to grass. It's never easy – especially when the memsahib is used to having everything done in her own precise way.'

Jim grinned. 'I know what you mean, sir.'

The grey eyes regarded Jim thoughtfully. 'I do understand the pressures you come under working here. We're helping service personnel who are suffering from a multitude of mental and physical problems, and there's always a very real danger that we are overwhelmed by it all if we try and take on too much. Especially if we have our own unresolved issues to deal with,' he added meaningfully.

'I am aware of that,' said Jim, feeling uncomfortable beneath that steady gaze. 'I do try and keep things on an impersonal footing, but sometimes it's a bit too close to home, and I admit to finding that hard.'

'There's no shame in it, Jim. Empathy and genuine understanding of what these men and women went through is at the core of our work. But that also applies to our staff and the volunteers – especially those who've recently seen the worst of the action. I have an open door, Jim, and any time you need to talk in private, I will gladly listen without prejudice or judgement. We need men like you.'

'That's kind of you to say, sir. I'll bear it in mind.'

Harry Field nodded and reached for his briefcase, signalling that the interview was almost over. 'I understand you're scheduled to visit Parkwood today. Let me know how Robert Simmons is getting on, will you? He was rather depressed the last time I saw him, poor chap.' He dug into the briefcase and pulled out a quarter bottle of whisky. 'This should cheer him up, although I know he's not really supposed to have it.'

'I'm sure he'll be most appreciative, sir.' Jim took the bottle and placed it in his own briefcase before leaving the room, his thoughts on Simmons.

He'd been a very junior officer in the Colonel's regiment during the first war and had lost both legs while leading his men in an assault on a gun emplacement during the second. The Colonel had followed his career and after his injuries had made sure he was well looked after at the residential home on the outskirts of Seahaven. This attention and care for one of his own was what made Jim admire the old man.

He placed the briefcase on the passenger seat, slipped off his hat and suit jacket and climbed into the Austin. The coastal journey across the hills to Seahaven was always a pleasure, and even more so when the sun was shining on the water from a clear sky and the hills looked as green and velvety as a billiard table.

He drove away from the headquarters building and out onto the main road which would take him several miles east of Tamarisk Bay and towards the large county town.

Seahaven had been planned as a new town shortly after the first war to accommodate returning soldiers and their families. The housing consisted mainly of brick bungalows set in small, well-tended gardens, sprawling on either side of a main road that ran in a straight line along the clifftops. It had recently become of interest to the town planners, who wanted to expand the whole area to provide much needed accommodation for those left homeless after this war.

A rather tired-looking parade of shops provided for most of the residents' needs, and there was an old-fashioned hotel that had seen better days but overlooked the beach, which was popular with the locals and any day trippers who found it more by accident than intent. A school had been built recently as the population grew, and there was a ramshackle pub that should have been pulled down years ago but still vied in popularity with the community hall as a place to go in the evening.

There were two churches – one on the Parkwood estate that was very old and rather picturesque, and a more modern one that, in Jim's opinion, resembled an ugly barn with fancy glass in the windows and a crooked wooden cross sticking out of its roof like a misshapen road sign.

Seahaven was an enigma, for it was sitting in the middle of nowhere, too big to be a village but not large enough to be a town, and most people passed through it without realising it was even there. Jim had always regarded the place unfavourably: unlike Cliffehaven, it was run-down, and the only access to the rock and pebble beach was from a very steep flight of crumbling concrete steps. There was no station, no port and no pier and the buses only ran twice a week, and now there were more cars about, the long, straight road was turning into a race track.

Jim finally turned off the coastal road to go down the narrow, winding lane that led into the valley nestled between the rolling hills. He passed the many rows of neat bungalows that all looked the same, and then drove deeper into the valley towards the forest before turning into the imposing gateway of the Parkwood estate.

Parkwood had once belonged to a wealthy family who'd had a long and distinguished military history, and when the last of them had died without an heir, he had gifted it in his will to the British Legion as a rest home and sanctuary for returning injured servicemen.

Jim drove slowly down the long, tree-lined driveway, admiring the manicured lawns and the well-tended flower beds, and pausing for a moment to look at the little Norman church behind its lych-gate. There were sheep grazing in a field beyond the formal gardens, and he could see four amputees in wheelchairs enjoying a riotous game of tennis on one of the two hard courts.

Jim admired their energy but feared for their lives in the way they were crashing into one another with such abandon, often ending up on the ground and having to be hauled back into their chairs by one of the beefy orderlies. He paused again to watch the fun and then his attention was drawn – as always – to the house. He loved looking at it, especially on a day like this when the mellow cream stone gleamed and the sun glinted in the many windows.

Parkwood House had been built in the seventeenth century as a gift from a grateful monarch for services rendered. It had been added onto with each succeeding generation and now boasted a round tower, several turrets and a very elegant terrace that swept the whole width of the building behind stone balustrades. Stone pots filled with greenery and the last of the summer's fading flowers were set on the balustrade's corner plinths, and there were more such pots gracing the curved line of the stairs which led up to the entrance.

In the centre of the driveway's turning circle there was a marble statue of a scantily clad young woman pouring water from a ewer into a large marble bowl, and as Jim parked the car and climbed out, he listened to the cool, pleasant sound of water trickling over the bowl and into the broad base of the fountain which held water lilies and other aquatic plants he couldn't begin to name.

He waved back to the small group of residents who were playing croquet on the lawn, and then reached into the car for his jacket, hat and briefcase. He would bring Peggy with him one day, he decided, for she'd love this house and grounds and would, no doubt, enjoy chatting to the residents who had some very tall tales to tell – not all of them totally true, but mostly highly elaborated to make a good story even better.

Resisting the temptation to reach for a restorative sip from the whisky flask he kept hidden in the glove box, he pulled on his jacket and hat, then walked past the flight of steps to the ramp which had been built out of sight and off to one side for those in wheelchairs. Reaching the terrace, he saw several residents sitting at the many tables, drinking tea, reading, or in deep conversation. He spotted Robert Simmons almost immediately, for he was sitting with two other wheelchair-bound men and enjoying an animated but friendly debate about the rights and wrongs of the refereeing at the latest big football match.

That was the good thing about Parkwood. The atmosphere was conducive to friendship, humour, and making the best of things – and despite the terrible injuries they'd all suffered, self-pity or gloominess had no place here.

'Hello, Robert,' said Jim, glad to see him looking cheerful. 'The Colonel sends his regards and asked me to give you this.' He handed over the whisky.

'God bless the old boy,' the man replied, taking the bottle. 'Look here, chums. This'll liven up the gnat's piss that passes for tea round here.'

'Just go steady,' warned Jim. 'That's strong stuff.'

'Aye, but it'll do us all good, Jim,' he replied. 'Who are you seeing today? That new fellow?'

Jim frowned. 'I didn't know there was one,' he replied. 'I'm here to see Barry Craven.'

The other man pulled a face. 'Barry's all right. His missus is taking him home any minute for a couple of weeks.' He winked. 'Nothing like a bit of rest and recuperation to cheer a chap up, if you know what I mean.

Could do with some of that myself, but as my missus fled the nest many moons ago, I suppose the whisky will have to do for now.'

Jim watched rather enviously as Robert tipped out the dregs of their tea and poured generous tots into the cups. They were clearly settling in for a good session. 'Tell me about this new arrival.'

Simmons sipped the whisky and smacked his lips appreciatively. 'None of us know anything about him, other than he seems to prefer his own company. He was brought in yesterday afternoon and we've not seen hide nor hair of him since.'

'Perhaps he's not well enough to be out and about,' said Jim.

Simmons took another drink of whisky. 'In that case he'd be in the infirmary – and he's not. Larry reckons he's got a face like a wet weekend, and is tight-lipped about who he is and why he's here.' He chuckled. 'Our Larry was quite put out about it as he loves nothing better than a good bit of gossip to spread around.'

Jim knew Laurence – or Larry – Dunning, who was one of the more popular orderlies, and as caring as any mother hen. Whoever this new chap was, he clearly had no idea of how to ingratiate himself with the man who would probably be his main carer. He would find it difficult to adapt to life here if he continued to be anti-social. But then the camaraderie and close-knit community of Parkwood wasn't for everyone – especially at first. In fact, Jim had learnt from some of the other residents that it could be quite daunting to turn up to a place where everyone already knew each other, and you felt exposed and outnumbered.

'What room is he in?'

'The garden room in the left wing,' replied Simmons, pouring more whisky.

Jim nodded and left them to their drinks. He knew the garden room well, for he'd been visiting the elderly Sam Frobisher in there since he'd begun working for the Legion. The old boy had been over ninety, but with a sharp wit and a gleam in his eyes as he told his many stories, which made him very entertaining company. Jim had been saddened to hear of his death the week before – but the man had lived a long and fulfilled life, and had confided in Jim that he was tired and ready to meet his maker.

Entering the large hall with its chequerboard tiled floor and gilt-framed paintings on the walls, he looked round in search of anyone who could give him more information about this latest arrival. It was most unusual for the Colonel not to mention a new resident, but then perhaps the man had come in as an emergency and the news hadn't filtered through to head office. It had happened before.

Jim could hear distant sounds of busy people, but there was no sign of anyone who might help him, so he made his way through the deserted drawing room and then through to the lounge bar.

Jim guessed it was styled like a gentlemen's club, for it was decked out with wood panelling, a billiard table, well-stocked bar and plenty of leather couches and club chairs. He nodded to the bored barman who was drying glasses and went through the swing doors into the corridor that led to the rooms in the left wing.

Passing the spacious dining room which overlooked the garden, he saw the maids in their black dresses and white aprons preparing the tables for lunch with crisp linen cloths and the heavy silverware the Legion had inherited along with the house and all its contents.

The whole place ran like a well-oiled machine under the auspices of a retired general and the very efficient housekeeper who had served in the Wrens as a senior officer, and now lived in one of the turret apartments.

Jim knew that there were forty men living in the comfortable apartment rooms that were spread throughout the house, and many more would come in each day to give respite to their families or for medical treatment. They were all looked after by a large, hand-picked staff that cooked, cleaned, saw to repairs on the house, and tended the gardens. There was no frosty matron here, that was for certain, he thought with a smile as he remembered his father's run-in at the General.

The numerous, highly qualified medical staff worked in shifts so that someone was always on call. The local vicar ran the services in the church and provided pastoral care, and the ladies of the Women's Institute came in once a month to teach arts and crafts, or entertain with a sing-song. A small surgery and operating theatre had been built at the back of the mansion for emergencies, and along with a makeshift cinema in the old ballroom, there was a gym and indoor pool in the annexe for physiotherapy sessions – or for supervised fun.

Jim understood that the residents saw this place as a refuge and a home, and were very aware of how lucky they were to have been given the chance to come here, for life beyond these elegant walls was fraught with difficulty for those with the kind of major injuries that he could see here.

His footsteps were muffled by the thick carpet that lined the wide, brightly lit corridor, and as he approached the door to the garden room, he thought he could hear the sound of a radio programme. He knocked and waited.

The radio was switched off, and a gruff voice shouted, 'What do you want? Go away.'

Jim frowned. The voice sounded strangely familiar – but he had to be mistaken. After all, it had been a long time since he'd heard it, and the last information he'd received was that he'd moved up north somewhere. He knocked again. 'Can I come in?'

'Please your bloody self. You will anyway, regardless of what I want,' the man replied sourly.

Jim stepped into the room and had to brace himself against the terrible shock of seeing his old mate, and how wasted and old he'd become since they'd fought together in Burma. He took a breath to regulate his rapid pulse and managed a weak smile as he approached the specially adapted wheelchair with its high headrest and restraining straps.

'Hello, Ernie, mate,' he managed weakly. 'Fancy seeing you here.'

'Jim Reilly,' he gasped. 'What the bloody hell are you doing here?'

Jim gave a brittle laugh, although the situation was far from funny. 'I might ask the same of you,' he replied, carefully circumnavigating the oxygen tank and taking a seat by the wheelchair to gently take his friend's hand. 'It's so good to see you again, Ernie.'

Ernie's weak fingers trembled as he tried to shake Jim's hand. 'I'm not a pretty sight stuck in this damned thing,' he replied, his voice unsteady. 'But it's a proper tonic to see you're still upright and breathing. Anyway, you didn't answer my question. What are you doing here?'

Jim's shock at finding his old pal here, and in such a state, was making it difficult to hold a sensible thought let alone a coherent conversation, but he knew he had to try. 'I work for the British Legion and come once a month to make sure everyone's got what they need.'

Jim did his best to keep his expression bland, but he could have wept as he looked into Ernie's pinched, sallow face etched with lines of pain. Ernie had never been a big man, but he was now so wizened, he was almost lost in that padded chair. Jim noted the withered legs tethered to the footrest, and the hands that were slowly curling inward because his spine had been severed by a hail of bullets – bullets he would have avoided if Jim had kept a closer eye on him.

'I told you I wasn't pretty,' rasped Ernie, 'so there's no need for the once-over. I don't want you feeling sorry for me, Jim – or blaming yourself. At least I'm alive, which is more than can be said for a lot of our mates.'

His breathing became laboured and he reached for the oxygen mask with some difficulty and took a couple of deep breaths which seemed to revive him a little.

Jim didn't offer to help as he knew instinctively it wouldn't be appreciated. Ernie had always been a fiercely proud little man. 'I wrote you lots of letters when I was in Singapore, but you never replied. Didn't you get them?'

'I meant to write back, but what could I say? I don't go anywhere or do anything. I don't see anyone, and as I'm stuck in this bloody thing, I can't do much for myself – not even wipe my own arse,' Ernie said with a snort.

Jim bowed his head in shame. 'I'm so sorry, Ernie. If I hadn't been so damned gung-ho during that Jap raid, you would never have been shot.'

Ernie's hazel eyes flashed with anger. 'Don't talk rubbish, Jim. I'd have got shot anyway. The Japs had us surrounded on that bloody ridge, but you got me out of there – under heavy fire – on your back and into the medics' tent. If you hadn't been there, I'd have died on that godforsaken hill and been left to rot along with the rest of our platoon.'

This long speech seemed to exhaust him, and Jim had painful flashes of memory as he waited for him to take another few breaths of oxygen.

'I hope they gave you a medal for that, mate,' Ernie wheezed, 'cos you damn well deserved one.'

Ernie didn't know it, but Jim had also been badly wounded that day and had earned a mention in dispatches and a promotion for what he'd done, but given half a chance, he would have given all that up to have his mate in one piece. 'Medals are just army flim-flam, Ernie. They don't mean much in the scheme of things.'

'Shame about your good looks being spoiled by that bullet,' said Ernie, eyeing the faint scar on his cheek and the missing earlobe. 'Apart from that you appear to have got through unscathed.'

Jim nodded. 'Yes. I was one of the lucky ones.'

'What about Big Bert? Did he make it through?'

Jim shook his head, saddened by the images of the terrible day when half the platoon had been slaughtered in a surprise attack by the Japs, and Big Bert had become a hero.

'But he was the bravest man I ever saw that day, Ernie. He went down fighting and took at least thirty Japs with him.' He cleared his throat and battled to keep his emotions in check. 'They awarded him a posthumous George Cross for all the bloody good it would do him.'

'Typical of Big Bert,' Ernie said with a wry smile. 'He always went looking for trouble, and I suppose it was inevitable he'd find it eventually.'

'So, Ernie. Why are you here? The last I heard, you'd left hospital and you and the wife moved up north to be nearer to her family.'

Ernie sat in silence for so long, Jim thought he didn't want to answer, but as he tried to think of something else to say, the other man gave a shallow, rattling sigh.

'Yeah, we did go north, but her lot weren't as helpful as we'd hoped. My missus did her best, Jim, but it proved too much in the end. I can't say I blame her, though,' he said sadly. 'I'm a moody sod at the best of times as you well know, and when the pain takes me or I get frustrated at not being able to do things, I'm the devil to live with.'

'I can imagine,' said Jim, remembering the many occasions that Ernie had flown into a raging temper and brought the wrath of his commanding officer down on his head by arguing the toss over some order he didn't agree with. 'But didn't you have a nurse coming in to help?'

'Only for an hour or two each day. But the missus was as trapped as me, stuck in the house and not able to go out unless she got someone in to keep me company, and her family were worse than useless at doing even that.' He grimaced. 'Maureen loved dancing, see, and going to the pictures, but that all had to stop because of me.'

Ernie took in some more oxygen. 'She tried very hard not to let me see how it was grinding her down, but I knew and it broke my heart, mate. So when she went out to the shops one day and didn't come back, it wasn't really a surprise – but it did hurt, I'm not ashamed to say. Cos I never really thought she'd just abandon me.'

'Oh, Ernie,' Jim sighed. 'I'm so very sorry, mate.'

Ernie shifted his shoulders in a weak shrug. 'She's better off without me, and I've landed on my feet here, so to speak.'

Jim decided that the best way forward was to be positive about things. 'You certainly have, Ernie, me old mucker, and you should be making the best of it instead of hiding away in here.'

'I need time to adjust,' said Ernie. 'They look a lively lot from what I've seen from the window, but it's been so long since I had any kind of social life that I'm almost frightened to mix again.' He shot Jim a rueful smile. 'Stupid, isn't it?'

'Not at all. Most men who come here feel exactly as you do at first, but they soon settle in – and so will you, Ernie.' Jim forced a grin and softly patted Ernie's trembling hand. 'You've never been the shy retiring type, so what's this Nervous Nelly lark? Get out there and enjoy all the things you can do here. It'll make you feel so much better, I promise.'

'I will when I'm ready,' he replied with familiar obstinacy. He regarded Jim evenly. 'So, Jim. How's civilian life treating you?'

'Better than I deserve,' he admitted.

'How so?'

Jim regarded the man he'd served with during his time in India and Burma, and realised he needed to be told the truth. 'I know how lucky I am to come home to a loving wife and good job, and although I might not be in the same state as you, you're not the only one who's been difficult to live with, Ernie, old son. There have been times when I really thought I was losing my mind, and my poor Peggy has had to put up with all sorts since I got home – which she really doesn't deserve.'

Ernie's gaze was steady and thoughtful. 'So you've had the nightmares too?' At Jim's nod, he grimaced. 'It's like you're back there again, isn't it? With all the noise and the smells of blood, cordite and rotting vegetation – and the sight of your mates being ripped to shreds.'

A shudder ran through Jim. 'That's it exactly,' he confessed. 'How do you cope, Ernie?'

'I don't really,' he admitted. 'I tried drinking, but it mucked up my medication and made me very ill. Fornication didn't work either as it's no longer physically possible, and I don't have the means or the ability to just end it all. And believe me, Jim, I did give it serious thought.'

Jim nodded, for he knew a lot of men who'd taken that way out. But it was not something he'd considered even for a second. He loved his family too much. 'So how do we deal with this thing gnawing away at us, Ernie? How do we stop the dreams and the memories – the dark days when all we want to do is hide away?'

'Perhaps us meeting again is a sign,' said Ernie thoughtfully. 'And as we both went through it, we might be able to find a way out together.' He held Jim's gaze with hope in his eyes.

Jim realised then that Ernie's physical problems were only a part of what ailed him, for his mind also bore the same deep scars as his own. They'd gone through almost the entire Asian campaign side by side, and now shared the aftermath of bad dreams and haunting memories.

He felt hope stirring in his heart that maybe Ernie was right. 'Like you, I've tried everything else, Ernie. If you're game to give this a go, then so am I.'

Ernie's pale, pinched face became wreathed in smiles. 'Damn right I am, Jim. We beat the Japs, so we'll beat this.'

13

Ruby had finally managed to stop crying and pull her emotions into some order. She'd left the doctor's surgery and hurried into the High Street to buy Ethel a couple of nightdresses, a dressing gown, hairbrush, slippers and washbag. Once the bank opened, she paid in the takings, and then dashed home to the Anchor.

It was still quite early, so she telephoned Brenda to remind her that she'd need Frank to help with the brewery delivery on the Thursday, and to ask her to come in the evenings rather than lunchtimes. This arrangement would suit her better as she could then visit Ethel in the afternoons and Brenda could open up while she was at the hospital in the early part of the evening.

Brenda hadn't sounded particularly enthused about the idea, but Ruby had promised her she could leave early each night once she'd come back from the hospital – and that hopefully, Ethel's stay in the General would be a short one. Ruby was aware of how exhausting all the rushing about would be, but the pub had to stay open and Ethel couldn't be abandoned.

With an hour to go before she opened at lunchtime, Ruby stripped Ethel's bed and propped the still-sodden mattress in front of the three-bar electric fire in the hope it would dry out before Ethel was allowed home. Not wanting to even think about the added cost to her electricity bill, she swept the floor and tidied the room, leaving the window open to clear the air of the unpleasant smells, and then loaded the washing machine again.

Once she was satisfied that there was little more to do, she dug out an overnight bag and packed the things she'd bought earlier, adding toothpaste and brush, shampoo, soap and flannel to the washbag – and then hunted out a few bits and pieces of make-up. Ethel had always liked to look her best, and perhaps they'd give her a bit of a boost.

She took the holdall into the sitting room and added a fresh roll of tobacco with a box of matches. As Ethel would be allowed to drink, she decided she'd take in a couple of bottles of milk stout when she went in tonight.

Feeling quite wrung out, she stripped off her clothes and ran a hot bath, but as she lay there she could only think of Ethel and what might be happening to her. Dr Darwin hadn't explained what the tests entailed and had been very cagey about what was actually wrong with her, which only made Ruby worry more. Perhaps Danuta would call in or ring to tell her what was going on? There again, she was a very busy district nurse, and the doctor had promised to pass on the test results as soon as he got them, so she'd just have to be patient.

Yet there was little doubt in Ruby's mind that her mother was seriously ill, and the guilt she was feeling about the way she'd treated her made her stomach tighten and her skin crawl. She'd seen the state she was in and had assumed it was the result of her drinking – had heard and not listened to the clues Ethel had tried to give her – but the fact of her mother's presence should have told her right from the start that she was in trouble, and she should have done something about it immediately. Not berated her over her drinking, or dragged up past sins and slights.

Ruby found it difficult to admit she didn't like her mother as a person, but, contrary to any logic, she did love her, and this was what would sustain her for whatever the future held.

Her troubled thoughts made it impossible to relax, so she climbed out of the bath and got ready for the lunchtime session which, being a Monday, would thankfully be fairly quiet. Half an hour later, she went down the stairs and locked the door to her rooms, then took the towels off the pumps, checked she had enough float in the till and gave the bar a quick dust.

The place could have done with a good sweep, and the diamond-paned windows weren't as clean as usual, but she was simply too downhearted to bother with the household chores, so went to unbolt the front door instead.

The first few regulars came in after a few minutes to take their usual places in the settles by the unlit fire to play dominoes and make their pints last as long as possible. Six of Solly's factory girls, all peroxide hair and heavy make-up, came in to order half-pints and then went into a giggling huddle at the end of the bar to discuss the merits of the rather handsome young arrival in the loading bay.

Ruby smiled inwardly as she poured their drinks. She didn't fancy the poor chap's chances of escaping that lot of man-eaters, but no doubt he would enjoy the chase.

She served a port and lemon and half a pint to the sweet elderly couple who came in every Monday like clockwork and had a bit of a natter with them before they went to their usual corner like Derby and Joan to play cards and keep an eagle eye on the comings and goings.

Ruby wondered what they did for the rest of the week, but as no one seemed to know who they were or where they lived, and they didn't give much away when she talked to them, she accepted their need for privacy. Not everyone wanted to discuss their business in a pub, or bend the barmaid's ear with tales of woe, and Mondays made a nice change because these particular regulars just wanted to drink in peace.

It was almost closing time when the familiar sound of high heels on the pavement and a determined stride alerted Ruby to the approach of someone she'd been hoping to avoid, and she steeled herself for the onslaught.

Gloria swept in, bosom to the fore, bracelets jangling, colourful scarves flying and earrings swinging. 'Ruby,' she yelled unnecessarily from the doorway before negotiating the two steps in her ridiculously high heels. 'Where is she?'

Before Ruby could reply, she'd sat herself down on a high stool and dumped her large handbag on the bar. 'Look, gel,' she said around the cigarette she was lighting. 'I know she's yer mum and all, but you can't be 'aving 'er 'ere. There's already talk, and it won't be long before it reaches the wrong ears.'

'Yeah, I know, but . . .'

'Knowing's one thing,' Gloria interrupted, undeterred. 'Doing something about it is quite another.' She leaned forward so her generous bosom pushed against the bar. 'So, what are yer doing, gel?'

'Nothing at the moment,' replied Ruby. 'You see . . .'

'Flaming Nora,' said Gloria in such exasperation her breasts almost escaped the skimpy blouse which had all of Ruby's male customers agog. Ignorant of the attention she was garnering, Gloria carried on.

'I thought you had yer wits about yer, Ruby. She can't stay 'ere, mate. Not if you want to keep this place.'

'I know,' said Ruby very firmly. 'And if you'd just let me get a word in, I'll tell you why I ain't done nothing.'

'Well?' Gloria folded her arms, her heavily made-up eyes gimlets in a sea of mascara and blue eyeshadow.

'She's in hospital,' said Ruby flatly. 'And I ain't discussing it here, Gloria,' she said through gritted teeth.

Gloria enjoyed a good shouting match, and seemed rather deflated by the news she wouldn't be having a run-in with Ethel this lunchtime. 'You'd better give us a gin then, while I wait 'til you close up,' she said, settling more firmly on the stool.

Ruby waved away her money. 'First one's on me,' she said.

'I pays me way, Rubes. You can't afford to be giving gin away at the prices you must be paying,' she retorted, shoving the money back across the counter. 'Which reminds me,' she began. 'There's this fella I know . . .'

'Hello, you two,' said Rosie, who'd slipped into the pub without either of them noticing. 'I thought I recognised your dulcet tones, Gloria, and I'm guessing this is about you know who. I'll have one of those as well,' she said, pointing at Gloria's glass of gin and tonic before gracefully perching on a stool.

'Not like you to be drinking at lunchtime,' said Gloria, her sharp gaze roving over her old rival and sparring partner. 'Yer looking a bit rough, if you don't mind me saying, Rosie. What's up, gel?'

'Ron's in hospital,' she replied, paying for her drink and taking a restorative sip.

'Blimey,' breathed Gloria. 'Sounds like half of blooming Cliffehaven's in the hospital.' She tipped her head towards Ruby who'd gone to serve the factory girls. 'Her mum's in there too,' she said with a roll of her eyes.

'I didn't realise,' Rosie murmured.

'So what's the matter with Ron? Caught fleas from one of his blasted ferrets?' She roared with laughter at her own joke and then saw how upset it had made Rosie and clammed up. 'Sorry, mate, but you gotta 'ave a laugh, ain't yer?'

'Not always,' said Rosie. 'Ron had an allergic reaction to penicillin and could have died if I hadn't got him into hospital in time.'

She turned to Ruby who'd finished serving drinks. 'I'm sorry to hear about your mum,' she said quietly, all too aware that the factory girls were listening to every word and would more than likely carry any bits of juicy gossip back to work with them.

Ruby just nodded. 'I'll tell you about it later.' She leaned closer to Rosie and lowered her voice. 'If you're going in to see Ron this afternoon, is there a chance you could find out where the Clarice Burnette Ward is? That place is a maze and I don't want to be wandering about getting lost.'

'Oh, but that's . . .'

Ruby eyed her sharply. 'That's what, Gloria?'

'Oh, nothing, mate,' she blustered. 'I 'ad a friend on that ward once, that's all,' she added before downing her drink.

Ruby eyed her suspiciously but Gloria seemed intent upon lighting another cigarette and wouldn't look at her.

'I'd be glad to look it up for you, but why aren't you going in this afternoon?' asked Rosie.

'We'll talk after I've closed,' said Ruby.

Gloria had had three gins by the time Ruby bolted the front door, and was getting loud and combatant again, so it was a good thing Ethel wasn't around. Rosie had stuck to just one as she wanted to keep a clear head for visiting time.

Once Ruby had collected the empty glasses, she poured herself a drink to be sociable and sat down with the other two women at the table vacated by the elderly couple. She told them about Ethel's arrival and the chaos she'd wrought in just two days, and then went on to talk about Danuta's intervention, what the doctor had said, and her worry over the tests she'd be having.

'I'm ever so sorry, Rubes,' said Gloria. 'Will you manage this place all right if she's sent home? Only I can spare my part-time barman for a couple of weeks if you need 'im – or even come in for a couple of shifts meself if things get too difficult.'

'Thanks, Gloria, I may take you up on that, but me and Brenda have worked out a plan. Let's see 'ow we get on, eh?'

'I could always lend a hand at lunchtime,' said Rosie. 'But only if Ron's still in there. I want to be at home when he's let out to make sure he doesn't get into any more trouble.'

'If she does come 'ome and it's as serious as what you think,' said Gloria, 'then how are you gunna manage? It'll be a full-time job looking after 'er, without running this place and all, Rubes.'

'I'll cross that bridge when I get to it, Gloria. But I do feel a lot better knowing I've got you both in my corner.'

'Peggy will be too, I'm sure of it,' said Rosie. 'I'll ring her tonight, if you don't mind, and let her know what's happening.' She looked at her watch. 'Sorry, Ruby, but it's almost visiting time. I'll pop in later to let you know where the ward is.' She gave Ruby a hug and gathered up her jacket and bag.

'I gotta go an' all,' said Gloria. 'I left young Chris on his own, and with that creep Phil Warner bending 'is ear at the bar, I need to check he ain't giving 'im free drinks.' She swung her handbag over her shoulder, gave Ruby a hearty hug and, with bracelets jangling, tottered across the uneven brick floor.

Ruby unbolted the door and then closed it behind them as they stepped out onto the pavement. But she'd forgotten she'd left the front window open to get rid of the cigarette smoke and therefore heard part of what Gloria was saying to Rosie as they stood outside.

'I swear I could 'ave bit me tongue off, Rosie,' she said before lowering her loud and very carrying voice to just above a murmur. 'Only that Clarice Burnette . . . is for . . . patients. My mate . . . Do you think Ruby . . .?'

Ruby heard Rosie shush to warn her she might be overheard, and then the sound of them walking away. But Ruby had heard enough to work out what Gloria had been saying. She leaned against the door and closed her eyes, the dread and guilt returning tenfold.

Jim had stayed with Ernie for almost two hours, which meant that the rest of his day's schedule was well out of kilter. But the long reminiscing and re-telling of events – funny, tragic, or the just plain ridiculous episodes of their time in Asia – had done them both a power of good. They'd laughed and shed a few tears, and when it was clear that Ernie had had enough, Jim had left his pal to the tender care of Larry with a promise that he would return the following day.

He took a hefty swig from the whisky flask before he drove away from Parkwood, his emotions torn between feeling pity for the man who'd fought so bravely and been brought so low, and enormous relief that they'd found one another again and could share their very personal experiences. The difficult conversation he'd had with his father had helped to a degree, but he'd held back on a great many things, whereas with Ernie there had been no holding back, no memory dismissed, or emotion glossed over. Hence the need for a drink to steady himself.

Ernie hadn't always been a good listener; rather, a man who acted with no thought for the consequences and little regard for what others might think of him. He'd been quick to lose his temper and find fault, and inclined to moan at the slightest thing, which hadn't made him particularly popular – especially with the Gurkhas, who kept their thoughts to themselves – but Jim had liked him, respected his bravery in a skirmish, and had taken him under his wing, realising a lot of it was mostly the bluster of a man way out of his depth.

Because of what had happened to him, Ernie had been forced to see the world in a different light, and instead of being bitter and angry at the injustice of his plight, he'd used that ingrained bloody-mindedness to fight against it. He'd also become more thoughtful and perceptive – more aware of the needs of others – which had surprised Jim, and made him like him even more.

Robert Simmons had been right about Barry Craven going home, so at least Jim hadn't needed to fit him in. He drove back towards Cliffehaven, stopping on the way to visit the other men on his list. They had differing problems: the first one with mobility after losing a leg, but he was learning how to use his crutches and would soon go back into Parkwood to be fitted with a prosthetic.

The second man, Sam Healey, had financial problems as he'd been blinded in one eye by a shell-blast that had ruined his face and had come home to find that he'd lost his deputy managerial post at the snooty bank in the county town because the posh customers didn't like looking at him. He was a father to two children, and his wife was just about coping on his small pension by teaching the piano and music appreciation in the local private girls' school.

Jim had tried to negotiate with the manager who'd sacked him, but had found the man to be so utterly unsympathetic and repellent in his attitude, he'd had a job to keep his fists from punching his smarmy face – but at least he'd cowed him enough to get a good reference for Sam out of him.

The third man had been in the navy, and when his ship had been torpedoed, he'd ingested oil and salt water which had left him with such damaged lungs, the slightest effort left him breathless and unable to do much. He'd just been released from hospital to an exhausted wife who was trying to keep her family fed by holding down two cleaning jobs and a night shift at Solly's factory.

By the time he'd seen them all, Jim was wrung out, but at least he'd had an idea which might help one of them. He drove over the hump-backed bridge into Cliffehaven's High Street and turned at the bottom into Camden Road, pulling up outside Solly's large factory which now sprawled between the fire station and the Lilac Tearooms and extended back as far as the gardens of the large houses that overlooked the promenade.

Chewing on a peppermint, he climbed out of the car and hurried across the front yard which encompassed the crèche where Daisy and Rose had once come and his other granddaughter Emily still attended. He ran up the flight of wooden stairs which led to the office and tapped on the door, then stepped inside.

'Is Solly in?' he asked the young woman who was bashing the typewriter keys with such venom, he kept his distance.

'Do you have an appointment?' she asked, head down and still furiously typing.

'No. But if he's in, he'll see me,' said Jim. 'Tell him it's Jim Reilly.'

She finally looked up, her gaze frosty. 'And what is your business, Mr Reilly?'

'That's between me and Solly, Miss . . .?'

'Mrs York,' she replied with emphasis on her marital status. She pushed back from her desk. 'I'll see if he wishes to be disturbed.'

Jim waited, wondering what had happened to the very pleasant Madge who used to work here.

Within seconds of her leaving the room, Solly Goldman appeared in the doorway; larger than life in a beautifully tailored suit that concealed his bulk, and with the inevitable cigar held between meaty fingers.

'My boy,' he said, swamping Jim in a bear hug. 'It's good to see you. Come in, come in. You've just missed Rachel, but I'm delighted we can catch up without her chattering on like a sparrow.'

'It's good to see you too.' Jim could have sworn he'd felt his ribs creak under the pressure of the older man's welcome, but he'd always got on well with Solly and admired him for the work he'd done during the war to bring Jewish children out of Europe before they fell prey to the Nazis.

Solly threw himself into his leather chair, making the springs complain alarmingly. 'How are you enjoying life outside the army, Jim?' he asked, offering him a cigar from the box on his desk.

'It's been interesting,' he replied, cutting the cigar and taking his time to light it and enjoy the rich taste. 'I suppose you know I'm working for the British Legion?' At Solly's nod, he continued. 'Well, it's the reason I've come to see you today.'

'I did wonder why you're here. Not that I don't appreciate a visit from an old friend,' Solly added hastily. He leaned back in his chair and narrowed his brown eyes against the smoke from his fragrant cigar, the diamond ring on his little finger winking in the light from the window.

'Rachel and I are familiar with the work done by the Legion, Jim. In fact, Rachel is holding a fundraising dinner and dance for them in November. What is it you want from me?'

'There's a man under my care who is out of work because his former boss didn't want his customers put off by the scars on his face and the patch he wears over his blind eye.'

'Go on,' murmured Solly.

'Sam Healey was injured while leading his men during the last push into Germany, and although he might not be as handsome as he was, he still has a very sharp mind and is desperate for a job.'

'And what does this Sam Healey do that I should want him to work for me?'

'He was the deputy manager of a bank and is an absolute wizard at accounting.' Jim puffed on the cigar. 'And as I happen to know you need someone to keep your books now the other chap's about to retire, I thought you might consider taking him on. You'd be saving a brave man's dignity and helping a little family who deserve a fresh start.'

Solly regarded him thoughtfully as he puffed on the cigar and filled the room with smoke. 'Running a bank is very different to keeping my books,' he murmured. 'And I would need references, Jim. In this business it's not wise to trust anyone.'

'His commanding officer gave him a superb reference, and I managed to rather forcefully persuade his former boss to write a decent one too.'

Solly grinned. 'Did you now? I'd have liked to see that. I hate bullies.'

'So, will you at least give him a trial? Say for a couple of weeks? Paid, of course.'

Solly's laugh was deep and rich. '*Oy vey*, Jim, you bargain like my Rachel, so how can I refuse? I'm out of the office tomorrow, so tell him to come at nine on Wednesday. I'll let him have a set of books to look over, and we'll go from there.'

'Thanks, Solly. You're a diamond, and I can assure you, you won't be disappointed.'

'I'm married to a woman who thinks shopping is a career and my wallet her private bank,' he said with his hands and shoulders rising. 'I'm always disappointed when my wallet is attacked.'

He sat forward. 'But I'm an honest man, Jim. I pay a decent wage for a decent day's work, and your Sam Healey will be no different.' He grinned and sat back again to reach for the decanter on top of the nearest filing cabinet. 'How about a glass of brandy for old times' sake?'

'I'm sorry, but I'd better not,' Jim replied, remembering the whisky he'd already drunk today, and the promise to Peggy which he'd now broken. He shot the older man a rueful smile. 'I've been hitting the bottle a bit too much since coming home, and it's not doing me or my family any good.'

'We all have our crosses to bear,' Solly replied on a sigh. 'My Rachel doesn't like me drinking either. Says it's not good for my blood pressure – but what does she know?' He shook his head and poured a generous slug of brandy into the snifter. '*L'chaim*,' he said, raising the glass.

'To life,' replied Jim, raising his cigar. He waited for the other man to fully enjoy his brandy before broaching another plea for help. 'You have a Mrs Rayner working a night shift on Tuesdays,' he began.

Solly pursed his lips, thought about it and then nodded. 'I do indeed. Pleasant little woman and excellent machinist, but always looks tired.' His eyes were bright with humour as he looked at Jim. 'Another of your lost souls?'

'In a way. Her husband's lungs were badly damaged after his ship went down and he'll never work again. Alice Rayner is trying to keep body and soul together working three jobs and looking after their two children.' He held Solly's gaze. 'I was wondering if you could offer her a full-time day-shift post and allow her to put her two kids into your crèche.'

'You ask a lot of me, Jim,' Solly murmured. 'I have all the staff I need on the day shift, and of course she'd be earning a better wage on nights. As to the crèche, there might be a few places going, I'd have to check with Rachel. She's in charge of all that.'

'Would you at least think about it, Solly? The poor woman is at her wits' end.'

'I will, Jim. But I make no promises.'

'Thanks, Solly, and I'm sorry to come here asking for favours, but times are very hard for so many, and it's a constant battle to try and ease things for these desperate families.'

Solly nodded and gave a deep sigh. 'The war might be over, but the fight for survival goes on. I will see what I can do for Alice Rayner, Jim, and look forward to meeting Sam Healey on Wednesday.'

Realising Solly meant what he said and was now eager to get back to work, Jim got to his feet. 'Thanks again, Solly. Now I'd better go before Peggy complains about me being late for tea.'

Solly chuckled as they warmly shook hands. 'Like it or not, we're ruled by our women, Jim. And although we complain about it, I suspect neither of us would have it any other way. I'll be in touch before the end of the week.'

14

Ron had woken that morning feeling as fit as a fiddle now his headache had gone and the awful itching had abated to a sporadic and minor irritation. He'd tried to persuade the very nice night sister that he was fully ready to be discharged, and although she agreed that he did indeed look remarkably robust, she wouldn't permit it until the doctor had given him the all-clear – and he wouldn't be on duty again until the following day. That was the moment he'd decided it was time to put an escape plan into action.

Fortunately for him, the night sister had been a very different kettle of fish to the one during the day, and he'd managed to charm her into letting him go to the bathroom on his own instead of having another detested bed bath and being forced to pee in a bottle. She'd also allowed him to go to the day room to smoke his pipe – and mercifully, had forgotten to ask for it back on his return.

Feeling armed and ready, he'd come back to the ward with a sense of achievement, for he'd used the short time away from the ward to prepare for something far bolder, and although it would cause untold ructions, he was feeling more than brave enough to withstand any flak that might come his way. Now it was a case of waiting until he could carry out his plan.

As the tea trolley was followed by the breakfast trolley and then the medicine trolley, he sat in the chair by his bed, acting the perfect patient, but poised like a coiled spring for the right moment. He watched the nurses and Sister Morgan in particular, for she was the danger that had to be avoided if his plan was to work. There was no sign of Matron, for that would have spiked everything – but the woman had a nasty trick of turning up at the very wrong moment, so he'd have to be careful.

He knew it was almost time to make his move when the lunch trays had been cleared away, and the midday medicines doled out, for Sister Morgan had left the ward with the other nurses to go for their meal break, leaving only a solitary probationer in charge. He felt a pang of guilt that the poor girl would get into trouble, but he really couldn't take any more of this torture, and needed to get home before Rosie came at visiting time.

Fortune seemed to smile on him, for one of the other men rang for a bedpan, and while the probationer was occupied behind the screens, Ron tightened the belt on his dressing gown, patted his pocket to ensure his pipe and tobacco pouch were secure, and briskly made his way down the ward and through the swing doors.

Quickly checking that there was no one in the sluice room, he hurried to the bathroom and locked the lavatory cubicle door behind him. His pulse was racing, but so far so good. He climbed onto the lavatory seat to retrieve the bundle of clothes he'd stashed on the high windowsill earlier, thankful that no one had spotted it – but then he'd learnt that very few people ever looked up, especially when they were occupied with more urgent concerns.

He dragged his trousers and shirt on over his pyjamas, shoved his slippers into his jacket pocket and rammed his feet into his shoes. With his precious pipe and tobacco safely secured in an inside pocket, he rolled his dressing gown under his arm, unlocked the door and stepped into the bathroom area.

'I expect my nurses to be prepared for the consultants' rounds, not sitting about gossiping over sandwiches.'

Matron's voice was unmistakable and Ron held his breath as he eased himself behind the open bathroom door and heard her stride down the corridor followed by a fluttering retinue of student nurses.

'You will find that the men's medical ward is one of the more difficult to maintain discipline,' Matron continued. 'The patients there seem to think they can lounge about and take advantage of one's good nature. But you will begin your ward training on Women's Surgical – a far gentler introduction to ward management, as you will discover.'

Their footsteps receded and Ron breathed again. He tiptoed round the door to take a quick peek down the corridor. The last of the student nurses was just disappearing into the women's ward at the far end, but as he had no idea how long Matron would stay with them there, he had to be quick. With his dressing gown tightly wedged under his arm, he hurried in the opposite direction, not really sure of where he was going, but needing to put a lot of distance between him and the matron.

Cliffehaven General was a maze of corridors and it would have been easy to get lost, but he'd been here before – had made a getaway before – and when he recognised a particular staircase, he quickly dived down it, knowing it would lead to the reception hall.

Fearing that at any moment he'd hear Matron's strident voice calling after him, he hurried across the vast space and weaved his way amongst the hurrying porters and nurses until he reached the short flight of steps down to the parking bays. He didn't dare look behind him, but as there was no hue and cry, he assumed he'd got away with it.

'Hello, Ron. You're in a hurry.'

He came to an abrupt halt and looked over his shoulder to see his pal, Harry Fuller, the porter, grinning at him. 'I've been discharged,' he fibbed, backing towards the gateway. 'And I want to get home to Rosie's cooking.'

'Can't say I blame you, mate,' the man replied. 'What they serve up here isn't fit to be called proper food.'

Ron reached the gateway. 'See you at the Anchor for a drink sometime,' he called and darted away down Camden Road, to home and freedom.

He reached Havelock Road and opened the gate, puzzled to hear the dogs barking from indoors. It wasn't like Rosie to keep them in when she was at home, and there was still an hour before visiting time, so where could she have gone?

That was when he realised he didn't have his bunch of keys. He rummaged about under the flower pots by the door looking for the spare, but it was nowhere to be seen, and he had a nasty suspicion that Rosie had carried out her threat and removed it as an added security precaution. With a sharp sigh of annoyance, he tramped round to the back of the house, thanking his lucky stars that the side gate hadn't been locked as well.

Harvey and Monty were barking fit to bust in the kitchen, but the French doors and all the windows were locked, apart from a small, high window in the downstairs cloakroom. He eyed it speculatively and realised that not even a miracle would get him through that narrow opening, so trudged moodily back to the kitchen window to try and placate the dogs.

Harvey had his front paws on the kitchen sink and was barking to be let out, and Monty was dashing back and forth as if it was a game.

Ron could see his keyring hanging from a hook, but it was of absolutely no use to him, which was very frustrating. 'Harvey, shut up, there's a good wee fellow,' he ordered sternly. 'To be sure you'll be having the neighbours complaining again, and I've enough on me plate without that.'

Harvey tilted his head, his intelligent amber eyes fixed on Ron as his ears twitched. He gave a single bark and got down from the sink, knocking crockery from the draining board as he did so which only made Monty bark sharply and carry on dashing about like a headless chicken.

'For all the saints, will you shut up, Monty?' Ron said in exasperation. 'Sit down, the pair of you, and behave. I'm going to my shed.'

This seemed to work and Ron was grateful for the silence as he moodily went to his shed in the hope he might find a forgotten packet of biscuits to stave off the hunger pangs. But of course he'd always made sure the shed was locked too, and as the key was on the ring with the others, he wasn't going to ruin a perfectly good and very new padlock to break in.

He sank onto one of the garden chairs and lit his pipe, thankful for small mercies – and then noted the dark clouds on the horizon which were drawing ever nearer, and the chill wind that was coming off the sea. Pulling up his jacket collar, he had the fleeting thought he'd have been better off in the warm dry of the hospital ward, and then promptly dismissed it. A bit of rain wouldn't hurt, Rosie would soon be back, and there was no place better than home – however difficult it was to actually get inside.

Rosie had bought an iced bun for Ron as a treat, and as she'd emerged from the Lilac Tearooms it was to discover it had started to rain quite heavily. Glad she'd thought to bring an umbrella, she'd run across the street and up the steps to the hospital reception area.

She'd still been troubled by what Gloria had revealed concerning the ward Ethel was being sent to, and although Gloria had given her a rough idea of where it was, she'd taken a few minutes to ask at reception to get her bearings so it was clear in her mind when she told Ruby.

Satisfied the girl could easily find her mother's ward, she hurried up the long flight of marble stairs and along the seemingly endless corridor to Spencer Ward. She was a bit out of breath as she pushed through the door, and wasn't at all prepared to find the hatchet-faced matron waiting for her with grim determination. Her spirits sank.

'What's he done now?' she asked wearily.

'Your husband has absconded,' she said in a furious hiss. 'And I will *not* have it. Do you understand?'

'Oh, I understand perfectly,' said Rosie. 'So what do you expect me to do about it?'

'Bring him back immediately.'

'And what if he refuses to come back?' Rosie matched her glare for glare, fully aware they had the breathless attention of every person in the room.

'Then I shall report him to the Board and he will be barred from darkening these doors ever again,' Matron retorted.

'You seem to hold a very high opinion of your status here, but I don't think even *you* can ban a sick man from this hospital,' Rosie replied calmly. 'And I find it not at all surprising that my husband felt unable to stay if he had to put up with your hectoring. This is not a prison – though you'd make a fine prison warden.'

'How *dare* you speak to me like that,' Matron hissed.

'Don't dish it out if you can't take the heat,' Rosie replied coolly. 'I shall be making my own complaint about the state of things here. The Governor of the Board happens to be a close friend, and I'm sure that once I've had a word, he'll realise there need to be changes made.' With that, she turned on her heel and left the ward.

Fury made her walk faster than usual, and she almost slipped on the stairs and only just saved herself by grabbing the handrail. It would be ironic if she broke or sprained something right now and had to have treatment, she thought with grim humour, because she'd probably find herself banned as well. That ridiculous bloody woman. Who in their right minds would put such a harridan in charge of this place? Hadn't Percy Bishop and the Board learnt from the mistakes of the last one? But that didn't excuse Ron – not at all – and he had a great deal of explaining to do.

She snapped her umbrella open and stalked down Camden Road, ready to do battle as the rain teemed down so hard it bounced off the pavement and dampened her good stockings. Her temper was at its peak when she reached the house and let herself in to the sound of the furiously barking dogs.

'Ron? Where are you? We need to have a word,' she shouted, kicking off her shoes and jamming the sodden umbrella in its stand.

There was no reply and she frowned as she pulled off her coat. If he hadn't come home from the hospital, then where would he have gone? There would only be Cordelia at home at Beach View, the pubs were shut, and he clearly hadn't taken the dogs out as they were trying to batter down the kitchen door.

She padded down the hallway in her slippers to open the door, but instead of flying out as she expected, they gathered at the side entrance and demanded to be let out. Puzzled, she unlocked the door, and they shot off round to the back garden. She wasn't about to follow them as the rain was coming down even harder, and she could only assume they were in pursuit of next door's cat which they both hated.

Rosie filled the kettle and switched it on, then padded into the sitting room to fetch a fresh pack of cigarettes. She stopped and stared at the bedraggled figure huddled on the patio with his dressing gown over his head and his dogs climbing all over him.

Ron's woebegone face turned towards her, his eyes pleading for clemency.

Rosie burst out laughing as she went to the French windows. 'It serves you right, you old escape artist,' she shouted through the glass. 'Do you realise the trouble you've caused?'

He looked suitably repentant but Rosie wasn't convinced, for despite being soaked to the skin, there was a gleam of mischief in his eyes. However, she was not yet ready to fully forgive him.

'You're not traipsing the wet through here,' she told him sternly. 'Come through the kitchen and dry off there – you and the dogs.'

She lit a cigarette and sat down to wait, unable to stay cross with him for very long, but still fizzing with righteous fury after her run-in with Matron.

Ron eventually appeared carrying a loaded tea tray which he set down on the low table in front of the couch. He'd stripped down to his slightly damp pyjamas and slippers, and both dogs had clearly had a good rub-down.

'To be sure, Rosie, I could stand it no longer in there. I'm sorry, darlin', but it was a misery.' He eyed her warily before carefully perching on the other end of the couch.

'It wasn't exactly a pleasure to be told off like a naughty child by that awful woman,' she replied, barely mollified. 'Why on earth do you do it, Ron?

Most normal people wait until they're discharged – not play bloody commando and go AWOL!'

He reached for her hand. 'Ach, Rosie, I'm sorry, but I missed you and just wanted to come home.'

She bit back a fit of giggles. 'Well, your timing was way off, and you clearly forgot you'd left your keys here.'

'I thought you'd be in,' he said woefully. 'And how was I to know you'd taken away the key by the front door, and the heavens were going to open?'

'That's the downfall of making plans without doing your research first,' she spluttered, no longer able to stop the laughter. 'Oh, Ron, you are the most impossible man.'

He grinned and pulled her to him. 'Aye, that I am, but you wouldn't want me any other way,' he murmured before kissing her into silence.

The clothing factory Peggy managed was only in production between nine and five. But Peggy had left on the dot of three so she'd be at the school gates to collect Daisy. She had negotiated the shorter hours with Solly when she'd taken up the post, knowing that when Daisy started school, her schedule would be in tatters. To make up the time, she would dispense with her tea breaks, start half an hour early each morning, and only take twenty minutes for her lunch – which she would probably eat at her desk. Doris's husband, John White, the factory estate administrator, had agreed to lock up each evening for her, so the arrangement worked to Solly's full satisfaction.

She ran through the pouring rain, wishing she had the car, but thankful she'd listened to the forecast and brought her brolly and her warm jacket.

There was a sea of black umbrellas outside the school gates, and Peggy finally saw Anne huddled amongst them as she waited with little Emily.

She kissed the child and received a scowl. 'Oh dear, Emily. You do look grumpy. Whatever's the matter?'

'I hate baby school,' she protested. 'I wanna go to big school with Rose and Daisy.'

'You will next year,' soothed Peggy, adjusting the ribbon in her dark curls and giving her a hug. 'But it won't be half as much fun as you have at nursery with all your friends.'

Emily didn't look at all impressed and turned away to peer longingly through the wire fence at the empty playground.

Peggy regarded Anne with some concern. 'You still look tired, love. Didn't you get your nap this afternoon?'

'I managed about half an hour and then got bored and restless.' Anne laughed. 'I'm not used to sitting around doing nothing, so I scrubbed the kitchen from top to bottom and did a great pile of ironing.'

'You're nesting,' murmured Peggy, remembering how she'd cleaned Beach View rigorously shortly before she'd given birth to all of her five children. 'It won't be long now, I bet.'

'I hope not,' sighed Anne. 'There's too much to do, and with Martin away so much at the moment, I really don't think I could cope with a new baby and Emily in a continuous strop.'

Their conversation was interrupted by the sound of children pouring out into the playground. Daisy and Rose raced towards them, and both women were almost knocked from their feet as the children flung themselves at them and began to talk over one another, nineteen to the dozen.

'Look what I drawed, Mum,' shouted Daisy, waving a piece of paper at Peggy that was filled with blotches of colour that resembled nothing Peggy could recognise.

'How lovely,' she said enthusiastically. 'What is it?'

'It's an ephalunt,' said Daisy crossly. 'Look. That's his trunk.'

Peggy forced herself to keep a straight face. 'Of course it is. How silly of me not to see.'

Rose was doing the same thing to Anne, chattering on about Miss Bell and how she'd known all her numbers up to ten. Standing glowering behind her was Emily, with her arms crossed as she scuffed her shoes against the kerb.

'It's time we got this lot out of the rain and home,' said Anne, reading the signs of a looming tantrum. 'Come on, all of you. Get in the car quickly so we can drop Grandma and Daisy off in time for their tea.'

'Are we going to have tea too?' asked Rose, clambering into the car.

'Of course; but not with Grandma today. I've bought special cake, and you wouldn't want to miss that, would you?'

Peggy climbed into the passenger seat, leaving the girls to sit in the back for the very short ride home. 'Thanks for mentioning cake,' she murmured drily beneath their bright chatter. 'I didn't have to time to buy any, and Daisy's bound to throw a fit about it.'

'Look in the glove box,' said Anne as they reached the end of the twitten.

Peggy found a cardboard box containing five iced buns. 'Oh, darling, how thoughtful. You must let me give you the money.'

'I won't hear of it, Mum. Just enjoy them, and I'll see you tomorrow.'

Peggy kissed her cheek, said goodbye to Rose and Emily and quickly shepherded Daisy down the twitten to the garden gate. As they approached the back door it opened and Cordelia was standing there, arms wide, to welcome Daisy home from her first day at school.

Peggy felt quite emotional as she watched the elderly woman cuddle her daughter with such love, and then take her hand as they slowly negotiated the concrete steps. Peggy hovered closely behind them in case Cordelia lost her balance, but they successfully reached the kitchen.

'We've got cake,' Daisy shouted, dropping her little case on the floor and discarding Amelia on a nearby chair. 'Can we have it now, Gan-gan?'

'You can have it after your tea,' said Peggy quickly. 'But first, I want you to go up and take off your uniform and get changed into something that won't matter if it gets food down it.

'Muuuuum. Do I have to?'

'Any moaning and I'll give your cake to Daddy,' Peggy threatened.

Daisy looked aghast. 'You wouldn't?'

'Don't try me, Daisy. Just do as you're told.'

The child scampered off and Cordelia chuckled. 'It's such fun having a young one in the house again. And by the sound of it, she enjoyed her first day.'

'Long may it last, Cordy. But I fear that Anne might have some problems with Emily. She's very jealous of Rose at the moment and inclined to throw lots of tantrums.'

'Anne's been a teacher for long enough to know how to handle her,' said Cordelia confidently. She sank down into her favourite chair by the range fire. 'How is she by the way? It can't be long now before she has that baby.'

'She's tired, of course, and is probably doing too much as we all do at that stage. But she's very capable and knows who to call if it all starts while Martin's away. Though I rather hope it isn't for another few days as there don't seem to be enough hours to get everything in at the moment, especially as Jim and I will have to pop in and visit Ron this evening.'

Cordelia laughed. 'Oh, you don't have to worry about Ron. The old rogue made a break for it around lunchtime and is back at home with Rosie. She phoned and told me all about it – and there's another thing I'm meant to tell you too, but for the life of me I can't remember what it was.'

'Don't worry about it and it will come back to you,' soothed Peggy. 'I'm just glad I don't have to go out again. It's raining cats and dogs out there.'

It was almost six o'clock when Jim and Charlie came home together. 'I picked this one up at the bus stop as he'd forgotten his coat and brolly,' said Jim cheerfully. 'Whew. What weather, eh? Only the ducks would enjoy it.'

Peggy smiled as he gave her a hug and a kiss, for there was a new light in his eyes, and his face was animated. 'So, what happened to you today, Jim Reilly? You're very cheerful.'

'I'll tell you about it later,' he said, joining his son at the bread bin in search of something to eat.

'There's fish pie for tea, so don't spoil your appetites,' Peggy warned, swiping the tea towel at both of them. 'Cordelia got Bertie to fetch the fish, and has spent the day preparing it.'

'But I'm hungry now,' moaned Charlie.

'You're always hungry,' she said fondly. 'Just hang on for five minutes so I can get the food onto the plates.'

'Where's my Daisy?' asked Jim.

'She wanted to wait up for you but was so tired after her exciting day she fell asleep right after her tea, so I put her to bed,' said Peggy. 'You can pop up to kiss her goodnight, but please don't wake her or she'll never settle again.'

With the plates of fragrant fish pie on the table, everyone dug in to enjoy it. The atmosphere was warm and loving as the radio played quietly in the background and the clock ticked to the accompaniment of cutlery clacking on china.

'I remember what it was Rosie told me,' said Cordelia suddenly, making them all jump. 'She said to tell you that Ruby's mother has been admitted to the General, and the poor girl is beside herself with worry.' Cordelia grimaced. 'Though I can't think why. That woman was always trouble.'

'Oh, poor Ruby,' sighed Peggy. 'It was bad enough that Ethel turned up, but this is going to cause her no end of problems.'

'Rosie said she and Gloria will help out at the pub,' said Cordelia. 'And of course she's got Brenda and Frank to lend a hand too.'

'Well of course we'll all rally round – that's what friends and family are for,' said Peggy. 'I have to say, Ethel did look dreadful when I bumped into them yesterday. Did Rosie mention what ward Ethel is on? It might give a clue as to what's wrong with her.'

'The Clarice something ward,' said Cordelia.

'Oh no,' gasped Peggy. 'Then I must pop in and see Ruby tonight to let her know I'll help as much as possible. The poor girl must be in shreds, with this coming so soon after losing her husband and baby, and she'll need some mothering.'

Jim chuckled. 'Once a mother hen, always a mother hen,' he said fondly.

'Peggy was more of a mother to Ruby than Ethel ever was,' said Cordelia stoutly. 'It's only right she should be with her in times of trouble.' She eyed Peggy over her half-moon glasses. 'What I don't understand,

Peggy, is why you've got so het up about the ward Ethel's gone into.'

Peggy quietly explained, and the silence that fell in her kitchen was sombre.

Ruby had still heard nothing from the doctor when Brenda arrived. 'Thanks for doing this, Brenda,' she said, giving her a swift hug. 'I really appreciate it.'

Brenda took off her soaking wet raincoat and hung up her umbrella. 'Frank's going to pop in to keep me company, if that's all right. And he said to tell you that of course he'll help with the deliveries, so you're not to worry.'

'Bless you, love,' Ruby sighed. 'Gloria and Rosie have offered their support too. Everyone is being very kind.'

'We all realise how difficult it must be for you, Ruby, and I'm sure that if we pull together, things won't seem half as bad.'

'I hope so,' she replied, reaching for her own raincoat and umbrella. She tied a scarf over her hair and then picked up the holdall. 'I'll be back in two hours. Lock this door after me, will you?'

'Good luck,' Brenda called as Ruby went out of the side door and dashed across the road in the teeming rain.

Rosie had telephoned to give her the instructions on how to find the ward, and then proceeded to regale her with Ron's latest exploit which, despite her terrible worry, had Ruby in fits of laughter. But she was sober enough now as she entered the General and made her way through to the back and the smaller wards that overlooked the gardens.

She pushed through the door to find a quiet room that didn't look like a hospital ward at all. The floor-to-ceiling windows could be opened during better weather onto a terrace that overlooked a private corner of garden. The curtains were bright with colourful flowers and they matched the eiderdowns on each of the eight beds as well as the screens that surrounded some of them. There were flowers in vases beside every bed, and more arranged on top of the nurses' table, which held a lamp and a pile of medical records.

The nurses, pretty and mostly youthful, wore pale pink candy-striped uniforms and white caps and aprons. They moved about the hushed room, their soft-soled shoes making no noise on the bright yellow linoleum.

As Ruby looked for Ethel, one of the nurses approached her. 'Are you here to see Mrs Sharp?'

'Yeah, how did you know?'

The girl smiled. 'I didn't recognise you as a regular, and as Ethel only came in today, I put two and two together and guessed you were her daughter.' She stuck out her hand. 'I'm Sister Anne Joyner. But please, call me Anne, we aren't formal in here.'

'Ruby Taylor. Pleased to meet you, Anne. How is she? Have the test results come back yet?'

'The doctor has prescribed something to help her sleep as she's had quite a busy day and was in some distress by the time she was admitted. As to the tests, it's a bit early to say, but I'm sure Dr Darwin will inform you the minute he has the results.'

'Yeah, that's what 'e said. But it's frustrating when no one will tell me anything for certain.'

The girl smiled in sympathy. 'I do understand; but we have to be careful not to rush into a diagnosis until we are absolutely sure we know what we're dealing with. It wouldn't be right to cause a lot of unnecessary worry to either the patient or their relatives.'

She looked down at the holdall Ruby was carrying. 'Is that for Ethel?'

'It's just some things I thought she might need as she's here overnight.' Ruby looked at the nurse squarely. 'It will just be overnight, won't it?'

The sister looked surprised. 'I'm sorry, Ruby, but I very much doubt it. Weren't you warned to expect her stay to be quite prolonged?'

Ruby shook her head, feeling a bit foolish. There were a lot more questions she wanted to ask, but she didn't quite have the courage to voice them as she'd already shown herself up. 'I put a couple of bottles of milk stout in the bag, for when Mum needs a drink. I 'ope that's all right?'

'I'll put it in the ward kitchen for now,' Anne said, taking charge of the holdall. 'She might not feel like it when she wakes up, but we'll keep it there just in case.'

'I'll be very surprised if she doesn't want it,' said Ruby. 'Mum is an alcoholic, you know,' she added in a whisper.

'Yes, we are aware of that, but sometimes the medication takes away the need for alcohol. We'll play it by ear, so don't worry.'

'Can I sit with her for a bit?'

'Of course,' the girl murmured. 'We don't keep regular visiting hours here. You can come and go whenever you please as long as it doesn't interfere with the doctors' rounds or the treatments. In which case there is a day room just down the corridor where you can wait, although a lot of our visitors prefer to go to the Lilac Tearooms across the road for a bit of a break. Visiting can be very tiring, and it's surprising how quickly a bit of cake and a cup of strong tea can revive the spirits,' she added with a smile.

Ruby had heard enough to know that this was a ward like no other, but still she was hesitant to ask exactly what everyone was in here for. She followed the girl to Ethel's bed and sat down in the nearby chair before her legs gave way beneath her. The nurse quietly carried off the holdall, and Ruby was left alone with her mother.

Ethel's hair had been brushed and she was wearing a pretty pink nightdress that must belong to the hospital. She looked so peaceful and quite rosy-cheeked, the lines of pain smoothed away from her face by whatever medication the doctors had given her. She looked more like the mother Ruby remembered, but her heart ached to see her so frail and defenceless beneath the pristine white sheets and pink blankets.

Wary of disturbing her, she resisted taking her hand but sat there tearfully watching her sleep, and praying that the doctors could make her whole again and bring her back to the Ethel who was proud and loud and a proper little battler.

Yet Ruby knew in her heart this was a false hope – a flight of fancy born from her own yearning – for the doctor had warned her that Ethel's health had reached the point of no return and there wasn't much they could do for her. But surely, with all the modern advances in medicine, there must be something?

As she sat there she slowly became aware of the other visitors who sat quietly talking to the occupants of the beds, their faces drawn with weariness, their stooped shoulders bearing the weight of sadness, their voices often broken with determinedly unshed tears.

Ruby turned her attention to each of the patients, seeing wan faces, thinning hair and skeletal arms resting on the pink covers. She saw the drips hanging above them, the oxygen bottles and heart monitors, the tubes snaking into arms and below the bedclothes, and the bags hanging beneath the beds filled with unmentionable fluids.

A chill ran through her and clutched at her heart. For all the flowers and pretty pink bedding, there were serious things going on in here and she needed to fully understand why her mother had been admitted. She quietly left Ethel's bedside and approached the sister – needing answers even though she dreaded hearing them.

'You need to tell me what this ward is,' she said firmly. 'And I don't want no waffle or double-talk. I need the truth.'

The young woman didn't flinch but met her gaze. 'This is the palliative care centre,' she replied quietly, so her voice didn't carry across the ward.

Ruby frowned. 'What's that when it's at 'ome?'

'We look after those who are dying, Ruby,' she said, reaching to take her hand. 'And to make sure that for the time they have left it's not spent in pain, discomfort or distress.'

Her worst suspicions confirmed, Ruby nodded and managed to stagger back to Ethel's bedside where she almost fell into the chair. 'Oh, Mum,' she whispered through her tears. 'I'm so sorry I was hard on yer. I didn't know. Really I didn't.'

The sister put a gentle hand on Ruby's shoulder. 'I'm sorry,' she murmured. 'Someone should have warned you so it wasn't such a shock.'

'I think I already knew,' Ruby said, hastily mopping at her tears. 'I just didn't want to admit it. It's no one's fault, cos I were afraid to ask, and Dr Darwin did try and warn me, only I weren't listening properly, were I?'

'You're not alone, Ruby. None of us really want to hear the truth when we'd prefer to cling on to what we want to believe. But there is a lot we can do to ease your mother's pain and distress and keep her comfortable. So she really is in the very best place.'

'Yeah, I suppose,' replied Ruby, wiping away her tears.

'Let me get you a cup of tea,' the sister offered.

'Thanks. I'd like that if it's not too much bother,' she managed as the tears flowed again.

The nurse gently squeezed her shoulder and moved away, leaving Ruby quietly sobbing as her mother slept on.

15

'I know it isn't far, but I really don't fancy walking,' said Peggy, looking out at the rain that was now blowing almost horizontally across the back garden. 'And I only have just enough petrol to get me to work tomorrow so I can fill up at Jack's garage.'

'I'm not supposed to use mine outside of working hours, but as it's such a short journey, I doubt anyone would mind this once,' replied Jim, who was feeling a little tense. It wasn't that he begrudged Peggy's desire to mother Ruby; it was just that he needed a bit of peace and quiet, and to settle by the fire instead of dashing out and having to be sociable after what had been quite a stressful day.

She looked up at him and frowned as they stood in the quiet kitchen. 'You're looking a bit fraught, love. Did something happen today that's playing on your mind?'

'Aye,' he said, putting his arm round her shoulders and drawing her close. 'I bumped into Ernie, and we spent most of the morning talking over old times.'

'Oh, I see,' she murmured. 'But I thought he and his wife had moved up north?'

Jim quietly explained the reason behind his old friend's arrival at Parkwood. 'He's a wreck physically,' he finished gruffly. 'And it broke my heart to see him so vulnerable. But it turns out that apart from his disabilities, he's suffering from the same anxieties, terrors and awful dreams as me.'

'Ah, that would explain it,' said Peggy. 'It can't have been easy to drag all that up.'

He held her close and nestled her head against his heart. 'No, it wasn't easy, but I think it helped us both to be able to talk today, because no one else can really understand. But it's left me a bit on edge, and not good company.'

She must have felt the tremor run through him, and Jim knew she would be torn between the desire to stay with him, and the need to be with poor little Ruby who must be feeling very much alone.

'You don't have to come with me, Jim. I can drive down in your car and be back before you know it.' She lifted her hand to his troubled face with a gentle caress. 'As to your experiences, only someone who was there could understand what you all went through. So, in that respect, I'm glad you and Ernie have caught up again.'

She held him tightly and he fought the shimmer of tension that ran through his body, knowing it would only worry her further. 'Of course I'll come with you,' he said. 'I'm not having you out on a night like this on your own.'

She nodded and leaned back from their embrace so she could look into his face. 'I'm really sad that poor Ernie's ended up there in such an awful state, but it's as if fate's offering you both a chance to come to terms with what's troubling you.'

'Ernie said that he'd seen a trick-cyclist who told him he had to face the memories head on, not bury them and pretend they hadn't happened. He'd advised Ernie to turn the negatives into positives.'

'I really don't understand how,' said Peggy with a frown.

'Think about it, Peggy. We relive situations in which we feared being killed and those moments return in vivid colour, with all the feelings, sights and sounds that overwhelmed us at the time. But despite the terror of those moments, we survived, and so the next time those memories come back we can face them in the knowledge that we don't need to fear them because we came through in one piece.'

He gave a trembling sigh. 'It's all mumbo-jumbo, really, but it seems to work for Ernie, so it's got to be worth a try, hasn't it?'

'Anything that might help is worth it, Jim. You both need to find peace of mind, and I really do hope this new way of thinking can be the start of it.'

'So do I,' he replied, kissing her softly and holding her close.

They stood there for a moment, safe in each other's arms, a close unit sharing their hope that things were about to change and that their love for one another would sustain them through whatever lay ahead.

'We'd better go,' said Jim eventually. 'I'll run up and warn Charlie he's in charge while we're out. Cordelia's gone to sleep in her chair again, and I doubt she'd hear Daisy if she cried out.'

Peggy wasn't at all sure it was wise for Jim to come with her, but as he seemed determined, she nodded and quickly wrote a note to let Cordelia know where they were, and then fetched her coat and outdoor shoes while Jim ran up the stairs to the top floor.

As she prepared to go back out into the awful night, her thoughts drifted from Jim to Ruby. She should be back from the hospital by now as it was well past visiting time, and Peggy wanted to make sure the girl was coping and knew that she'd always help in any way she could – though with work, school and keeping the house going, she'd be run ragged. But Ruby was one of her beloved chicks, and come hell or high water, she'd do what she could for her.

Peggy was suddenly reminded of her own mother's slow and very sad descent into her final illness and the awful void it had left in her heart as well as in her life; and although Ethel hadn't been the best or most caring mother in the world, the girl would be filled with regrets that they hadn't been close, and remorse for the bitter words they'd probably exchanged – but it was the awful dread for what was to come that would be the hardest to bear.

Jim came back into the kitchen and pulled on his heavy raincoat then reached for Peggy's hand. They went out into the black, wintry night, still holding each other's hand, and ran down the steps to the car.

The drive was a short one down Camden Road, and Jim parked right outside the Anchor where the warm, welcoming glow of lamplight spilled from the diamond-paned windows onto the slick, wet pavement, above which the ancient sign creaked and swayed on its wrought-iron moorings.

'We won't stay long, Jim,' she said, smearing the condensation from the car window.

'Don't worry about me, Peg. I'm fine, really, and young Ruby needs you, so you take as long as you like. But just wait in the car until I've opened your door. I don't want you getting soaked through.'

He climbed out, opened the big black umbrella and held it over them both as they dashed across the pavement and into the warm fug of the almost deserted bar. One glance was all it took to realise that Ruby had yet to return.

Peggy could see from Jim's relaxed shoulders and easy manner that it was a huge relief to him that the place wasn't packed and noisy. She shed her coat and smiled at Brenda, who was serving one of the four customers, and watched Jim greet his older brother.

'Hello, Frank,' he said warmly as he approached the bar. 'It's been a while. I bet you're glad you're not out fishing in this.'

Frank rose from the bar stool and slapped Jim on the back as he embraced him. 'It's good to see you too,' he replied with a grin. 'And yes. It's not fit for man or boat out there tonight.'

Peggy had always liked Frank, for he was utterly dependable and as sturdy as a granite rock when it came to family loyalties. It was why he'd put up with his awful wife, Pauline, for so many years – it must have been a huge relief to him when she'd finally upped and left him.

Frank was the elder brother by five years. He and Jim shared the same height but Frank was much broader in girth, his hands roughened by years of hard labour on the fishing boat. His dark hair was now liberally sprinkled with silver, which enhanced the startling blue of his eyes and tanned, weathered face which would often be wreathed in smiles now he was free of Pauline. Like all the Reilly men, he was handsome and gifted with a charm inherited from their Irish ancestors, and Peggy could fully understand why Brenda was so smitten.

'Have you any idea of when Ruby might be back?' she asked Brenda.

'I expected her a couple of hours ago,' Brenda said fretfully. 'I do hope nothing bad has happened over there.'

'I'm sure she would have telephoned if that was the case,' soothed Peggy. 'I'll have a gin and tonic while I wait, please.'

'I might have a pint,' said Jim, shooting Peggy a questioning glance. At her nod, he grinned and slapped his brother on the shoulder. 'And one for your man here, Brenda.'

Peggy sipped her drink as the time went by, but kept an eye on Jim's intake as the brothers ordered a second pint. Jim seemed much more relaxed, and she supposed a couple of beers wouldn't do him any harm – but she knew how quickly he and Frank could get into a drinking session, and in Jim's fragile state, it wouldn't be at all helpful.

She tried to relax, but keeping an eye on Jim's drinking and worrying about Ruby was making it impossible. She'd almost reached the point of going across to the hospital to try and find her when she heard the side door slam, and with relief and some trepidation hurried into the hallway to meet her.

Ruby stood there, glassy-eyed, pale and tear-streaked, seemingly frozen to the door for support.

'Oh, love,' breathed Peggy, taking her in her arms. 'It's all right. I'm here, Ruby. I'm here.'

Ruby burst into tears and clung to her, her words incoherent as she tried to speak.

'Shoosh, shoosh, there, there,' soothed Peggy. 'Don't try and talk.'

When the first storm of tears finally abated, Peggy took her hand and led her to the door leading to her rooms. 'Open the door, love, and let's go up.'

Ruby shook her head, clearly struggling to find some sort of calm within the storm that must be raging through her. 'I have to relieve Brenda,' she managed. 'I said I wouldn't be long, and it's been hours.'

'Brenda's coping just fine,' said Peggy firmly. 'It's not busy in there and she's got Frank and Jim for company. Besides, you're in no fit state to face anyone, so come on, upstairs.'

Reluctantly, Ruby opened the door and led the way. Reaching her sitting room, she shed her wet coat and umbrella and kicked off her shoes before sinking onto the couch.

Peggy put the gas fire on to take the chill off the room, closed the curtains against the foul night, and then went into the kitchen to make a pot of tea.

'Here we are,' she said minutes later. 'This should warm you up a bit.' She handed Ruby a mug of strong tea and sat down beside her to light them both a cigarette.

'I was planning to come back ages ago,' Ruby said after she'd taken several sips of the hot tea. 'But just as I was about to leave, Mum woke up, so I 'ad to stay and keep her company. She didn't understand why she was there, or what was happening to her, and I 'ad a bit of a job explaining it all as I didn't know much either.'

'Of course you did, love,' murmured Peggy. 'I know what ward's she's on, by the way. I'm so sorry you're having to go through this, Ruby. If there's anything I can do . . .'

'There isn't much anyone can do, Auntie Peg. Whatever's wrong with Mum can't be fixed. I know that now.' She raised a tear-streaked face to regard Peggy with love and gratitude. 'But I'm so glad I've got you, Peggy,' she said, reaching for her hand. 'I don't think I could have coped otherwise.'

'You're stronger than you think, darling, and you don't have to go through this alone. We love you as one of the family, and we'll be with you every step of the way.'

'Everyone is being so kind,' Ruby said, mopping at fresh tears. 'Rosie and Gloria stopped by this afternoon, and the nurses are so lovely and understanding, and they didn't mind me making a fool of meself by crying all over the place and asking stupid questions. I mean, how was I to know what that ward was for?'

'The doctor should have warned you,' said Peggy. 'But of course the nurses understand that you're confused and frightened by it all – they must have to deal with so many emotions on that ward.'

Ruby stubbed out her cigarette and took a drink of her tea. 'I'm sure Dr Darwin didn't mean to keep me in the dark,' she said. 'He were ever so kind and gentle about it all, but I was in such a state I never took in half of what he said.'

'Yes, I've heard he's a good man to have in your corner at times like these,' said Peggy. 'I'm sure he never meant to mislead you in any way.'

Ruby fell silent for a moment. 'I can visit whenever I want,' she said eventually. 'So it will make running things here a bit easier, and let Brenda off the hook too. I'll go in for the morning, and then back in the afternoons.' There was a hitch in her voice as she continued, 'And when it looks like she's . . . well, you know. I'll stay with her until . . .'

'I'll be here,' said Peggy. 'And so will the others.'

Ruby offered her cigarettes to Peggy, and once they were lit, they sat cuddled up on the couch, garnering warmth and comfort from each other as they became lost in their separate thoughts.

Peggy stroked the girl's hair as she rested her head on her shoulder. The sadness and fear of this latest disaster seemed to radiate from her, and Peggy thought how tragic it was that one so young should have gone through so much. Life really was so unfair – and it put her own cares very much in the shadows.

Eventually, Ruby eased herself from their embrace and ran her fingers through her hair. 'I'd better go down,' she said, glancing at the mantel clock. 'Poor Brenda will think I've deserted her.'

'She won't think that at all,' said Peggy. 'Will you be all right here on your own tonight? Because I could always stay and keep you company.'

Ruby gave her a hug. 'Bless you, Auntie Peg, but I'll be fine, really I will. I need time to think and take it all in, so I want you to go home and get a good night's sleep.' She kissed Peggy's cheek. 'And thanks again, Auntie Peg – for everything.'

That first sip of beer had been like nectar to Jim. It coursed through him, easing the tension that had been tightening its grip on him throughout the day. He sat next to Frank and leaned against the bar as he watched him flirting with Brenda, glad that his brother had found someone who seemed to genuinely care for him – even if she was over a decade younger than him.

When Brenda moved away to clear the empty glasses, Jim nudged his brother's arm. 'You're a lucky man, Frank. She's a real little smasher, even if she is far too young for you.'

Frank grinned. 'Jealousy will get you nowhere, little brother. Some of us have got it, and others haven't. That's all I can say.' He finished the pint and placed his glass on the bar. 'Another round please, love,' he said to Brenda on her return. 'And whisky chasers on the side. We need something to warm us on this horrid night.'

'I'd have lit the fire if I'd known it was going to be so bad,' she replied, 'but as it's almost closing time, it's not worth the bother.' She poured the drinks and glanced back at the clock, but made no comment on Ruby and Peggy's continued absence.

Jim raised his glass in salute and savoured the glorious warmth of the whisky going down. 'How's Brendon managing on that fancy new boat, Frank?'

'Taken to it like a real Reilly,' Frank replied. 'And thank God for it. With a whole new crew, I couldn't have managed both boats on my own.' He sipped his whisky. 'He and Betty brought their little Joseph over yesterday and Brenda cooked a marvellous roast chicken with all the trimmings.'

'We had pheasant,' said Jim. 'Da brought it back from one of his walks and said Harvey had caught it.' He chuckled. 'As if. Harvey's getting much too old to be catching pheasants.'

Frank grinned back. 'Da was probably up to his old tricks, and who can blame him with the price of everything these days?' He chuckled. 'I heard about his latest escapade. How's the old rogue doing?'

'Well enough to have Rosie looking after him instead of that matron,' Jim replied. 'That one's a right tartar, and I don't blame him for escaping her clutches.'

He swallowed the last of the whisky and took a sip of beer. 'Talking of difficult women. Have you heard anything from Pauline since the divorce?'

'Only through Brendon. He feels it's his duty to see her now and then, even though she caused such awful hurt over his little Betty.' Frank grimaced. 'Still, she is his mother, and he's the only son she's got left. It's a great shame she doesn't appreciate him as much as she damned well should,' he added bitterly. 'How any mother could treat her son and grandson as she's done is beyond me, Jim.'

Jim had always disliked Pauline and thought she was an utter bitch for all the years of misery she'd caused Frank with her histrionics and self-pitying tantrums. But it had been the way she'd so cruelly taken against Brendon's wife Betty and her own grandchild that had been the final straw for Jim.

Betty was a schoolteacher and had been disabled through childhood polio. She wore a calliper and special boot, but her mind was as sharp as a tack, her intelligent and lively personality shone through, and Brendon clearly adored her. They'd met in Devon during Brendon's service with the Royal Naval

Reserve. His ship had been delayed on his final tour of duty, and Joseph had been born before the wedding could take place.

Pauline had never forgiven them for having the child out of wedlock and had taken it personally that she and Frank hadn't been invited to the service when it did finally take place – despite the fact it had been held in Devon and the travelling restrictions had made it impossible for them to attend.

On their return home to Cliffehaven, Pauline had accused Betty of trapping her son into marriage and had even questioned if Brendon was actually Joseph's father. It had been hurtful and totally unnecessary, and had caused untold misery to everyone, for which neither Jim nor Peggy could ever forgive her.

But he kept these thoughts to himself as he was fairly certain that his brother felt the same, and rather wished he hadn't broached the subject at all. 'I think we're all better off without her,' he said quietly.

Frank nodded and drained his glass. 'If she hadn't left me for that fancy job with the Red Cross, I'd never have got to know Brenda properly. And I thank my lucky stars I did.' He placed the glass on the bar and regarded Jim from beneath his heavy brows. 'Another?'

'I'd better not,' Jim replied with some reluctance. 'I've got to be at work early tomorrow and need to keep my head clear.'

'I probably shouldn't either,' Frank murmured. 'We're taking the boats out on the high tide first thing if this weather clears.'

Jim was about to change his mind and order another whisky for them both when Peggy and Ruby came into the bar. The girl looked completely washed out, poor little thing, and his Peggy didn't look that lively either. Whatever was happening with Ethel, he'd no doubt soon find out. But for now it was time to get Peggy home and hope the whisky would give him a sleep free of dreams.

The nightmare crept up on him just as it always did, and with it came the growing terror that he was about to die. He was in the jungle, feeling the damp heat, the sweat and the sting of insects. Every sound was magnified, every colour brighter than it should be as they crept through the stinking undergrowth on full alert. He was so tense that the slightest sound made him flinch and his stomach clench into a tight knot. But there would be no turning back, no hiding from the onslaught to come, for they would soon be at the top of the ridge, and the Japs were lying in wait to slaughter them all.

The monsoon rain was beating down on his hat and running in rivers beneath his boots, making it hard to get a reliable toehold on the steep slope. He knew what was coming and tried to brace himself against the thunder of surrounding gunfire and the screaming emergence of the enemy with their swords and bayonets.

He reached a defile in the ground and threw himself onto his belly in the hope the scant shelter might protect him. But he knew without a doubt that he was going to die here, and the terror made his heart thud so rapidly he could barely breathe, let alone focus through the gunsights at the surrounding enemy.

The sapper lying next to him caught a bullet in the head, spraying Jim with brains and blood, and Jim began to shake, the tremors growing by the second as he scrambled away from the gore. That could have been him.

And then he saw that Ernie had been hit and was fully exposed to enemy fire as he tried to crawl for cover. Jim knew he had to get to him – even though the chances of surviving such a move were zero.

Crawling over the dead man he'd shared breakfast with only hours ago, he slithered on his belly from the narrow defile which had become a charnel house and managed to reach Ernie, who was desperately trying to find cover behind a boulder.

'I've got you, mate,' he rasped. 'Come on, Ernie. Stop fighting me. I'm trying to get you out of here.'

That was when he felt the punch of something in his own back. Letting rip with a string of oaths, he ignored the pain and grabbed Ernie so he could roll him onto his back. Thanking his lucky stars that his mate was a lightweight, he held tightly to Ernie's hands and crabbed into the meagre shelter of the surrounding boulders where he waited as the bullets zinged and whined around them, and wounded men screamed for a medic.

His breathing was rapid and shallow. They were both about to die. Any minute now one of those bullets would find its mark and he'd never get home to Peggy. But despite the terror, he found the courage and strength to use a lull in the barrage to carry Ernie down to the medics' tent where everything suddenly turned black and he knew no more.

Jim reared up in bed, fully awake, pulse thudding and mouth dry as cold sweat ran down his body. The darkness was real. But he wasn't in the jungle but at home and it was the middle of the night, and instead of gunfire he could hear the sharp rattle of the rain against the windows.

Aware of Peggy sleeping beside him, he tried to control his breathing and regain some sort of equilibrium so he could separate the dream from his present reality. He was still alive. He'd come through despite the bullet the medics had had to dig out – and he was at home with his Peggy, not buried in a jungle grave with only a coordinate on a map to mark the spot.

He sat in the darkness listening to the rain and the soft breathing of his darling Peggy. He'd saved Ernie that day, but what a terrible price the man had paid. Whereas he'd survived to fight another day – and another – and endless days after that.

He swung his legs out of the bed, careful not to disturb Peggy, and shoved on his slippers and the old tartan dressing gown that had seen better days. Peggy had used it during his years away as a form of comfort and he could still catch her scent in the cloth, which in turn brought him a sense of ease.

He crept out of the bedroom and went downstairs, his tread making no sound on the new carpet. Feeling his way across the hall in the darkness, he went into the kitchen, closed the door and switched on the light.

Blinking from the glare, he put the kettle on, made a cup of tea and sat at the table. It was the same old table they'd always had, but Charlie had done an excellent job of painting it, and the chairs. It had seen a lot of use over the years, as had the two recovered chairs by the fire.

As he sipped the tea and smoked a cigarette, he took stock of the kitchen, and realised that although things had been renovated and moved around, it still held the essence of home, for the years of family gatherings at this table were embedded in the very fabric of the room. There had been happy days and sad days – and days when tempers had been frayed only to be soothed – but through it all, they'd stuck together, and this kitchen epitomised the family's growth and change as they were about to enter a new decade in a world of hard-won peace.

Jim felt much calmer, for the vestiges of his nightmare had fragmented and faded into nothing, leaving him clear-headed and ready to fully examine what was happening to him. It had been a huge relief to discover he wasn't alone in the terrors, and that he and Ernie shared the same nightmares, but he realised it could take a long time before either of them would really be free – and although the alcohol tonight might have offered a brief respite to the edginess he'd been feeling, it had been a mistake to think it was the answer.

Perhaps Ernie's psychologist had known what he was talking about after all, he mused. For he'd gone to bed already tense against the prospect of having a bad dream, and when it had come he'd had no strength to fight against the threat of death it always brought. But the man was right. He had survived. He'd come home to Peggy and his family. He was fit and healthy and no longer in danger of flying bullets or murderous Japs, so there was no need to let past terrors control his dreams, or his life.

Facing the reality of his situation, and continuing to remind himself of it without any of the survivor's guilt, would help him to face those demons and see them for what they were – shadows from the past – sights and sounds he could no longer hear – dead comrades he would always remember as the living, breathing men he'd fought beside – and a cruel enemy defeated.

Jim took a deep breath. He stubbed out the cigarette and washed the mug, leaving it on the draining board, then switched off the light and slowly made his way back upstairs, tired and ready to sleep. It would be a better day tomorrow.

16

Ruby had been exhausted after the long hours at her mother's bedside and had expected to fall into bed and go straight to sleep. But sleep wouldn't come, and she'd become so restless she'd gone back downstairs to the bar and cleaned the place from top to bottom. Not that it had really needed it, for Brenda had done a good job, but having something physical to do was the medicine Ruby had needed, and when she'd finally returned to her bed in the early hours, she'd slept deeply and without dreams.

She was woken by the sound of someone banging on the front door and, stumbling out of bed, she rushed to the sitting-room window to see who was making such a racket.

'Bloody hell,' she breathed, recognising her visitor and realising she must look a right sight in her nightclothes. She opened the window. 'I'll be down in a minute,' she shouted and quickly shut it again before he could fully take in her dishevelled state.

A glance at the bedside clock told her it was well after eight, so the day was already racing away with her. She pulled on her clothes and shoes and ran a brush through her tousled hair. She'd slept in much later than usual and there was no time for make-up, so he'd have to put up with her puffy eyes and pale face – not that she was particularly bothered about what he thought of her – it wasn't a social call.

Leaving her hair loose about her shoulders, she ran down the stairs to let him in.

'Sorry, Dr Darwin. I don't usually sleep so late,' she said breathlessly. 'Please come in. I'll make us both a cup of tea.'

'Thank you, that would be welcome,' he replied, taking off his Harris tweed hat as he stepped over the threshold into the bar.

Ruby led him upstairs to her sitting room, giving it a hasty once-over in case she'd left underwear lying about. Relieved that it looked tidy enough for such an important visitor, she went to put the kettle on.

'I'm surprised you haven't got surgery this morning,' she said in an attempt to stave off any serious discussion before she'd had some tea and got her nerves under control.

'One of the other partners is taking it this morning,' he said as he dithered in the centre of her sitting room and fiddled with his hat. 'This is all very nice,' he murmured, looking round. 'It's been a while since I came to the Anchor, but of course I didn't know Rosie well enough to ever be invited up here.' He shot her a beaming smile and she immediately felt a bit more at ease.

'I bought the pub and the furniture as a job lot,' she confessed, 'so all of this is Rosie's. But as it's to my taste, I count meself lucky.'

Her hands weren't quite steady as she made the pot of tea and loaded up a tray with everything to go with it. Her nerves were jangling, and she was dreading what was to come.

'Here, let me take that before you drop it,' he said, his rich, deep voice sounding oddly comforting in this very feminine room.

Ruby let him take it and place it on the low table between the couches.

'Shall I be mother?' he asked with a twinkle in his brown eyes. 'I think my hands might be just a little steadier.'

'You'd better if you want yer tea in the cup,' she replied with a nervous giggle. 'I'm likely to pour it all over the carpet.'

He poured the tea, added milk and sugar and finally sat down. After taking a sip, he placed the cup and saucer back on the tray. 'Of course you know why I'm here, Mrs Taylor, and I'm sure you don't want to prolong this difficult moment,' he said, 'so I'll come straight to the point.' He looked at her hesitantly. 'If that's all right?'

Ruby nodded and knotted her hands in her lap to stop them from trembling. 'I know she's dying, cos you wouldn't have put her in that ward if she weren't. What I wanna know is what's killing her, and what you're going to do about it.'

'It's cancer, Mrs Taylor. A particularly virulent cancer that has spread to her lungs and bones.' He took a shallow breath and kept his kindly gaze fixed on her. 'Your mother's liver has been badly damaged from her years of drinking, and unfortunately her kidneys are also struggling. I'm very much afraid there is nothing we can do to improve the outcome.'

'It's worse than I thought,' Ruby managed through the overwhelming rise of emotions. 'She must be in the most terrible pain, even though she never let on to me.'

He shook his head. 'She's in no pain at all, Mrs Taylor, so please don't worry about that. The medication she's on is very strong, and she will stay on it until . . .'

'How long?' she whispered.

'A matter of days,' he replied solemnly. 'Perhaps a week – but probably no longer.'

'Days? A week?' The words echoed through her head as Ruby stared at him in shock. 'So soon? But it were only the other day when she was 'aving a scrap at the council laundry.'

'I'm sorry,' he said. 'Every patient is different and your mother is a terrific fighter, so maybe . . .'

'Yeah, but she ain't strong enough to beat this, is she?'

He didn't give her an answer, but just looking at his expression, she knew what it would have been.

'I'd better rearrange things 'ere so I can stay with her,' she said tearfully. 'We never 'ad what you might call a close relationship, but she is me mum, and it's the very least I can do for her.'

'I am sorry this has come as such a shock, Mrs Taylor. Please be assured that I'll call into the hospital regularly, and should you need me, then I'm at the end of the telephone.' He reached into an inside pocket of his tweed jacket and pulled out a card. 'My private number is on there.'

'Thanks ever so.' She placed the card on the table and picked up her cup of tea with a hand that shook so much she slopped most of it in the saucer. 'We'd better drink this before it gets cold. It would be a shame to waste it at the price they charge these days,' she stuttered before bursting into tears and clattering the cup back into the saucer.

He sipped the cooling tea in silence as she wept, and when it became obvious that she didn't have a handkerchief, he offered her his.

'I already got one of yours,' she sobbed. 'I meant to wash it and give it back, but with all what's going on . . .'

'Don't worry about it,' he replied softly. 'I have plenty more where that came from. It seems people think a man can never have too many handkerchiefs.'

Ruby finally managed to pull herself together, mopped her tears and finished her tea which was now cold.

'Would you like me to prescribe you something to help you sleep, Mrs Taylor? Only hospital visiting can be very hard, both physically and emotionally, and you will also have the responsibility of running this place.'

'I never needed nothing after I lost Mike and me baby, so I won't start now,' she said firmly. 'Mum will need me to be clear-headed, and I'll make sure I grab some sleep whenever I can.'

'You must eat properly too,' he said earnestly. 'It's all too easy to forget to look after yourself when caring for others – and you'll do your mother no good if you get ill.'

Ruby grinned despite the seriousness of the occasion. 'You sound like Auntie Peggy. She's always fussing about getting enough food and sleep.'

'She's clearly a very wise woman,' he replied. 'I understand from Danuta that you both once lived at Beach View as evacuees. It's good that you have the Reillys on your side – you're going to need them in the days to come, Mrs Taylor.'

'Yes, I struck very lucky when they took me in,' she replied. She looked back at him and gave him a watery smile. 'You and Danuta seem to do an awful lot of talking. Is there anything you don't know about me?'

He reddened. 'It might sound as if we've been gossiping, but I'm still trying to acquaint myself with my patients, and need all the help I can get. I assure you, Mrs Taylor, nothing we say will ever become public, and I'm sorry if you think Danuta and I have overstepped the mark.'

Ruby liked this man for his decency and kindness – and that smile which had the power to warm and put her at ease. She surprised herself by grinning at him. 'As long as you keep everything you've heard to yourself, I don't mind. But do you think we can stop being so formal with each other as we're about to set out on this difficult journey?' she asked boldly. 'My name's Ruby. What's yours?'

He looked momentarily startled and then grinned back. 'Alistair McDuff Darwin. My friends call me Duffer,' he said bashfully.

Ruby managed a short chuckle. 'I think I'll stick to Alistair. I don't want a duffer for a doctor.'

He tipped back his head and laughed. 'Oh, very clever, Ruby. I can see we're going to get along just fine.'

Ruby realised things were getting a bit out of hand, so tucked her hair behind her ears and met his gaze. 'I ain't as daft as egg-looking, as me mum would say, Alistair. We girls from the East End are sharper than you might think.'

'I never doubted that for a moment,' he replied, still smiling as he stood up and carried the tray back to the kitchen.

Ruby stood and waited for him to return, anxious now for the meeting to be over so she could call Brenda and the others to let them know she'd need all the help she could get over the next few days.

He seemed to realise she needed to be alone, for he picked up his hat from the arm of the couch. 'I'll call in to the hospital when I do my local rounds.' He stuck out his hand. 'Good luck, Ruby. Keep that East End spirit flying. You're going to need it.'

She shook his hand, struck once again by how warm and capable it was. 'I'll do me best,' she said with some bravado before leading the way down the stairs and letting him out of the side entrance.

But with the door shut and the silence of the pub surrounding her, she began to shiver. It had nothing to do with the wind outside, or the chill that seeped from the flagstone floor through her shoes and into her feet.

It was the arctic blast of an imminent death – a terrible herald announcing the final days of the only family member she had left.

Peggy suspected Jim must have got up in the night, for there was a mug on the draining board and cold tea in the pot when she'd come down that morning. But as he seemed quite cheerful, she had said nothing and just got on with preparing breakfast.

The usual early morning chaos had ensued with lost homework, forgotten sports kit and misplaced keys. Peggy made the sandwiches for the lunch boxes and started a long list in her head of things she'd have to buy if everyone was to be fed tonight, but was constantly distracted by the others demanding her attention.

Cordelia was all of a dither because she'd had a letter from her distant relatives in Canada who were planning a trip to England next spring, and Daisy was in a lather of excitement at the prospect of another school day with Rose Margaret, and wouldn't sit still or stop talking. Charlie was moaning because his sports kit hadn't been washed – which was his own fault because he hadn't put it in the laundry basket after his Saturday match – and Jim was muttering as he tried to sew a button back on his jacket and stabbed himself with the needle.

Peggy finally managed to get Charlie and Jim out of the house on time, soothed Cordelia's fears over the proposed visit, scooped up the pile of lovely letters that had just arrived, and got Daisy in the car.

Arriving at the school, she saw Anne parking just up the road and waited for her to clamber out and waddle towards her. The two little girls raced towards each other and ran into the playground, thoroughly at home in their new environment.

'You look as if you're about to go pop,' said Peggy fondly.

'I feel like it too,' Anne moaned, pressing a hand into her back. 'I can't stop, Mum, sorry. But I'm due at the clinic in twenty minutes.'

Peggy kissed her and waved her off before climbing back into her car and pausing for a moment as she saw the rather handsome Dr Darwin emerging from the Anchor's side door. It wasn't a good sign, and with Ethel in that ward, poor little Ruby must be beside herself with worry. But she was already pushed for time, so even a quick visit to console Ruby was out of the question. At least she had the lovely doctor to advise her, but it wasn't the same as family, and Peggy couldn't banish the stab of guilt as she drove towards the industrial estate.

She got Jack to fill the tank with petrol and passed the time of day with him before driving round to the back of the clothing factory into her designated parking bay. Clambering out, she took a breath and hurried inside to telephone Ruby before the machinists arrived.

Their conversation was necessarily brief because they were both short of time. Having assured Ruby she'd help as much as possible, she reminded her to eat properly and promised to pop into the ward during the evening visiting hours to make sure Ethel had everything she might need. Feeling a little bit better from having spoken to her, Peggy went to find Gracie, one of her favourite machinists, to make sure she was all right. She'd heard through the grapevine that Gracie had recently become entangled with Phil Warner, which could only be bad news. Gracie was a young widow with a little son, and knowing Warner, he was after something. Peggy could only hope Gracie kept a sensible head on her shoulders and didn't let things go too far.

The telephone rang just as she'd finished going through the order book for the past week. 'Hello, Rosie,' she said in surprise. 'It's not like you to ring me here. What's up?'

'You haven't seen Ron, have you?' she asked, sounding anxious.

'No,' said Peggy. 'Why? Was he planning to come up here?'

'I don't know what he was planning,' Rosie said with a degree of exasperation. 'He just said he had something important to do and not to expect him back for lunch.'

'I'm sorry, Rosie. I don't know what to say. But if he does turn up here, I'll let you know – though I can't think why he should,' Peggy added in puzzlement.

'I'm just worried he's up to some sort of mischief,' said Rosie. 'And he's not fully recovered from his allergic reaction, despite his argument to the contrary. He was very restless last night, and up before it was even light.'

'Ron being up to something is nothing new, Rosie,' Peggy soothed. 'You should know that.'

Rosie heaved a sigh. 'Of course I do, but he's taken the dogs with him, and if he's off poaching, there'll be hell to pay. That new gamekeeper is young and keen, and not at all likely to turn a blind eye.'

'I doubt he'll be poaching,' said Peggy, suddenly remembering the pheasant they'd eaten on Sunday and instantly feeling guilty. 'And even if he is, he's wily enough to evade any gamekeeper. Sorry, Rosie,' she added on a sigh. 'I'm not much help, am I?'

'I'm sorry for disturbing you at work, Peggy. I'll let you get on.'

The call was disconnected and Peggy replaced the receiver with a frown. 'Honestly, Ron, your shenanigans are making life very difficult for everyone,' she murmured. Glancing out of the window, she noticed the line manager standing in a huddle with one of the cutters, apparently having a serious discussion.

Peggy headed out to talk to her. 'What's the matter, Flo?'

'Beryl went to look for that bolt of sprigged cotton which came in on Friday, and it seems to have gone missing,' the woman replied quietly. 'I've checked against the order and got the storeman to help me search for it. But it's nowhere to be found, and I'm worried it's been stolen.'

Peggy knew this wasn't the first time things had gone missing, but it was usually off-cuts, or from the collection of seconds which had been put aside to sell on market stalls. A blind eye was usually turned to this petty thieving, but losing a whole bolt of expensive cloth was a serious matter that could not be ignored, and ultimately it would be Peggy's responsibility.

She turned to Beryl, who was their most experienced and reliable cutter. 'Carry on with a different pattern and material,' she ordered quietly, realising they were being watched and listened to by Gracie and Edna whose work station was nearby.

She then steered Flo away from the cutting table and into the storeroom. 'Let's have another look before we jump the gun,' she murmured. 'A whole bolt of fabric is too unwieldy to smuggle out of here, and could have fallen down the back of something.'

The search took up most of the morning but yielded nothing, so Peggy decided it might be wise to check the inventories against what was in the storeroom in case other bolts had disappeared. It took several hours, and revealed the loss of two bolts of white satin, one of lace, and several items of haberdashery. With a sick feeling in her stomach, she went to telephone Solly.

But Solly was out of his office, and when she telephoned his house, Rachel confirmed that he was up in London for a business meeting. Having discussed the situation with Rachel, Peggy had no choice but to inform the police.

Once she'd made the call, she sat at her desk and frantically checked all the time-sheets again to see who'd been in on Friday. The bolts of satin and lace, and that particular cotton, had come in late that afternoon just before they'd closed for the weekend, and Peggy had seen them in and ticked them off the list, so they had to have been taken sometime during the past three days.

She suspected someone had broken in over the weekend, but there had been no sign of a forced entry, which meant whoever it was had used a key – but how? She and Solly were the main key-holders, and the third set was kept in John White's safe up in the administration office so he could lock up at the end of the shift now that Peggy left early – and if that had gone missing he'd have told her immediately.

It was all very worrying. She had a niggling suspicion that the thief had an accomplice amongst Solly's employees, and what was worse, she thought she knew who that person might be. Although it was way past her lunchtime, she found she had little appetite for the tomato sandwiches she'd made. She poured a cup of tea from her flask and went outside for a calming cigarette as she waited for the police to arrive.

Ron had tramped from home, up the hill past the factory estate with the dogs at his heels, before he began the long, steep climb to Chalky White's smallholding which lay in a valley to the west of Cliffehaven.

His chest felt tight and his lungs were struggling a bit, so it took him much longer than usual. By the time he'd reached halfway he was completely out of breath and feeling rather light-headed, and he started to wish he'd borrowed Rosie's car to drive up here, for he was definitely not as fit as before his run-in with the penicillin. But he'd come too far to turn back now, and the prospect of a cup of tea and a long sit-down with his old pal kept him going.

The dogs ran ahead as he approached the ramshackle collection of barns and pens that spread beyond the sprawling stone farmhouse, and he saw Chalky emerge from his smokehouse to stand and watch Ron's laboured trek across the valley floor.

'Age getting to you at last, is it?' he called. 'Join the club, old friend.'

'I've got eight years on you yet,' Ron panted. 'So less of the old.' He sank down on a wooden bench and wiped the sweat from his face with a grubby handkerchief, struggling to get his breath back.

'Well, I never thought I'd see you in this state,' muttered Chalky, his mop of pure white hair blowing in the light wind. 'I'll fetch you a drop of my home-made elderflower wine. That'll stoke your boiler.'

Ron would have preferred a cup of tea, but as Chalky rarely offered his hooch, he was reluctant to cause offence by turning down the chance. As the other man ducked into the farmhouse and the dogs went off to explore, Ron sat and moodily regarded Chalky's smallholding as the ache in his chest eased and his head cleared.

The chickens were kept in a large fenced-off area, the ducks were free range and enjoying the rather muddy pond at the bottom of the vegetable garden, and there were a couple of goats tethered in a nearby field. A sow and her piglets snuffled about in a pen, and homing pigeons cooed in a large aviary and loft that Ron had helped to build by the back door of the farmhouse.

As usual there was no sign of Chalky's nagging wife, who seemed to have taken up permanent residence with her sister who lived thirty miles away. But Chalky was quite content with his own company, and Ron suspected he enjoyed her absence so he could do as he pleased without her interference.

Chalky White had joined up at the same time as Ron, Stan from the station, Fred the Fish and Alf the Butcher, and together they'd seen action throughout the First World War and managed to scrape through it without any serious injuries. Fred and Alf had originally come from London and decided to settle in Cliffehaven after the war, and Chalky and Stan had been born here, and so had picked up the threads of their old lives. These friendships were a mainstay in helping them all to recover from the horrors of the trenches, and Ron could only hope that his son Jim would find such support.

Chalky appeared with ham bones for the dogs and two large bottles. 'Here you are, Ron. Take it easy, though. It has a kick like a mule.'

Ron knew from past experience that Chalky's home brews could be lethal and needed careful handling, so he took the bottle and had an experimental swig. It was chilled and welcoming and slipped down far too easily. Feeling a bit of a buzz as it hit the spot, he set the bottle to one side and concentrated on filling his pipe as the dogs chewed on the bones.

'If it's chickens you're after, you've come to the wrong place,' said Chalky, rolling a cigarette. 'I've told you before, Ron. They're all accounted for by the rationing people, and it's more than my life's worth to start selling them off.'

Ron eyed his old pal from beneath his brows as he lit his pipe and got the tobacco burning satisfactorily. 'Come on, Chalky. We both know there are always extras that missed the count,' he rumbled. 'To be sure, I'll pay you a fair price for 'em.'

'That's not the point, Ron. If we get caught, we'll be up before the magistrate quicker than you can blink.'

'I'm not going to tell anyone,' Ron replied. 'And I doubt you will, either.'

'Maybe not, but those chickens will be seen and someone will report them, as sure as eggs are eggs,' persisted Chalky, who'd always been a bit of a pessimist.

'They'll just be replacing the ones the foxes got,' said Ron. 'And . . .'

Chalky held his hands up. 'I don't want to know the whys and wherefores, Ron.' He gave a deep sigh of capitulation. 'But as it's you, and I know from past experience that you won't stop badgering me, I'll let you have two for half a crown each.'

'That's daylight robbery, Chalky. How about two bob each?'

'Take it or leave it, Ron. Can't say fairer than that.'

Ron took a deep swig of the home-made wine. 'I think two bob is quite fair enough,' he grumbled.

'Supply and demand, me old son.' Chalky grinned. 'Two and six each, and we've got a deal.' He held out his work-hardened and rather dirty hand.

Reluctantly, Ron shook it. 'Remind me never to do business with you again, you wee scoundrel,' he growled. 'And as you're charging an arm and a leg, I'll pick out the ones I'm taking, and have a bag of feed while I'm at it.'

Chalky smiled, his weathered face wrinkling into lines and creases gained from many years of an outdoor life. 'Feed is sixpence a bag.'

Ron glared at him. 'You're really trying it on today, Chalky. I thought we were friends?'

'We are,' said Chalky. 'But chicken feed and hens cost money, and as it is I'll come out of this at a loss.'

'To be sure, you drive a hard bargain,' Ron complained.

Chalky shrugged. 'These are hard times, Ron, old pal. Now, I have a special pen for the extras. You'd better come and have a look.'

Ron finished the bottle of hooch and, with his head now in a whirl, staggered to his feet. He ordered the dogs to stay where they were (needlessly, since they were still occupied with the bones and had no intention of going anywhere).

Ron mopped his sweating face again and then settled his battered hat on his head before following Chalky to the copse that grew in a deep fold further down the valley.

A rough pen had been built of chicken wire and wood and the ten birds were happily pecking away at their feed when the men approached.

'I'm keeping the rooster,' said Chalky, 'but you can have your pick of the hens. They're all this year's crop of chicks and proving to be good layers.'

Ron eyed the preening rooster with his bright feathers and red coxcomb and then regarded the fine-looking brown hens. He picked the fattest two, and once Chalky had opened the gate, went in to catch them.

This proved to be a hard task, for the hens didn't want to be caught and the rooster seemed determined to keep them to himself. With Chalky keeping the rooster at bay, Ron eventually managed to round up the two hens, which he then carefully stuffed into separate inside pockets of his poacher's coat.

Chalky locked the gate, Ron handed over the money, and they walked back to where the dogs had abandoned the bones and were showing far too much interest in Chalky's ducks. 'If they snaffle one of them, it'll cost you a crown,' he said.

Ron quickly called them to heel and, once Chalky had given him the bag of feed, shook his hand. 'Thanks, Chalky. They're going to a good home, so there's no need to fret.'

'I always fret when you come calling, Ron, but I suppose I should be used to it by now,' Chalky replied wearily.

Ron grinned and, with the dogs at his heels once more, set off towards home.

Harvey and Monty carried their precious bones with them and scampered ahead as he slowly climbed the hill, the chickens fussing and squawking in his pockets, the bag of feed weighing more than he'd expected.

He'd have to go the long way back to Beach View, he realised, for the complaining hens would attract attention if he went through the town, and that was the last thing he wanted.

Ron reached the top of the hill which gave him a bird's-eye view of the town and then slowly traversed the plateau which formed the northern edge until he reached the old drovers' track which would eventually lead to the country road from where it was just a short dash to the back of Beach View.

Ron paused to catch his breath as he reached the end of the drovers' track. He was hot and his chest hurt again, and the combination of bright sun, Chalky's lethal brew and the effort of getting across the hills was taking its toll. He eased off his heavy poacher's coat, rubbed his eyes and shook his head, but it made little difference to his blurred sight or the darkness now swirling in his head.

With a massive effort, he managed to set aside his coat to protect its precious cargo and called out to

Harvey to stay. And then the vertiginous darkness took over and he crumpled to the ground in a dead faint.

'Ron. Ron. What are you doing? What has happened?'

He opened his eyes and blearily looked up at Danuta in confusion. 'What? Why?' He struggled to understand what was going on and to get to his feet, but she firmly pressed him back down into the grass.

'You must have fainted,' she said, holding his wrist to take his pulse. 'What on earth are you doing out here?'

He tried to wave her away and sit up, but she was having none of it.

'I hear the chickens,' she said sternly. 'Have you been poaching again?'

'No,' he protested. 'I bought them fair and square as a present for Peggy.'

'Mama Peggy will not like them if they are stolen,' she said fiercely. 'Come. I help you up and drive you to Beach View.'

'I don't need help,' he rasped as he struggled to get to his feet, grab his coat, and placate the whining and fretful dogs.

'Yes, you do,' she retorted, taking hold of his arm and forcibly steering him towards her little car. 'You are lucky I saw you.'

'What are you doing all the way out here, anyway?' he asked as she bundled him into the car and shooed the dogs onto the back seat.

'I have a patient in cottage up the road,' she said, reaching for a canteen of water. 'Drink this,' she ordered. 'All of it, mind. You are very dehydrated.'

With that, she started the engine and drove him to Beach View.

*

The arrival of the police had caused a stir and disrupted production to the point where it was hardly worth finishing the shift. The two constables had taken statements from everyone – including John White, who'd promptly produced his set of keys. They'd poked about the storeroom and loading bay, leaving a trail of mess behind them before they finally went back to the station with promises that they'd follow up any leads and get back to Peggy.

Peggy had kept quiet about her suspicions as to who might have been involved in the robbery and planned to take the person concerned to one side during the afternoon tea break, to have a quiet word. She didn't want to believe the woman was guilty as she'd been a long-term employee with never a hint of wrongdoing, but unfortunately all the signs were there that she was somehow involved.

The telephone rang just as she was about to leave her office. 'Mum? It's Anne.'

Peggy was immediately on alert. 'Have you started?'

'Yes. I've left a message at the clinic for Danuta, but please can you pick the girls up and keep them until Martin comes home? He's been delayed by bad weather and doesn't expect to get back until tomorrow now.'

She sounded so fraught that Peggy's first instinct was to drive over there to be with her. But the more practical side of her knew it was far more helpful to do as she'd asked. 'Of course I will, darling. How far on are you, do you think?'

'Every ten minutes, and as regular as clockwork. I just hope Danuta gets here in time. I don't fancy doing it on my own,' she said between gritted teeth as another pain swept through her. 'Thanks, Mum.'

Peggy was left with a dead line. She replaced the receiver, looked at her watch and decided the awkward interview with Gracie would have to wait. It was almost time to pick up the girls.

Ron was feeling very much better, so he was quite cheerful as he thanked Danuta for the lift and made his way down the twitten to the back gate. The dogs retrieved their ham bones and ran ahead of him, eagerly anticipating another treat at Beach View.

Ron quickly freed the birds from his pocket and set them squawking and indignant into the coop which he'd cleaned, repaired and restocked with fresh straw the previous week. Having filled the water bowl and scattered the feed, he used his spare key to let himself into Peggy's spotless basement to stow away the rest of the feed in one of her laundry cupboards.

Harvey and Monty saw this as an open invitation and raced up the cellar steps straight into the kitchen.

'Ooh. What's going on?' screeched Cordelia.

Ron hurried up the steps. 'Sorry, old girl. I didn't know you'd be here.'

Cordelia, still bleary from her afternoon nap, and disorientated by the dogs' fulsome greetings, tried to retrieve her knitting from the floor and put her glasses straight. 'And where else would I be, Ronan Reilly?' she snapped.

Ron quickly shooed the dogs back down the steps. 'To be sure 'tis sorry I am we disturbed your beauty sleep, Cordelia,' he said, shooting her his most charming smile. 'But I've brought Peggy a gift, and was just putting away the feed.'

'Tweed? What tweed?' She frowned and twiddled with her hearing aid. 'Why would I want tweed?'

'Chicken feed,' he said, raising his voice. 'I've brought Peggy two chickens and the rest of the bag of feed is in a cupboard downstairs.'

She eyed him sternly over her half-moon glasses. 'Bought or pinched?'

'Bought with hard cash,' he replied, rather hurt that she was the second person today to accuse him of theft. 'But if anyone asks, they were the only survivors of the fox attack and they've been here a long time.'

She heaved a sigh and then broke into a giggle. 'Nothing is ever straightforward with you, is it?'

'Hard times call for diversionary tactics,' he replied with a wink.

'You're a rogue and a scoundrel,' she replied, wagging a finger at him. 'But while you're here, you might as well make yourself useful and put the kettle on. Then you can telephone Rosie. She's been sick with worry about where you've been all day.'

Ron filled the kettle and plonked it on the hob, then went to phone Rosie, all too aware that Cordelia was earwigging from the kitchen doorway.

It wasn't an easy conversation, and Ron could barely get a word in edgewise as Rosie tore him off several strips and ordered him home immediately.

17

Jim had had a busy and fulfilling day, for he'd managed to secure an earlier date for the amputee to be fitted with his new prosthetic, arranged some decent housing for another of the families under his care, and had spent a very enlightening hour with Ernie and a psychiatrist who went under the rather unfortunate sobriquet of 'Squiffy'.

Dr Sam Squires was a very tall, slender man of indeterminate age with pebble-thick glasses and a sleepy left eye which wandered quite disconcertingly until you got used to it. He wore a tweed jacket with leather patches on the elbows, corduroy trousers, and an overlarge jumper over his check shirt. His manner was mild, his voice surprisingly deep, but he seemed to know all the right questions to ask, and listened attentively to the answers.

Once Jim had stopped fighting his long-held prejudice against what he called 'trick-cyclists', he started to relax and found the man surprisingly easy to talk to. He'd come from that meeting an hour later feeling calm, and as if a great weight had been lifted from his shoulders. He thanked Ernie for arranging it all and promised to make time for further visits to the doctor, then headed for home, impatient to tell Peggy all about it.

But as he opened the front door to Beach View, he found it was in chaos. Emily was having a tantrum, Rose and Daisy were squabbling over a doll and

Peggy was ignoring it all as she scrubbed at her kitchen floor.

'Look at my floor,' she shouted above the noise as he walked into the kitchen. 'Your blessed father has tramped half the hills in with his blasted dogs, and frightened poor Cordelia to death. Apart from that, he's dumped chickens in our pen, and has been missing all day. Rosie's been at her wits' end with him. And we've had the police in at the factory, so it's been one disaster after another.'

Jim broke out in a cold sweat. He felt as if he was under fire, the noise echoing in his head and making him want to run for cover. He glanced at Cordelia who'd clearly turned off her hearing aid and was peacefully reading her library book. He envied her. There was no sign of Charlie, and Jim didn't blame him from escaping the bedlam.

He tried to emulate Peggy and ignore the high-pitched shrieking and loud squabbling, but it was hurting his head, and the calm he'd felt on his arrival had been replaced by an overwhelming tension.

'Will you stop that screaming, Emily?' he shouted. 'And you two girls should know better than to fight. Stop it. Stop it now.'

They took absolutely no notice, so Jim grabbed the doll that was being fought over, chucked it to one side, hoisted both girls up and dumped them forcibly onto chairs.

'Sit. Stay, and don't say another word,' he ordered before turning to Emily who was still screeching. 'Be quiet,' he roared.

Emily stared at him in shock and then burst into hysterical tears – which started the other two off.

'Now look what you've done,' hissed Peggy, rushing to try and soothe all three. 'Honestly, Jim. What's got into you, shouting at them like that?'

Jim began to shake. He had to escape before he completely lost control. He turned on his heel, went down the cellar steps and slammed his way out into the back garden, desperate for fresh air and silence.

Yet he could still hear the loud sobbing, so he marched up the path and went into the twitten, putting as much space as he could between him and the chaos of that kitchen.

Reaching the bombed-out ruins of the house on the corner of Camden Road, he stood in the cool, deep shadows and leaned his forehead against the rough remains of a wall. He closed his eyes, concentrated on the relative peace that surrounded him and took a series of deep, shuddering breaths as Squiffy had advised and tried to quell the tremors that shook him. He knew he had to separate the noise of the children from the noise of battle and accept it for what it was – an everyday hazard of living with small girls which posed no mortal danger – but it was easier said than done.

He had no idea of how long he stood there, but gradually his shoulders relaxed and the tremors faded as the tension eased from his spine, and he managed to uncurl his fists. Jim slowly sank onto a pile of rubble and began the familiar ritual of rolling and lighting a cigarette. His hands were still a little unsteady, but the calm had returned and his head was once again clear.

'Jim?'

He looked up to see Peggy standing there in the fading light. 'I'm sorry, Peggy,' he murmured, standing to take her hands. 'I just couldn't take all that noise.'

'I realised that, which is why I left you alone for a while.' She sat beside him on what had once been a concrete step leading to a basement. 'I'm sorry you had to come home to that, Jim,' she murmured. 'But Anne went into labour this afternoon, and as Martin's been delayed I had to keep the girls.'

He mashed out the stub of his cigarette under his heel and put his arm round her shoulders to draw her near. 'It sounds as if you've had one hell of a day,' he said. 'Do you want to tell me about it?'

Peggy shook her head. 'It's not over yet, Jim. I still have to get the girls to bed which will probably turn into a tussle, and I promised Ruby I'd go and see her at the hospital this evening.'

'What's she doing in hospital?'

Peggy told him about Ethel's rapid decline. 'I never liked the woman, but I wouldn't wish that on anybody,' she added. 'And I feel very guilty about not being able to do much to help Ruby when she needs it the most.'

'I think you have quite enough on your hands at the moment,' he replied, kissing the side of her head. 'My darling little mother hen, I am sorry for making things worse earlier.'

She looked up at him. 'But you're all right now?'

He nodded. 'I met a man today who I think can really help me,' he said quietly. 'He's a strange man, but there's a calm about him that's most reassuring, and I get the sense that he really understands what Ernie and I went through.'

'Tell me about him.'

Dusk had turned into darkness and the streetlamps had come on by the time they brushed themselves down and peacefully made their way, hand in hand, home to Beach View.

Ruby had spent the remainder of the morning by Ethel's bedside, returning again after she'd closed the pub at two. Alistair Darwin had called in for twenty minutes during what must have been a busy afternoon, and she'd been glad of his quiet company as they'd sat beside Ethel who had tubes snaking from beneath the bedclothes and several drips attached to her arms. An oxygen mask helped Ethel to breathe, and Alistair explained how the newfangled dialysis machine was cleansing her damaged kidneys in an effort to keep them working. And through it all Ethel was oblivious in her drug-induced sleep.

Ruby had rushed to the shops and bought some scented soap and hand cream for Ethel, and then returned to the pub to make sure Brenda had everything she needed for the evening session. Now she was back in the hushed ward, sitting in the high-backed and not very comfortable bedside chair. She'd brought a book to read but simply couldn't concentrate on it, so set it aside and watched the comings and goings of the nurses and visitors while her mother slept on to the regular beeping of the machines that were keeping her alive.

'Here we are, Ruby dear,' said the lovely plump Jamaican nurse whose smile could light up any room. 'A cup of tea to bring some cheer,' she said, putting the cup and saucer on the nightstand.

'Oh, that's ever so welcome, thanks, Jasmine.'

Jasmine checked Ethel's pulse and temperature, and then changed one of the drips. 'Would you like something to eat? I brought some johnny cakes from home tonight.'

Ruby smiled back at her. 'Thank you, but the tea will be just fine.'

'You don't know what you're missing, girl,' she replied cheerfully. 'My johnny cakes have won prizes.'

Ruby giggled. 'What is a johnny cake when it's at 'ome?'

'I'll bring you a couple,' Jasmine replied and bustled off without waiting for a reply.

Ruby sipped the lovely hot, strong tea and leaned back in the chair. Everyone was being so kind, but they'd been right to warn her of how tiring it was to sit hour after hour at a bedside, especially when the patient was comatose and unreachable. Throughout the day she had found herself checking that Ethel was still breathing, for the shallow rise and fall of her narrow chest was scarcely visible beneath the bedclothes.

'Here we are, honey. This will put some meat on those bones. You English girls are far too skinny.' Jasmine had returned carrying a tray. On it was a glass of milk, what looked like two plump pancakes and a small bowl of something fragrant which made Ruby's mouth water.

'That's my special chilli,' Jasmine said proudly, handing her a spoon and a linen napkin.

Ruby hesitated, for she'd never had chilli and wasn't at all sure if she'd like it. But it smelled delicious and Jasmine was standing over her, arms folded beneath her large bosom, her smile encouraging her to dip the spoon in.

The first taste was warm and delicious, heavy with garlic, onion and herbs. But as she took a second mouthful, the heat increased and it felt as if her mouth was on fire. 'It's burning me,' she gasped.

'Drink some milk, honey,' said Jasmine. 'That will help it down, and use the johnny cake to mop up the best bits.'

Ruby drank some milk and found the combination of the pancake, milk and chilli formed a harmony of sensations in her mouth so tantalising they encouraged her to eat the whole bowl.

'I didn't realise how hungry I was,' she admitted. 'But that was the best thing I've tasted in a long time,' she added, setting the empty bowl back on the tray. 'You must give me the recipe.'

Jasmine beamed in delight. 'I have a whole heap of recipes from home – though it's difficult to find a lot of the ingredients over here. Tomorrow you will try my jerk chicken.' She whipped away the tray and was gone.

Ethel stirred and her eyes fluttered open as she grappled to get the oxygen mask off her face.

Ruby gently stilled her hands. 'Leave it on, Mum. It's helping you to breathe.'

'What's goin' on, Rubes? Who you talking to?' she asked weakly, her voice muffled by the mask.

Ruby took her hand, careful of the drip which was attached to a bag hanging from a metal stand. 'You're in hospital, Mum, and I was just thanking Jasmine for the delicious supper she give me,' she replied.

Ethel grimaced. 'I can smell it,' she muttered. 'Reminds me of the caffs down the docks.'

Ruby knew what she meant, for those eating places were popular with the foreign sailors, and the smells emanating from them were always enticing.

'How are you feeling, Mum? Fancy a sip of milk, or something to eat?'

Ethel shook her head. 'Don't want nothing. Too tired,' she murmured before closing her eyes.

Ruby thought she'd gone to sleep again, so was startled when she suddenly felt her mother's grip tighten on her hand.

'I'm going soon, ain't I?'

'You're not going nowhere for a while yet, Mum.'

Ethel's eyes opened. 'The doc told me at the prison,' she managed, the oxygen mask fogging with her breath. 'That's why I come to find yer.'

'Then why didn't you tell me sooner, Mum?' Ruby asked tearfully. 'I could 'a helped you and not been such a cow.'

'I were 'oping to just slip away when I was at the last hostel,' Ethel said on a sigh. 'But I wanted to see yer first.'

'Oh, Mum. I'm just glad you found me. I'd never forgive meself if you'd gone through this on yer own.'

'Wanted to see you one more time,' she whispered. 'Say I were sorry for not bein' the mum you should've 'ad.'

'I love yer anyway,' said Ruby. 'You're me mum, and always will be.'

Ethel's grip tightened again momentarily and then her hand fell back onto the bedclothes. 'Feels like comin' 'ome with you 'ere,' she whispered.

Ruby held back her tears and was about to reply when she realised Ethel had fallen asleep again. She studiously watched the rise and fall of her chest as she held her hand and let the tears roll unheeded down her face.

There were so many things she wanted to say that might heal the awful rift that had grown between them. So much they should have shared in the past and never got around to it. They were alike in many ways, she realised, for they both put up a façade of being proud and stubborn and confident they could go it alone, when in reality they were just two women who'd seen too much of a dark and cruel world and simply stumbled through it as best they could.

'Hello, Ruby, love.' Peggy slid into the chair next to her and touched her arm.

Ruby's tears were flowing freely as she turned to hug Peggy with a fierceness that startled them both. 'Oh, Auntie Peggy,' she sobbed. 'I'm ever so glad to see you.'

'I'm sorry I couldn't come earlier, but it's been one of those days. There, there, love, you let it all out, that's a good girl,' she crooned.

They eventually drew apart and as Peggy waited for Ruby to compose herself, she regarded Ethel and the machines and tubes that surrounded her. 'How is she doing?'

'As well as possible in the circumstances,' said Ruby, quoting the doctors. 'I ain't had much chance of talking to her cos she's drugged up to the eyeballs, but she just told me she knew she was dying, and that's why she come down 'ere to find me.'

'Oh, Ruby, love,' Peggy sighed.

'At least I were here and not in Canada,' Ruby continued. 'I dunno how I would've felt if she'd 'ad to go through this alone.'

'Thank God for small mercies that she doesn't have to,' said Peggy. 'And you're not to blame yourself for any of this, Ruby, sweetheart. You've done what you could for her, and I'm sure that now she's found you she'll be at peace.'

'That's what Alistair said.'

Peggy frowned.

'Alistair Darwin. The doctor. He was 'ere this afternoon and we had a long chat. He's ever so kind.'

Peggy made no comment, just squeezed her hand in sympathy.

'Alistair said she's not in any pain, which is a huge relief. But he warned me she could linger for a few days yet, and probably not make much sense if she does wake. It's the drugs she's on, see.'

She gave a shuddering sigh. 'I'm just 'oping I get the chance to talk to her again, cos there's lots of things I want to tell her – clear the air, like – make up for all the hurtful things what I said – what we both said.'

'I suspect it's water under the bridge for both of you, love. Ethel wouldn't have come to find you if she thought she'd be turned away – and you wouldn't have taken her in if you really meant what you'd said about never wanting to see her again.'

'Yeah, that's what Alistair said,' she murmured.

Peggy smiled. 'I'm glad you and he are getting on so well,' she said blithely.

'Yeah. He's a nice bloke, and don't put on any airs and graces like most doctors.' Ruby cocked her head, a smile tweaking her lips. 'But I know you, Auntie Peg, and if you think there's anything more goin' on, then you're sorely mistaken.'

Peggy kept her expression innocent. 'As if I would.'

'Oh, you would all right,' Ruby chuckled and gave her another hug. 'I do love you, Auntie Peg. Please don't ever change.'

They were sitting close together and holding hands when Alistair Darwin arrived at the end of the bed. He looked rather startled – or was it disappointed? – to see Peggy there. 'You must be Mrs Reilly,' he said, quickly recovering his cheerful demeanour.

'Indeed I am,' she replied, giving him the once-over and finding the view very pleasant. 'I've just popped in to keep Ruby company, but if you want to see to Ethel, then of course I'll leave.'

'No, it's just a social visit, really,' he replied, his soft brown gaze drifting to Ruby. 'I didn't want Ruby to think she'd been abandoned, but as you're here . . .'

'Why don't you join us?' said Peggy, who'd seen the look that had passed between them.

'I have evening surgery, actually.' He picked up the chart at the end of Ethel's bed, flicked through the sheets of paper fixed to it and put it back. 'That all seems to be fine,' he muttered. 'Goodnight then, ladies. I'll see you tomorrow, Ruby.' He nodded to Peggy and hurried away.

'That was nice of him to call in again,' murmured Peggy.

'Yeah, he's kind like that,' said Ruby, busily digging in her handbag for something.

Peggy was smiling to herself as she walked up Camden Road an hour later. Ruby might not be aware of it yet, but there was definitely something going on there. Alistair's name kept cropping up in her conversation, and when he'd arrived unexpectedly during her visit, Peggy had seen the way he'd looked at Ruby before he'd beaten a hasty retreat. If that wasn't a man smitten, she'd eat her hat. Not her wedding hat, of course. That might soon become rather useful.

She trudged up the cellar steps to the kitchen to find Solly and Jim sitting at the table wreathed in cigar smoke and in deep conversation. 'Hello, you two. What have you done with Cordelia?'

'She went to bed with her library book, saying she needed some peace and quiet after the tantrums earlier. The girls are finally asleep, and as Charlie has homework, he's gone up too.'

Peggy turned to greet Solly. 'I was wondering if you'd call round.'

'The police telephoned me,' he said, rising to his feet to kiss her on each cheek, his Polish ancestral chivalry still to the fore despite the fact he'd been born and raised in England. 'It seems they have two suspects and plan to speak to them tomorrow.'

'One is Gracie Smith, isn't it?' Solly nodded, and Peggy continued, 'I hoped it wasn't. That girl's been through enough without being arrested.'

'I'm not familiar with her background,' said Solly. 'With so many women on my payroll it's hard to keep up with them all.'

'She's twenty-six. Married in haste at twenty and had her son five months later. Her husband was killed in Normandy, and her house was bombed in the last raid we had here. She and her little boy are sharing a house with another woman and her three children and she's been struggling to keep body and soul together ever since. She's a good machinist, a team player with no previous hint of wrongdoing, and popular with everyone.'

Peggy gave a sigh. 'Unfortunately, she's recently got involved with Phil Warner – ex-convict, fly-by-night and ne'er-do-well. I wouldn't mind betting he had a hand in all this.'

'But how would either of them have got hold of the keys?' Solly asked.

'That's what I don't understand,' she said. 'They rarely leave my side, and John White is meticulous about keeping his set in his office safe.'

'Perhaps the police know more than they're letting on,' he said gruffly. 'They didn't tell me much on the telephone.' He stubbed out the remains of his cigar. 'But if they know about Gracie's connection to Warner, they're probably searching both their places right now.'

'Warner wouldn't be stupid enough to leave stolen goods anywhere that would lead back to him,' Peggy said. 'He's more likely to have hidden them in some lock-up – or they could even be on their way to London to flog at the markets.'

'I've already put the word out in London,' Solly said. 'If that material ends up there, I'll hear about it.' He got to his feet and shook Jim's hand. 'Thanks for your company, Jim. And I'll get back to you on the matter of hiring your Sam Healey by the end of the week. I'll need someone reliable now Farley's retiring.'

Peggy helped him on with his heavy camel coat and handed him his brown fedora. 'I am sorry this has happened, Solly.'

'*Oy vey*, Peggy. It's not your fault. In this business there are always thieves and they seem to be getting more cunning. I'll pop up to see you at the factory tomorrow.'

Jim and Peggy saw him to the front door and watched him climb into his Rolls-Royce. The expensive engine purred as he drove down the cul-de-sac, headlights blazing, heading for Rachel and home.

Jim put his arm around Peggy and closed the door behind him. 'I don't know about you, but I've had enough for one day – and it looks as if tomorrow isn't going to be any easier, especially for you. Early night?'

'That would be lovely,' she sighed, 'but I have ironing to do, and Charlie's games kit is still in the washing machine.'

He smiled down at her fondly. 'Tell you what, Peggy. How about I do the ironing and you finish up whatever else there is to do?'

'You? Ironing?' she gasped in disbelief.

'We Chindits can turn our hands to anything. And it has been said that I'm a dab hand at ironing, so don't mock.'

She laughed. 'As if I would,' she said, nudging him gently in the ribs. 'I'll get the ironing board out and you can show me just how clever you are. You never know – you might earn a Brownie badge.'

'I can think of something better than a badge to earn,' he replied, playfully grabbing her bottom.

'Jim Reilly, behave yourself,' she giggled, slapping away his roving hands.

18

Rosie was not in the best of moods. She'd spent the day hunting high and low for Ron, and getting increasingly worried as the light faded and there was still no sign of him. When he'd finally telephoned from Beach View she'd let rip, and now, as she heard his key in the front door, she was fully prepared to really give him what for.

The dogs came rushing in, took one look at her and sensed trouble. With their tails between their legs, they beat a hasty retreat.

'Hello, my wee girl,' he said, coming into the room rather unsteadily but with a smile so lacking in guilt, she could have slapped him.

'Don't wee girl me,' she retorted. 'You've been missing all day. And look at the state of you. Where have you been?'

'Ach, to be sure I was fetching hens from Chalky's place. It took a bit longer than I expected, but they're safe and sound at Peggy's now.' He took a step towards her. 'Are you not going to give me a kiss, darlin'?'

Rosie folded her arms and glared at him. 'It's after eight,' she said. 'You telephoned from Beach View at two in the afternoon. Where have you been since then?'

He backed off and wouldn't meet her gaze. 'It was thirsty work walking all that way,' he mumbled. 'So I had a cup of tea with Cordelia to keep her company, and then stopped off to see Stan for a drop of beer up at his allotment. We got talking and the time sort of ran away with me.'

'I see,' she fumed. 'So you went for a beer with Stan, even though you knew I'd been worried sick about you all day?'

He eyed her warily from beneath his brows. 'Ach, Rosie. To be fair, darlin', I told you I was fine, but you sounded so cross, I thought I'd give you a bit of time to cool down before I got home.'

'Cool down?' she snapped. 'How can I ever be cool when married to a man who thinks and acts like a naughty schoolboy? Damn right I'm cross,' she continued furiously. 'And you still haven't told me what happened to you up in those blasted hills.'

He frowned. 'Happened?'

'Don't act the innocent, Ron. It won't wash.'

'Oh, that,' he breathed with a wide-eyed look that didn't fool her one bit. 'That was nothing. I just decided to have a bit of a rest, but I'm fine now.' He frowned again. 'But how did you know?'

'Danuta rang to ask if you were all right after she had to revive you and drive you to Peggy's. She said she'd found you slumped in a heap in the middle of nowhere, and in a dead faint.'

'Aye, well, she was exaggerating a bit, to be sure. It was a hot day and I was feeling a bit under the weather, so I thought a wee sleep might improve things,' he muttered, reaching into his pocket for his pipe and tobacco.

'Feeling the effects of Chalky's home brew more like,' she snapped.

'Ach, to be sure, the wee man's tipple has a fierce kick to it, so it does.' He fiddled with his pipe and shot her a hopeful smile. 'But all's well that ends well, Rosie. I'm home now.'

Rosie refused to be charmed out of her bad mood. 'Home, you might be. But what will you be up to tomorrow or the next day?' she said flatly. 'I'm sick of it, Ron. Sick of putting up with all your stupid pranks and thoughtless carryings-on. Any more of it and I'll pack your bags and send you back to Peggy – if she'll have you.'

He looked at her like a cowed puppy. 'Ach, Rosie, love, you don't mean that.'

He tried to reach for her hand but she snatched it away. 'I wouldn't put it to the test,' she warned. 'Because I *do* mean it this time. And if there's one more incident involving matrons, hens, illicit booze or disappearing for hours, those bags will be on the doorstep and I'll change the locks.'

He looked at her aghast. 'But I love you, Rosie,' he managed.

'I love you too, God help me,' she sighed. 'But you'd exhaust the patience of a saint, and I really have had enough of it all.'

'Oh, darling,' he murmured, tenderly taking her into his arms. 'I'm sorry.'

She remained unyielding within his embrace. 'I know you are,' she said wearily. 'You're always sorry after the event, but that doesn't stop you from repeating it over and over again, does it? Why can't you be like other men of your age and just behave yourself?'

He nuzzled her neck. ''Tis the awful legacy of the Irish in me,' he murmured. 'Born with too much imagination, and a liking for a bit of mischief to liven things up now and again. Besides, Rosie, you wouldn't love me as much if I was like other men and life became boring.'

She began to giggle, and he seemed to sense she was weakening, for he held her closer and nuzzled her neck again.

'Stop that,' she protested weakly.

'Ach, you know you like it,' he replied.

Rosie tried to resist, but it was impossible. 'Life is certainly never boring with you,' she admitted reluctantly. 'But please, just for once, try not to get into any more trouble.'

'Rosie, my wee girl, I'll do me best, but fate seems to have a habit of tripping me up, and before I know it, I'm in the soup again.'

She eased herself from his embrace before things got out of hand. 'Talking of trouble,' she said, rather breathlessly, 'Matron telephoned. You left your overnight bag in the locker, and she expects you to fetch it from her office tomorrow at ten sharp.'

She saw the pleading look in his eyes. 'No, I'm not going to do it, Ron. You will. And you'll apologise to her while you're at it.'

Ron gave a huge sigh to show he was utterly defeated. 'To be sure that woman is a punishment in herself.'

'And one you absolutely deserve,' she managed before bursting into a fit of giggles.

The telephone rang early the next morning and Peggy dashed in from feeding the chickens to answer it; knowing it could mean only one thing.

'Mama Peggy? Is Danuta. Anne is well and has a beautiful baby boy.'

'Oh, Danuta, how lovely. Are they both well? How much did he weigh?'

'They are both well, but Anne had to be admitted to hospital.' She hurried on before Peggy could panic. 'She is fine. But baby was too big and took too long to be born. She have to have caesarean.'

'I must go to her,' breathed Peggy.

'No, Mama Peggy. She not see visitors until this evening. It was a very long labour and she needs to rest.'

'But she's all right? There are no complications?' Peggy fretted.

'Everything is very fine. Please not worry, Mama Peggy. I would not lie to you. But she ask if you could keep girls for one more night, please. Martin is home late this evening.'

'Of course I will,' she replied, wondering how the rest of the family would feel about that after the shenanigans of last night. 'Are you visiting Anne today?'

'I will see her on my usual rounds. I will of course send her your love and tell her the girls are very happy to be with you. Congratulations, Mama Peggy. Your grandson is fine bouncing boy of eight pounds nine ounces. Anne said to tell you his name is Oscar James.'

'Oscar? Where on earth did she get that from?'

'I not know, but is fine name, yes? I must go. Another patient is in need of me. I will call in to see you when I can.'

Danuta cut the connection and Peggy gave a sigh as she replaced the receiver.

'I heard most of that,' said Jim, who'd followed her into the hall. 'I take it we're the proud grandparents of a boy called Oscar.'

'Oscar James, actually,' she said, beaming up at him. 'Eight pounds nine ounces, he was, and very reluctant to face the world. No wonder poor Anne needed a caesarean.'

'It sounds to me as if there's more hospital visiting on the cards,' said Jim dourly. 'Better get the breakfast on, Peg. We'll need something to fortify us for another busy day.'

Peggy bustled into the kitchen. 'Anne's had her baby,' she announced joyfully. 'Eight pounds and nine ounces. They're calling him Oscar James.'

'Oh, how lovely,' twittered Cordelia. 'I must finish that matinee jacket I was knitting.'

Peggy fervently hoped that Cordelia wouldn't notice that she'd actually unravelled it and started it again, leaving only a few rows of knitting for her to finish off. 'She'll love it,' she said enthusiastically.

Turning to the three little girls who were sleepily eating their bowls of cereal, she said, 'Rose, Emily. You have a little brother. Isn't that wonderful?'

'Can we go and see him?' asked Rose excitedly.

'I don't want a brother,' said Emily moodily. 'Why can't I have a puppy instead?'

'Is he my brother too?' piped up Daisy.

'A brother is far more exciting than a puppy,' Peggy said cheerfully to Emily. 'We'll all go and see him and your mum this evening. Won't that be lovely? And no, Daisy, he's not your brother. He's your cousin – or your . . .' She looked at Jim because she wasn't absolutely sure what he must be.

He frowned as he thought about it and was saved by Charlie. 'Anne is mine and Daisy's sister, therefore Oscar is our nephew, just as Rose and Emily are our nieces. Why on earth did they pick such an odd name?'

'Who knows,' said Jim. 'Just be thankful he's arrived safely, and your sister's all right.' He ruffled Charlie's hair and earned himself a scowl. 'Think of all that babysitting pocket money you'll be earning, lad, and cheer up.'

Charlie carefully smoothed his hair back into place, glowered at everyone and continued eating his cereal in his usual early morning silence.

Peggy went to the fridge and dug out the bacon rashers and the week's egg rations, then fetched another tin of baked beans and the bread. 'Get me some of the last tomatoes from the garden, will you, Jim? This calls for a celebration, and a proper fry-up.'

She concentrated on cooking the breakfast and getting all the lunch boxes ready, but her mind was flitting between Anne and the problems she'd have to face in the factory later. Something Solly had said the night before had sparked a flare of elusive memory that simply wouldn't fully reveal itself, and it was driving her round the bend trying to think what it could mean – and how it could possibly have any connection to the robbery.

The three little girls eyed Jim warily as he moved about the kitchen – perhaps remembering his anger of the previous evening – whatever it was, they sat, good as gold, waiting for Peggy to put the plates of breakfast in front of them.

'What were all those letters that came, yesterday, Peggy?' asked Cordelia once she'd perused the headlines of the newspaper.

'I haven't had a chance to even open them yet,' said Peggy, putting the last of the plates on the table and sitting down. 'From the handwriting, I'd say they were from Jane and Sarah, and Fran. You can read them if you want,' she offered. 'I doubt I'll have much time to myself today either.'

'I'd like the ones from Sarah and Jane,' Cordelia replied. 'My great-nieces seem to have such exciting lives over there in America, and it quite makes me want to travel.' She gave a little sigh. 'But I suppose I've left it far too late to be gallivanting halfway across the world. I've never really been anywhere, you know. Only here and London, and I didn't think much of London.'

'According to Cissy, London is the place to be right now,' said Peggy, tucking into the hearty meal. 'Which reminds me, I must telephone and tell her Anne's news.'

She reached across and stilled Emily's hand as she began to bang her spoon on the table. 'We don't do that, Emily,' she said calmly. 'If you've finished your breakfast you can get down from the table.'

'But I want toast,' she replied moodily.

'If you say please, then you might get some,' replied Peggy with a steady look.

Emily glanced at Jim from beneath her eyelashes before answering. 'Please,' she said begrudgingly, and put down the spoon.

Peggy kept putting the slices of bread in her swanky new toaster until everyone had enough, and then sat down to finish her cooling breakfast and enjoy a cup of tea. Once her plate was empty, she dug into her handbag to retrieve the letters and, with some reluctance, handed them to Cordelia, hoping they contained good news. There was too much drama in her life at the moment, and she certainly didn't need any more.

Keeping an eye on the time, she managed to get everyone ready. Once she'd seen Jim and Charlie off, she kissed Cordelia goodbye and chivvied the girls out of the house and into the car. The weather was unpredictable at the moment, so she made sure they all had raincoats, and stowed the big black umbrella on the parcel shelf at the back of the car just in case.

Having dropped Emily at the crèche without too much kerfuffle, she took the girls to school, and then headed for the factory estate. She would ring Cissy and Ron from the office if she had time, and perhaps even phone Auntie Vi down in Somerset so she could pass Anne's news on to Bob, who would be busy with the harvesting.

However, the best laid plans were hostages to fate, and it appeared that Solly and the police were already at the factory.

Peggy parked between the Rolls-Royce and the police car, and sat for a long moment in deep thought.

The silence and calm of the deserted estate finally gave her the time and space to unearth the elusive fragments of information from her mind and slot them together like a jigsaw puzzle. What they revealed was quite startling, but at last it all made sense.

Fearing she might just be fitting things together to suit her need to protect Gracie's reputation, she ran through the scenario once more. Now, quite certain that she was right but dreading having to face Solly with it, she climbed out of the car and walked into the cavernous factory, her footsteps echoing in the heavy silence.

Sergeant Mayhew and Solly were in her office, making themselves at home with cups of tea and cigars. She went in and greeted Solly warmly, then opened the window to let the smoke out and stared at Mayhew until he reluctantly moved from her chair to a less comfortable one.

She hadn't taken to the young and rather arrogant Mayhew on their first meeting, for he'd been seconded down here from London, thought they all had straw in their hair and regarded himself as far too superior to be dealing with what he clearly saw as petty theft amongst the local yokels.

She sat down, placed her bag on the desk, and looked at him squarely. 'I understand you have two suspects,' she began. 'Phil Warner and Gracie Smith.'

'That's right,' said Mayhew. 'We've interviewed them both and released them under police bail until they can be questioned further.'

'And did your search of their premises find anything incriminating?'

Mayhew's gaze shifted. 'We searched all known premises linked to both of them but found nothing,' he said reluctantly. 'But we know the two of them are in a relationship, and with Warner's record of robbery and house-breaking, it's only a matter of time before we can tie them in with it.'

'But what if it isn't Gracie Smith who is involved?' asked Peggy.

She turned to Solly, who'd so far remained silent, allowing her to lead the conversation. 'There is someone else, Solly. But you're not going to like it.' She took a breath and named the man she suspected of being in cahoots with Warner.

Solly looked startled. 'Surely you can't really suspect him of having anything to do with this, Peggy? He's been with me for years.'

'I know, but if you hear me out, Solly, you'll understand why I'm certain he's far more involved in the robbery than Gracie ever was.'

Solly and Mayhew remained silent as Peggy outlined her reasons for the surprising accusation, and although Solly's expression darkened throughout the telling, she could see that he was beginning to understand how Peggy had put the pieces of random information together to make an unsavoury picture.

'It sounds as if you've really thought about this,' rumbled Solly. 'But I still don't understand how he could have been so stupid as to have got involved with Warner in the first place.'

'Warner was blackmailing him,' said Peggy.

'How the hell do you know that?' breathed Solly.

'I hear things, Solly. In here, in the pub, and in the queues outside the shops. I don't take much notice of it, but now and again someone lets something slip and I realise it isn't tittle-tattle but a useful piece of information to ferret away in case it's needed later. Warner had obviously heard it too, because I overheard a snatch of conversation between the two men that morning outside Plummers, and Warner's attitude was definitely menacing as he took charge of a large envelope.'

She took a deep breath. 'I didn't take much notice at the time as I was occupied in a rather heated exchange with someone else, but even so, it struck me as very suspicious.'

'I really think you've let your imagination run away with you, Peggy,' said Solly. 'I know you think a lot of Gracie Smith, but really, what you're suggesting is preposterous.'

'Oh, I'm not saying she's entirely innocent,' she replied quickly. 'But pillow talk is a dangerous thing, and knowing Warner, he probably wheedled a lot of information out of her about the way we do things here without her realising what he was up to.'

She could see that Solly didn't really want to believe what she was telling him, so she hurried on. 'Warner would realise that his relationship with Gracie would be common knowledge, so she would be the first person to be suspected of aiding and abetting in the crime should he be hauled in by the police. But once he had the information he needed from Gracie, he used blackmail to get hold of the keys.'

'Well, it's all supposition at the moment,' said Mayhew, 'and my money's still on Warner and Smith. But I suppose it wouldn't hurt to do a background check on this man and see what he has to say. Where does he live?'

Peggy gave him the address and then turned to Solly. 'Jim said you were going to give one of his men a trial at doing your books. Can I suggest you give him a set from here just to check that nothing else is amiss?'

'I really don't like what you're implying, Peggy,' he said. 'But as I've never had cause to distrust your judgement, you'd better give me the books for the past year and I'll let Jim's chap go through them.'

He gave a deep sigh. 'I really don't want to believe all this, Peggy. That man's been with me almost from the start of my business down here. I've been good to him, trusted him. I hope to God you're wrong.'

'I'll go and interview him and see what he has to say,' said Mayhew, closing his notebook with a snap. 'But in the meantime, I suggest you keep a more watchful eye on what comes in and goes out of this factory, Mrs Reilly.'

He strode out of the office and she and Solly sat in silence as they heard the police car's tyres screeching on the tarmac as he drove away at speed.

'I'm so sorry, Solly. He's right. I should have kept a closer eye on things. And I feel quite ill about it all, but if justice is to be served, then surely it's right to make absolutely sure the police get the real culprits?'

'Peggy, you're the most reliable, honest and loyal person I know, but I do wish you'd said something to me when you first suspected he was up to no good.'

'But I didn't, don't you see?' she protested. 'It was two fleeting instances, and a snippet of gossip. It wasn't until you visited last night that they began to make sense.'

He heaved a great sigh, mashed out his cigar in the ashtray and put on his hat. 'Give me the books, Peggy. I need to get back to the other factory and see if this chap of Jim's is as good as he says. If your suspicions turn out to be right, then my faith in my fellow man will never be the same.'

Peggy opened the safe and handed him the ledgers. 'I'm so sorry,' she said again.

'Enough already with the apologies, Peggy,' he said. 'What is done is done.'

Peggy watched him stride away, his shoulders slumped in disappointment that someone he'd trusted for years could have cheated him.

She closed the office door, resumed her seat behind her desk and lit a cigarette, not caring that she wasn't really supposed to smoke in here. But it had been one heck of a morning, Solly and Mayhew had already filled the room with their cigar smoke, and she needed ten minutes of peace to calm down and prepare for a very tricky conversation with Gracie Smith – if the girl turned up for her shift – which was highly unlikely in the circumstances.

However, as the women began to pour into the factory, it was clear that word of the robbery and those suspected of it had travelled fast and become the most eagerly discussed topic as they took their time to settle down behind their machines.

Peggy didn't see Gracie amongst them but heard her name being mentioned several times, and knew that if she didn't say something there'd be little work done today, and the girl's reputation would be in ruins. She stubbed out her cigarette, tugged her jacket straight and headed purposefully for the front of the factory floor.

The chattering died to a whisper and she finally had their attention. 'You all know the police have been asking questions about the missing bolts of fabric,' she said, her voice echoing in the stillness of the vast room. 'And I'd just like to warn you that salacious gossip and unsubstantiated rumour will not help anyone's cause – in fact, it could make things far worse. It's up to the police to do the detective work, not you. So, I'd like you all to keep your opinions to yourself and get on with your work without any further delay.'

Peggy saw several of the women glance towards Gracie Smith's empty chair before they reluctantly started their machines. But it seemed her little ticking off had worked for now, and she breathed a sigh of relief.

'Flo. Could you come into my office, please?'

Peggy followed the line manager in and closed the door. 'It's going to be difficult to stop the rumour mill,

I'm afraid, Flo, but until this is resolved, we'll just have to put up with it. Did Gracie say anything to you about all this once the theft had been discovered?'

Florence Hillier was a woman in her forties who'd once been in charge of an ATS platoon and, although fair in her judgements, expected a high standard of discipline from those in her charge and stood no nonsense. But Peggy knew she'd taken Gracie under her wing when she'd first started here, and probably knew more about her than anyone.

'She never said anything to me, but now I think about it, she was looking a bit green around the gills when she heard the cloth was missing, and after we'd all been questioned by the police, her work was not her usual high standard.'

Peggy knew Flo would have questioned Gracie about that, but it seemed she was reluctant to say more. 'If you know something, Flo, then please tell me. It's important.'

Flo gave a sigh. 'She just said she had a terrible headache and asked me if she could go home half an hour early. She certainly didn't look right, and it could explain the poor work she'd done that day.'

She took a quick breath. 'Mrs Reilly, I know she's involved with Warner, and I did try to put her straight about him, but he can be a charmer when he needs to be, and she was lonely and flattered by his attention. You don't really think she's involved, do you?'

'I certainly don't want her to be,' admitted Peggy. She looked back at the other woman and smiled. 'Thanks, Flo. You can go back to your duties now.'

It was five minutes to ten and Ron was in great danger of being late for his appointment with Matron, but he was in no real hurry. He returned from walking the dogs to find a note from Rosie telling him she'd gone to the Town Hall to catch up on some work before popping in to see Ruby, and wanted him to meet her at the Officers' Club for lunch at one o'clock.

Ron groaned at this, for it meant he'd have to smarten up if they were going there – and probably even to have a shave. Feeling hard done by, he took his time to feed the dogs and check on his ferrets. Then he sat down to a welcome cup of tea.

Without bothering to change out of his disreputable clothes just yet, he rammed his battered hat onto his head and left the house at five past ten. It was only a short walk to the hospital – and what was six minutes in the grand scheme of things?

However, he hadn't factored in meeting his pal Harry who was coming down the steps as he was about to go up them. 'Hello, Harry,' he said, coming to a halt. 'Do you make a habit of hanging about out here?'

'It's better than hanging about in there and being at everyone's beck and call.' Harry lit a cigarette. 'What you doing back so soon, Ron? I'd have thought you'd seen enough of this place.'

'I've got an appointment with Matron,' he replied.

Harry clapped him on the shoulder. 'Bad luck, mate. But if you will cause ructions, what do you expect? You're the talk of the hospital, you know.'

'Glad I'm famous for something,' Ron said. The scent of Harry's cigarette was making him wonder if he should risk a quick puff on his pipe before he went in to face the music. But the echoes of Rosie's telling-off the previous evening warned him it would probably be foolhardy, so he didn't tempt fate.

'You're getting to be a proper Houdini, Ron. Perhaps you should take it up as a new career?'

'It wouldn't be half the fun if I had to do it every day,' he replied. 'Besides, it gets me into trouble with the wife.'

'Tell me about it,' said Harry with a wink. 'My missus is always on at me for something or other.' He clucked his tongue. 'Women, eh?'

'I'd better get going or I'll be late,' said Ron as the Town Hall clock struck quarter past ten.

Harry shot him a broad grin. 'Let me know how it went,' he said. 'I'll be out here when you get back – if you get back. That one could strike a man dead with one look.'

Ron stomped up the steps thinking that Harry was on to a good thing working here. Not that he ever seemed to actually do any work, but spent most of his time gossiping and smoking with the other porters and ambulance crews. He was a lazy so-and-so really, and Ron didn't blame his missus for constantly nagging him.

He ambled towards Matron's office, which was on the ground floor. He'd been there before when the last one had been in charge, and that hadn't been a particularly pleasant experience, so he didn't expect this one to be either. He rapped on the door, knowing he was late, but not particularly bothered by whatever trouble it might cause.

The door opened and Matron stood there grim-faced and smelling of carbolic soap and disinfectant, her starched cap positively trembling with annoyance. 'You're late,' she said by way of greeting.

'Ach, to be sure it's only by a few minutes,' Ron replied with a winning smile.

'Sixteen minutes, to be exact,' she snapped. 'I have a busy hospital to run and do not appreciate having my schedule disrupted by the likes of you.'

He decided discretion was the better part of valour and kept his mouth shut.

'I am waiting,' she said, looking down her nose at him.

He frowned. 'For what?

'For an apology,' she replied tartly.

'I'm not apologising,' he said, raising himself to his full height and filling her doorway with his breadth. 'I have no regrets about leaving these premises, and certainly have no wish to converse further with you. Give me my property, and I'll leave you to your schedule.'

She tried to stare him down but it had no effect, and they both became aware of the attention they were drawing from the slow-moving stream of people going to and fro in the corridor.

Ron glared back, perfectly willing to stand there all day if necessary. He'd faced far worse enemies than Matron, and a lifetime's experience of dealing with bullies had imbued him with endless, stubborn patience.

She was the first to break eye contact. She stuck out her foot and shoved his overnight bag towards him with such force it shot into the corridor and almost tripped up a hurrying nurse. Before Ron could react, she'd slammed the door in his face.

Ron apologised to the nurse, picked up his bag and marched back down the corridor with a broad grin on his face.

'Good morning again, Harry,' he said cheerfully as he ran down the steps. 'Don't you ever have any work to do?'

Harry grinned back at him. 'Not if I can help it.' He cocked his head. 'You look remarkably cheerful for a man who's been in the lion's den.'

'She's no lion, Harry. Just a rather sour puss. See you around.' He swung the overnight bag over his shoulder and whistled a happy tune as he strolled out of the hospital grounds and headed for home. It was a lovely day, Matron was back in her lair, Rosie had forgiven him, and all was right with his world.

Rosie's business at the Town Hall took less than an hour as most of the other councillors were still in Bournemouth, and there were only a couple of letters to deal with. Having dictated the replies to her secretary, she avoided bumping into anyone who might tell her off for missing the conference and then popped round the back of the Crown to see Gloria.

'Blimey,' Gloria said upon opening the door. 'You're out and about early, Rosie.'

'I have things to do,' she replied, taking in the flimsy wrap over the flimsier nightdress – which left little to the imagination in the bright sunlight – the high-heeled mules with their swansdown fluff at the toes, and the bristle of curlers beneath the headscarf.

'Pushing it a bit for time, aren't you, Gloria? You're due to open in less than an hour.'

'It don't take me long to put the slap on,' she replied. 'Wanna join me for a cuppa while I get ready?'

'I can't stop as I'm on my way to see Ruby at the hospital. I just wanted you to know that Ethel is dying, and the poor girl is spending every hour she can by her bedside. I'm sure she'd appreciate us popping in from time to time with little treats, or just for a bit of company.'

'Yeah, of course. I'll drop in this afternoon.' Gloria leaned nonchalantly against the door jamb, seemingly unaware she was all but naked and on view to anyone who passed by the open back gate. 'What about the pub?'

'Brenda's managing at the moment, but she might need some help if Ethel lingers for too long.' Rosie took a breath. 'I know it sounds heartless, but I hope she goes quickly. Poor Ruby's had enough to cope with these past two years, and that mother of hers doesn't deserve all that devotion.'

'I'm with you there,' said Gloria around the cigarette she was lighting. 'And having to pay Brenda a full-time wage ain't gunna help her bank balance, neither.' She stood straight and stuck two fingers up at a man who'd paused, open-mouthed, to ogle her.

'Tell you what, Rosie. I'll go round just before two and have a chat with Brenda. See if she'll agree to me taking on the evenings. I got enough staff 'ere for the rest of the week, it's just the weekends what might cause a problem.'

'Yes, it's a busy time,' murmured Rosie. 'I'd offer to do a shift, but Ron needs me at home.'

'Yeah, I 'eard he was under the weather.' Gloria grinned. 'Didn't stop him doing a runner from the hospital, though, did it?'

Rosie sighed in exasperation. 'I didn't realise his latest escapade had become common knowledge.'

Gloria laughed and mashed out her cigarette beneath the toe of her high-heeled mule, the swansdown in danger of being set alight. 'This town's lifeblood is gossip, Rosie. You should know that by now.'

'I'd better let you get on,' said Rosie, eager to be gone. 'If you need me, you know where I am.'

She hurried out of the gate and down the alley into the High Street. Gloria had a heart of gold, but she did wish she wouldn't flaunt herself like that. Anyone would think she was on the game – which was entirely the wrong impression, for Rosie knew Gloria kept her favours strictly for one man, and had done for years. The fact it was a secret still was a minor miracle considering how quickly gossip could spread in this town of busybodies.

Rosie stopped off to buy some flowers and a bar of Five Boys chocolate, and then hurried on to the hospital. She made her way to Ethel's ward and pushed open the door. She'd never been in here before and was pleasantly surprised to find how bright and airy it was compared to the other wards.

'I've come to see Ethel Sharp,' she told the nurse who came to greet her.

'Ethel's asleep but Ruby is with her, and will probably appreciate a visit. She's been here since before dawn and is looking very tired,' she confided quietly.

'I'll see if I can persuade her to come with me to the Lilac Tearooms,' replied Rosie.

The nurse nodded and led the way down the ward to where the flower-printed screens were shielding the bed. 'I'll take these and put them in water,' she said, reaching for the flowers before bustling quietly off.

Rosie stepped warily around the screens, not at all sure of what she'd find. When she saw that Ruby was asleep in the bedside chair, she stayed where she was and took in the scene.

Ethel was almost hidden by the oxygen mask and pile of bedding and seemed to have shrunk in the two days since she'd last seen her. There were tubes and bags and pipes and weird machines softly thrumming, and she wondered for a moment if Ethel was already dead. But a closer look confirmed she was still breathing, so with a sigh of relief, Rosie turned her attention to Ruby.

Ruby's head was resting against the wing of the high-backed chair, her hair hanging over her shoulders in disarray, her dark lashes not quite hiding the bruises of tiredness beneath her eyes, or the paleness of her face. She looked so very young and vulnerable, it twisted Rosie's tender heart.

Deciding not to wake her, she quietly backed out from the screens and came face to face with Danuta. She quickly put her finger to her lips and indicated they should talk elsewhere. Having left the chocolates and books she'd brought with the nurse, she followed Danuta through a side door and out into the back garden.

'I never knew this was here,' she said in astonishment as she took in the bright flower beds and the pleasant terrace with its comfortable chairs.

'It's for the patients like Ethel, and their visitors,' said Danuta. 'I am guessing that Ruby is sleeping. How does she look?'

'Worn out and vulnerable,' replied Rosie. 'And it's only been four days since Ethel first put in an appearance.'

'She's young and strong and will survive. It's always harder on the visitors than it is on the patients, Rosie. Ethel is heavily medicated and will know nothing of what Ruby is going through.'

'How long do you think it'll be before . . .?'

'Not long,' Danuta replied. She smiled at Rosie. 'By the way, congratulations.'

'What for?'

'Mama Peggy did not tell you?' she asked in amazement.

'Tell me what? Come on, Danuta, spit it out.'

'Anne has had baby boy. A new great-grandson for you and Ron,' she replied with a beaming smile.

The news made Rosie feel positively ancient. 'How lovely,' she said, trying her best to be enthusiastic – although being a great-grandmother by proxy before she'd turned sixty was not her idea of fun. 'Ron will be over the moon to have another boy in the family after all those girls. But I'm really surprised Peggy didn't tell us.'

'I telephone her very early this morning, but perhaps she is busy at work. I hear there has been a robbery at the factory.'

'That'll be it then,' Rosie said. 'This robbery, what was taken, do you know?'

'Bolts of expensive cloth is what I heard. The police are most interested in one of the girls on the machines and a man called Philip Warner.'

'Well, I'm not surprised to hear he's involved. Phil Warner was the boyfriend of Ethel's pal, Olive. It was suspected he helped to fence the stuff they stole from the Red Cross collection centre. The police didn't have enough to arrest him, and as Ethel and Olive refused to admit he was part of it all, he got away with it.'

Danuta nodded solemnly. 'This I have heard. But only one month later he was caught stealing a shipment of cigarettes and alcohol, and went to prison for four years.'

'My word,' breathed Rosie. 'You do get to hear a lot, don't you?'

Danuta shrugged. 'People talk. It is part of my job to listen.' She looked at her watch. 'I must go. I have baby clinic.'

Rosie gave her a quick hug. 'I'll just pop in and see if Ruby's awake, then I'm meeting Ron at the Officers' Club for lunch. Try not to work too hard, Danuta, and give that lovely husband of yours my very best wishes.'

'Thank you. I will tell him.'

Danuta hurried away and Rosie returned to the ward to discover that Ruby was awake, but not alone.

'Hello, Dr Darwin. I'm sorry, am I interrupting?'

'Och, no, not at all,' he replied, colour rising in his tanned face as he shot to his feet. 'I was just checking on Ethel and making sure Ruby has everything she needs.'

Rosie smiled and waited for him to make his rather hurried exit, then sat in the vacated chair next to Ruby. 'Well, you're looking much better,' she said to Ruby after giving her a hug. 'It's amazing what a visit from our young and unattached Alistair Darwin can do.'

'Don't talk daft, Rosie,' she retorted. 'Honestly, you're as bad as Auntie Peggy. He were just here to check on Mum, and cos he woke me up, he stopped for a bit of a chat.'

Yes, thought Rosie. *And pigs might fly*. 'Of course he did,' she said. 'I've brought you some books to read and a bar of Five Boys chocolate. And there should be some flowers somewhere,' she added, looking round for them.

'Jasmine put them with the others on the windowsill out there,' Ruby said. 'There ain't no room in 'ere what with all the machines and that.'

'I went to see Gloria this morning,' Rosie began. 'We're both worried you're doing too much and overspending on wages. She suggested she'd do the evening shifts until Thursday night to save you having to pay Brenda, but the weekend could be a problem as she'll be busy at the Crown and won't be able to spare any of her bar staff.'

'I can afford it, Rosie, really I can, so neither of you needs to worry on that score.' Ruby gave a regretful sigh and regarded the still figure on the bed. 'I doubt she'll see in the weekend, so nothing much else matters really.'

'Have you managed to talk to her at all since she's been in here?'

'A couple of times. But since then she ain't made much sense – just muttering and talking gibberish.'

They sat together and listened to the machines whirring and the soft murmurs and rustles of the nurses moving about on the other side of the screens.

Rosie decided Ruby needed cheering up a bit, so told her about the latest run-in she'd had with Ron, and the trouble he'd caused at the hospital.

'I'm glad that Matron never comes in 'ere,' said Ruby at the end of the long and amusing story. 'She sounds a right tartar.'

'Oh, I think Ron has her measure. He's usually very good at dealing with women like that, and I suspect he came out of that meeting the victor.'

She looked at her watch. 'I'm sorry, love, but I have to go. Gloria promised to drop in to see you this afternoon, and I expect Peggy will too after she's visited her newest grandson.'

Ruby's face lit up. 'Oh, she will be relieved he's arrived at last. I know she was worried about how long Anne was carrying.'

Rosie hugged her. 'Don't you worry about Peggy. She frets enough for everyone, and it's mostly unnecessary. I'll leave her to tell you all about the new baby and pop in again tomorrow. Should you need anything in the meantime, just telephone me.'

19

Peggy was relieved to see it was almost time for her to get out of her office and collect the girls. The atmosphere was still heavy with rumour and dour mutterings; there had been no further word from the police, and she'd been fretting all day about what the new man at Solly's might find in those account ledgers.

She put down the receiver, frustrated by the fact she couldn't get hold of Cissy, Rosie or Ron, but at least she'd managed to spread the word about baby Oscar to the rest of the family, so no doubt they'd hear about it soon enough.

Gathering up her things, she carefully locked the office door and hurried across the factory floor to the main exit, her mind already occupied with the best way of getting everything accomplished in time to be able to visit Anne and see the new baby.

It had suddenly struck her that as Anne had had a caesarean, she'd be stuck in hospital for at least ten days, and with Martin flying all hours, it would be impossible for him to take Rose and Emily home and do the school run each day. With a heavy sigh she rejigged her plans, and was about to climb into her car when she heard someone call her name.

She looked round and there was Doris hurrying towards her. 'That's all I need,' she muttered. 'I'm just off to pick the children up,' she said as Doris came within earshot.

'This won't take a minute.' Doris came to an abrupt halt, her gaze steely. 'I am not at all happy that you've involved my husband in this disgraceful affair,' she said. 'For a man of his standing, that sort of scandal could ruin him.'

'Doris,' Peggy said carefully. 'John was only involved because he's a key-holder. No scandal or blame is attached to him. I really don't see why you're getting so het up about it.'

'Mud sticks,' hissed Doris. 'Everyone would have seen the police coming to our office, and probably put two and two together and made five as usual. One has to be so careful when one is dealing with these sorts of people.'

'They were all over my office too,' said Peggy with as much calm as she could muster. 'And had the entire factory almost at a standstill as they did a very messy search.'

'That's only to be expected,' Doris huffed. 'With the class of people you employ, it's hardly surprising to discover the place is a den of thieves.'

Peggy gave an exasperated sigh. 'You're talking nonsense as usual, Doris, and I really haven't got the time to stand here listening to it.'

'Well, I'm sorry if it's inconvenient for you,' Doris snapped. 'But I'm sick with worry that my John will get dragged into this disgraceful business. I *knew* you weren't up to managing that ghastly factory, and I wish you'd never become involved in it. It's hardly the most salubrious of jobs, after all.'

Peggy opened her car door. 'Thanks for your vote of confidence, Doris. I knew I could always rely on you to stick the knife in.'

Before Doris could react, she climbed into the car and slammed the door, determined not to be drawn any further. Turning the key, she revved the engine to warn Doris to get out of the way, and as her sister leapt to one side, she drove at speed out of the estate. From a glance in her rear-view mirror, she saw Doris stomp back towards the stairs leading to her office, all elegance lost in her fury at being bested.

Peggy let out a breath of annoyance, then gathered her thoughts and went to pick up the girls. Once she'd got them in the car, she drove out of Cliffehaven to the tiny hamlet where Anne and Martin lived.

Their house stood in a large plot of land at the end of a dirt track, and had been renovated from top to bottom once the wartime tenants had left. The trees surrounding it were still lush and green, and the sheltered front garden was ablaze with late summer colour. There was no sign of Martin's car, but then he wasn't expected home until late this evening, and Anne's little run-around was parked in front of the garage door.

Peggy parked by the front steps, and as the children scrambled out, she used her spare key to open the door. 'Come into the kitchen and I'll get you a drink and a biscuit,' she said, leading them down the hall. 'Then I want you to play nicely while I get some things together for Mummy.'

'Are we staying here?' asked Rose.

'No, you're coming to live with Granny for a bit.'

'Where's Daddy? I want my daddy,' grumbled Emily.

'He'll be home later,' Peggy replied distractedly as she doled out glasses of squash, some rather stale biscuits, and found colouring books and pencils in the big toy-box under the stairs. 'Now, be good girls. I won't be long.'

Having settled the girls at the table, she hurried upstairs to find Anne's bedroom in some disarray. Quickly changing the sheets and making the bed, she tidied up as best she could and hunted out clean underwear, nightdresses and slippers. She found a holdall on top of the wardrobe and packed everything, then added Anne's hand and face cream, hairbrush, washbag and the bottle of perfume she found on the dressing table.

It didn't take long to collect what the girls might need for the next week, and she hurried back downstairs with the two heavy bags. The girls were behaving themselves, so she took the empty glasses to give them a wash before mopping up the biscuit crumbs and making sure nothing had gone off in the fridge. The rest of the house was as neat as a pin, a sign that Anne had been nesting again before she went into labour.

'Will Grandpa be cross with us again?' asked Emily.

'Only if you don't behave yourself,' Peggy replied, before chivvying them out of the door. She grabbed their overcoats and wellingtons on the way and dumped everything in the boot of the car.

The girls began to squabble over a toy on the drive back and by the time Peggy had reached Beach View, she'd had enough. She parked the car in the cul-de-sac and turned to glare at them.

'Stop that at once. I will *not* have you fighting all the time,' she said sternly. 'If there's any more of it, then you will go to bed with no tea and not visit the new baby. Is that understood?'

There were muttered replies and lots of shifting about on the back seat.

'I didn't hear you,' she said flatly.

'Yes, Grandma,' they said in unison.

'Daisy?'

'Yes, Mum,' she said sweetly.

Peggy wasn't fooled for a minute, but collected the things from the boot and then steered the girls up the steps into the hall, where she dumped the bags. 'Daisy and Rose, I want you to go upstairs and get changed out of your uniforms. Emily, you can come with me and help to prepare tea.'

Emily looked rather sulky about this, but Peggy gave her a quick hug which made her smile, and they went into the kitchen to find Gracie Smith breaking off a conversation with Cordelia and getting quickly to her feet.

Rather startled to see her there, Peggy let go of Emily's hand and the child went straight to Cordelia and clambered onto her lap for a cuddle. 'Careful, Emily. Gan-gan isn't strong enough to have you climbing all over her.' She turned to Gracie.

'Gracie? What brings you here?'

'I'm ever so sorry if I'm intruding, Mrs Reilly, but I just had to come and see you.'

Gracie was a pretty, petite blonde, with delicate features and large grey eyes fringed with dark lashes, and Peggy could see how worried and upset she was. 'That's all right, Gracie. Just let me organise things here, and then we'll go in the other room.'

Peggy turned to Cordelia. 'The other two will be down in a minute. Can you get them to set the table, and then perhaps read them a story?'

Cordelia nodded. 'As long as it's not too drawn out. They can be a bit of a handful at times.'

'I doubt I shall be long, and we'll only be in the other room if things get out of hand,' she assured her.

Peggy put her handbag on a chair, pulled out her cigarettes and lighter, and indicated for Gracie to follow her across the hall to the dining room. It struck her as quite chill after the warmth of the kitchen, but she wasn't planning on staying more than a few minutes. Peggy sat down, lit a cigarette and waited for Gracie to settle in the other chair.

'I didn't rob the factory,' Gracie blurted out, the ready tears glistening on her lashes. 'I know you all think I helped Phil do it, but I didn't, really, I didn't.'

'All right, Gracie,' she soothed. 'Try to calm down, dear, and tell me why I should believe you.'

Gracie hunted up her cardigan sleeve for a handkerchief and gradually got herself under control. 'I really liked Phil,' she began. 'He was good with my boy, and ever so generous with taking me out and buying me little presents.'

Peggy stayed silent as Gracie took a shaky breath.

'I can see now what he was really up to, and I feel such a fool. Flo warned me he was never up to any good, and had only just come out of prison. I should never have trusted him.'

The large grey eyes regarded Peggy sorrowfully. 'But I was lonely, Mrs Reilly. Since Tom was killed and we lost our home, things have been so hard, and I've felt so alone. He was good company and made me feel special.'

'I can understand that, Gracie,' murmured Peggy, saddened by the fact that her suspicions seemed to have been proven right.

'I didn't realise what he was up to when he asked me about my work, the people there, and the daily routine. I just thought he was interested in what I was up to, and it was lovely to have someone to share my day with again when I got home.'

She mangled the sodden handkerchief. 'Now I see how stupid I was to tell him about the new cloth that had just come in, and prattling on about the expensive satin and lace which I was looking forward to sewing into the new line of christening gowns. I even made a stupid joke about how lovely it would look as a wedding dress.'

As the girl collapsed once more into a storm of tears, Peggy's soft heart ached for her in her loneliness and cruel betrayal. She perched on the arm of Gracie's chair and quickly enfolded her in her arms. 'It's all right, Gracie. Really it is.'

'But it's not, is it?' she sobbed, raising her tear-streaked face. 'The police questioned me for ages, searched the house and even the shed and outside lav. All the neighbours were watching, and Bessie, my housemate, got very po-faced about it all. She even threatened to tell our landlord and have me and my Bobby chucked out.'

The sobs got louder and more hysterical. 'Now I'm out on bail and facing a prison sentence. And what will happen to my boy? He'll be put into a home, because I've got no other family and Bessie already has three kids and . . . and . . .'

'Stop it, Gracie,' Peggy said firmly. 'You're getting all worked up and seeing things far too bleakly. There are solutions, you know, and I'll do my best to help you as long as you can promise you've told me the absolute truth.'

'You'd do that?' she gasped. 'You'd really help me after all I've told you?'

'If it's the truth.'

'It is. I promise you on my boy's life it is,' she said fervently, grasping Peggy's hand, her big eyes innocent of any guile.

'Very well, Gracie. Now dry your eyes and pull yourself together. I expect Bobby will be home from school by now, and you won't want him seeing you like this, will you?'

Gracie shook her head, mopped up her tears and took several deep breaths. 'You're ever so kind, Mrs Reilly. Flo said you'd understand.'

Peggy wasn't at all surprised that Flo had been behind this surprise visit, and she was glad she'd stood by Gracie. 'Flo's clearly a good friend to have in times of trouble, Gracie, and I can be too. Now you go home and stay there until the police have finished their enquiries, and then I think you'll find things won't be half as bad as you feared.'

'What do you mean?'

'You'll find out very soon, I'm sure.' Peggy stood and led the way back into the hall. Opening the door, she squeezed the girl's arm in encouragement. 'Try not to worry, Gracie.' She stood in the doorway and watched as the girl ran down the steps and hurried away.

Closing the door, she gave a deep sigh. Warner had chosen a prime target in poor little Gracie. Peggy gritted her teeth and thought how satisfying it would be to punch Warner as hard as she could on the nose. But he would get his comeuppance, she was certain of it.

Ethel seemed to have suddenly rallied a bit, for she opened her eyes and slapped Ruby's hand away as she tried to be rid of the oxygen mask. 'Gerroff,' she snarled.

'You've got to keep it on, Mum.'

'I don't want the bloody thing,' she rasped breathlessly, snatching it from her face and trying to push herself up the pillows. 'Help me, Ruby. I can't do this on me own.'

'Careful, Mum. You'll pull out all the lines and feeding tubes they've stuck in you.'

'Don't care,' she gasped, still struggling.

Ruby quickly lifted her as gently as possible until she was more upright. Ethel weighed next to nothing, and her skin had taken on an unhealthy yellow tone that was mirrored in what had once been the whites of her eyes. Alistair had explained about the jaundice caused by her damaged liver, and it was clearer than ever today – which Ruby knew wasn't a good sign.

'There you go. Better?'

Ethel nodded and placed the oxygen mask briefly over her face to take a couple of breaths, then let it fall into her lap. She reached for Ruby's hand. 'I'm sorry to cause you bother, gel,' she wheezed. 'But you're all I got in this world, and I wanted to be with you until . . .'

'You're all I got, too, Mum, so I do understand.'

Ethel gave a weak shrug, took another few breaths of oxygen and carried on talking in broken sentences. 'I weren't cut out to be a mum. Never really got the 'ang of it. You might think I didn't love yer. But I did, Rubes – in me own way – and I'm sorry I weren't always around for yer. Gawd knows 'ow, but you turned out a proper treat. I'm ever so proud of yer.'

Ruby's eyes filled with tears as she gently squeezed the bony hand, noticing how it trembled. 'Oh, Mum. That means so much to me, really it does – especially now. I never stopped loving you, cos you was the only mum I had, and I knew you didn't really mean half of what you said. I didn't mean none of it either, Mum, and I'm ever so sorry I was nasty to yer when you come to the Anchor.'

The oxygen came into play again, and Ruby could see Ethel was struggling. 'Don't talk no more, Mum, it's making you tired. We've made our peace, and that's all that matters.'

'Tell me about Mike,' Ethel panted into the oxygen mask.

Ruby fixed it back behind Ethel's ears. 'Slow breaths, Mum. You know what the doctor said.'

Once Ethel's breathing was more regular, Ruby told her about how she'd met Mike when he was in hospital recovering from a disastrous beach landing in France. Ethel seemed calmer and far more alert than she had been, so Ruby went on to tell her how she'd lost Mike and their daughter, and the journey she'd made back to Cliffehaven and Beach View.

'That Peggy's a good woman,' said Ethel. 'I'm glad you got 'er to look after yer when I'm gone.' She closed her eyes momentarily and then gripped Ruby's hand. 'But you gotta watch out for Phil Warner,' she rasped urgently. 'He's dangerous.'

'What do you mean by dangerous? I thought he was just a petty thief you and Olive were in cahoots with when you nicked all that stuff?'

'Old history,' panted Ethel. 'Thinks I come back to squeal on 'im. Give me a thumping to keep me gob shut.'

Ruby suddenly understood where those fresh bruises had come from. 'Bastard,' she breathed.

'Yeah, you got that right.'

Ruby spun round to find Gloria standing at the end of the bed, laden with flowers and an enormous box of chocolates. 'How much of that did you hear?'

'Enough to bar the bastard from my pub for the rest of his natural,' she replied tartly before dumping the gifts on the spare chair and sitting down. 'I come to see if either of you need anything,' she said, 'and to check on how Ethel's getting on, of course.'

She glanced at Ethel and received a scowl followed by a mutter which they both interpreted as a string of curses.

'Glad to see you ain't lost yer flair fer languages, Et,' Gloria said cheerfully. 'But you'd have to do better than that to find one I ain't heard.'

'Don't be like that, Gloria,' Ruby protested quietly.

'You don't mind, Et, do ya? Cut from the same cloth, you and me. Tell it like it is, eh, and no offence?'

Ethel seemed to gather all her strength. 'Bugger off, Gloria. And me name's Ethel. Not flaming Et.'

Gloria grinned. 'Knew I'd get you with that,' she said. 'Still, I'm glad there's life enough in yer to talk back, *Ethel*.'

Ruby chuckled as the two old enemies glared at each other. If nothing else, Gloria's visit had certainly enlivened her mother.

She turned to Gloria. 'Thanks ever so for coming in,' she said quietly, noting that Ethel had closed her eyes and slumped further down the bed again. 'And for offering to do the evening sessions. It's really kind of you, Gloria, and I'm so grateful. But Brenda needs the money, and I've got enough to pay her until . . . Well, you know.'

Gloria nodded, her gaze flitting to Ethel who seemed to have fallen asleep. 'I'd be glad to do it for yer, love,' she said quietly. 'And actually, I dropped in to see Brenda before I come in 'ere, and she turned me down flat saying she'd promised to look after your place until you could take over again and weren't about to break her word.'

Gloria shook her head, making her dangling earrings sway. 'She's a good girl, that one. Honest and loyal. You're lucky.'

'Yeah, I know.' Ruby reached for Gloria's hand. 'And I'm lucky to have such good friends, too. You and Mum never got on, so it were lovely of you to pop in and see 'er. Though by the looks of it you've worn her out.'

'Nah,' said Gloria and grinned. 'That one won't go down without a fight.'

'Ain't you gone yet?' Ethel growled, her eyes still tightly shut.

Gloria raised her heavily plucked eyebrows. 'See? Told ya.'

She scrabbled about in her large handbag and pulled out something wrapped in white butcher's paper. 'I made a meat and onion pie for yer. It's already cooked, so you can eat it now or heat it up later. Just make sure you eat it, though. That's a week's meat ration in there,' she said with a grin.

'Oh Gloria, that's so kind.'

Gloria waved away her thanks and got to her feet. 'I'd better get off.' She swamped Ruby in a hug perfumed with cheap scent, face powder and hair lacquer. 'Ring me if you need me,' she murmured, and stole away on tiptoe, chastened by the sad and solemn atmosphere of this quiet ward.

Jim had done his usual morning rounds and then headed for Parkwood and Ernie. Having spent another hour with him and Squiffy, he finished off the visits to the other men on his list and returned to Cliffehaven and the head office.

He sat and filled in all his reports, adding suggestions as to how some of his men could be better assisted in their many needs, and then sat for a long moment in deep thought before going in search of the Colonel.

'Ah, Jim. Good to see you,' the older man said, rising to greet him with a handshake.

'I hope you feel the same way after I've said what I've come to say,' said Jim nervously, for he was suddenly afraid he was making a huge error of judgement.

'You'd better sit down and get on with it then. There's no point in shilly-shallying when something is important.' The Colonel sat in his large swivel chair and eyed Jim thoughtfully. 'And I get the feeling this is important, Jim. So fire away.'

Jim realised he needed to keep things simple. 'I need help,' he said.

'Yes. I thought you might.' The Colonel leaned his forearms on the desk, his expression concerned. 'What brought you to this conclusion, Jim?'

Jim told him about the nightmares; the loud noises that had him cowering and whimpering; the flashbacks of terrifying moments in Burma when he thought he was about to die; the images of those prisoners of the Japanese and the massacre at Rangoon.

'That's quite understandable and not uncommon,' said the Colonel. 'And what else is bothering you?'

Jim was surprised the old man was so astute. He thought carefully how to put into words the different emotions he'd felt ever since coming home from Singapore.

'I miss the adrenaline rush of battle; the camaraderie of my mates; the rules and regulations of army life, and the knowledge that I was part of something far bigger than any of us.' He regarded the Colonel. 'Does that sound strange?'

He slowly shook his head. 'Not at all. You were indeed part of something that was bigger than us all, and of course you miss that rush, and even the fear you experienced each time you went into battle. Over time those two things can become almost addictive, as I know from my own experience.'

He leaned back in his chair. 'The army taught you discipline, gave you strict boundaries to abide by so you could become a fighting man who went to war in the knowledge the men around you had your back, as you had theirs. There's nothing like that feeling, Jim, so I fully understand what you're talking about.'

He took a breath and regarded Jim with kindness. 'Now, suddenly you're back in a different world with no one to give you orders – no enemy to kill – and only the day-to-day routine to look forward to. But you are not alone, Jim. We are here to watch your back, and give you all the help you need to ease you into civilian life.'

'I haven't doubted it,' said Jim. 'And I'm very grateful for your understanding.'

'As I said before, Jim. We don't want to lose you.' The Colonel opened a drawer and pulled out what looked like a letter, but merely laid it face down on the desk. 'I understand our most recent resident at Parkwood fought alongside you in India and Burma. It must have been difficult for you to find him so disabled.'

'It was a shock, yes. But Ernie's a tough little man, and it's helped us both to talk over what we went through.'

'Indeed, and I hope that continues, but of course you must realise that Ernest is terminally ill?'

Jim nodded. 'I'm hoping to spend as much time with him as I can for as long as he's still with us.' He hesitated for a moment. 'Ernie introduced me to someone who I think will help us both. So with your permission, I'd like to ask for two hours a week to see Dr Squires.'

The Colonel turned the letter over. 'I received this yesterday. It's written on behalf of Ernest who dictated it to Laurence, his nurse. Ernest is making the same request, citing the fact that your visits have improved his mental well-being, and together you wish to recover from what has been termed by the Americans as "battle fatigue" rather than what we called shell shock in the previous shout. He wishes to live out what's left of his life in peace, and not to be continually haunted by the past – and wants the same for you.'

'I didn't know,' breathed Jim. 'Bless him for that.'

'Well, I think it's a capital idea. As long as you fulfil your duties with us, of course you may attend these sessions with Ernest and Dr Squires.'

He shot Jim a beaming smile. 'We take care of our own,' he said. 'What's the phrase? Physician, heal thyself. The men who work for us need to be at peace with themselves before they can help to heal others. And perhaps, once you feel able, we might ask you to pass on the wisdom you've learnt from Dr Squires so others may gain from it.'

'There's a way to go before that, Colonel.'

'I agree.' He got to his feet and stuck out his hand. 'I'm glad you felt able to talk to me at last, Jim. Finally acknowledging you have a problem is the first step towards recovery. The second is asking for help. You're already on your way, Jim. Good luck, and call in any time. My door is always open.'

Jim shook his hand and, feeling lighter of heart and spirit, headed home to Peggy.

20

It was threatening to rain again, so Peggy helped Cordelia into her car, with Jim squashed in the back with the three little girls. Charlie had opted to stay at home as he had little interest in babies and a lot of homework to do.

Peggy drove the short distance from Beach View, down Camden Road and into the hospital grounds to drop everyone off as the first drops of rain splattered the windscreen, and then managed to find a parking space in the road. The lack of parking at the hospital had always been a thorny issue, but one that would probably never be resolved as there was no spare ground in which to put a car park.

As she opened her umbrella to run through the rain into the vast reception hall, she spotted Rosie and Ron.

'Oh, I'm so glad you're here,' she said, giving them both a hug. 'I've been trying all day to get hold of you and tell you the news.'

'Danuta told me this morning when I popped in to see Ruby,' said Rosie, 'and we've been out most of the afternoon, having a long lunch at the Officers' Club.'

'You lucky things,' sighed Peggy. 'I've had nothing but trouble today.' She decided not to dampen the enthusiasm for what lay ahead, and turned to Ron. 'Congratulations, Great-Grandpa,' she said.

'Ach, to be sure, it makes me feel old,' he moaned dramatically.

'But you are old,' teased Jim, nudging him with his elbow. 'Come on, ancient one, you can help me escort Cordelia up in the lift.'

As the men went off with Cordelia and the children, Peggy and Rosie slowly began to climb the stairs. 'How were things with Ruby when you saw her this morning?' Peggy asked.

'No real change, but then there probably won't be, will there?' Rosie said on a sigh. Then her expression brightened. 'But there is something that might make you smile, Peggy. The good doctor Darwin was with her, and they looked very cosy.'

Peggy giggled. 'Yes, he seems to have become a regular visitor. Wouldn't it be lovely if . . .?'

'Forever the romantic, Peggy,' Rosie said fondly. 'But things have to settle down for Ruby. She's had far too much to cope with lately and will need time to catch her breath before she can even begin to think of her future.'

They reached the second floor to find the others waiting for them outside the doors to the maternity ward.

Jim took charge. 'We'd better get organised and decide who's going in first as they won't allow all of us at the same time.'

'You and Peggy take the children, we'll wait here with Cordelia,' said Rosie, plumping down on one of the chairs that lined the corridor.

Jim picked up Emily and held Daisy's hand as Peggy took charge of Rose Margaret. The little girls were positively buzzing with excitement as they entered the flower-filled ward, and when they saw their mother, they scrambled to her side.

'Hello, my darlings,' said a delighted Anne, gathering them into her arms for a kiss, and at the same time trying to keep them from climbing all over her sore stomach. She looked over their heads. 'Mum, Dad. It's lovely to see you. Thanks so much for taking care of my two. I know it can't be easy.'

They kissed her and assured her they were managing all right as they coaxed the girls to stay off the bed and be content with holding their mother's hand.

'I brought you some things from home,' said Peggy, opening the holdall and unpacking it into the bedside locker. 'And this is from me and Jim. Sorry about the paper, but it was all I could find.'

Anne opened the parcel wrapped in old Christmas paper to reveal the hand-knitted layette Peggy had been working on for weeks. 'Oh, Mum,' she breathed, holding up the lacy white shawl, and then the tiny blue cap, mittens, leggings and matinee jacket. She grinned. 'How did you know it was going to be a boy?'

Peggy laughed. 'I didn't,' she admitted. 'But I like blue, and I thought it wouldn't really matter if it was a girl.' She looked round. 'Where's Oscar?'

'They'll be bringing in the babies from the nursery any minute,' Anne replied. 'And before you ask, we chose to call him Oscar because we like the name. Luckily it seems to suit him as you'll see when he's brought in.'

'Oscar James Black certainly has a ring to it,' said Peggy. 'By the way, Ron, Rosie and Cordelia are waiting outside, so once we've all had a chance to coo over him, we'll swap over.' She reached for Anne's hand. 'How are you, darling?'

'I daren't cough or laugh or move too quickly because it hurts like billy-o,' she replied, 'but apart from being a bit tired still, I'm just glad it's all over. They're keeping me in for about ten days, Mum. Do you think you and Dad can survive my two for that long?'

'We'll manage,' said Jim blithely.

'Of course we will,' said Peggy. 'I'm just relieved they're at school all day, otherwise it could get complicated.'

The nursery doors opened and the parade of nurses entered the ward, each pushing a see-through cot. Silence fell amongst the visitors and then a chorus of oohs and aahs greeted the babies as they were delivered to each bed.

'Oh, Anne,' breathed Peggy. 'He's gorgeous, and look at all that hair!'

'He's a big lad,' said Jim in admiration. 'What do you think, girls?'

They seemed to be struck dumb and simply stared at this new arrival in awe until Daisy hesitantly put her finger against the tightly closed little fist, and Oscar grabbed it. And then the other two started to push and shove to do the same.

'Right, that's enough,' said Jim, hastily pulling them away from the cot before they knocked it flying. 'Come on, girls. It's time to let the others in.'

There were loud protests, but Jim bore them off determinedly, and within minutes, Ron came in with Cordelia.

Ron leaned over the cot and clucked his tongue. 'Too be sure, Anne, he's a grand lad, so he is. That's a fine mop of hair too. A proper Reilly if I'm not mistaken.'

Anne giggled. 'I wouldn't let Martin hear you say that. He's a Black, and only part Reilly.'

Cordelia looked down at Oscar with tears in her eyes. 'Dear little thing,' she murmured. 'How lovely and bonny he is. I wouldn't mind betting he'll win all the local baby shows next year.'

She plonked down into the chair next to Peggy and pulled out the matinee jacket from her handbag. 'I only finished it this afternoon,' she said, handing it to Anne. 'I do hope you like it.'

Anne admired the pale yellow jacket with the wobbly stiches around the neck, and the gap where the sleeve didn't quite meet the front panel, and gave Cordelia a kiss. 'It's beautiful. Thank you, Grandma Cordy.'

Peggy could see that Anne was getting tired, so she got to her feet. 'I'll swap over with Rosie,' she said. 'And help Jim with the girls.' She kissed Anne's rather warm cheek. 'Well done, darling. He's perfect.'

Leaving Ron and Cordelia to coo over Oscar, Peggy went out into the corridor to find the three little girls nestled sleepily between Jim and Rosie as he read them a story.

'Your turn, Rosie,' said Peggy. 'I think Jim and I should get the girls home before they go to sleep. One of us will come back to pick up Cordelia.'

Rosie reluctantly went into the maternity ward and hugged Anne before making all the right noises over Oscar. And yet the sight of the lovely, perfect baby tugged at her heart, for she'd never been blessed, and now never would. The only time she'd come close to having her own was when she'd tried to adopt a little girl, but she had been cruelly cheated out of the chance by her nefarious brother Tommy.

She sat back and let the conversation swirl around her in that overheated ward, her thoughts returning to the past heartache she'd suffered because Tommy's illegitimate child had gone to someone else. However, time had mostly healed her, so when she finally got to meet Mary, who'd grown into a lovely, caring young woman, it was a joy to know that she'd been loved. They had remained in touch ever since, and on

Mary's brief visits to Cliffehaven she would come to stay.

Tuning in once more to the conversation, she congratulated Anne again and cooed over the baby, then left the ward.

'Are you all right, Rosie?' asked a concerned Ron minutes later.

'I'm fine, really,' she assured him. 'I just get a bit sentimental when I see a new baby, and it takes me back a bit.'

He put his arm about her. 'Well, you've got me to look after you now, and I'm sure Mary will soon come to visit again with her little boy.'

Rosie nodded. 'I know. Let's go home, Ron. I need a bit of a cuddle.'

He chuckled. 'Well now, Rosie. That I can supply, and to be sure we all need a cuddle now and again.'

Phil Warner was not having a good night. He'd been barred from the Crown, and that oversized man-mountain, Frank Reilly, had refused to let him into the Anchor. He'd been evicted from his scruffy bedsit on his return from the police station, and the bossy cow who shared the two-up two-down with Gracie had slammed the door in his face.

The rain was coming down so hard it was bouncing off the pavements and gushing out of the drainpipes to sweep the debris along the gutters, so he pulled up his coat collar, tipped his hat over his eyes, and sought the meagre shelter of a shop doorway. All he possessed was stuffed in a battered suitcase at his feet, and with only a few shillings in his pocket, he couldn't afford to pay for a room, and certainly didn't intend to doss down at the local Sally Army hostel.

The police had released him on bail, which had surprised him because he had a long list of previous convictions behind him, and they must have suspected he'd do a runner. And indeed, his first thought had been to catch the next train to London where he could lose himself amongst people who wouldn't grass on him. However, there had been several rather unfortunate things which had prevented this.

Firstly, there were no more trains to London until tomorrow. Secondly, he'd spent a good deal on that silly tart Gracie so was down to his few last pennies, and thirdly, the blackmail money and bolts of cloth had already gone to pay off his debts. There were certain people you didn't owe money to, and the robbery at the factory had been his only way of getting them off his back. But he'd never dare grass them up, for he knew what they were capable of. However, his life was unravelling; he was stuck in a town he'd come to loathe, and he felt cornered.

He took a swig from the small bottle of gin he'd nicked from the off-licence and stared moodily out at the glistening pavements and shuttered shops. It had been stupid to come back here, he realised. He'd never particularly liked the place – or the people – and it seemed that every time he got the chance to make a bit of money, something or someone spiked it. Still, he'd ensured that Ethel would keep her mouth shut, and as Olive had died in prison, there was no one left to tie him in with the crime they'd gone down for.

He took another swig of gin, returned the bottle to his coat pocket and picked up his suitcase. There was only one place left to go where he was certain of not being turned away – not if the man wanted to keep his good looks, he thought grimly.

It was getting late and the streets had been deserted even by the usual slinking cats; the shops were shuttered, and every window blanked by curtains. There'd be no chance of house-breaking tonight as everyone would be indoors, so there was no point in even considering the idea.

Unaware that he was being followed, Phil Warner weaved through the alleys and back streets to the house where he knew he would not be denied refuge, but when it was finally in sight, he came to an abrupt halt. Two police cars were in the driveway; a Black Maria was parked at the kerb and light flooded out from the open front door.

Phil eased into the dark shadows of a hedge and watched as his mark was brought out of the house and shoved into the Black Maria. As the police van drove off, it became clear that the house was being thoroughly searched. There'd be no sanctuary there for him tonight.

He turned away and hurried to put some distance between himself and all those coppers. He turned sharply into a dark, narrow alleyway which would lead him back to the High Street, his mind churning over where he could go for the night. The only place he could think of was the large storage shed behind the Crown. It would mean scaling the high gate, but as Gloria didn't have a guard dog or security lights, and he'd kept himself as fit as a butcher's dog during his last prison term, it wouldn't pose a problem.

He didn't hear the quiet footsteps behind him and was totally unaware of the two large men who moved as swiftly and silently as shadows in the dark alley.

The kick in the back of his knee sent him stumbling, the punch in the kidneys catching him before he fell to the ground.

Phil Warner knew what was coming and curled into a ball, his arms protectively over his head, his knees to his chest as the men closed in. He couldn't see who they were. Had no idea who had sent them – or why

– but as the rain thundered down and the kicking began in earnest, all he could focus on was the awful pain they were inflicting.

The rain of the previous night seemed to have washed Cliffehaven clean, and the streets and pavements shone brightly as the late September sun briefly appeared through the clouds that Thursday afternoon. The air seemed fresher too, and smelled of the sea, so Peggy had opened her office window to clear the stale smell of Solly's cigars that still lingered.

She was feeling tired after all the running about she'd had to do over the last two days, and although she was looking forward to getting home, she knew there wasn't much chance of a quiet evening until she'd got the girls to bed. All three children were crotchety after their school day, and overexcited about the new baby, so there had been quite a few tiffs between them. She'd come to the decision that she'd take them straight to the hospital after school and then get them home for their tea, baths and beds. It would leave her free to pop in on Ruby, and give Jim the chance to unwind.

Peggy was in the pre-packing area with Flo, checking over the collection of garments that would have to be sold as seconds. Some of the sewing was appalling, and when she read the machinist's label, it didn't come as a surprise to see who was to blame. 'It's not good enough, Flo, and it's been going on for too long. I think it's time we let Sarah go.'

'I agree. I thought she'd improve, but she's too busy gossiping and minding everyone else's business to concentrate on her work. I'll tell her at the end of this shift.'

'Thanks, Flo. It's a job I loathe.'

'It will mean we'll be two machinists short if Gracie doesn't come back,' Flo warned.

'Yes, I know, but I think Solly has someone in mind to fill one gap, and I'm hoping Gracie will be able to return once all this robbery business is cleared up.'

She looked up at Flo who was a good three inches taller. 'She came round to Beach View to see me, in an awful state. Do you know how she is today?'

Flo looked a bit embarrassed. 'She's doing all right now I've moved her and Bobby into my spare room. It's a bit of a squash, but I don't mind, and if that Warner comes looking for her he won't find her.'

Peggy was startled and concerned, for this possibility hadn't occurred to her. 'You think he might?'

'I know for a fact that he went round to her old place late last night, but luckily he was shown the door in no uncertain terms by Gracie's fellow lodger.' Flo regarded Peggy evenly. 'I hope you don't mind, Mrs Reilly, but I thought it best to keep her and the boy safe while all this is going on.'

Peggy nodded. 'You did the right thing, Flo. Well done.'

She led the way onto the shop floor and was about to head for her office when she caught the unwelcome sight of Sergeant Mayhew striding into the factory.

'Let's hope he's got some good news for us,' Peggy murmured to Flo before hurrying towards him.

Mayhew seemed to realise it wasn't wise to say anything in front of the machinists, and waited until Peggy had shut her office door before speaking. 'I thought you'd want to know we've caught the culprit, Mrs Reilly. John Farley was taken into custody late last night and was charged with various offences this morning.'

'So I was right, then. What does he have to say for himself?'

Mayhew was preening as he smoothed back his oiled hair and fiddled with the knot in his silk tie. 'He's singing like a bird in the hope he'll get a lighter sentence, but with the other charges against him, I doubt he'll be out for a long time.'

Peggy nodded. 'And Warner?'

'Ah, that's a different story,' he said, his expression grim. 'He was found by a member of the public late last night and taken to hospital by ambulance. He'd been badly beaten, and will have to stay there for a while under guard until he's well enough to stand trial.'

'Who do you think attacked him?'

'Warner mixed with a dangerous crowd and made some nasty enemies,' he said. 'I doubt he'll ever tell us, for fear of further reprisals. But we have enough on him to put him away, now Farley's talking.'

'So, Gracie's clear?'

'That will be up to the courts,' he replied. 'But as she has no history of criminal activity and was clearly used by Warner to get the inside information, it will probably be up to Mr Solomon to press any charges.'

'I see,' murmured Peggy. 'Have you spoken to Mr Solomon yet?'

'I have informed him of the situation,' he said stiffly, 'and it was he who suggested I come to put you in the picture.' He got to his feet. 'As Farley is turning King's evidence, and it looks as if Warner will plead guilty to protect the people he was working for, I doubt there will even be a trial.' He shook her hand. 'I wish you good day,' he said before marching out of her office like a toy soldier.

'Silly, self-satisfied man,' muttered Peggy as she closed the door behind him and went back to her desk to telephone Solly.

'Good afternoon, Peggy, my dear,' he boomed down the telephone. 'I take it you've had a visit from the rather pompous Sergeant Mayhew?'

'I certainly did. It looks as if it's at an end. Except for what will happen to young Gracie,' she added.

'Silly girl to get her head turned like that,' rumbled Solly. 'But I'm a fair man, Peggy. The girl's a good worker and we all make mistakes, so I'll give her a second chance and not press charges.'

'Oh, that is a relief. Thanks, Solly.'

'It's not me you should be thanking, Peggy. My Rachel has been giving me earache since this started, and I wouldn't dare go against her wish to keep the girl.'

Peggy smiled, hearing Solly puffing on his cigar at the other end of the line, and the low murmur of another voice. 'I'll leave you to get on then,' she said.

'No, wait, Peggy. Is there a chance that you could fit in another full-time machinist? Only your Jim was most anxious I should give this person more work, and there is room at the crèche for her children.'

'As a matter of fact, I will have by the end of today.' She went on to tell him about Sarah. 'Who is this girl? Does she know what she's doing, Solly?'

'It's Alice Rayner. A quiet and efficient little machinist who desperately needs more hours now her husband is unable to work. She won't let you down.'

'Ask her to come in tomorrow, and if she's as good as you say, then I'll be pleased to take her on full-time. Is there any news about replacing the christening gown fabric? Only we're getting a lot of orders.'

'My London contacts tell me it should arrive before the weekend. It's all good news, Peggy, but I have to get on. Goodbye.'

Ruby had spent the previous night at the hospital hoping that her mother would speak to her again, but those few moments of lucidity had exhausted her. The doctors had done the rounds, her medication had been discussed and the dosage increased. Ethel had slept throughout the night as Ruby had kept watch and dozed fitfully.

She'd left the hospital early that Thursday morning to oversee the arrival of the drayman, but she needn't have worried, for both Frank and Ron had turned up to make sure the barrels were safely delivered into the cellar, and the bottles of beers and mixers were neatly stowed away.

Thanking them both, she'd gone upstairs to have a long bath, wash her hair and change into fresh clothes. The hospital smell seemed to cling to her and she was so strained and tired that she had little appetite for the lovely breakfast Brenda had taken so much trouble to prepare for her.

Now it was late evening and she was once again at Ethel's bedside, trying to concentrate on the book she'd brought, and finding that the print was blurring so much it was becoming impossible to understand any of it. She stood and dug her hands into her trouser pockets, feeling restless and uneasy. Ethel's colour was still a concerning yellow, and her breathing was so ragged it sounded as if she had to fight for every ounce of oxygen.

Feeling the need to walk off the stiffness and to get some fresh air, she slung a cardigan over her shoulders and headed for the day room to make a cup of tea, and then went out into the quiet garden. It smelled lovely after the rain, and she took in a deep breath, noting scents of late honeysuckle, wet grass and rich, damp earth.

Feeling refreshed by it, she managed to find a dry bench beneath the awning so she could sit and have a moment of quiet before she returned to her vigil.

Ruby looked up to watch the clouds scudding across the hazy moon against the starless blackness beyond.

She gave a deep sigh. It was so peaceful out here, and wonderfully cool after the dry, stifling heat of that ward.

The lateness of the hour meant there were few sounds to break the silence of a slumbering Cliffehaven – merely the skitter of something small in the nearby flower bed, the distant bark of a dog, and the rustle of a sleepy bird in the tree – and as she sat there she felt her inner peace restored and the strength of purpose she'd always relied upon, return.

The coming days wouldn't be easy, but she would face them as she'd faced all the dark moments in her life, with determination to get through it, no matter how hard, for experience had taught her that she would ultimately survive the storm and be stronger because of it.

Ruby sat there smoking and thinking and remembering the past as the Town Hall clock struck the quarter hours. It was only when she realised it had started to rain again that she left that quiet haven and returned to the ward to once again keep vigil over her mother.

21

It was Saturday morning on the first day of October, and everyone at Beach View had been run ragged by the three little girls racing about the house and yelling at the tops of their voices. Cordelia had taken out her hearing aids and shut herself in the dining room; Charlie had shot off early to Ron's with the excuse he might need help with something before he had to go to his rugby match, and Jim was sitting at the kitchen table with his head in his hands.

'Can't you stop them, Peggy?' he pleaded.

'I've tried everything,' she replied, closing the kitchen door so their noise was muffled as they rampaged about upstairs. 'I've threatened, glared and shouted, but they're out of control, and I really don't know what to do about it.'

She put her hand on Jim's shoulder. 'Why don't you go out for a walk along the seafront? That might help clear your head.'

'No need for that,' said Martin as he came through from the basement. 'I'll take the little blighters with me and keep them for the rest of the weekend.'

'Oh, Martin, would you?' Peggy breathed with enormous relief as she gave her son-in-law a huge hug. 'I don't know what the matter is with them,' she said helplessly.

'Don't worry, Peg. They're just overexcited to all be together, and what with school and the new baby, it's probably proving too much.'

He sat down at the table and accepted a cup of tea. 'Sorry, Jim,' he murmured. 'I know this is an awful imposition, but I'm hoping it won't continue for much longer.'

Jim shook his head. 'I should be used to it after having five of my own, but I don't remember them making so much noise.'

'It's because little girls have this awful habit of screaming,' said Martin calmly. 'It goes right through one's head.'

'I'm aware of that,' Jim said dourly just before the door opened and the three girls charged in shrieking.

On seeing their father, Emily and Rose threw themselves at him in delight and began to talk over one another until they were yelling to be heard.

Martin drank down his tea and stood up. 'Right, that's quite enough, you two. I'm taking you out to the car and you will stay there until I come back to drive you home.'

He ignored their loud protests and turned to Peggy. 'If you could pack up their things for me? That would be an enormous help.'

Peggy didn't need asking twice, and hurried upstairs as Martin marched the girls out of the house to the car.

Jim decided the walk could wait for a while, so pulled a disappointed and tearful Daisy onto his knee and coaxed her into listening to a story from her favourite picture book in the hope it would take her mind off things.

Minutes later, he looked up as Peggy returned to the kitchen with the bags of the girls' things. 'Perhaps we could all go for a bit of a stroll along the prom as it's stopped raining,' he said hopefully.

'That sounds lovely,' she replied. 'Although a lie-down in a darkened room for two hours sounds far more tempting.' She giggled as Jim wriggled his eyebrows and grinned suggestively. 'Keep your mind clean, Jim Reilly. I didn't mean what you think I meant.'

Martin returned, looking rather frazzled. 'I've locked them in the car so they can't escape,' he said, 'but I daren't leave them too long as they're bound to get up to some mischief or other.'

'Are they always so noisy and naughty?' asked Jim.

'Only when their mother isn't around,' sighed Martin. 'She knows how to handle them, whereas I don't really have a clue. Thanks so much for looking after them. I realise it must have been difficult, and so I'm in the process of trying to sort out things which will help us all until Anne can come home. Hopefully, that will mean you won't have to put up with them after today.'

'Oh, but I've loved having them,' protested Peggy.

'No, you haven't,' he replied, grinning as he gave her a hug. 'They're a couple of terrors – especially Emily – and only digestible in very small doses.' He shook Jim's hand, picked up the bags and went down the cellar steps, slamming the door behind him.

The silence in the kitchen was quite deafening after the days of noise, and Peggy slumped into the chair beside Jim and leaned against his shoulder. 'Peace. Perfect peace,' she sighed.

The telephone rang stridently from the hall, and Jim kissed Peggy's forehead, eased Daisy from his lap and went to answer it.

'If it's anyone asking for help, I'm not here,' shouted Peggy after him. She gave Daisy a cuddle and pulled her onto her lap. 'We've had more than enough drama to last us a lifetime, haven't we, Daisy?' she murmured into her hair.

'What's drama?' the child asked.

'Four days of three little girls in one house,' she replied wearily. 'All I can say, Daisy, is I'm glad I'm past having more children.'

Daisy frowned up at her, and then slid off her lap to go and play with the toys that lay scattered across the hallway floor.

'That was Solly,' said Jim, as he came back and leaned against the range. 'You remember me telling you about Sam Healey?'

'The chap with the scarred face and eye-patch who's a wizard with numbers?'

'That's the one. Solly is delighted with him and has taken him on permanently. So with Alice Rayner settled up at your place, her kids in the crèche and Sam gainfully employed again, it's been a very successful week.'

He came to sit beside her again and took her hand. 'And you, Mrs Reilly, are a very clever woman,' he said proudly.

She looked at him and laughed. 'If you think flattery is going to get me up in that bedroom, you've got another think coming,' she replied. 'I've got the week's washing to do, beds to change and the house to tidy from top to bottom.'

He shook his head. 'It's not flattery, but the truth. You see, you were right all along about Farley. Sam found several anomalies in the account books. Farley had been siphoning off money for about three months.'

'Yes, I suspected he might have been,' said Peggy. 'Oh, dear, poor Solly. All this must have been a terrible blow to him after trusting Farley for so many years.'

Jim checked that Daisy wasn't up to any mischief and then sat back and lit a cigarette. 'You never did tell me the full story of how you came to suspect Farley in the first place. What was it that alerted you?'

Peggy got up to pour more boiling water over the tea leaves before sitting down again to light a cigarette. 'It was a combination of things really,' she replied. 'About four months ago, I was standing in a queue for tins of baked beans when I overheard someone talking very quietly behind me. My ears pricked up, of course, and I discovered she was discussing some police raid at a club further along the coast. It was the Pink Pussycat.'

'That's a club for men of a certain persuasion,' muttered Jim. 'Is Farley one of them?'

'Whether he is or not is not our business,' she replied dismissively. 'But I did hear that he was seen leaving the place seconds before the police raid and therefore escaped prosecution.'

She puffed on her cigarette as she put her thoughts in order. 'The second thing that meant nothing much at the time was about three weeks later. I'd been going through the weekly invoices with Farley when I was called out to see to a girl who'd fainted in the lavatories and banged her head quite badly on the floor. It took a while to give her first aid, and by the time I got back, I noticed my bunch of keys weren't where I'd left them. Farley explained they'd got in the way and he'd shifted them to clear the desk. It was a logical explanation, so I thought no more about it.'

She flicked ash into the ashtray, and poured out the tea which was now the colour of dirty dishwater. 'Shortly afterwards, I noticed there was something sticky on the key to the main entrance which made it difficult to turn properly. It looked like plasticine, or that stuff you put round windows when you're fitting them.' She took a breath. 'Anyway, it was only a tiny bit, so I scraped it off, and again thought no more about it.'

Peggy sipped her tea. All this talking was making her thirsty.

'And then, only last Saturday, I saw Farley in a huddle with Warner who was definitely acting in a threatening sort of way towards him. It was only a brief glimpse as I was stalking off in a huff after rowing with Doris. But it struck me as most odd because the two men are chalk and cheese, and I was surprised they even knew each other.'

She stubbed out her cigarette. 'When I got to my car, I glanced back and saw Farley hand Warner an envelope which he stuffed quickly out of sight, and they hurried off in opposite directions.'

Jim grinned. 'This is better than an Agatha Christie,' he said, settling into his chair in anticipation of more. 'Go on, Peg.'

She drank some more tea. 'When the theft at the factory came to light and Warner and Gracie became prime suspects, it got me thinking. Gracie might have been flattered into pillow talk, but she's an honest girl at heart, and I couldn't believe she'd knowingly played a part in the robbery.

'And then I remembered Solly saying Farley was about to retire. But he's only in his fifties, and had been with the same accountancy firm since he'd qualified – he told me that when we first met – so why retire so early and risk losing his pension?'

'It's certainly a foolhardy step,' muttered Jim.

'That was what triggered off the chain of memories, really, and suddenly it all made sense. Warner had somehow discovered Farley's illegal secret and blackmailed him into taking a casting of the main factory key and getting it copied. Warner had already weaselled his way into Gracie's life to find out the factory's schedule and what was being delivered, so he knew when to strike.'

'You're a proper Miss Marple, aren't you?' said Jim in admiration. 'But what I don't understand is why Farley was retiring so early.'

'Ah, well,' she said with a flourish of her hand. 'I telephoned a friend of mine after the police had left the factory. She's been a secretary at Farley's accountants for donkey's years, and knows far more than her bosses would like. She told me in the strictest confidence that the partners had got to hear of Farley's liking for clubs like the Pink Pussycat, and he'd been asked very quietly to leave immediately, and not expect a company pension.'

'So the man had no income, other than what he was stealing from Solly; was fired without a pension to look forward to; was being blackmailed by Warner – and had the dark shadow of the law hanging over him because of his sexual preferences.' Jim shook his head. 'It almost makes me feel sorry for him.'

'Well, you shouldn't,' said Peggy as she poured out more tea into their cups. 'Solly trusted him, and if he'd been truly honest, he would have told Solly immediately when Warner threatened to blackmail him, and something could have been done about it. The man was a fool.'

'That's a bit harsh, Peg,' Jim admonished gently. 'He was probably terrified to tell anyone, let alone Solly, who is inclined to go off at the deep end, and is quite daunting when he does.'

'It's really no excuse,' persisted Peggy.

Jim gave a sigh. 'It's time they changed the law, and accepted these men into society. I met quite a few during the war, and they were unstintingly brave, going unarmed into fierce battle situations to rescue and treat the wounded. Most of them were conscientious objectors; others were rejected by the forces as perverts, or devout Christians who refused to kill, but their work as volunteer stretcher bearers, nurses and medics was quite astounding.'

She looked at him in astonishment. 'You used to be so scathing about men like that.'

He shrugged and looked a bit embarrassed. 'Well, the war changed my outlook on many things, and the sooner that ridiculous law is changed, the better. It just opens them up to blackmailers like Warner, and ruins lives.'

'I do love you, Jim Reilly,' she murmured, kissing his cheek, and quickly escaping his clutches. 'Now I must get on with my housework if we're going to take this walk. You can help by starting to clear up all the children's toys. Get Daisy to join in and make it a game. It'll take half the time.'

He caught her mid-flight towards the cellar door and held her close. 'And after our walk?'

'We'll have lunch,' she replied, wriggling away and dashing down the cellar steps in a fit of giggles.

Ron had been delighted to see Charlie turn up early that Saturday morning. Since Rosie had gone out to do the shopping, they could spend a sociable few hours happily pottering about in his vegetable garden and shed as the dogs lay slumbering in the weak sunshine.

It soon became clear to Ron that the lad needed to get things off his chest, so he let him talk as they weeded and hoed.

'I'm just realising how much more is expected of me now I'm in the Lower Sixth,' said Charlie, pausing for a moment to ease his back. 'The subjects I'm studying for my exams next year are much harder too.'

'That's only to be expected,' said Ron as he carefully planted out his winter vegetable seedlings. 'Mind you, I left school when I was eleven and went straight onto my da's fishing boat. But that was a different world back then, and you're in a lucky position, wee Charlie. The work might be hard, but you have the brains to deal with it, and it'll give you a much better future than I could ever have dreamed of.'

'Yes, I do realise that,' he replied, leaning on the hoe. 'And I want to do well. But there's so much noise at home, it's difficult to concentrate on my homework.'

He paused and then blurted out, 'And I'm also worried about Dad. He hasn't been right ever since he came home from Singapore, and although Mum makes light of it, I know she's struggling.'

Ron stopped what he was doing and laid his large and rather dirty hand on his grandson's broad shoulder. 'Your da knows how hard it's been for everyone, Charlie. But it's been far tougher for him, you know. He's been haunted by the sort of horrors none of us can fully understand, and is trying his very best to overcome them. But at the same time, he's seen how it's affected his family, and it cuts him to the quick.'

He paused to light his pipe. 'He told me yesterday that he's now in regular touch with a pal of his who went through the exact same thing, and is also struggling with it. So, through this man, he's finally gone to the right people to ask for the help he needs to come to terms with everything he's been through.'

Ron puffed on his pipe and stared out to sea. 'He's desperate to repair the damage he realises he could do to those he loves most, and I believe he will do it, Charlie. But it will take time, and we, as a family, must be patient and understanding, and give him all the love and support we can.'

Charlie nodded, his gaze fixed on the newly dug-over vegetable plot.

Ron put his arm round his shoulders and gave him a quick hug. 'The last thing he'd want is for you to worry about him to the point where your schooling suffers. He's so proud of you, Charlie – and so am I.'

Charlie kept his head bowed as he sniffed and rapidly swiped his face with the back of his dirty hand. 'Yeah, I know. But it's difficult not to worry, Grandad. And those girls don't help with all their screeching and thundering about the house. Dad's going mad with it, Mum's at the end of her tether, and how the heck am I supposed to be able to concentrate when they do nothing but scream and squabble?'

'That's easily solved,' said Ron. 'You can bring your homework here. Rosie and I lead a mostly quiet life, and there's the spare bedroom upstairs we could kit out for you.'

'Really?' Charlie looked up, his eyes hopeful. 'You wouldn't mind?'

'I wouldn't have offered if I minded. And don't worry about Rosie. She'll be only too pleased to help out, I can assure you.'

'That would be a huge help, Grandad,' he said on a grateful sigh.

'Think nothing of it. Now get hoeing. I need to get these seedlings planted before you go rushing off to rugby.'

They shared a grin and worked in harmony for the next hour. Rosie returned with the grocery shopping, and after agreeing wholeheartedly to the idea of turning the spare bedroom into Charlie's study, made them each a doorstep sandwich of cheese and homemade pickle, which they washed down with tumblers of Ron's elderflower cordial.

'Thanks, Rosie,' said Charlie as he drained the glass. 'That hit the spot. But I'd better get going. The charabanc is due in half an hour to take us to our match, and I daren't miss it.'

Ron went with him to the gate, the dogs following at their heels – no doubt in the hope they'd get another walk.

'Good luck, Charlie. And remember, those girls won't be at Beach View for ever, but there will always be a quiet workspace for you here.' He handed Charlie the spare door key.

Charlie shoved it into his pocket and threw his arms about him in an awkward hug. 'Thanks for everything, Grandad. I feel so much better about things now,' he muttered before picking up his kitbag and hurrying towards the recreation ground.

Ron shooed the disappointed dogs back into the garden and firmly fastened the gate before he led them back indoors.

'That was a good idea of yours, Ron,' said Rosie as she finished the washing-up and stripped off the rubber gloves. 'I'm glad we could do something to help the lad. It can't be easy for him at home.'

'I've given him a key to let himself in if we're out,' said Ron, gathering her into his arms. 'And I was wondering if you'd be inclined to agree to another good idea I had this morning.'

'That depends entirely on what it is,' she replied, smiling up into his eyes.

'I thought we might take that holiday we talked about. As long as it won't interfere with your council work, that is,' he added hurriedly.

'There are lots of meetings this coming week because we have to discuss the autumn budget and get things moving on highway repairs and the final passing of those plans for the new council housing estate behind the station. But I'll clear my diary for next weekend and the following Monday, so we can have a decent length of time away. Will that suit you, do you think?'

He gave her a squeeze and kissed her soft, powdered cheek. 'Aye, that'll do nicely,' he murmured into her hair. 'I'll telephone the hotel we stayed in before and make the booking. But for now, I want to show you how very much I love you.'

It had taken a while to tidy the house and get a week's worth of washing done, but now the washing was blowing very satisfactorily on the line and the house was clean, Peggy decided it was time for them all to get some fresh air.

'I think I'll stay here and finish my library book,' said Cordelia. 'It's a bit too bracing out there today.'

Peggy gave her a gentle hug before she coaxed Daisy into her coat and mittens and rammed a woolly hat over her head as Jim dragged on an extra sweater to wear beneath his heavy overcoat. Wrapped up warm in her overcoat, which rather swamped her now she'd lost so much weight, she tied a scarf over her hair, pulled on gloves and found her sturdiest walking shoes.

'Right,' she said once everyone was ready. 'As Cordelia said, it's going to be a bit bracing, but I think if we walked to the end of the prom and back up Camden Road, we'll have earned a cup of tea and a sticky bun at the Lilac Tearooms.'

They set off down the twitten and as they reached the end were met with a blustery wind that came up from the sea. It was so strong that as they began to descend the hill to the seafront, Peggy's scarf flapped about, Daisy was almost knocked over, and Jim had to hold onto his fedora.

They both held tightly to Daisy as they went down the steep hill, and upon reaching the promenade, paused for a moment to catch their breath and watch

Frank, Brendon and the rest of the fishing crew haul their boats up above the high-tide line and anchor them firmly into the shingle. The sea was grey, the icy waves curling in rapid succession to crash into foam on the beach – and out on the horizon, they could see the ominous dark clouds of an approaching storm.

'Are you sure about this, Peggy?' asked Jim, who'd now squashed his hat into a coat pocket to save it from blowing away.

Peggy laughed in delight. 'Absolutely,' she shouted back above the sound of the wind and the sea. 'It's on days like this that you feel most alive.'

Jim was actually half-frozen, but as Peggy seemed to be so happy, he said nothing as they went along the narrow track in front of what had once been fishermen's cottages, to speak to Frank and Brendon.

'How's it going?' he asked his brother.

'Too rough, and the forecast is for a real hooley to come blowing in from France, so we'll have to batten everything down.' He grinned at Jim. 'Still, it'll give me a chance to help Brenda at the pub tonight.'

'Have you heard how things are with Ruby?' asked Peggy.

'She told Brenda she didn't think it would be long,' said Frank. 'Ethel rallied for a bit, but since then, things haven't looked too good.'

'Oh, dear. I'd better pop in later and give her some support,' said Peggy.

'Actually, Auntie Peg, she asked me to tell everyone she didn't want any more visitors.' At Peggy's frown, he continued, 'She needs quiet time with her mother just now.'

Peggy nodded sadly. 'Yes, I can understand that. It was the same for me when my poor mother was dying.'

'Talking about support,' said Brendon. 'Martin's been in touch with my Betty, and it sounds as if you've been relieved of grandparent duties.'

'How so?' asked Jim, stamping his feet in an effort to keep warm.

'As Betty teaches the juniors, she'll drive them in and pick them up each day, and then keep them until Martin comes home. He's arranged with Roger and the others to stick to doing admin and give up flying for a few weeks so he can look after them and Anne and the new baby when they come home.'

'Are you sure your Betty can handle those two as well as little Joseph?' asked Peggy fretfully.

Brendon grinned. 'She might be small, but she's very capable and knows exactly how to keep them all in line. That's why she's such a good teacher, and so popular with all the children.'

'Well, I have to say, that's an enormous relief,' said Peggy. 'Thank her for me, will you?' She tucked her hand into the crook of Jim's elbow and gave it a tug. 'We'd better get going before you freeze to death,' she said, her words snatched away by the wind.

'Thank the Lord for that,' he muttered, pulling up his coat collar. 'I'd forgotten how bitter that wind can be after all my years in the tropics.'

With Daisy's hands firmly held between them, they headed back down the track and started to walk along the seafront where there were already piles of shingle being flung by the rising tide.

Peggy knew that Jim wasn't enjoying it much, but she found it bracing and life-giving after a week of office, home and hospital visits. She looked out to sea at the threatening sky, watching the seabirds swoop and battle against the wind as their mournful cries filled the air, then along the shoreline where the old pier had once been. The rusting remnants had been dismantled and there was talk of building a new one, but she doubted it would be any time soon, as there were far more important things to be done to bring Cliffehaven back to its former glory.

They fought their way against the wind as they passed the bomb craters and ruins of the once elegant hotels and guest houses, and then turned their backs to it as they headed for Camden Road and the warm shelter of the Lilac Tearooms.

Peggy was now very ready for that tea and bun, and suspected the others would be too, but she paused in the doorway and looked up at Jim, hoping the love she had for him showed in her eyes.

'It's so lovely to have you home with me again, Jim,' she said softly. 'And I want you to know that whatever happens, I will always be by your side.'

Jim kept hold of Daisy's hand and smiled down at Peggy with such love it made her heart beat a little faster. 'This is where I belong, Peggy, and where I'll stay. For this is the place I call home, and you, my darling, are the heart of it.'

It was two o'clock the following morning when Ruby realised the end was near. The screens were once more pulled round the bed and the nurses had come in more regularly to check on Ethel and the medication that was slowly being delivered through the drips. The hospital doctor came for a moment, his expression solemn as he examined Ethel. He squeezed Ruby's shoulder to give her courage, and then held a murmured conversation with the ward sister before he left.

All Ruby could do now, she realised, was to steel herself for what was to come. She had no regrets about asking to be left alone for these last hours, for she wanted the chance to share these quiet but heart-breaking moments with just Ethel, and not be distracted.

In the hope that Ethel could hear her, she held tightly to her hand and talked to her about their life together in the East End, dredging up memories of people and places they'd had in common, and retelling the story of how she'd found sanctuary at Beach View with Peggy and the lovely Reilly family.

Ethel was unresponsive, and the dialysis machine began to make strange and alarming noises, which immediately alerted the nurses. Sister Jasmine supervised the turning off of the machine and the emptying of the bag that had collected the fluid from Ethel's failing kidneys, and then sat down next to Ruby and took her hand.

'There is no more to be done, Ruby,' she said softly. 'Your mother is close to the end now, so I'm going to make her as comfortable as possible.'

'But won't she be in pain now you've turned that machine off?'

Jasmine shook her head. 'She's beyond feeling anything now, Ruby. And I promise you, she will pass peacefully.'

Ruby watched through her tears as Jasmine tenderly brushed back Ethel's hair from her forehead, murmured a few words that might have been a prayer, and then blocked Ruby's view momentarily before slipping quietly away beyond the screens.

Ruby took hold of her mother's hands. She prayed to a God she'd not believed in since childhood, and waited for the awful moment when her mother would be gone from her for ever.

Ethel lifted her chin as if she could hear Ruby reciting the childhood prayer, and then raised a hand, her fingers trying to reach for something above her before it flopped back onto the covers. She took a breath – and then another – and with a sigh, was gone.

Ruby burst into tears and gathered her into her arms, holding her like a baby, her tears falling on Ethel's lifeless face. 'I'm sorry I couldn't do more,' she sobbed. 'But I hope that wherever you are, you're finally at peace. I love you, Mum, and I'm glad you aren't in any more pain, but oh, I'm going to miss you.'

She sat cradling Ethel, who weighed less than a child, and whose fiery spirit was finally extinguished.

But eventually, her tears abated, and she gently settled Ethel back against the pillows. She kissed the cheek that was already cooling, and slumped down into the chair, unsure of what she was supposed to do now.

Jasmine must have been waiting for this moment, because she came in and took Ruby's hand. 'I've brought the holdall, Ruby,' she said quietly. 'So when you're ready, gather up your mother's things, and then come to see me. I have pamphlets that will help you make all the necessary arrangements, but I suggest you leave them to read until tomorrow and try to get some sleep for now.'

'What about Mum?'

'The doctor has to come to sign the death certificate, and then I will tend to her before she is taken downstairs. We can arrange for an undertaker to collect her if you'd like?'

Ruby nodded. 'Thank you,' she whispered.

Jasmine patted her hand and closed the screens to give her privacy.

Ruby's hands were shaking and her vision was blurred by tears as she emptied the bedside locker of the clothes and toiletries that Ethel had never had the chance to use. She added the books she'd brought to read, and tidied away the old newspaper and sweet wrappers into the paper bag clipped to the small cupboard.

Leaving the holdall on the chair, she took Ethel's hand once more and held it to her heart. 'Goodbye, Mum,' she whispered.

Softly tucking Ethel's hand beneath the covers, Ruby turned to pick up her coat, handbag and holdall, and then caught sight of the large box of chocolates Gloria had brought in. Tucking it under her arm, she took one last lingering look at her mother and pushed her way out through the screens.

'Please take this and share it with the other nurses, Jasmine,' she said, handing over the chocolates. 'You've all been so kind, and there ain't really the words to tell you how much I appreciate all you done fer me and Mum.'

She didn't wait for a reply, but headed through the swing doors and into the corridor before the tears returned. Her footsteps echoed in the silence of that great hospital as she slowly made her way to the main entrance, and they seemed to emphasise the fact that she was truly alone in the world – and that what she'd just lost would never be found again.

She went down the steps to discover that it was softly raining, which seemed appropriate, but instead of running across to the Anchor, she stood for a moment and let the cooling rain drench her face and hair as the tears coursed down her cheeks.

She looked up at the sky, but again there were no stars, just the golden reminder of the hidden moon at the ragged edges of the scudding clouds. She walked slowly away from the hospital and across a deserted Camden Road, noting the silence in the sleeping town, and how her lonely footsteps echoed once again.

Ruby unlocked the side door and stepped into the familiar and welcoming hallway. Placing the bag at her feet, she bolted the door and breathed a trembling sigh as she leaned back on it. This was where she belonged, and she would see to it that Ethel would be laid to rest in the peace and quiet of Cliffehaven's oldest churchyard – far from the noise and smog and bad memories of London. For this was the place she called home, and it was where they both would stay.

WELCOME TO
Cliffehaven
ELLIE DEAN

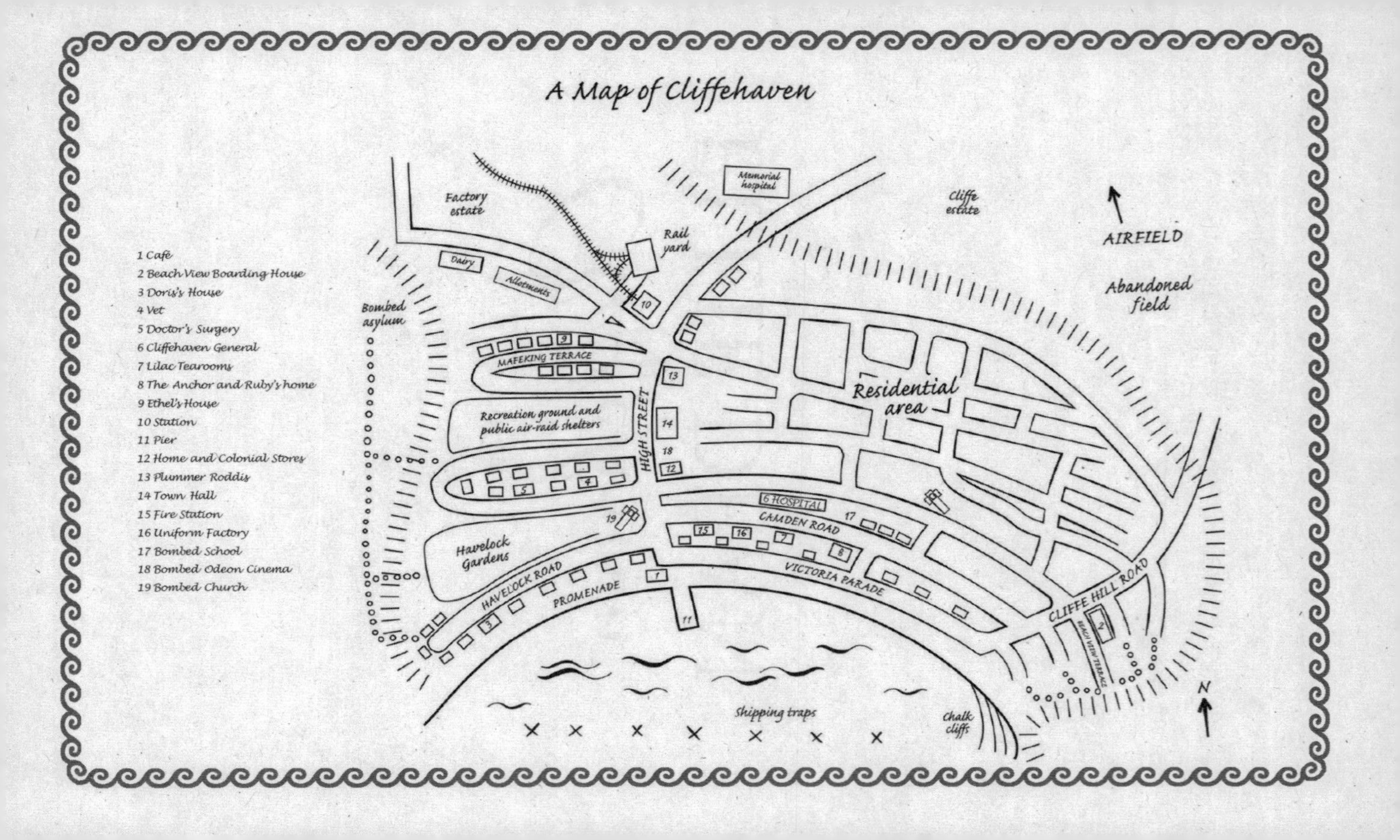

A Map of Cliffehaven
1 Café
2 Beach View Boarding House
3 Doris's House
4 Vet
5 Doctor's Surgery
6 Cliffehaven General
7 Lilac Tearooms
8 The Anchor and Ruby's home
9 Ethel's House
10 Station
11 Pier
12 Home and Colonial Stores
13 Plummer Roddis
14 Town Hall
15 Fire Station
16 Uniform Factory
17 Bombed School
18 Bombed Odeon Cinema
19 Bombed Church
Factory estate
Dairy
Allotments
Rail yard
Memorial hospital
Cliffe estate
AIRFIELD
Abandoned field
Bombed asylum
MAFEKING TERRACE
Recreation ground and public air-raid shelters
HIGH STREET
Residential area
6 HOSPITAL
CAMDEN ROAD
Havelock Gardens
HAVELOCK ROAD
PROMENADE
VICTORIA PARADE
CLIFFE HILL ROAD
BEACH VIEW TERRACE
Shipping traps
Chalk cliffs
N

MEET THE CLIFFEHAVEN FAMILY

PEGGY REILLY is in her early forties, and married to Jim. She is small and slender, with dark, curly hair and lively brown eyes. As if running a busy household and caring for her young daughter wasn't enough, she also runs the local uniform factory and still finds time to offer tea, sympathy and a shoulder to cry on when they're needed. She and Jim took over the running of Beach View Boarding House when Peggy's parents retired. When war was declared and the boarding house business no longer became viable, she decided to take in evacuees.

Peggy can be feisty and certainly doesn't suffer fools, and yet she is also trying very hard to come to terms with the fact that her family has been torn apart by the war. She is a romantic at heart and can't help trying to match-make, but she's also a terrible worrier, always fretting over someone – and as the evacuees make their home with her, she comes to regard them as her chicks and will do everything she can to protect them.

JIM REILLY is in his mid-forties and was a young engineer in the last days of the first war, where he served alongside his elder brother, Frank, and father Ron. Now he's fighting for king and country in India and Burma.

Jim is handsome, with flashing blue eyes and dark hair, and the gift of the Irish blarney he'd inherited from his Irish parents, which usually gets him out of trouble. He enjoys the camaraderie of being a soldier, but the conditions and dangers he's encountering in the jungles have somewhat dampened his enthusiasm, and he treasures the letters and cards from home.

RONAN REILLY (Ron) is a sturdy man in his sixties who often leads a very secretive life away from Beach View now that his experience and skills from the previous war are called upon during the hostilities. Widowed several decades ago, he has recently married the luscious Rosie Braithwaite who owns the Anchor pub.

Ron is a wily countryman; a poacher and retired fisherman with great roguish charm who tramps over the fields with his dog, Harvey, and two ferrets. He doesn't care much about his appearance, much to Peggy's dismay, but beneath that ramshackle old hat and moth-eaten clothing, beats the heart of a strong, loving man who will fiercely protect those he loves.

ROSIE REILLY is in her fifties and has recently married Ron, after her husband died following many years in a mental asylum. She took over the Anchor pub twenty years ago and has turned it into a little gold-mine. Rosie has platinum hair, big blue eyes and an hour-glass figure – she also has a good sense of humour and can hold her own with the customers.

HARVEY is a scruffy, but highly intelligent brindled lurcher, with a mind of his own and a mischievous nature – much like his owner, Ron.

DORIS WILLIAMS is Peggy's older sister and for many years she has been divorced from her long-suffering husband, Ted, who died very recently. She used to live in the posh part of town, Havelock Road, and look down on Peggy and the boarding house.

But her days of snooty social climbing and snobbishness are behind her. Having lived with Peggy at Beach View Boarding House after bombs destroyed her former neighbourhood, Doris has softened and although she's still proud of her connections to high society, she's also on much better terms with her sister and the rest of the family. But despite all this, Doris is still rather lonely, especially with her only son now married and moved away. Could her recent change of heart also lead to a new romance?

FRANK REILLY has served his time in the army during both wars, but now he's been demobbed due to his age and is doing his bit by joining the Home Guard and Civil Defence. He's married to Pauline and they live in Tamarisk Bay in the fisherman's cottage where he was born.

CORDY FINCH is a widow and has been living at Beach View for many years. She is in her eighties and is rather frail from her arthritis, but that doesn't stop her from bantering with Ron and enjoying life to the full. She adores Peggy and looks on her as a daughter, for her own sons emigrated to Canada many years before and she rarely hears from them. The girls who live at Beach View regard her as their grandmother, as does Peggy's youngest, Daisy.

ANNE is married to Station Commander Martin Black, an RAF pilot, and they have two small girls. Anne has moved down to Somerset for the war, teaching at the local village school.

CICELY (Cissy) is a driver for the WAAF and is stationed at Cliffe aerodrome. She once had ambitions to go on stage, but finds great satisfaction in doing her bit, and is enjoying the new friendships she's made. She has fallen in love with a young American pilot, Randolf Stevens, but now he's been sent to Biggin Hill, they rarely see one another.

BOB and **CHARLIE** are Peggy's two young sons, who are also living in Somerset for the duration. Bob is serious and dedicated to running the farm, while Charlie is still mischievous, and when not causing trouble, can be found most of the time under the bonnet of some vehicle, tinkering with the engine.

DAISY is Peggy's youngest child, born the day Singapore fell. She can sleep through air raids and simply adores pulling Ron's wayward eyebrows. She and Harvey are best of friends, but she has yet to truly know her father, or her siblings.

RITA SMITH came to Beach View after her home in Cliffehaven was flattened by an air raid. Rita is small and an energetic tomboy who is a fully qualified mechanic, having been taught from an early age by her father. She can usually be seen in heavy trousers and boots, and a First World War leather jacket and flying helmet.

FRAN is from Ireland and works as a theatre nurse at Cliffehaven General. She has been living with Peggy since before the war, and has become an intrinsic part of the family. She plays the violin at the Anchor for the sing-songs, and has fallen in love with Robert – an MOD colleague of Anthony Williams.

SARAH FULLER and her younger sister, **JANE**, came to England and Beach View after the fall of Singapore. They are the great-nieces of Cordelia Finch who has welcomed them with open arms. Sarah works for the Women's Timber Corps, and Jane has now left Cliffehaven for a secret posting where she's deciphering codes.

IVY is from the East End of London and was billeted for a time with Doris where she was expected to skivvy. She's stepping out with Fire Officer Andy, who is the nephew of Gloria Stevens who runs the Crown pub in Cliffehaven High Street. She and Rita are best friends and the untidiest pair Peggy has ever met – other than Ron and Harvey.

Lose yourself in the
There'll be Blue Skies
It's 1939 and the first evacuees are arriving at Beach View boarding house . . .
Ellie Dean
Far From Home
Will she ever see her loved ones again?
Ellie Dean
Ellie DEAN
She swore she would never lose heart . . .
Keep Smiling Through
War can bring hope as well as heartache
Ellie Dean
Some Lucky Day
The Sunday Times Top Ten Bestselling author
Ellie Dean
While We're Apart
The Sunday Times Bestselling Author
Can you forgive and forget in a time of war?
Ellie Dean
Sealed With a Loving Kiss
Ellie DEAN
Can love survive in a time of war?
Where the Heart Lies
United by love, separated by war...
Ellie Dean
Always in my Heart
It was a time of friendship, family, love and loss...
Ellie Dean
All My Tomorrows
Find Love. Find Hope.
Find Cliffehaven.